Oblivion

Stories

David Foster Wallace

BACK BAY BOOKS
Little, Brown and Company
New York   Boston

Back Bay Books / Little, Brown and Company
Hachette Book Group
1290 Avenue of the Americas, New York, NY 10104
www.hachettebookgroup.com

Originally published in hardcover by Little, Brown and Company, June 2004
First Back Bay paperback edition, August 2005

Back Bay Books is an imprint of Little, Brown and Company. The Back Bay Books name and logo are trademarks of Hachette Book Group, Inc.

Versions of some of these stories first appeared in the following publications, to whose editors grateful acknowledgment is made: *AGNI, Black Clock, Colorado Review, Conjunctions, Esquire, McSweeney's,* and *The O. Henry Prize Stories 2002.* One or two tiny parts of "Philosophy and the Mirror of Nature" make uncited use of Gordon Grice's *The Red Hourglass: Lives of the Predators* (Delacorte Press, 1988). "The Suffering Channel"'s snippet of Jonathan Swift's "The Lady's Dressing Room" is from *Swift: Poetical Works,* ed. Herbert Davis (Oxford University Press, 1968).

Library of Congress Cataloging-in-Publication Data

Wallace, David Foster.
   Oblivion / David Foster Wallace. — 1st ed.
     p. cm.
   ISBN 978-0-316-91981-4 (hc) / 978-0-316-01076-4 (pb)
   I. Title.
PS3573.A425635O35 2004
813'.54 — dc22   2003027135

20 19 18 17

LSC-C

Book designed by Marie Mundaca

Printed in the United States of America

Contents

For Karen Carlson and Karen Green

Oblivion

Mister Squishy

The Focus Group was then reconvened in another of Reesemeyer Shannon Belt Advertising's nineteenth-floor conference rooms. Each member returned his Individual Response Profile packets to the facilitator, who thanked each in turn. The long conference table was equipped with leather executive swivel chairs; there was no assigned seating. Bottled spring water and caffeinated beverages were made available to those who thought they might want them. The exterior wall of the conference room was a thick tinted window with a broad high-altitude view of points NE, creating a spacious, attractive, and more or less natural-lit environment that was welcome after the bland fluorescent enclosure of the testing cubicles. One or two members of the Targeted Focus Group unconsciously loosened their neckties as they settled into the comfortable chairs.

There were more samples of the product arranged on a tray at the conference table's center.

This facilitator, just like the one who'd led the large Product Test and Initial Response assembly earlier that morning before all the members of the different Focus Groups had been separated into individual soundproof cubicles to complete their Individual Response Profiles, held degrees in both Descriptive Statistics and Behavioral Psychology and was employed by Team Δy, a cutting-edge market research firm that Reesemeyer Shannon Belt Adv. had begun using almost exclusively in recent years. This Focus Group's facilitator was a stout, palely freckled man with an archaic haircut and a warm if somewhat nervous and complexly irreverent manner. On the wall next to the door behind him was a presentation whiteboard with several Dry Erase markers in its recessed aluminum sill.

The facilitator played idly with the edges of the IRPs forms in his folder until all the men had seated themselves and gotten comfortable. Then he said: 'Right, so thanks again for your part in this, which as I'm pretty sure Mr. Mounce told you this morning is always an important part of deciding what new products get made available to consumers versus those that don't.' He had a graceful, practiced way of panning his gaze back and forth to make sure he addressed the entire table, a skill that was slightly at odds with the bashful, somewhat fidgety presentation of his body as he spoke before the assembled men. The fourteen members of the Focus Group, all male and several with beverages before them, engaged in the slight gestures and expressions of men around a conference table who are less than 100% sure what is going to be expected of them. The conference room was very different in appearance and feel from the sterile, almost lablike auditorium in which the PT/IR had been held two hours earlier. The facilitator, who did have the customary pocket-protector with three different colored pens in it, wore a crisp striped dress shirt and wool tie and cocoa-brown slacks, but no jacket or sportcoat. His shirtsleeves were not rolled up. His smile had a slight wincing quality, several members observed, as of some vague diffuse apology. Attached to the breast pocket on the same side of his shirt as his nametag was also a large pin or button emblazoned with the familiar Mister Squishy brand icon, which was a plump and childlike cartoon face of indeterminate ethnicity with its eyes squeezed partly shut in an expression that somehow connoted delight, satiation, and rapacious desire all at the same time. The icon communicated the sort of innocuous facial affect that was almost impossible not to smile back at or feel positive about in some way, and it had been commissioned and introduced by one of Reesemeyer Shannon Belt's senior creative people over a decade ago, when the regional

Mister Squishy Company had come under national corporate owner-ship and rapidly expanded and diversified from extra-soft sandwich breads and buns into sweet rolls and flavored doughnuts and snack cakes and soft confections of nearly every conceivable kind; and with-out any particular messages or associations anyone in Demographics could ever produce data to quantify or get a handle on, the crude line-drawn face had become one of the most popular, recognizable, and demonstrably successful brand icons in American advertising.

Traffic was brisk on the street far below, and also trade.

It was, however, not the Mister Squishy brand icon that concerned the carefully chosen and vetted Focus Groups on this bright cold No-vember day in 1995. Currently in third-phase Focus Testing was a new and high-concept chocolate-intensive Mister Squishy–brand snack cake designed primarily for individual sale in convenience stores, with twelve-pack boxes to be placed in up-market food retail outlets first in the Midwest and upper East Coast and then, if the test-market data bore out Mister Squishy's parent company's hopes, nationwide.

A total 27 of the snack cakes were piled in a pyramidal display on a large rotating silver tray in the center of the conference table. Each was wrapped in an airtight transpolymer material that looked like paper but tore like thin plastic, the same retail packaging that nearly all US confections had deployed since M&M Mars pioneered the composite and used it to help launch the innovative Milky Way Dark line in the late 1980s. This new product's wrap had the familiar distinctive Mis-ter Squishy navy-and-white design scheme, but here the Mister Squishy icon appeared with its eyes and mouth rounded in cartoon alarm be-hind a series of microtextured black lines that appeared to be the bars of a jail cell, around two of which lines or bars the icon's plump and dough-colored fingers were curled in the universal position of inmates everywhere. The dark and exceptionally dense and moist-looking snack cakes inside the packaging were *Felonies!*® — a risky and multi-valent trade name meant both to connote and to parody the modern health-conscious consumer's sense of vice/indulgence/transgression/ sin vis à vis the consumption of a high-calorie corporate snack. The name's association matrix included as well the suggestion of adulthood and adult autonomy: in its real-world rejection of the highly cute, cartoonish, *n*- and *oo*-intensive names of so many other snack cakes, the product tag *'Felony!'* was designed and tested primarily for its appeal to the 18–39 Male demographic, the single most prized and fictile demo-target in high-end marketing. Only two of the present Focus Group's members were over 40, and their profiles had been vetted not once but twice by Scott R. Laleman's Technical Processing team during the intensive demographic/behavioral voir dire for which Team Δy Focus Group data was so justly prized.

Inspired, according to agency rumor, by an R.S.B. Creative Director's epiphanic encounter with something billed as Death by Chocolate in a Near North café, *Felonies!* were all-chocolate, filling and icing and cake as well, and in fact all-real-or-*fondant*-chocolate instead of the usual hydrogenated cocoa and high-F corn syrup, *Felonies!* conceived thus less as a variant on rivals' Zingers, Ding Dongs, Ho Hos, and Choco-Diles than as a radical upscaling and re-visioning of same. A domed cylinder of flourless maltilol-flavored sponge cake covered entirely in 2.4mm of a high-lecithin chocolate frosting manufactured with trace amounts of butter, cocoa butter, baker's chocolate, chocolate liquor, vanilla extract, dextrose, and sorbitol (a relatively high-cost frosting, and one whose butter-redundancies alone required heroic innovations in production systems and engineering — an entire production line had had to be remachined and the lineworkers retrained and production and quality-assurance quotas recalculated more or less from scratch), which high-end frosting was then also injected by high-pressure confectionery needle into the 26 × 13mm hollow ellipse in each *Felony!*'s center (a center which in for example Hostess Inc.'s products was packed with what amounted to a sucrotic whipped lard), resulting in double doses of an ultrarich and near-restaurant-grade frosting whose central pocket — given that the thin coat of outer frosting's exposure to the air caused it to assume traditional icing's hard-yet-deliquescent marzipan character — seemed even richer, denser, sweeter, and more felonious than the exterior icing, icing that in most rivals' Field tests' IRPs and GRDS was declared consumers' favorite part. (Hostess's lead agency Chiat/Day I.B.'s 1991–2 double-blind

Behavior series' videotapes recorded over 45% of younger consumers actually peeling off Ho Hos' matte icing in great dry jagged flakes and eating it solo, leaving the low-end cake itself to sit ossifying on their tables' Lazy Susans, film clips of which had reportedly been part of R.S.B.'s initial pitch to Mister Squishy's parent company's Subsidiary Product Development boys.)

In an unconventional move, some of this quote unquote Full-Access background information re ingredients, production innovations, and even demotargeting was being relayed to the Focus Group by the facilitator, who used a Dry Erase marker to sketch a diagram of Mister Squishy's snack cake production sequence and the complex adjustments required by *Felonies!* at select points along the automated line. The relevant information was relayed in a skillfully orchestrated QA period, with many of the specified questions supplied by two ostensible members of the Targeted Focus Group who were in fact not civilian consumers at all but employees of Team Δy assigned to help orchestrate the unconventionally informative QA, and to observe the deliberations of the other twelve men once the facilitator left the room, taking care not to influence the Focus Group's arguments or verdicts but later adding personal observations and impressions that would help round and flesh out the data provided by the Group Response Data Summary and the digital videotape supplied by what appeared to be a large smoke detector in the conference room's northwest corner, whose lens and parabolic mike, while mobile and state-of-the-art, invariably failed to catch certain subtle nuances in individual affect as well as low-volume interchanges between adjoining members. One of the UAFs,* a slim young man with waxy blond hair and a complexion whose redness appeared more irritated than ruddy or hale, had been allowed by Team Δy's UAF Coordinator to cultivate an eccentric and (to most Focus Group members) irritating set of personal mannerisms whose very conspicuousness served to disguise his professional

---

*Team Δy's term for their Focus Groups' moles was *Unintroduced Assistant Facilitators,* whose identities were theoretically unknown to the facilitators in pure double-blinds, though in practice they were usually child's play to spot.

identity: he had small squeeze bottles of both contact lens lubricant and intranasal saline before him on the table, and not only took written notes on the facilitator's presentation but did so with a Magic Marker that squeaked loudly and had ink you could smell, and whenever he asked one of his preassigned questions he did not tentatively raise his hand or clear his throat as other UAFs were wont but rather simply tersely barked out, 'Question:', as in: 'Question: is it possible to be more specific about what "natural and artificial flavors" means, and is there any substantive difference between what it really means and what the average consumer is expected to understand it to mean,' without any sort of interrogative lilt or expression, his brow furrowed and rimless glasses very askew.

As any decent small-set univariable probability distribution would predict, not all members of the Targeted Focus Group were attending closely to the facilitator's explanation of what Mister Squishy and Team Δy hoped to achieve by leaving the Focus Group alone very shortly *in camera* to compare the results of their Individual Response Profiles and speak openly and without interference amongst themselves and attempt to come as close as possible to a unanimous univocal Group Response Data Summary of the product along sixteen different radial Preference and Satisfaction axes. A certain amount of this inattention was factored into the matrices of what the TFG's facilitator had been informed was the actual test underway on today's nineteenth floor. This secondary (or, 'nested') test sought quantifiable data on quote unquote Full-Access manufacturing and marketing information's effects on Targeted Focus Groups' perceptions of both the product and its corporate producer; it was a double-blind series, designed to be replicated along three different variable grids with random TFGs throughout the next two fiscal quarters, and sponsored by parties whose identities were being withheld from the facilitators as (apparently) part of the nested test's conditions.

Three of the Targeted Focus Group's members were staring absently out the large tinted window that gave on a delicately muted sepia view of the street's north side's skyscrapers and, beyond and between these, different bits of the northeast Loop and harbor and several feet of

severely foreshortened lake. Two of these members were very young
men at the extreme left of the demotarget's x axis who sat slumped in
their tilted swivels in attitudes of either reverie or stylized indifference;
the third was feeling absently at his upper lip's little dent.

The Focus Group facilitator, trained by the requirements of what
seemed to have turned out to be his profession to behave as though he
were interacting in a lively and spontaneous way while actually remaining inwardly detached and almost clinically observant, possessed
also a natural eye for behavioral details that could often reveal tiny
gems of statistical relevance amid the rough raw surfeit of random
fact. Sometimes little things made a difference. The facilitator's name
was Terry Schmidt and he was 34 years old, a Virgo. Eleven of the
Focus Group's fourteen men wore wristwatches, of which roughly one-
third were expensive and/or foreign. A twelfth, by far the TFG's oldest
member, had the platinum fob of a quality pocketwatch running diagonally left-right across his vest and a big pink face and the permanent
benevolent look in his eyes of someone older who had many grandchildren and spent so much time looking warmly at them that the expression becomes almost ingrained. Schmidt's own grandfather had
lived in a north Florida retirement community where he sat with a
plaid blanket on his lap and coughed constantly both times Schmidt
had ever been in his presence, addressing him only as Boy. Precisely
50% of the room's men wore coats and ties or had suitcoats or blazers
hanging from the back of their chairs, three of which coats were part
of an actual three-piece business wardrobe; another three men wore
combinations of knit shirts, slacks, and various crew- and turtleneck
sweaters classifiable as Business Casual. Schmidt lived alone in a condominium he had recently refinanced. The remaining four men wore
bluejeans and sweatshirts with the logo of either a university or the
garment's manufacturer; one was the Nike Swoosh icon that to
Schmidt always looked somewhat Arabic. Three of the four men in conspicuously casual/sloppy attire were the Focus Group's youngest members, two of whom were among the three making rather a show of not
attending closely. Team Δy favored a loose demographic grid. Two of
the three youngest men were under 21. All three of these youngest

members sat back on their tailbones with their legs uncrossed and their hands spread out over their thighs and their faces arranged in the mildly sullen expressions of consumers who have never once questioned their entitlement to satisfaction or meaning. Schmidt's initial undergraduate concentration had been in Statistical Chemistry; he still enjoyed the clinical precision of a lab. Less than 50% of the room's total footwear involved laces. One man in a knit shirt had small brass zippers up the sides of low-cut boots that were shined to a distracting gleam, another detail possessed of mnemonic associations for Schmidt. Unlike Terry Schmidt's and Ron Mounce's, Darlene Lilley's own marketing background was in computer-aided design; she'd come into Research because she said she'd discovered she was really more of a people person at heart. There were four pairs of eyeglasses in the room, although one of these pairs were sunglasses and possibly not prescription, another with heavy black frames that gave their wearer's face an earnest aspect above his dark turtleneck sweater. There were two mustaches and one probable goatee. A stocky man in his late twenties had a sort of sparse, mossy beard; it was indeterminable whether this man was just starting to grow a beard or whether he was the sort of person whose beard simply looked this way. Among the youngest men, it was obvious which were sincerely in need of a shave and which were just affecting an unshaved look. Two of the Focus Group's members had the distinctive blink patterns of men wearing contact lenses in the conference room's astringent air. Five of the men were more than 10% overweight, Terry Schmidt himself excluded. His high-school PE teacher had once referred to Terry Schmidt in front of his peers as the Crisco Kid, which he had laughingly explained meant *fat in the can*. Schmidt's own father, a decorated combat veteran, had recently retired from a company that sold seed, nitrogen fertilizer, and broad-spectrum herbicides in downstate Galesburg. The affectedly eccentric UAF was asking the men on either side of him, one of whom was Hispanic, whether they'd perhaps care for a chewable vitamin C tablet. The Mister Squishy icon also reappeared in the conference room as the stylized finials of two fine beige or tan ceramic lamps on side tables at either end of the windowless interior wall. There were two African-American males in the Targeted Focus Group, one over 30, the one under 30 with a shaved head. Three of the men had hair classifiable as brown, two gray or salt/pepper, another three black (excluding the African-Americans and the Focus Group's lone oriental, whose nametag and overwhelming cheekbones suggested either Laos or the Socialist Republic of Vietnam — for complex but solid statistical reasons, Scott Laleman's team's Profile grids specified distributions for ethnicity but not national origin); three could be called blond or fair-haired. These distributions included the UAFs, and Schmidt felt he already had a good idea who this Group's other UAF was. Rarely did R.S.B. Focus Groups include representatives of the very pale or freckled red-haired physical type, though Foote, Cone & Belding and D.D.B. Needham both made regular use of such types because of certain data suggesting meaningful connections between melanin quotients and continuous probability distributions of income and preference on the US East Coast, where over 70% of upmarket products tested. Some of the trendy hypergeometric techniques on which these data were based had been called into question by more traditional demographic statisticians, however.

By industry-wide convention, Focus Group members received a per diem equal to exactly 300% of what they would receive for jury duty in the state where they resided. The reasoning behind this equation was so old and tradition-bound that no one of Terry Schmidt's generation knew its origin. It was, for senior test marketers, both an in-joke and a plausible extension of verified attitudes about civic duty and elective consumption, respectively. The Hispanic man to the off-blond UAF's left, who did not wear a wristwatch, had evidence of large tattoos on his upper arms through the fabric of his dress shirt, which fabric the natural lighting's tinted hue rendered partly translucent. He was also one of the men with mustaches, and his nametag identified him as *NORBERTO*, making this the first Norberto to appear in any of the over 845 Focus Groups that Schmidt had led so far in his career as a Statistical Field Researcher for Team Δy. Schmidt kept his own private records of correlations between product, Client agency, and certain variables in Focus Groups' constituents and procedures. These were run through various discriminant-analysis programs on his Apple-brand computer at home and the results collected in three-ring binders which he labeled and stored on a set of home-assembled gray steel shelves in the utility room of his condominium. The whole problem and project of descriptive statistics was discriminating between what made a difference and what did not. The fact that Scott R. Laleman now both vetted Focus Groups and helped design them was just one more sign that his star was ascending at Team Δy. The other real comer was A. Ronald Mounce, whose background was also in Technical Processing. 'Question:' 'Question:' 'Comment:' One man with a kind of long chinless face wished to know what *Felonies!'* retail price was going to be, and he either didn't understand or disliked Terry Schmidt's explanation that retail pricing lay outside the purview of the Group's focus today and was in fact the responsibility of a whole different R.S.B. research vendor. The reasoning behind the separation of price from consumer-satisfaction grids was technical and parametric and was not included in the putative Full-Access information Schmidt was authorized to share with the Focus Group under the terms of the study. There was one obvious hairweave in the room, as well as two victims of untreated Male Pattern Baldness, both of whom — either interestingly or by mere random chance — were among the Group's four blue-eyed members.

When Schmidt thought of Scott Laleman, with his all-season tan and sunglasses pushed musslessly up on his pale hair's crown, it was as something with the mindless malevolence of a carnivorous eel or skate, something that hunted on autopilot at extreme depths. The African-American male whose head was unshaved sat with the rigidity of someone who had back problems and understood the dignity with which he bore them to be an essential part of his character. The other wore sunglasses indoors in such a way as to make some unknown type of statement about himself; there was also no way of knowing whether it was a general statement or one specific to this context. Scott Laleman was only 27 and had come on board at Team Δy three years after Darlene Lilley and two and one-half years after Schmidt himself, who had helped Darlene train Laleman to run chi-square and t distributions on raw phone-survey data and had taken surprising satisfaction in watching the boy's eyes glaze and tan go sallow under the fluorescent banklights of Δy's data room, until then one day Schmidt had needed to see Alan Britton personally about something and had knocked and come in and Laleman was sitting in the office's recliner across the room and he and Britton were both smoking very large cigars and laughing.

The figure that began its free climb up the building's steadily increscent north facet just before 11:00 AM was outfitted in tight windproof Lycra leggings and a snug hooded GoreTex sweatshirt w/ fiber-lined hood up and tied tight and what appeared to be mountaineering or rock-climbing boots except that instead of crampons or spikes there were suction cups lining the instep of each boot. Attached to both palms and wrists' insides were single suction cups the size of a plumber's helper; the cups' color was the same shrill orange as hunting jackets and road crews' hardhats. The Lycra pants' color scheme was one navy-blue leg and one white leg; the sweatshirt and hood were blue with white piping. The mountaineering boots were an emphatic black. The figure moved swiftly and with numerous moist popping suction-noises up the display window of the Gap, a large retail clothier. He then pulled himself up and over onto the narrow ledge at the base of the second-floor window, rose complexly to his feet, affixed his cups, and swarmed up the pane's thick glass, which gave onto the Gap's second floor but had no promotional items displayed within. The figure presented as lithe and expert. His manner of climbing appeared almost more reptilian than mammalian, you'd have to say. He was halfway up the window of a management consulting firm on the fifth floor when a small crowd of passersby began to gather on the sidewalk below. Winds at ground level were light to moderate.

In the conference room, the north window's tint made the northeastern half-cloudy sky seem raw and the froth of the waves on the distant windblown lake look dark; it brindled the sides of the other tall buildings in view, as well, which were all partly in one another's shadow. Fully seven of the Focus Group's men had small remains of *Felonies!* either on their shirtfront or hanging from the hairs on one side of their mustache or lodged at the inner corner of their mouth or in the small crease between the fingernail of their dominant hand and that nail's surrounding skin. Two of the men wore no socks; both these men's shoes were laceless leather; only one pair had tassels. One of the youngest men's denim bellbottoms were so terrifically oversized that even with his legs out splayed and both knees bent his sock-status was unknown. One of the older men wore black silk or rayon socks with tiny lozenges of dark rich red upon them. Another of the older men had a mean little slit of a mouth, another a face far too saggy and seamed for his demographic slot. As was often the case, the youngest men's faces appeared not quite yet fully or humanly formed, with the clean generic quality of products just off the factory floor. Terry Schmidt sometimes sketched his own face's outlines in caricature form as he spoke on the phone or waited for software programs to run. One of the group's men had a pear-shaped head, another a diamond- or kite-shaped face; the room's second-oldest consumer had cropped gray hair and an overdeveloped upper lip that lent him a simian aspect. The men's demoprofiles and initial Systat scores were in Schmidt's valise on the carpet next to the whiteboard; he also had an over-shoulder bag he kept in his cubicle. I was one of the men in this room, the only one wearing a wristwatch who never once glanced at it. What looked just like glasses were not. I was wired from stem to stern. A small LCD at the bottom of my right scope ran both Real Time and Mission Time. My brief script for the GRDS caucus had been memorized in toto but there was a backup copy on a laminated card just inside my sweater's sleeve, held in place with small tabs I could release by depressing one of the buttons on my wristwatch, which was really not a watch at all. There was also the emetic prosthesis. The cakes, of which I had already made a show of eating three, were so sweet they hurt your teeth.

Terry Schmidt himself was hypoglycemic and could eat only confections prepared with fructose, aspartame, or very small amounts of $C_6H_8(OH)_6$, and sometimes he felt himself looking at trays of the product with the expression of an urchin at a toystore's window.

Down the hall and past the MROP* Division's green room, in another R.S.B. conference room whose window faced NE, Darlene Lilley was leading twelve consumers and two UAFs into the GRDS phase of Focused Response without any structured QA or ersatz Full-Access background. Neither Schmidt nor Darlene Lilley had been told which of today's TFGs represented the nested test's control group, though it was pretty obvious. You had to work on the upper floors for some time before you noticed the very slight sway with which the building's structural design accommodated winds off the lake. 'Question: just what exactly *is* polysorbate 80?' Schmidt was reasonably certain that none of the Focus Group felt the sway. It was not pronounced enough even to cause movement in the coffee in any of the iconized mugs on the table that Schmidt, standing and rotating the Dry Erase marker in his hand in an absent way that connoted both informality and a slight humanizing nervousness in front of groups, could see down into. The conference table was heavy pine with lemonwood inlays and a thick coat of polyurethane, and without the window's sepia tint there would be blinding pockets of reflected sun that changed angle as one's own angle with respect to the sun and table changed. Schmidt would also have had to watch dust and tiny clothing fibers swirl in columns of direct sunlight and fall very gently onto everyone's heads and upper bodies, which occurred in even the cleanest conference rooms and was one of Schmidt's least favorite things about the untinted interiors of certain other agencies' conference rooms around the Loop and metro area. Sometimes when waiting or on Hold on the phone Schmidt would put his finger inside his mouth and hold it there for no good reason he could ever ascertain. Darlene Lilley, who was married and the mother of a large-headed toddler whose photograph adorned her desk and hutch at Team Δy, had, three fiscal quarters past, been subjected to unwelcome sexual advances by one of the four Senior Research Directors who liaisoned between the Field and Technical Processing teams and the upper echelons of Team Δy under Alan Britton, advances and duress more than sufficient for legal action in Schmidt's and most of

---

* = Market Research Oversight and Planning

the rest of their Field Team's opinions, which advances she had been able to deflect and defuse in an enormously skillful manner without raising any of the sort of hue and cry that could divide a firm along gender and/or political lines, and things had been allowed to cool down and blow over to such an extent that Darlene Lilley, Schmidt, and the three other members of their Field Team all now still enjoyed a productive working relationship with this dusky and pungent older Senior Research Director, who was now in fact overseeing Field research on the Mister Squishy–R.S.B. project, and Terry Schmidt was personally somewhat in awe of the self-possession and interpersonal savvy Darlene had displayed throughout the whole tense period, an awe tinged with an unwilled element of romantic attraction, and it is true that Schmidt at night in his condominium sometimes without feeling as if he could help himself masturbated to thoughts of having moist slapping intercourse with Darlene Lilley on one of the ponderous laminate conference tables of the firms they conducted statistical market research for, and this was a tertiary cause of what practicing social psychologists would call his MAM* with the board's marker as he used a modulated tone of off-the-record confidence to tell the Focus Group about some of the more dramatic travails Reesemeyer Shannon Belt had had with establishing the product's brand-identity and coming up with the test name *Felony!*, all the while envisioning in a more autonomic part of his brain Darlene delivering nothing but the standard minimal pre-GRDS instructions for her own Focus Group as she stood in her dark Hanes hosiery and the burgundy high heels she kept at work in the bottom-right cabinet of her hutch and changed out of her crosstrainers into every morning the moment she sat down and rolled her chair with small pretend whimpers of effort over to the hutch's cabinets, sometimes (unlike Schmidt) pacing slightly in front of the whiteboard, sometimes planting one heel and rotating her foot slightly or crossing her sturdy ankles to lend her standing posture a carelessly demure aspect, sometimes taking her delicate oval eyeglasses off and not chewing on the arm but holding the glasses in such a way

---

* = Manual Adjusting Mechanism

and in such proximity to her mouth that one got the idea she could, at any moment, put one of the frames' arm's plastic earguards just inside her mouth and nibble on it absently, an unconscious gesture of shyness and concentration at once.

The conference room's carpeting was magenta pile in which wheels left symmetrically distended impressions when one or more of the men adjusted their executive swivel chairs slightly to reposition their legs or their bodies' relation to the table itself. The ventilation system laid a pale hum over tiny distant street and city noises which the window's thickness itself cut to almost nothing. Each of the Targeted Focus Group's members wore a blue-and-white nametag with his first name inscribed thereon by hand. 42.8% of these inscriptions were cursive or script; three of the remaining eight were block capitals, with all the block-cap first names, in a remarkable but statistically meaningless coincidence, beginning with *H*. Sometimes, too, Schmidt would as it were take a step back inside his head and view the Focus Group as a unit, a right-angled mass of fleshtone busts; he'd observe all the faces at once, qua group, so that nothing but the very broadest commonalities passed through his filter. The faces were well-nourished, mid- to upscale, neutral, provisionally attentive, the blood-fed minds behind them occupied with their own owners' lives, jobs, problems, plans, desires, & c. None had been hungry a day in their lives — this was a core commonality, and for Schmidt this one did ramify. It was rare that the product ever truly penetrated a Focus Group's consciousness. One of the first things a Field Researcher accepts is that the product is never going to have as important a place in a TFG's minds as it did in the Client's. Advertising is not voodoo. The Client could ultimately hope only to create the impression of a connection or resonance between the brand and what was important to consumers. And what was important to consumers was, always and invariably, themselves. What they conceived themselves to be. The Focus Groups made little difference in the long run — the only true test was real sales, in Schmidt's personal opinion. Part of today's design was to go past lunch and keep the members eating only confections. Assuming a normal breakfasttime prior to arrival, one could expect their blood sugar to start heading down sharply by 11:30. The ones who ate the most *Felonies!* would be hit the hardest. Among other symptoms, low blood sugar produces oscitance, irritability, lowered inhibitions — their game-faces would begin to slip a bit. Some of the TFG strategies could be extremely manipulative or even abusive in the name of data. A bleach-alternative detergent's agency had once hired Team Δy to convene primipara mothers aged 29 to 34 whose TATs had indicated insecurities at three key loci and to administer questionnaires whose items were designed to provoke and/or heighten those insecurities — Do you ever have negative or hostile feelings towards your child? How often do you feel as if you must hide or deny the fact that your parenting skills are inadequate? Have teachers or other parents ever made remarks about your child which embarrassed you? How often do you feel as if your child looks shabby or unclean in comparison to other children? Have you ever neglected to launder, bleach, mend or iron your child's clothes because of time constraints? Does your child ever seem sad or anxious for no reason you can understand? Can you think of a time when your child appeared to be frightened of you? Does your child's behavior or appearance ever provoke negative feelings in you? Have you ever said or thought negative things about your child? & c. — which, over eleven hours and six separate rounds of carefully designed questionnaires, brought the women to such an emotional state that truly invaluable data on how to pitch Cheer Xtra in terms of very deep maternal anxieties and conflicts emerged ... data that so far as Schmidt had been able to see went wholly unexploited in the campaign the agency had finally sold P. & G. on. Darlene Lilley had later said she had felt like calling the Focus Group's women and apologizing and letting them know that they'd been totally set up and manhandled, emotionally speaking.

Some of the other products and agencies whose branding campaigns Terry Schmidt and Darlene Lilley's Field Team had also worked on for Team Δy were: Downyflake Waffles for D'Arcy Masius Benton & Bowles, Diet Caffeine Free Coke for Ads Infinitum US, Eucalyptamint for Pringle Dixon, Citizens Business Insurance for Krauthammer-Jaynes/SMS, the G. Heileman Brewing Co.'s Special

Export and Special Export Lite for Bayer Bess Vanderwarker, Winner International's *HelpMe* Personal Sound Alarm for Reesemeyer Shannon Belt, Isotoner Comfort-Fit Gloves for PR Cogent Partners, Northern Bathroom Tissue for Reesemeyer Shannon Belt, and Rhône-Poulenc Rorer's new Nasacort and Nasacort AQ Prescription Nasal Spray, also for R.S.B.

The only way for an observer to detect anything unusual or out of the ordinary about the two UAFs' status would be to note that the facilitator never once looked fully or directly at them, whereas on the other hand Schmidt did look at each of the other twelve men at various intervals, making brief and candid eye-contact with first one man and then another at a different place around the conference table and so on, a subtle skill (there is no term for it) that often marks those who are practiced at speaking before small groups, Schmidt neither holding any man's eye for so long as to discomfit nor simply panning automatonically back and forth and brushing only lightly against each man's gaze in such a way that the men in the Focus Group might feel as though this representative of Mister Squishy and *Felonies!* were talking merely at them rather than to or with them; and it would have taken a practiced small-group observer indeed to notice that there were two men in the conference room — one being the terse eccentric member surrounded by personal-care products, the other a silent earnest-eyed bespectacled man who sat in blazer and turtleneck at the table's far corner, which latter Schmidt had decided was the second UAF: something a tiny bit too composed about the man's mien and blink-rate gave him up — on whose eyes the facilitator's never quite did alight all the way. Schmidt's lapse here was very subtle, and an observer would have to be both highly experienced and unusually attentive to extract any kind of meaning from it.

The exterior figure wore also a mountaineer's tool apron and a large nylon or microfiber backpack. Visually, he was both conspicuous and complex. On each slim ledge he again appeared to use the suction cups on his right hand and wrist to pull himself lithely up from a supine position to a standing position, cruciform, facing inward, hugging the glass with his arms' cups engaged in order to keep from falling backward as he raised his left leg and turned the shoe outward to align the instep's cups with the pane's reflective surface. The suction cups appeared to be the kind whose vacuum action could be activated and deactivated by slight rotary adjustments that probably took a great deal of practice to learn to perform as deftly as the figure made them look. The backpack and boots were the same color. Most of the passersby who looked up and stopped and accreted into a small watching crowd found their attention most fully involved and compelled by the free climb's mechanics. The figure traversed each window by lifting his left leg and right arm and pulling himself smoothly up, then attaching his dangling right leg and left arm and activating their cups' suction and leaving them to hold his weight while he deactivated the left leg's and right arm's suction and moved them up and reactivated their cups. There were high degrees of both precision and economy in the way the figure orchestrated his different extremities' tasks. The day was very crisp and winds aloft were high; whatever clouds there were moved rapidly across the slim square of sky visible above the tall buildings that flanked the street. The autumn sky itself the sort of blue that seems to burn. People with hats tipped them back on their heads and people without hats shaded their eyes with their gloves as they craned to watch the figure's progress. The clabbering skies over the lake were not visible from the buildings' rifts or canyon's base. Also there was one large additional suction cup affixed to the back of the hood with a white Velcro strap. When the figure cleared another ledge and for a moment lay on his side facing out into the chasm below, those onlookers far enough back on the sidewalk to have some visual perspective could see another large orange suction cup, the hood's cup's twin, attached to his forehead by what was presumably also Velcro although this Velcro band must have run beneath the hood. And — there was general assent among the watching group — either reflective goggles or very odd and frightening eyes indeed.

Schmidt was simply giving the Focus Group a little extra background, he said, on the product's genesis and on some of the marketing challenges it had presented, but he said that in no way shape or form was he giving them anything like the whole story, that he wouldn't want to pretend he was giving them anything more than little pieces here and there. Time was tight in the pre-GRDS orientation phase. One of the men sneezed loudly. Schmidt explained that this was because Reesemeyer Shannon Belt Adv. wanted to make sure to give the Focus Group a generous interval to convene together *in camera* and discuss their experiences and assessments of *Felonies!* as a group, to compare notes if you will, on their own, qua group, without any marketing researchers yammering at them or standing there observing as if they were psychological guinea pigs or something, which meant that Terry would soon be getting out of their hair and leaving them to perpend and converse in private amongst themselves, and that he wouldn't be coming back until whatever foreman they elected pushed the large red button next to the room's lights' rheostat that in turn activated — the red button did — an amber light in the office down the hall, where Terry Schmidt said he would be twiddling his metaphorical thumbs waiting to come collect the hopefully univocal Group Response Data Summary packet, which the elected foreman here would be receiving ex post hasto. Eleven of the room's men had now consumed at least one of the products on the table's central tray; five of them had had more than one. Schmidt, who was no longer playing idly with the Dry Erase marker because some of the men's eyes had begun to follow it in his hand and he sensed it was becoming a distraction, said he now also proposed to give them just a little of the standard spiel on why after all the solo time and effort they'd all already put in on their Individual Response Profiles he was going to ask them to start all over again and consider the GRDS packet's various questions and scales as a collective. He had a trick for disposing of the Dry Erase marker where he very casually placed it in the slotted tray at the bottom of the whiteboard and gave the pen's butt a hard flick with his finger, sending it the length of the tray to stop just short of shooting out off the other end altogether, with its cap's tip almost precisely aligned with the tray's end, which he performed with TFGs about 70% of the time, and did perform now. The trick was even more impressively casual-looking if he performed it while he was speaking; it lent both what he was saying and the trick itself an air of nonchalance that heightened the impact. Robert Awad himself — this being the Team Δy Senior Research Director who would later harass and be so artfully defused by Darlene Lilley — had casually performed this little trick in one of his orientation presentations for new Field Team researchers 27 fiscal quarters past. This, Schmidt said, was because one of Reesemeyer Shannon Belt Advertising's central tenets, one of the things that set them apart from other agencies in their bailiwick and so was of course something in which they took great pride and made much of in their pitches to clients like Mister Squishy and North American Soft Confections Inc., was that IRPs like the 20-page questionnaires the men had so kindly filled out in their separate airless cubicles were of definite but only partial research utility, since corporations whose products had national or even regional distribution depended on appealing not just to individual consumers but also of course it almost went without saying to very large groups of them, groups that were yes comprised of individuals but were nevertheless groups, larger entities or collectives. These groups as conceived and understood by market researchers were strange and protean entities, Schmidt told the Focus Group, whose tastes — referring to groups, or small-m markets as they were known around the industry — whose tastes and whims and predilections were not only as the men in the room were doubtless aware subtle and fickle and susceptible to influence from myriad tiny factors in each individual consumer's appetitive makeup but were also, somewhat paradoxically, functions of the members of the group's various influences upon one another, all in a set of interactions and recursively exponential responses-to-responses so complex and multifaceted that it drove statistical demographers half nuts and required a whole Sysplex series of enormously powerful low-temperature Cray-brand supercomputers even to try to model.

And if all that just sounded like a lot of marketing doubletalk, Terry Schmidt told the Focus Group with an air of someone loosening his tie after something public's end, maybe the easiest example of what R.S.B. was talking about in terms of intramarket influences was probably say for instance teenage kids and the fashions and fads that swept like wildfire through markets comprised mostly of kids, meaning high-school and college kids and markets such as for instance popular music, clothing fashions, etcetera. If the members saw a lot of teenage kids these days wearing pants that looked way too big for them and rode low and had cuffs that dragged on the ground, for one obvious example, Schmidt said as if plucking an example at random out of the air, or if as was surely the case with some of the more senior men in the room (two, in fact) they themselves had kids who'd taken in the last couple years to suddenly wanting and wearing clothes that were far too big for them and made them look like urchins in Victorian novels even though as the men probably knew all too well, with a grim chuckle, the clothes cost a pretty penny indeed over at the Gap or Structure. And if you wondered why your kid was wearing them of course the majority of the answer was simply that other kids were wearing them, for of course kids as a demographic market today were notoriously herdlike and their individual choices in consumption were overwhelmingly influenced by other kids' consumption-choices and so on in a fadlike pattern that spread like wildfire and usually then abruptly and mysteriously vanished or changed into something else. This was the most simple and obvious example of the sort of complex system of large groups' intragroup preferences influencing one another and building exponentially on one another, much more like a nuclear chain reaction or an epidemiological transmission grid than a simple case of each individual consumer deciding privately for himself what he wanted and then going out and judiciously spending his disposable income on it. The wonks in Demographics' buzzword for this phenomenon was Metastatic Consumption Pattern or MCP, Schmidt told the Focus Group, rolling his eyes in a way that invited those who were listening to laugh with him at the statisticians' jargon. Granted, the facilitator went on, this model he was so rapidly sketching for them was overly simplistic — e.g., it left out advertising and the media, which in today's hypercomplex business environment sought always to anticipate and fuel these sudden proliferating movements in group choice, aiming for a tipping point at which a product or brand achieved such ubiquitous popularity that it became like unto actual cultural news and-slash-or fodder for cultural critics and comedians, plus also a plausible placement-prop for mass entertainment that sought to look real and in-the-now, and so thereupon a product or style that got hot at a certain ideal apex of the MCP graph ceased to require much paid advertising at all, the hot brand becoming as it were a piece of cultural information or an element of the way the market wished to see itself, which — Schmidt gave them a wistful smile — was a rare and prized phenomenon and was considered in marketing to be something like winning the World Series.

Of the 67% of the twelve true Focus Group members who were still concentrating on listening closely to Terry Schmidt, two now wore the expressions of men who were trying to decide whether to be slightly offended; both these men were over 40. Also, some of the individual adults across the conference table from one another began to exchange glances, and since (Schmidt believed) these men had no prior acquaintance or connection on which to base meaningful eye-contact, it seemed probable that the looks were in reaction to the facilitator's analogy to teen fashion fads. One of the group's members had classic peckerwood sideburns that came all the way down to his mandibles and ended in sharp points. Of the room's three youngest men, none were attending closely, and two were still established in postures and facial configurations designed to make this apparent. The third had removed his fourth *Felony!* from the table's display and was dismantling the wrapper as quietly as possible, looking furtively around to determine whether anyone cared that he'd exceeded his technical product-share. Schmidt, improvising slightly, was saying, 'I'm talking here about juvenile fads, of course, only because it's the simplest, most intuitive sort of example. The marketing people at Mister Squishy know full well that you gentlemen aren't kids,' with a small slight smile at the younger members, all three of whom could after all vote, purchase alcohol, and enlist in the armed forces; 'or nor that there's anything like a real herd mentality we're trying to spark here by leaving you alone to confer amongst yourselves qua group. If nothing else, keep in mind that soft-confection marketing doesn't work this way; it's much more complicated, and the group dynamics of the market are much harder to really talk about without computer modeling and all sorts of ugly math up on the board that we wouldn't even dream of trying to get you to sit still for.'

A single intrepid sporting boat was making its way right to left across the portion of the lake the large window gave out on, and once or twice an automobile horn far below on E. Huron sounded at such insistent length that it intruded on the attention of Terry Schmidt and some of the well-vetted consumers in this conference room, a couple of whom Schmidt had to admit to himself that he felt he might frankly dislike — both of them somewhat older, one the man with the hairweave, something hooded about their eyes, and the way they made little self-satisfied adjustments to parts of themselves and their wardrobes, sometimes in a very concentrated way, as if to communicate that they were men so important that their attention itself was highly prized, that they were old and experienced hands at sitting in rooms like this having earnest young men with easels and full-color charts make presentations and try to solicit favorable responses from them, and that they were well above whatever mass-consumer LCD Schmidt's clumsy mime of candid spontaneity was pitched at, that they'd taken cellular phone calls during or in fact even walked out of far more nuanced, sophisticated, assuasive pitches than this. Schmidt had had several years of psychotherapy and was not without some perspective on himself, and he knew that a certain percentage of his reaction to the way these older men coolly inspected their cuticles or pinched at the crease in the trouser of the topmost leg as they sat back on their coccyx joggling the foot of their crossed leg was his own insecurity, that he felt somewhat sullied and implicated by the whole enterprise of contemporary marketing and that this sometimes manifested via projection as the feeling that people he was just trying to talk as candidly as possible to always believed he was making a sales pitch or trying to manipulate them in some way, as if merely being employed, however ephemerally, in the great grinding US marketing machine had somehow colored his whole being and that something essentially shifty or pleading in his expression now always seemed inherently false or manipulative and turned people off, and not just in his career — which was not his whole existence, unlike so many at Team Δy, or even all that terribly important to him; he had a vivid and complex inner life, and introspected a great deal — but in his personal affairs as well, and that somewhere along the line his professional marketing skills had metastasized throughout his whole character so that he was now the sort of man who, if he were to screw up his courage and ask a female colleague out for drinks and over drinks open his heart up to her and reveal that he respected her enormously, that his feelings for her involved elements of both professional and highly personal regard, and that he spent a great deal more time thinking about her than she probably had any idea he did, and that if there were anything at all he could ever do to make her life happier or easier or more satisfying or fulfilling he hoped she'd just say the word, for that is all she would have to do, say the word or snap her thick fingers or even just look at him in a meaningful way, and he'd be there, instantly and with no reservations at all, he would nevertheless in all probability be viewed as probably just wanting to sleep with her or fondle or harass her, or as having some creepy obsession with her, or as maybe even having a small creepy secretive kind of almost shrine to her in one corner of the unused second bedroom of his condominium, consisting of personal items fished out of her cubicle's wastebasket or the occasional dry witty little notes she passed him during especially deadly or absurd Team Δy staff meetings, or that his home Apple PowerBook's screensaver was an Adobe-brand 1440-dpi blowup of a digital snapshot of the two of them with his arm over her shoulder and just part of the arm and shoulder of another Team Δy Field-worker with his arm over her shoulder from the other side at a Fourth of July picnic that A.C. Romney–Jaswat & Assoc. had thrown for its research subcontractors at Navy Pier two years past, Darlene holding her cup and smiling in such a way as to show almost as much upper gum as teeth, the ale's cup's red digitally enhanced to match her lipstick and the small scarlet hairbow she often wore just right of center as a sort of personal signature or statement.

The crowd on the sidewalk's growth was still inconstant. For every two or three passersby who joined the group of onlookers craning upward, someone else in the crowd suddenly looked at his watch and detached from the collective and hurried off either northward or across the street to keep some type of appointment. From a certain perspective the small crowd, then, looked like a living cell engaged in trade and exchange with the linear streetside flows that fed it. There was no evidence that the climbing figure saw the fluctuantly growing mass so far below. He certainly never made any of the motions or expressions people associate with someone at a great height looking down at them. No one in the sidewalk's group of spectators pointed or yelled; for the most part they just watched. What children there were held their guardians' hand. There were some remarks and small conversations between adjoining onlookers, but these took place out of the sides of their mouths as all parties looked up at what appeared to be a sheer and sky-high column of alternating glass and prestressed stone. The figure averaged roughly 230 seconds per story; a commuter timed him. Both his backpack and apron looked full of some kind of equipment that caused them to bulge. There were loops along his GoreTex top's shoulders and also — unless it was a trick of the building's windows' refracted light — small strange almost nipplelike protuberances at the figure's shoulders, on his knees' backs, and in the center of the odd navy-and-white bullseye design at the figure's seat. The crampons on mountaineering boots can be removed with a small square tool so that they can be sharpened or replaced, a long-haired man supporting an expensive bicycle against his hip told the people around him. He personally felt he knew what the protuberances were. New members of the crowd always asked the people around them what was going on, whether they knew anything. The costume was airtight, the guy was inflatable or designed to look that way, the long-haired man said. He appeared to be talking to his bicycle; no one acknowledged him. His pantcuffs were clipped for easy cycling. On every third or fourth floor, the figure paused for a time on his back on the narrow ledge with scrollwork at the cornices, resting. A man who had at one time driven an airport shuttlebus opined that the figure on the ledge looked to be purposely idling, timing out his ascent to conform to some schedule; the child attached to the hand of the woman he said this to looked briefly over at him with his face still upturned. Anyone looking straight down would have seen a shifting collection of several dozen watching faces with bodies so foreshortened as to be mere suggestions only.

'Probably only up to a certain point,' Terry Schmidt said then in response to a sort of confirmational question from the tall man with the kite-shaped face and a partly torn tag (two of the room's six cursive nametags were ripped or sectional, the result of accidents during their removal from the adhesive backing) that read *FORREST*, a 40ish fellow with large and hirsute hands and a slightly frayed collar, whose air of rumpled integrity — along with two separate questions that had actually helped advance the presentation's agendas — made this fellow Schmidt's personal choice for foreman. 'What it is is just that R.S.B. feels your Focus Group responses qua group instead of just as the sum of your personal individual responses is an equally important market research tool for a product like the *Felony!*. "GRDS as well as IRPs" as we say in the trade,' with a breeziness he did not feel. One of the younger members — age 22 according to the tiny Charleston code worked into the scrollwork at his nametag's lower border, and handsome in a generic way — wore a reversed baseball cap and a soft wool V-neck sweater with no shirt underneath, displaying a powerful upper chest and forearms (the sleeves of the sweater were carefully pushed up to reveal the forearms' musculature in a way designed to look casual, as if the sweater's arms had been thoughtlessly pushed up in the midst of his thinking hard about something other than himself), and had crossed his leg ankle-on-knee and slid so far down on his tailbone that his cocked leg was the same height as his chin, thereupon holding the salient knee with his fingers laced in such a way as to apply pressure and make his forearms bulge even more. It had occurred to Terry Schmidt that even though so many home products, from Centrum Multivitamins to Visine AC Soothing Antiallergenic Eye Drops to Nasacort AQ Prescription Nasal Spray, now came in conspicuous tamperproof packaging in the wake of the Tylenol poisonings of a decade past and Johnson & Johnson's legendarily swift and conscientious response to the crisis — pulling every bottle of every variety of Tylenol off every retail shelf in America and spending millions on setting up overnight a smooth and hassle-free system for every Tylenol consumer to return his or her bottle for an immediate NQA refund plus an added sum for the gas and mileage or US postage involved in the return, writing off tens of millions in returns and operational costs and recouping untold exponents more in positive PR and consumer goodwill and thereby actually enhancing the brand Tylenol's association with compassion and concern for consumer wellbeing, a strategy that had made J. & J.'s CEO and their PR vendors legends in a marketing field that Terry Schmidt had only just that year begun considering getting into as a practical and potentially creative and rewarding way to use his double major in Descriptive Statistics + Bv. Psych, the young Schmidt imagining himself in plush conference rooms not unlike this one, using the sheer force of his personality and command of the facts to persuade tablesful of hard-eyed corporate officers that legitimate concern for consumer wellbeing was both emotionally and economically Good Business, that if, e.g., R. J. Reynolds elected to be forthcoming about its products' addictive qualities, and GM to be upfront in its national ads about the fact that vastly greater fuel efficiency was totally feasible if consumers would be willing to spend a couple hundred dollars more and settle for slightly fewer aesthetic amenities, and shampoo manufacturers to concede that the 'Repeat' in their product instructions was hygienically unnecessary, and Tums' parent General Brands to spend a couple million to announce candidly that Tums-brand antacid tablets should not be used regularly for more than a couple weeks at a time because after that the stomach lining automatically started secreting more HCl to compensate for all the neutralization and made the original stomach trouble worse, that the consequent gains in corporate PR and associations of the brand with integrity and trust would more than outweigh the short-term costs and stock-price repercussions, that yes it was a risk but not a wild or dicelike risk, that it had on its side both precedent cases and demographic data as well as the solid reputation for both caginess and integrity of T. E. Schmidt & Associates, to concede that yes gentlemen he supposed he was in a way asking them to gamble some of their narrow short-term margins and equity on the humble sayso of Terence Eric Schmidt Jr., whose own character's clear marriage of virtue, pragmatism, and oracular marketing savvy were his best and final argument; he was saying to these upper-management men in their vests and Cole Haans just what he proposed to have them say to a sorry and cynical US market: Trust Me You Will Not Be Sorry — which when he thinks of the starry-eyed puerility and narcissism of these fantasies now, a rough decade later, Schmidt experiences a kind of full-frame internal wince, that type of embarrassment-before-self that makes our most mortifying memories objects of fascination and repulsion at once, though in Terry Schmidt's case a certain amount of introspection and psychotherapy (the latter the origin of the self-caricature doodling during downtime in his beige cubicle) had enabled him to understand that his professional fantasies were not in the main all that unique, that a large percentage of bright young men and women locate the impetus behind their career choice in the belief that they are fundamentally different from the common run of man, unique and in certain crucial ways superior, more as it were central, meaningful — what else could explain the fact that they themselves have been at the *exact center* of all they've experienced for the whole 20 years of their conscious lives? — and that they can and will make a difference in their chosen field simply by the fact of their unique and central presence in it . . . ; and but so (Schmidt also still declaiming professionally to the TFG all this while) that even though so many upmarket consumer products now were tamperproof, Mister Squishy–brand snack cakes — as well as Hostess, Little Debbie, Dolly Madison, the whole soft-confection industry with its flimsy neopolymerized wrappers and cheap thin cardboard Economy Size containers — were decidedly not tamperproof at all, that it would take nothing more than one thin-gauge hypodermic and 24 infinitesimal doses of KCN, As_2O_3, ricin, $C_{21}H_{22}O_2N_2$, acincetilcholine, botulinus, or even merely Tl or some other aqueous base-metal compound to bring almost an entire industry down on one supplicatory knee; for even if the soft-confection manufacturers survived the initial horror and managed to recover some measure of consumer trust, the relevant products' low price was an essential part of their established Market

Appeal Matrix[*], and the costs of reinforcing the Economy packaging or rendering the individual snack cakes visibly invulnerable to a thin-gauge hypodermic would push the products out so far right on the demand curve that mass-market snacks would become economically and emotionally untenable, corporate soft confections going thus the way of hitchhiking, unsupervised trick-or-treating, door-to-door sales, & c.

At various intervals throughout the pre-GRDS presentation the limbic portions of Schmidt's brain pursued this line of thinking — while in fact a whole other part of his mind surveyed these memories and fantasies and was simultaneously fascinated and repelled at the way in which all these thoughts and feelings could be entertained in total subjective private while Schmidt ran the Focus Group through its brief and supposedly Full-Access description of Mister Squishy's place in the soft-confection industry and some of the travails of developing and marketing what these men were experiencing as *Felonies!* (referring offhandedly to nascent plans for bite-sized *misdemeanors!* [*sic*] if the original product established a foothold), at least half the room's men listening with what's called half an ear while pursuing their own private lines of thought, and Schmidt had a quick vision of them all in the conference room as like icebergs and/or floes, only the sharp caps showing, unknown and -knowable to one another, and he imagined that it was probably only in marriage (and a good marriage, not the decorous dance of loneliness he'd watched his mother and father do for seventeen years but rather true conjugal intimacy) that partners allowed each other to see below the berg's cap's public mask and consented to be truly *known*, maybe even to the extent of not only letting the partner see the repulsive nest of moles under their left arm or the way after any sort of cold or viral infection the toenails on both feet turned a weird deep yellow for several weeks but even perhaps every once in a while sobbing in each other's arms late at night and pouring out the most ghastly private fears and thoughts of failure and impotence and terrible and thoroughgoing *smallness* within a grinding professional machine you can't believe you once had the temerity to think

---

[*]also, somewhat confusingly, = MAM

you could help change or make a difference or ever be more than a tiny faceless cog in, the shame of being so hungry to make some sort of real impact on an industry that you'd fantasized over and over about finally deciding that making a dark difference with a hypo and eight cc's of castor bean distillate was better, was somehow more true to your own inner centrality and importance, than being nothing but a faceless cog and doing a job that untold thousands of other bright young men and women could do at least as well as you, or rather now even better than you because at least the younger among them still believed deep inside that they were made for something larger and more central and relevant than shepherding preoccupied men through an abstracted sham-caucus and yet at the same time still believed that they could (= the bright young men could) begin to manifest their larger potential for impact and effectiveness by being the very best darn Targeted Focus Group facilitator that Team Δy and R.S.B. had ever seen, better than the nested-test data they'd seen so far had shown might even be possible, establishing via manifest candor and integrity and a smooth informal rhetoric that let their own very special qualities manifest themselves and shine forth such a level of connection and intimacy with a Focus Group that the TFG's men or women felt, within the special high-voltage field of the relationship the extraordinary facilitator created, an interest in and enthusiasm for the product and for R.S.B.'s desire to bring the product out into the US market in the very most effective way that matched or even exceeded the agency's own. Or maybe that even the mere possibility of expressing any of this childish heartbreak to someone else seemed impossible except in the context of the mystery of true marriage, meaning not just a ceremony and financial merger but a true communion of souls, and Schmidt now lately felt he was coming to understand why the Church all through his childhood catechism and pre-Con referred to it as the Holy Sacrament of Marriage, for it seemed every bit as miraculous and trans-rational and remote from the possibilities of actual lived life as the crucifixion and resurrection and transubstantiation did, which is to say it appeared not as a goal to expect ever to really reach or achieve but as a kind of navigational star, as in in the sky, something high and untouchable and miraculously beautiful in the sort of distant way that reminded you always of how ordinary and unbeautiful and incapable of miracles you your own self were, which was another reason why Schmidt had stopped looking at the sky or going out at night or even usually ever opening the lightproof curtains of his condominium's picture window when he got home at night and instead sat with his satellite TV's channel-changer in his left hand switching rapidly from channel to channel to channel out of fear that something better was going to come on suddenly on another of the cable provider's 220 regular and premium channels and that he was about to miss it, spending three nightly hours this way before it was time to stare with drumming heart at the telephone that wholly unbeknownst to her had Darlene Lilley's home number on Speed Dial so that it would take only one moment of the courage to risk looking prurient or creepy to use just one finger to push just one gray button to invite her for one cocktail or even just a soft drink over which he could take off his public mask and open his heart to her before quailing and deferring the call one more night and waddling into the bathroom and/or then the cream-and-tan bedroom to lay out the next day's crisp shirt and tie and say his nightly dekate and then masturbate himself to sleep again once more. Schmidt was sensitive about the way his weight and body fat percentage increased with each passing year, and imagined that there was something about the way he walked that suggested a plump or prissy fat man's waddle, when in fact his stride was 100% average and unremarkable and nobody except Terry Schmidt had any opinions about his manner of walking one way or the other. Sometimes over this last quarter, when shaving in the morning with WLS News and Talk Radio on over the intercom, he stopped — Schmidt did — and would look at his face and at the faint lines and pouches that seemed to grow a little more pronounced each quarter and would call himself, directly to his mirrored face, *Mister Squishy*, the name would come unbidden into his mind, and despite his attempts to ignore or resist it the large subsidiary's name and logo had become the dark part of him's latest taunt, so that when he thought of himself now it was as something he called *Mister Squishy*, and his own face and the plump and wholly innocuous icon's face tended to bleed in his mind into one face, crude and line-drawn and clever in a small way, a design that someone might find some small selfish use for but could never love or hate or ever care to truly even know.

Some of the shoppers inside the first-floor display window of the Gap observed the mass of people on the sidewalk craning upward and wondered, naturally, what was up. At the base of the eighth floor, the figure shifted himself carefully around so that he was seated on the ledge facing outward with his bicolored legs adangle. He was 238 feet up in the air. The square of sky directly above him a pilot-light blue. The growing crowd watching the figure's climb could not discern that there was in turn a growing collection of shoppers inside looking out at them because the building's glass, which appeared tinted on the inside, was reflective on the outside; it was One Way Glass. The figure now crossed his legs lotus-style on the ledge beneath him, paused, and then in one lithe movement drove himself upright, losing his balance slightly and windmilling his arms to keep from pitching forward off the ledge altogether. There was a brief group-exhalation from the sidewalk's crowd as the figure now snapped its hooded head back and with a tiny distant wet noise affixed the suction cup at his head's rear to the window. A couple young men in the crowd cried up at the eighth floor for the figure to jump, but their tone was self-ironic and it was plain that they were simply parodying the typical cry of jaded onlookers to a figure balanced on a slim ledge 240 feet up in a high wind and looking down at a crowd on the plaza's sidewalk far below. Still, one or two much older people shot optical daggers at the youths who'd shouted; it was unclear whether they knew what self-parody even was. Inside the window of the building's north facet's eighth floor — which space happened to comprise the circulation and subscription departments of *Playboy* magazine — the employees' reaction to the sight of the back of a lithe blue-and-white figure attached to the window by a large suction cup on its head can only be imagined. It was the Gap's floor manager in Accessories who first called the police, and this merely because the press of customers at the window's display clearly bespoke some kind of disturbance on the street outside; and because the nature of that disturbance was unknown, none of the roving television vans who monitored the city's police frequencies were alerted, and the scene remained media-free for a good 1500 feet in every direction.

What Terry Schmidt sketched from memory for the all-male Focus Group was a small eddy or crosscurrent in the tide that demomarketers called an MCP — these were known as Antitrends, or sometimes Shadow Markets. In the area of corporate snacks, Schmidt pretended to explain, there were two basic ways a new product could position itself in a US market for which health, fitness, nutrition, and attendant indulgence-v.-discipline conflicts had achieved a metastatic status. A Shadow snack simply worked to define itself in opposition to the over-all trend against HDL fats, refined carbs, transfatty acids, i.e. against the consumption of what some subgroups variously termed *empty calories, sweets, junk food,* or in other words the whole brilliantly orchestrated obsession with nutrition and exercise and stress-management that went under the demographic heading Healthy Lifestyles. Schmidt said he could tell from the Focus Group's faces — whose expressions ranged from sullen distraction in the youngest to a kind of studious anxiety in the older men, faces tinged with the slight guilt-about-guilt that Schemm Halter/Deight's legendary E. Peter Fish, the mind behind both shark cartilage and odor-free garlic supplements, had called at a high-priced seminar that both Scott Laleman and Darlene Lilley had attended '. . . the knife edge that Healthy Lifestyles Marketing ha[d] to walk along,' which unfortunate phrase was reproduced by a Hewlett Packard digital projector that cast Fish's key points in bold-fonted outline form against one wall to facilitate effective note-taking (the whole industry seminar business was such bullshit, Terry Schmidt believed, with its leather binders and mission statements and wargame nomenclature, marketing truisms to marketers, who when all was said and done were probably the most plasticly gullible market around, although at the same time there was no disputing E. P. Fish's importance or his statements' weight) — Schmidt said he could tell from their faces that the men knew quite well what Antitrend was about, the Shadow Markets like Punk contra Disco and Cadillacs contra high-mileage compacts and Sun and Apple contra the MS juggernaut.

He said they could if the men wished talk at some length about the stresses on individual consumers caught between their natural God-given herd instincts and their deep fear of sacrificing their natural God-given identities as individuals, and about the way these stresses were tweaked and-slash-or soothed by skillfully engineered trends, and that but then, by sort of the Third Law of Motion of marketing, the MCP trends spawned also their Antitrend Shadows, the spin inside and against the larger spin of in this instance Reduced-Calorie and Fat-Free foods, nutritional supplements, Lowcaf and Decaf, Nutra-Sweet and Olestra, jazzercise and liposuction and kava kava, good v. bad cholesterol, free radicals v. antioxidants, time management and Quality Time and the really rather brilliantly managed stress that everyone was made to feel about staying fit and looking good and living long and squeezing the absolute maximum productivity and health and self-actuation out of every last vanishing second, Schmidt then backing off to acknowledge that but of course on the other hand he was aware that the men's time was valuable and so he'd . . . and here one or two of the older Focus Group members who had wristwatches glanced at them by reflex, and the overstylized UAF's pager went off by prearrangement, which allowed Schmidt to gesture broadly and pretend to chuckle and to concede that yes yes see their time *was* valuable, that they all felt it, that they all knew what he was talking about because after all they all lived in it didn't they, and to say that so in this case it would perhaps suffice just to simply for example utter the illustrative words Jolt Cola, Starbucks, Häagen-Dazs, Ericson's All Butter Fudge, premium cigars, conspicuously low-mileage urban 4WDs, Hammacher Schlemmer's all-silk boxers, whole Near North Side eateries given over to high-lipid desserts — enterprises in other words that rode the transverse Shadow, that said or sought to say to a consumer bludgeoned by herd-pressures to achieve, forbear, trim the fat, cut down, discipline, prioritize, be sensible, self-parent, that hey, you deserve it, reward yourself, brands that in essence said what's the use of living longer and healthier if there aren't those few precious moments in every day when you stopped, sat down, and took a few moments of hard-earned pleasure just for you? and various myriad other pitches that aimed to remind the consumer that he was at root an individual, one with individual tastes and preferences and freedom of individual choice, that he was not a mere herd animal who had no choice but to go go go on US life's digital-calorie-readout treadmill, that there were still some rich and refined and harmless-if-judiciously-indulged-in pleasures out there to indulge in if the consumer'd snap out of his high-fiber hypnosis and realize that life was also to be enjoyed, that the un-enjoyed life was not worth living, &c. &c. That, as one example, just as Hostess Inc. was coming out with low-fat Twinkies and cholesterol-free Ding Dongs, Jolt Cola's own branders had hung its West Coast launch on the inverted All the Sugar Twice the Caffeine, and that meanwhile the stock of Ericson's All Butter Fudge and individual bite-sized Fudgees' parent company US Brands had split three times via D.D.B. Needham's series of ads that featured people in workout clothes running into each other in dim closets where they'd gone to eat Ericson's A.B.F. in secret, with all the ingenious and piquant taglines that played against the moment the characters' mutual embarrassment turned to laughter and a convolved esprit de corps. (Schmidt knew full well that Reesemeyer Shannon Belt Adv. had lost the US Brands/Ericson account to D.D.B. Needham's spectacular pitch for a full-out Shadow strategy, and thus that the videotape of his remarks here would raise at least three eyebrows among R.S.B.'s MROP team and would force Robert Awad to behave as though he believed Schmidt hadn't known anything about the Ericson–D.D.B. Needham thing and to come lean pungently over the wall of Schmidt's cubicle and try to quote unquote 'fill in Terry' on certain facts of life of interagency politics without unduly damaging Schmidt's morale over the putative boner, and so on.)

Nor in fact was the high-altitude figure gazing down at them, the street's keener onlookers saw — what he was actually doing was look-ing down at himself and gingerly removing a shiny packet of what ap-peared to be foil or Mylar from his mountaineer's tool apron and giving it a delicate little towel-like snap to open it out and then reach-ing up with both hands and rolling it down over his head and hood and fixing it in place with small snaps or Velcro tabs at his shoulders and throat's base. It was some sort of mask, the long-haired cyclist who always carried a small novelty-type spy telescope in his fannypack opined, though except for two holes for eyes and a large one for his forehead's cup the whole thing appeared too wrinkled and detumesced-looking to be able to make out who or what the shapeless arrangement of microtextured lines on the Mylar was supposed to represent, but even at this distance the mask looked frightening, baggy and hydro-cephalic and cartoonishly inhuman, and there were now some louder and less self-ironic shouts and cries, and several members of the watching crowd involuntarily stepped back into the street, fouling traffic and causing a brief discordance of horns as the figure placed both hands on his head's white bag and with something like a wet kissing noise from his skull's rear suction cup performed a lithe *contra face* that left him now facing the window with the sagged mask's nose and lips and forehead's very orange cup pressed tight against it — again provoking God only knows what reaction from the *Playboy* mag-azine corporate staff on the glass's inside — whereupon he now reached around and removed from the backpack what appeared to be a small generator or perhaps scuba-style tank with a slender hoselike attach-ment that was either black or dark blue and ended in a strange sort of triangular or arrowhead- or Δ-shaped nozzle or attachment or mor-tise, which tank he connected with straps and a harness to the back of his GoreTex top and allowed the dark hose and nozzle to hang unfet-tered down over his concentricized rear and the leggings' tops, so that when he resumed his practiced-looking opposite-leg and -arm climb up the eighth-floor window he now also wore what appeared to be a deflated cranial mask or balloon, dorsal airtank, and frankly demonic-looking tail, and presented an overall sight so complex and unlike any-thing from any member of the (now much larger and more diffuse, some still in the street and beginning to roil) crowd's visual experience that there were several moments of dead silence as everyone's individ-ual neocortices worked to process the visual information and to scan their memories for any thing or combination of live or animated things the figure might resemble or suggest. A small child in the crowd began to cry because someone had stepped on its foot.

Now that he appeared less conventionally human, the way the figure climbed by moving his left arm/right leg and then right arm/left
leg looked even more arachnoid or saurian; in any event he was still
just lithe as hell. Some of the shoppers inside the display windows of
the Gap had now come out and joined the sidewalk's crowd. The figure scaled the eighth–twelfth floors with ease, then paused while attached to the thirteenth- (perhaps called the fourteenth-) floor window
to apply some kind of adhesive or cleaner to his suction cups. The
winds at 425 feet must have been very strong, because his caudal hose
swung wildly this way and that.

It was also impossible for some people in the front portion of the
street and sidewalk's crowd to resist looking at their own and the
whole collective's reflection in the Gap's display window. There were
no more screams or cries of *Jump!*, but among some of the crowd's
younger and more media-savvy members there began to be specula-
tion about whether this was a PR stunt for some product or service or
whether perhaps the climbing figure was one of those renegade urban
daredevils who scaled tall buildings and then parachuted to the ground
below and submitted to arrest while blowing kisses to network news
cameras. The well-known Sears Tower or even Hancock Center would
have been a far better high-visibility site for a stunt like this if such a
stunt it was, some of them opined. The first two squad cars arrived as
the figure — by this time quite small, even through a novelty telescope,
and obscured almost wholly from view when he negotiated ledges —
was hanging attached by his forehead's central cup to the fifteenth-
floor window (or perhaps sixteenth, depending whether the building
had a thirteenth floor; some do and some don't) and appeared to be
pulling more items from his nylon pack, fitting them together and using both hands to telescope something out to arm's length and then attaching various other small things to it. It was probably the squad cars
and their garish lights at the curb that caused so many other cars on
Huron Ave. to slow down or even pull over to see if there'd been a
death or an arrest, forcing one of the officers to spend his time trying
to control traffic and keep cars moving so that the avenue remained
passable. It was an older African-American woman who'd been one of

the very first pedestrians to stop and look up and was now using broad motions of all four limbs to report or re-create for a policeman all she had witnessed up to the present who'd paused to ask whether to the officer's knowledge the strangely costumed figure's climb could possibly be a licensed stunt for a feature film or commercial television or cable program, and this was when it occurred to some of the other spectators that the lithe figure's climb was conceivably being filmed from the upper stories of one of the other commercial skyscrapers on the street, and that there might in particular be cameras, film crews, and/or celebrities in the tall gray vertiginously flèched older building directly opposite 1101 E. Huron's north facet; and a certain percentage of the crowd's rear turned around and began craning and scanning windows on that building's south side, none of which were open, although this signified nothing because by City Ordinance 920-1247(d) no commercially zoned structure could possess, nor authorize by terms of lease or contract any lessee to possess, operable windows above the third floor. It was not clear whether this older opposite building's glass was One Way or not because the angle of the late-morning sun, now almost directly overhead in the street's slot of sky, caused blinding reflections in that older spired building's windows, some of which brilliant reflections the windows focused and cast almost like spotlights against the surface of the original building which even now the masked figure with the tank and tail and real or imitation semiautomatic weapon — for verily that is what the new item was, slung over the subject's back at a slight transverse angle so that its unfolded stock rested atop the small blue-and-white tank for what might even conceivably be a miniaturized combat-grade gas mask or even maybe Jaysus help us all if it was a flamethrower or Clancy-grade biochemical aerosol nebulizer gizmo thing, the officer with the Dept.-issue high-× binoculars reported, using a radio that was somehow attached like an epaulette to his uniform's shoulder so that he had only to cock his head and touch his left shoulder to be able to confer with other officers, whose blue-and-white bored-out Montegos' sirens could be heard approaching from what sounded like Loyola U. — continued to scale, namely 1101 E. Huron, so that squares and small rectangles and parallelograms

of high-intensity light swam around him and lit up the sixteenth-
or seventeenth-floor window he was even then scaling with nerveless
ease, the fully automatic–looking M16's barrel and folded stock inserted through several presewn loops along the left shoulder of his
GoreTex top so that he retained full use of his left arm and hand's
cup as he scaled the window and sat once again on the next story's
ledge, the long nozzle arranged beneath him and only a couple feet
of it protruding from between his legs and wobbling stiffly in the
wind. Reflected light aswim all around him. A group of pigeons or
doves on the ledge of the adjoining window was disturbed and took
flight across the street and reassembled on a ledge at the exact same
height on the opposite building. The figure appeared now to have
removed some sort of radio, cellular phone, or handheld recording
device from his mountaineer's apron and to be speaking into it. At no
time did he look down or in any way acknowledge the sidewalk and
street's crowds, their shouts and cheers as each window was traversed,
or the police cruisers which by this time were parked at several different angles on the street, all emitting complex light, with two more
squad cars now blocking off E. Huron at the major intersections on
either side.

A C.F.D. truck arrived and firefighters in heavy slickers exited and
began to mill about for no discernible reason. There were also no evident media vans or rigs or mobile cameras at any time, which struck
the savvier onlookers as further evidence that the whole thing could be
some sort of licensed prearranged corporate promotion or stunt or
ploy. A few arguments ensued, mostly good-natured and inhibited by
the number of auditors nearby. A stiff new ground-level breeze carried
the smell of fried foods. A foreign couple arrived and began to hawk
T-shirts whose silkscreen designs had nothing to do with what was
going on. A detachment of police and firefighters entered 1101's north
facet in order to establish a position on the building's roof, the fire-
men's axes and hats causing a small panic in the Gap and causing a
jam-up at the building's revolving door that left a man in Oakley sunglasses slumped and holding his chest or side. Several people in the
crowd's rear cried out and pointed at what they claimed had been

movement and/or the flash of lenses on the roof of the opposite building. There was counterspeculation in the crowd that the whole thing was maybe designed to maybe only *look* like a media stunt and that the weapon the figure was now sitting uncomfortably back against was genuine and that the idea was for him to look as eccentric as possible and climb high enough to draw a large crowd and then to spray automatic fire indiscriminately down into the crowd. The driverless autos along the curb at both sides of the street now had tickets under their windshield wipers. A helicopter could be heard but not seen from the canyon or crevasse the commercial structures made of the street below. One or two fingers of cirrus were now in the sky overhead. Some people were eating vendors' pretzels and brats, the wind whipping at the paper napkins tucked into their collars. One officer held a bullhorn but seemed unable to activate it. Someone had stepped backward onto the steep curb and injured his ankle or foot; a paramedic attended him as he lay on his topcoat and stared straight upward at the tiny figure, who by this time had gained his feet and was splayed beneath the seventeenth/eighteenth floor, appearing to just stay there, attached to the window and waiting.

Terry Schmidt's father had served in the US armed forces and been awarded a field commission at the age of just 21 and received both the Purple Heart and the Bronze Star, and the decorated veteran's favorite civilian activity in the whole world — you could tell by his face as he did it — was polishing his shoes and the buttons on his five sportcoats, which he did every Sunday afternoon, and the placid concentration on his face as he knelt on newspaper with his tins and shoes and chamois had formed a large unanalyzable part of the young Terry Schmidt's determination to make a difference in the affairs of men someday in the future. Which was now: time had indeed slipped by, just as in popular songs, and revealed Schmidt fils to be neither special nor exempt.

In the last two years Team Δy had come to function as what the advertising industry called a Captured Shop: the firm occupied a contractual space somewhere between a subsidiary of Reesemeyer Shannon Belt and an outside vendor. Under Alan Britton's stewardship, Team Δy had joined the industry's trend toward Captured consolidation and reinvented itself as more or less the research arm of Reesemeyer Shannon Belt Advertising. Team Δy's new status was designed both to limit R.S.B.'s paper overhead and to maximize the tax advantages of Focus Group research, which now could be both billed to Client and written off as an R&D subcontracting expense. There were substantial salary and benefit advantages to Team Δy (which was structured as an employee-owned S corporation under U.S.T.C. §1361-1379) as well. The major disadvantage, from Terry Schmidt's perspective, was that there were no mechanisms in place by which a Captured Shop employee could make the horizontal jump to Reesemeyer Shannon Belt itself, within whose MROP division the firm's marketing research strategies were developed, thereby enabling someone like T. E. Schmidt to conceivably have at least some sort of impact on actual research design and analysis. Within Team Δy, Schmidt's only possible advancement was to the Senior Research Director position now occupied by the same swarthy, slick, gladhanding émigré (with college-age children and a wife who always appeared about to ululate) who had made Darlene Lilley's professional life so difficult over the past year; and of course even if the Team did vote in such a way as to pressure Alan Britton to ease Robert Awad out and then even if (as would be unlikely to say the least) the thunderingly unexceptional Terry Schmidt were picked and successfully pitched to the rest of Team Δy's upper echelon as Awad's replacement, the SRD position really involved nothing more meaningful than the supervision of sixteen coglike Field Researchers just like Schmidt himself, plus conducting desultory orientations for new hires, plus of course overseeing the compression of TFGs' data into various statistically differentiated totals, all of which was done on commercially available software and entailed nothing more significant than adding four-color graphs and a great deal of acronym-heavy jargon designed to make a survey that any competent tenth-grader could have conducted appear sophisticated and meaningful. Although there were also of course the preliminary lunches and golf and gladhanding with R.S.B.'s MROPs, and the actual three-hour presentation of Field Research results in the larger and more expensively appointed conference room upstairs where Awad, his mute and spectrally thin A/V technician, and one chosen member of the relevant Field Team presented the numbers and graphs and helped facilitate R.S.B.'s MROPs and Creative and Marketing heads' brainstorming on the research's implications for an actual campaign that in truth R.S.B. was already at this stage far too heavily invested in to do anything more than modify some of the more ephemeral or decorative elements of. (Neither Schmidt nor Darlene Lilley had ever been selected to assist Bob Awad in these PCAs[*], for reasons that in Schmidt's case seemed all too clear.) Meaning, in other words, without anyone once ever saying it outright, that Team Δy's real function was to present to Reesemeyer Shannon Belt test data that R.S.B. could then turn around and present to Client as confirming the soundness of the very OCC[†] that R.S.B. had already billed Client in the millions for and couldn't turn back from even if the actual test data turned out to be resoundingly grim or unpromising, which it was Team Δy's unspoken real job to make sure never happened, a job that Team Δy accomplished simply by targeting so many different Focus Groups and foci and by varying the format and context of the tests so baroquely and by facilitating the different TFGs in so many different modalities that in the end it was child's play to selectively weight and rearrange the data in pretty much whatever way R.S.B.'s MROP division wanted, and so in reality Team Δy's function was not to provide information or even a statistical approximation of information but rather its entropic converse, a cascade of random noise meant to so befuddle the firm and its Client that no one would feel anything but relief at the decision to proceed with an OCC which in the present case the Mister Squishy Company itself was already so heavily invested in that it couldn't possibly turn away from and would in fact have fired R.S.B. if its testing had indicated any substantive problems with, because Mister Squishy's parent company had very strict normative ratios for R&D marketing costs (= RDM) to production volume (= PV), ratios based on the Cobb-Douglas Function whereby $\frac{RDM(x)}{PV(x)}$ must, after all the pro forma hemming and hawing,

---

be $0 < \frac{RDM(x)}{PV(x)} < 1$, a textbook formula which any first-term MBA student had to memorize in Management Stats, which was in fact where North American Soft Confections Inc.'s CEO had almost surely learned it, and nothing inside the man or at any of the four large US corporations he had helmed since taking his degree from Wharton in 1968 had changed; no no all that ever changed were the jargon and mechanisms and gilt rococo with which everyone in the whole huge blind grinding mechanism conspired to convince each other that they could figure out how to give the paying customer what they could prove he could be persuaded to believe he wanted, without anybody once ever saying stop a second or pointing out the absurdity of calling what they were doing collecting information or ever even saying aloud — not even Team Δy's Field Researchers over drinks at Beyers' Market Pub on E. Ohio together on Fridays before going home alone to stare at the phone — what was going on or what it meant or what the simple truth was. That it made no difference. None of it. One R.S.B. Senior Creative Director with his little gray ponytail had been at one upscale café someplace and had ordered one trendy dessert on the same day he was making notes for one Creative Directors' brainstorming session on what to pitch to the Subsidiary PD boys over at North American Soft Confections, and had had one idea, and one or two dozen pistons and gears already machined and set in place in various craggy heads at R.S.B. and North American's Mister Squishy had needed only this one single spark of $C_{12}H_{22}O_{11}$-inspired passion from an SCD whose whole inflated rep had been based on a concept equating toilet paper with clouds and helium-voiced teddy bears and all manner of things innocent of shit in some abstract Ur-consumer's mind in order to set in movement a machine of which no one single person now — least of all the squishy Mr. T. E. Schmidt, forgetting himself enough almost to pace a little before the conference table's men and toying dangerously with the idea of dropping the whole involved farce and simply telling them the truth — could be master.

Not surprisingly, the marketing of a conspicuously high-sugar, high-cholesterol, Shadow-class snack cake had presented substantially more challenges than the actual kitchenwork of development and production.

As with most Antitrend products, the *Felony!* had to walk a fine line between a consumer's resentment of the Healthy Lifestyles trend's ascetic pressures and the guilt and unease any animal instinctively felt when it left the herd — or at least perceived itself as leaving the herd — and the successful Shadow product was one that managed to position and present itself in such a way as to resonate with both these inner drives at once, the facilitator told the Focus Group, using slight changes in intonation and facial expression to place scare quotes around *herd.* The perfectly proportioned mixture of shame, delight, and secret (literally: closeted) alliance in the Ericson-D.D.B.N. spots was a seminal example of this sort of multivalent pitch, Terry Schmidt said (tweaking Awad again and letting the small secret thrill of it almost make him throw a puckish wink at the smoke detector), as too was Jolt Cola's brand name's double entendre of a 'jolt' both to the individual nervous system and to the tyranny of dilute and innocuous soft drinks in an era of trendy self-denial, as well of course as Jolt's well-packaged can's iconic face with its bulging crossed eyes and electricized hair and ghastly fluorescent computer-room pallor — for Jolt had worked to position itself as a recreational beverage for digital-era phreaks and dweebs and had managed at once to acknowledge, parody, and evect the computer-dweeb as an avatar of individual rebellion.

Schmidt had also adopted one of Darlene Lilley's signature physical MAMs when addressing TFGs, which was sometimes to put one foot forward with his or her weight on its heel and to lift the remainder of that foot slightly and rotate it idly back and forth along the x axis with the planted heel serving as pivot, which in Lilley's case was slightly more effective and appealing because a burgundy high heel formed a better pivot than a cocoa-brown cordovan loafer. Sometimes Schmidt had dreams in which he was one of a Focus Group's consumers being led by Darlene Lilley as she crossed her sturdy ankles or rotated her 9DD high heel back and forth along the floor's x axis, and she had her eyeglasses off, which were small and oval with tortoiseshell-design frames, and was holding them in a MAM such that one of the glasses' delicate arms was in very close proximity to her mouth, and the whole dream was Schmidt and the rest of the Focus Group for the nameless product hovering right on the edge of watching Darlene actually put the glasses' arm inside her mouth, which she came incrementally closer and closer to doing without ever quite seeming to be aware of what she was doing or the effect it was having, and the feeling of the dream was that if she ever did actually put the plastic arm in her mouth something very important and/or dangerous would happen, and the ambient unspoken tension of the dream's constant waiting often left Schmidt exhausted by the time he awoke and remembered again who and what he was, opening the lightproof curtains.

In the morning at the sink's mirror shaving sometimes Schmidt as *Mr. S.* would examine the faint lines beginning to appear and to connect the various dots of pale freckle in meaningless ways on his face, and could envision in his mind's eye the deeper lines and sags and bruised eye-circles of his face's predictable future and imagine the slight changes required to shave his 44-year-old cheeks and chin as he stood in this exact spot ten years hence and checked his moles and nails and brushed his teeth and examined his face and did precisely the same series of things in preparation for the exact same job he had been doing now for eight years, sometimes carrying the vision further all the way and seeing his ravaged lineaments and bloblike body propped upright on wheels with a blanket on its lap against some sundrenched pastel backdrop, coughing. So that even if the almost vanishingly unlikely were to happen and Schmidt did somehow get tagged to replace Robert Awad or one of the other SRDs the only substantive difference would be that he would receive a larger share of Team Δy's after-tax profits and so would be able to afford a nicer and better-appointed condominium to masturbate himself to sleep in and more of the props and surface pretenses of someone truly important but really he wouldn't be important, he would make no more substantive difference in the larger scheme of things than he did now. The almost-35-year-old Terry Schmidt had very nearly nothing left anymore of the delusion that he differed from the great herd of the common run of men, not even in his despair at not making a difference or in the great hunger to have an impact that in his late twenties he'd clung to as evidence that even though he was emerging as sort of a failure the grand ambitions against which he judged himself a failure were somehow exceptional and superior to the common run's — not anymore, since now even the phrase *Make a Difference* had become a platitude so familiar that it was used as the mnemonic tag in low-budget Ad Council PSAs for Big Brothers/Big Sisters and the United Way, which used Make a Difference in a Child's Life and Making a Difference in Your Community respectively, with B.B./B.S. even acquiring the telephonic equivalent of *DIF-FER-ENCE* to serve as their Volunteer Hotline number in the metro area. And Schmidt, then just at the cusp of 30, at first had rallied himself into what he knew was a classic consumer delusion, namely that the B.B./B.S. tagline and telephone number were a meaningful coincidence and directed somehow particularly at him, and had called and volunteered to act as Big Brother for a boy age 11–15 who lacked significant male mentors and/or positive role models, and had sat through the two three-hour trainings and testimonials with what was the psychological equivalent of a rigid grin, and the first boy he was assigned to as a Big Brother had worn a tiny black leather jacket with fringe hanging from the shoulders' rear and a red handkerchief tied over his head and was on the tilted porch of his low-income home with two other boys also in expensive little jackets, and all three boys had without a word jumped into the back seat of Schmidt's car, and the one whose photo and heartbreaking file identified him as Schmidt's mentorless Little Brother had leaned forward and tersely uttered the name of a large shopping mall in Aurora some distance west of the city proper, and after Schmidt had driven them on the nightmarish I-88 tollway all the way to this mall and been directed to pull over at the curb outside the main entrance the three boys had all jumped out without a word and run inside, and after waiting at the curb for over three hours without their returning — and after two $40 tickets and a tow-warning from the Apex MegaMall Security officer, who was completely indifferent to Schmidt's explanation that he was here in his capacity as a Big Brother and was afraid to move the car for fear that his Little Brother would come out expecting to see Schmidt's car right where he and his friends had left it and would be traumatized if it appeared to have vanished just like so many of the other adult male figures in his case file's history — Schmidt had driven home; and subsequent telephone calls to the Little Brother's home were not returned. The second 11–15-year-old boy he was assigned to was not at home either of the times Schmidt had come for his appointment to mentor him, and the woman who answered the apartment door — who purported to be the boy's mother although she was of a completely different race than the boy in the file's photo, and who the second time had appeared intoxicated — claimed to have no knowledge of the appointment or the boy's whereabouts or even the last time she'd seen him, after which Schmidt had finally acknowledged the delusory nature of the impact that the Ad Council's PSAs had made on him and had — being now 30 and thus older, wiser, more indurate — given up and gone on about his business.

In his spare time Terry Schmidt read, watched satellite television, collected rare and uncirculated US coins, ran discriminant analyses of TFG statistics on his Apple PowerBook, worked in the small home laboratory he'd established in his condominium's utility room, and power-walked on a treadmill in a line of eighteen identical treadmills on the mezzanine-level CardioDeck of a Bally Total Fitness franchise just east of the Prudential Center on Mies van der Rohe Way, where he sometimes also used the sauna. Favoring beige, rust, and cocoa-brown in his professional wardrobe, soft and round-faced and vestigially freckled, with a helmetish haircut and a smile that always looked pained no matter how real the cheer, Terry Schmidt had been described by one of Scott R. Laleman's toadies in Technical Processing as looking like a '70s yearbook photo come to life. Agency MROPs whom Terry'd worked with for years had trouble recalling his name, and always greeted him with an exaggerated bonhomie designed to obscure this fact. Ricin and botulinus were about equally easy to cultivate. Actually they were both quite easy indeed, assuming you were comfortable in a laboratory environment and exercised due care in your procedures. Schmidt himself had personally overheard some of the other young men in Technical Processing refer to Darlene Lilley as

Lurch or *Herman* and make fun of her height and physical solidity, and had been outraged enough to have come very very close indeed to confronting them directly.

41.6% of what Schmidt mistakenly believed were the TFG's twelve true sample consumers were presenting with the classic dilated eyes and shiny pallor of low-grade insulin shock as Schmidt announced that he'd decided to 'privately confide' to the men that the product's original proposed trade name had actually been *Devils!*, a cognomen designed both to connote the snack cake's chocolate-intensive composition and to simultaneously invoke and parody associations of sin, sinful indulgence, yielding to temptation, & c., and that considerable resources had been devoted to developing, refining, and target-testing the product inside various combinations of red-and-black individual wrappers with various cartoonishly demonic incarnations of the familiar Mister Squishy icon, presented here as rubicund and heavy-browed and grinning fiendishly instead of endearingly, before negative test data scrapped the whole strategy. Both Darlene Lilley and Trudi Keener had worked some of these early Focus Groups, which apparently some inträagency political enemy of the Creative Packaging Director at Reesemeyer Shannon Belt who'd pitched the trade name *Devils!* had used his (meaning the CPD's enemy's) influence with R.S.B.'s MROP coordinator to stock heavily with consumers from downstate IL — a region that as Terry Schmidt knew all too well tended to be Republican and Bible-Beltish — and without going into any of the Medicean intrigues and retaliations that had ended up costing three midlevel R.S.B. executives their jobs and resulted in at least one six-figure settlement to forestall WT* litigation (which was the only truly interesting part of the story, Schmidt himself believed, jingling a pocket's contents and watching his cordovan rotate slowly from 10:00 to 2:00 and back again as straticulate clouds in the lake's upper atmosphere began to lend the sunlight a pearly cast that the conference room's windows embrowned), the nub was that the stacked Groups' responses to taglines that included Sinfully Delicious, Demon-

---

* = Wrongful Termination

ically Indulgent, and Why Do You Think It's Called [in red] **Temptation**?, as well as to video storyboards in which shadowed and voice-distorted figures in hoods supposedly confessed to being regular upstanding citizens and consumers who unbeknownst to anyone 'worshipped the Devil' in 'secret orgies of indulgence,' had been so uniformly extreme as to produce markedly different Taste and Overall Satisfaction aggregates for the snack cakes on IRPs and GRDSs completed before and after exposure to the lines and boards themselves, which after much midlevel headrolling and high-level caucuses had resulted in the present *Felonies!*®, with its milder penal and thus renegade associations designed to offend absolutely no one except maybe anticrime wackos and prison-reform fringes. With the facilitator's stated point being that please let none of those assembled here today doubt that their judgments and responses and the hard evaluative work they had already put in and would shortly plunge into again qua group in the vital GRDS phase were important or were taken very seriously indeed by the folks over at Mister Squishy.

Showing as yet no signs of polypeptide surfeit, a balding blue-eyed 30ish man whose tag's block caps read *HANK* was staring, from his place at the corner of the conference table nearest Schmidt and the whiteboard, either absently or intently at Schmidt's valise, which was made of a pebbled black synthetic leather material and happened to be markedly wider and squatter than your average-type briefcase or valise, resembling almost more a doctor's bag or computer technician's upscale toolcase. Among the periodicals to which Schmidt subscribed were *US News & World Report, Numismatic News, Advertising Age,* and the quarterly *Journal of Applied Statistics,* the last of which was divided into four stacks of three years each and as such supported the sanded pine plank and sodium worklamp that functioned as a laboratory table with various decanters, retorts, flasks, vacuum jars, filters, and Reese-Handey–brand alcohol burners in the small utility room that was separated from Schmidt's condominium's kitchen by a foldable door of louvered enamel composite. Ricin and its close relative abrin are powerful phytotoxins, respectively derived from castor and jequirity beans, whose attractive flowering plants can be purchased at most commercial nurseries and require just three months of cultivation to yield mature beans, which beans are lima-shaped and either scarlet or a lustrous brown and historically were, Schmidt had gotten that eerie Big Brothers/Big Sisters–like sensation again when he discovered during his careful researches, sometimes employed as rosary beads by medieval flagellants. Castor beans' seed hulls must be removed by soaking 1–4 oz. of the beans in 12–36 oz. of distilled water with 4–6 tablespoons of NaOH or 6–8 ts. of commercial lye (the beans' natural buoyancy requiring here that they be weighted down with marbles, sterilized gravel, or low-value coins combined and tied in an ordinary Trojan condom). After one hour of soaking, the beans can be taken out of solution and dried and the hulls carefully removed by anyone wearing quality surgical gloves. (NB: Ordinary rubber household gloves are too thick and unwieldy for removing castor hulls.) Schmidt had step-by-step instructions stored on both the hard drive and backup disks of his Apple home computer, which possessed a three-hour battery capacity and could itself be set up right there on the pine worktable in order to keep a very precise and time-indexed experimental log, which is one of the absolutely basic principles of proper lab procedure. A blender set on Purée is used to grind the hulled beans plus commercial acetone in a 1:4 ratio. Discard blender after use. Pour castor-and-acetone mixture into a covered sterile jar and let stand for 72–96 hours. Then attach a sturdy commercial coffee filter to an identical jar and pour mixture slowly and carefully through filter. You are not decanting; you're after what is being filtered out. Wearing two pairs of surgical gloves and at least two standard commercial filtration masks, use manual pressure to squish as much acetone as possible out of the filter's sediment. Bear down as hard as due caution permits. Weigh the remainder of the filter's contents and place them in a third sterile jar along with × 4 their weight in fresh CH_3COCH_3. Repeat standing, filtering, and manual squishing process 3–5 times. The residue at the procedures' terminus will be nearly pure ricin, of which 0.04 mg is lethal if injected directly (note that 9.5–12 times this dose is required for lethality through ingestion). Saline or distilled water can be used to load a 0.4 mg ricin solution in a standard fine-gauge hypodermic injector, available at better pharmacies everywhere under Diabetes Supplies. Ricin requires 24–36 hours to produce initial symptoms of severe nausea, vomiting, disorientation, and cyanosis. Terminal VF and circulatory collapse follow within twelve hours. Note that *in situ* concentrations under 1.5 mg are undetectable by standard forensic reagents.

More than a few among the crowds and police initially used the words *sick, sickening,* and/or *nasty* when the tank's deltate nozzle was affixed to the protuberance at the center of the figure's rear end's white-and-navy bullseye design. All such expressions of distaste were silenced by the subsequent inflation. First the bottom and belly and thighs ballooned, forcing the figure out from the window and contorting him slightly to keep his forehead's cup affixed. The airtight Lycra rounded and became shiny. The long-haired man on Dexedrine patted his bicycle's slim rear tire and told the young lady he'd lent the field glasses to that he'd figured all along what they (presumably meaning the little protuberances) were. One shoulder's valve inflated the left arm, the other the right arm, & c., until the figure's entire costume had become large, bulbous, and doughily cartoonish. There was no coherent response from the crowd, however, until a nearly suicidal-looking series of nozzle-to-temple motions from the figure began to fill the head's baggy mask, the crumpled white Mylar at first collapsing slightly to the left and then coming back up erect as it filled with gas, the face's array of patternless lines rounding to resolve into something that produced from 400+ ground-level US adults loud cries of recognition and an almost childlike delight.

. . . And that the time, Schmidt told the Focus Group, had — probably not at all to their disappointment, he said with a tiny pained smile — that the time had now arrived for them to elect a foreman and for Schmidt himself to withdraw and allow the Focus Group's constituents to take counsel together here in the darkening conference room, to compare their individual responses and opinions of the Taste, Texture, and Overall Satisfaction of *Felonies!* and to try now together to come up with agreed-upon GRDS ratings for same. In some of the fantasies in which he and Darlene Lilley were having high-impact intercourse on the firms' conference tables Schmidt kept finding himself saying *Thank you, oh thank you* in rhythm to the undulatory thrusting motions of the coitus, and was unable to stop himself, and couldn't help seeing the confused and then distasteful expression that the rhythmic *Oh God, thank you*s produced on Darlene Lilley's face even as her glasses fogged and her crosstrainers' heels drummed thunderously on the table's surface, and sometimes it almost wrecked the whole fantasy. If, after time and a reasonable amount of discussion, the Focus Group by chance for whatever reason found that they couldn't get together on a certain specific number to express the whole group's true feelings, Schmidt told them (by this time three of the men actually had their heads down on the table, including the overeccentric UAF, who was also emitting tiny low moans, and Schmidt had decided he was going to give this fellow a very low TFG Performance Rating indeed on the evaluations all Team Δy facilitators had to fill out on UAFs at the end of a research cycle), what he'd ask is that the Focus Group then just go ahead and submit two separate Group Response Data Summaries, one GRDS comprising each of the numbers on which the Focus Group's two opposed camps had settled — there was no such thing as a hung jury in TFG testing, he said with a grin that he hoped wasn't rigid or pained — and that if splitting into even two such subgroups proved unfeasible because one or more of the men at the table felt that neither subgroup's number adequately captured their own individual feelings and preferences, why then if necessary three separate GRDSs should be completed, or four, and so on — but with the overall idea being please keep in mind that Team Δy, Reesemeyer Shannon Belt, and the Mister Squishy Co. were asking for the very lowest possible number of separate GRDS responses an intelligent group of discerning consumers could come up with today. Schmidt in fact had as many as thirteen separate GRDS packets in the manila folder he now held rather dramatically up as he mentioned the GRDS forms, though he removed only one packet from the folder, since there was no point in proactively doing anything to encourage the Focus Group to atomize and not unite. The fantasy would of course have been exponentially better if it were Darlene Lilley who gasped *Thank you, thank you* in rhythm to the damp lisping slapping sounds, and Schmidt was well aware of this, and of his apparent inability to enforce his preferences even in fantasy. It made him wonder if he even had what convention called a Free Will at all, deep down. Only two of the room's fifteen total males noticed that there had been no hint of distant window-muffled exterior noise in the conference room for quite some time; neither of these two were actual test subjects. Schmidt knew also that by this time — the exordial presentation had so far taken 23 minutes, but it felt, as always, much longer, and even the more upright and insulin-tolerant members' restive expressions indicated that they too were feeling hungry and tired and probably thinking this preliminary background was taking an oppressively long time (when in reality Robert Awad had explicitly told Schmidt that Alan Britton had authorized up to 32 minutes for the putatively experimental Full-Access TFG presentation, and had said that Terry's reputation for relative conciseness and smooth preemption of digressive questions and ephemera was one of the reasons he [meaning R. Awad] had selected Schmidt to facilitate the quote unquote experimental TFG's GRDS phase) — Schmidt also knew that by this time Darlene Lilley's own Focus Group was *in camera* and deeply into its own GRDS caucus, and that Darlene was thus back in the R.S.B. Research green room making a brisk cup of Lipton tea in the microwave, what she liked to call her grownup shoes off and resting — one perhaps on its burgundy side — with her briefcase and purse beside one of the comfortable chairs opposite the green room's four-part viewing screen, Darlene at this moment facing the microwave and with her great broad back to the door so that Schmidt would have to sigh loudly or cough or jingle his keys as he came down the hall to the green room in order to avoid making her jump and lay her palm against the flounces of her blouse's front by 'com[ing] up behind [her] like that,' as she'd accused him of doing once during the six-month period when SRD Awad really had been coming up stealthily behind her all the time and her own and everyone else's nerves were understandably strung out and on edge. Schmidt would shortly then pour a cup of R.S.B.'s strong sour coffee and join Darlene Lilley and today's so-called experimental project's other two Field Researchers and perhaps one or two silent and very intense young R.S.B. Market Research interns in the row of cushioned chairs before the screens, Schmidt next to Lilley and somewhat in the shadow of her very tall hair, and Ron Mounce would as always produce a pack of cigarettes, and Trudi Keener would laugh at the way Mounce always made a show of clawing a cigarette desperately out of the pack and lighting it with a tremorous hand, and the fact that neither Schmidt nor Darlene Lilley smoked (Darlene had grown up in a household with heavy smokers and was now allergic) would cause a slight alliance of posture as they both leaned slightly away from the smoke. Schmidt had once swallowed hard in his chair and mentioned the whole smoking issue to Mounce, gallantly claiming the allergy as his own, but since R.S.B. equipped its green room with both ashtrays and exhaust fans and it was eighteen floors down and 100 yards out the Gap's rear service doors into a small cobbled area where people without private offices gathered on breaks to smoke, it wasn't the sort of issue that could really be pressed without appearing either like a militant crank or like someone putting on a show of patronizing chivalry for Darlene, who often crossed her legs ankle-on-knee-style and massaged her instep with both hands as she watched her Focus Group's private deliberations and Schmidt tried to focus on his own TFG. There was never much conversation; the four facilitators were still technically on, ready at any moment to return to their respective groups' conference rooms if the screen showed their foreman moving to press the button that the Groups were told activated an amber signal light.

Team Δy chief Alan Britton, M.S. & J.D., of whom one sensed that no one had ever even once made fun, was an immense and physically imposing man, roughly 6'1" in every direction, with a large smooth shiny oval head in the precise center of which were extremely tiny close-set features arranged in the invulnerably cheerful expression of a man who had made a difference in all he'd ever tried.

In terms of administration there was, of course, the ramified problem of taste and/or texture. Ricin, like most phytotoxins, is exceedingly bitter, which meant that the requisite 0.4 mg must present for ingestion in a highly dilute form. But the dilution seemed even more unpalatable than the ricin itself: injected through the thin wrapper into the 26 × 13 mm ellipse of *fondant* at the *Felony!*'s hollow center, the distilled water formed a soggy caustic pocket whose contrast with the deliquescent high-lipid filling itself fairly shouted adulteration. Injection into the moist flourless surrounding cake itself turned an area the size of a 1916 Flowing Liberty Quarter into maltilol-flavored sludge. A promising early alternative was to administer six to eight very small injections in different areas of the *Felony!* and hope that the subject got all or most of the snack cake down (like Twinkies and Choco-Diles, the *Felony!* was designed to be a prototypical Three-Biter but also to be sufficiently light and saliva-soluble that an ambitious consumer could get the whole thing into his mouth at once, with predictably favorable consequences for IMPCs* and concomitant sales volume) before noticing anything amiss. The problem here was that each injection, even with a fine-gauge hypodermic, produced a puncture of .012 mm diameter (median) in the flimsy transpolymer wrapper, and in home tests of individually packaged cakes at average Midwest–New England humidity levels these punctures produced topical staleness/desiccation within 48–72 hours of shelving. (As with all Mister Squishy products, *Felonies!* were engineered to be palpably moist and to react with salivary ptyalin in such a way as to literally 'melt in the mouth,' qualities established in very early Field tests to be associated with both freshness and a luxe, almost sensual indulgence.†) The botulinus exotoxin,

---

* = Intervals of Multiple Product Consumption

†The emetic prosthesis consisted of a small polyurethane bag taped under one arm and a tube of ordinary clear plastic running up the rear of the left shoulder blade to emerge from the turtleneck through a small hole just under my chin. The contents of the bag were six of the little cakes mixed with mineral water and real bile harvested by means of OTC emetic first thing this AM. The bag's power cell and vacuum were engineered for one high-volume emission and two or three smaller spurts and dribbles afterward; they were to be activated by a button on my watch. The material wouldn't actually be coming out of my mouth, but it was a safe bet that nobody would be looking closely at the point of exit; people's automatic reaction is to avert their eyes. The C.P.D.'s transmitter's clear earpiece was attached to my glasses. The scope's Mission Time said 24:31 and change, but the presentation already seemed much longer. We were all of us anxious to get down to business already.

being tasteless as well as 97% lethal at .00003 g, was thus rather more practical, though because its source is an anaerobe it must be injected into the direct center of the product's interior filling, and even the microscopic air pocket produced by evacuation of the hypodermic will begin to attack the compound, requiring ingestion within one week for any predictable result. The anaerobic saprophyte *Clostridium botulinum* is simple to culture, requiring only an airtight home-canning jar in which are placed 2–3 ounces of puréed Aunt Nellie–brand beets, 1–2 oz. of common cube steak, two tablespoons of fresh topsoil from beneath the noisome pine chips under the lollipop hedges flanking the pretentiously gated front entrance to Briarhaven Condominiums, and enough ordinary tap water (chlorinated OK) to fill the jar to the absolute top. This being the only exacting part: the absolute top. If the water's meniscus comes right to the absolute top of the jar's threaded mouth and the jar's lid is properly applied and screwed on very tightly w/ vise and wide-mouth Sears Craftsman pliers so as to allow 0.0% trapped O_2 in the jar, ten days on the top shelf of a dark utility closet will produce a moderate bulge in the jar's lid, and extremely careful double-gloved and -masked removal of the lid will reveal a small tan-to-brown colony of *Clostridium* awash in a green-to-tan penumbra of botulinus exotoxin, which is, to put it delicately, a byproduct of the mold's digestive process, and can be removed in very small amounts with the same hypodermic used for administration. Botulinus had also the advantage of directing attention to defects in manufacturing and/or packaging rather than product tampering, which would of course heighten the overall industry impact.

The real principle behind running Field research in which some of the TFGs completed only IRPs and some were additionally convened in juridical groups to hammer out a GRDS was to allow Team Δy to provide Reesemeyer Shannon Belt with two distinct and statistically complete sets of market research data, thereby allowing R.S.B. to use and evince whichever data best reinforced the research results that they believed Mister Squishy and N.A.S.C. most wanted to see. Schmidt, Darlene Lilley, and Trudi Keener had all been given tacitly

to understand that this same principle informed the experimental
subdivision of today's TFG juries into so-called No-Access and Full-
Access groups, which latter were to be given what the members were
told was special behind-the-scenes information on the genesis, production, and marketing goals of the product — meaning that, whether
retroscenic access to marketing agendas created substantive differences in the Focus Groups' mean GRDSs or not, Team Δy and R.S.B.
clearly wanted access to different data fields from which they could
pick and choose and use slippery hypergeometric statistical techniques
to manipulate as they believed Client saw fit. In the green room, only
A. Ronald Mounce, M.S. — who is Robert Awad's personal mentee
and probable heir apparent and is also his mole among the Field Researchers, whose water cooler chitchat Mounce distills and reports via
special #0302 *Field Concerns and Morale* forms that Awad's earnest
young Administrative Asst. provides Mounce with in the same manila
envelopes all the day's IRP and GRDS packets are distributed to Field
Teams in — only Mounce has been told privately that the unconventional Full- and No-Access Mister Squishy TFG design is in fact part
of a larger field experiment that Alan Britton and Team Δy's upper
management's secret inner executive circle (said circle incorporated by
Britton as a §543 Personal Holding Company under the dummy name
Δy^2 Associates) is conducting for its own sub rosa research into TFGs'
probable role in the ever more complex and self-conscious marketing
strategies of the future. The basic idea, as Robert Awad saw fit to
explain to Mounce on Awad's new catamaran one June day when they
were becalmed and drifting four nautical miles off Montrose-Wilson
Beach's private jetties, was that as the ever-evolving US consumer
became more savvy and discerning about media and marketing and
tactics of product positioning — a sudden insight into today's average
individual consumer mind which Awad explained he had achieved in
his health club's sauna one day after handball when the intellectual
property attorney he had just decisively trounced was praising an A.C.
Romney–Jaswat campaign for the new carbonated beverage *Surge*
whose tightly demotargeted advertisements everyone had been seeing

all over the metro area that quarter, and remarked (the nude and per-
spiring intellectual property attorney* had) that he probably found all
these modern youth-targeted ads utilizing jagged guitar riffs and epi-
thets like *dude* and the whole ideology of rebellion-via-consumption
so fascinating and got such a hoot out of them because he himself was
so far out of the demographic (using the actual word *demographic*) for
a campaign like *Surge*'s that even as an amateur he found himself dis-
interestedly analyzing the ads' strategies and pitches and appreciating
them more like pieces of art or fine pastry than like mere ads, then had
(meaning the attorney had, right there in the sauna, wearing only plastic thongs and a towel wrapped Sikh-style around his head, according to
Awad) proceeded casually to deconstruct the strategies and probable
objectives of the *Surge* campaign with such acuity that it was almost
as if the fellow had somehow been right there in the room at A.C.
Romney–Jaswat's MROP team's brainstorming and strategy confabs
with Team Δy, who as Mounce was of course aware had done some
first-stage Focus Group work for A.C.R.-J./Coke on *Surge* six quarters
past before the firm's gradual emigration to R.S.B. as a Captured Shop.
Awad, whose knowledge of small craft operation came entirely from a
manual he was now using as a paddle, told Mounce that the idea's gist's
thrust here involved what was known in the industry as a Narrative
(or, 'Story') Campaign and the concept of making some new product's
actual marketers' strategies and travails themselves a part of that product's
essential Story — as in for historic examples that Chicago's own Keebler
Inc.'s hard confections were manufactured by elves in a hollow tree, or
that Pillsbury's Green Giant–brand canned and frozen vegetables
were cultivated by an actual giant in his eponymous Valley — but with
the added narrative twist or hook now of, say for instance, advertising
Mister Squishy's new *Felony!* line as a disastrously costly and labor-
intensive ultra-gourmet snack cake which had to be marketed by beleaguered legions of nerdy admen under the thumb of, say, a tyrannical

---

*(who in fact, unbeknownst to Awad, was an old friend and Limited Partnership crony
of Alan Britton from way back in the previous decade's Passive-Income Tax Shelter
heyday)

mullah-like CEO who was such a personal fiend for luxury-class chocolate that he was determined to push *Felonies!* into the US market no matter what the cost- or sales-projections, such that (in the proposed campaign's Story) Mister Squishy's advertisers had to force Team Δy to manipulate and cajole Focus Groups into producing just the sort of quote unquote 'objective' statistical data needed to greenlight the project and get *Felonies!* on the shelves, all in other words comprising just the sort of arch and tongue-in-cheek pseudo-behind-the-scenes Story designed to appeal to urban or younger consumers' self-imagined savvy about marketing tactics and 'objective' data and to flatter their sense that in this age of metastatic spin and trend and the complete commercialization of every last thing in their world they were unprecedentedly ad-savvy and discerning and canny and well nigh impossible to manipulate by any sort of clever multimillion-dollar marketing campaign. This was, as of the second quarter of 1995, a fairly bold and unconventional ad concept, Awad conceded modestly over Ron Mounce's cries of admiration and excitement, tossing (Mounce did) another cigarette over the catamaran's side to hiss and bob forever instead of sinking; and Awad further conceded that obviously an enormous amount of very carefully controlled research would have to be done and analyzed in all sorts of hypergeometric ways before they could even conceive of possibly jumping ship and starting their own R. Awad & Subordinates agency and pitching the idea to various far-sighted companies — certain of the US Internet's new startups, with their young and self-perceivedly renegade top management, looked like a promising market — yes to various forward-looking companies that craved a fresh, edgy, cynicism-friendly corporate image, rather like Subaru's in the previous decade, or also for example FedEx and Wendy's in the era when Sedelmaier's own local crew had come out of nowhere to rule the industry. Whereas in point of fact none of what Robert Awad had brought his mentee four miles out onto the lake to whisper in Mounce's big pink ear was true or even in any sense real except as the agreed-upon cover narrative to be fed to select Team Δy SRDs and Field Researchers as part of the control conditions for the really true Field experiment, which Alan Britton and Scott R. Laleman (there was really no §543-structured Δy^2 Associates; that little fiction was part of the cover narrative that Britton had fed to Bob Awad, who unbeknownst to him [= Awad] was already being gradually eased out in favor of Mrs. Lilley, who Laleman said was a whiz on both Systat and HTML, and on whom [= Darlene Lilley] Britton had had his eye ever since he'd sent Awad around with covert instructions to behave in such a way as to test for faultlines in Field Team morale and the girl'd shown such an extraordinary blend of personal stones and political aplomb in defusing Awad's stressors) so but yes which field experiment Britton and his mentee Laleman had been told by no less a personage than T. Cordell ('Ted') Belt himself was designed to produce data on the way(s) certain received ideas of market research's purposes affected the way Field Researchers facilitated their Targeted Focus Groups' GRDS phase and thus influenced the material outcome of the TFGs' *in camera* deliberations and GRDSs. This internal experiment was the second stage of a campaign, Britton had later told Laleman over near-zeppelin-sized cigars in his inner office, to finally after all this time start bringing US marketing research into line with the realities of modern hard science, which had proved long ago (science had) that the presence of an observer affects any process and thus by clear implication that even the tiniest, most ephemeral details of a Field test's setup can impact the resultant data. The ultimate objective was to eliminate all unnecessary random variables in those Field tests, and of course by your most basic managerial Ockham's Razorblade this meant doing away as much as possible with the human element, the most obvious of these elements being the TFG facilitators, namely Team Δy's nerdy beleaguered Field Researchers, who now, with the coming digital era of abundant data on whole markets' preferences and patterns available via cybercommerce links, were soon going to be obsolete (the Field Researchers were) anyway, Alan Britton said. A passionate and assuasive rhetor, Britton liked to draw invisible little illustrations in the air with his cigar's glowing tip as he spoke. The mental image Scott Laleman associated with Alan Britton was of an enormous macadamia nut with a tiny little face painted on it. Laleman did unkind impersonations of Britton's speech and gestures for some of the boys in Technical Processing when he was sure Mr. B. was nowhere around. Because the whole thing from soup to nuts could soon be done via computer network, as Britton said he was sure he didn't have to sell Laleman on. Scott Laleman didn't really even like cigars. Meaning the coming www-dot-slash-hypercybercommerce thing, which there'd already been countless professional seminars on and all of US marketing and advertising and related support industries were terribly excited about. But where most agencies still saw the coming www primarily as just a new, fifth venue* for high-impact ads, part of your more forward-looking Reesemeyer Shannon Belt–type vision for the coming era involved finding ways to exploit cybercommerce's staggering research potential as well. Undisplayed little tracking codes could be designed to tag and follow each consumer's w^3 interests and spending patterns — here Laleman once again told Alan Britton what these algorithms were commonly called and averred that he personally knew how to design them; he of course did not tell Britton that he had already secretly helped design some very special little tracking algorithms for A.C. Romney–Jaswat & Assoc.'s sirenic Chloe Jaswat and that two of these quote unquote Cookies were even at that moment nested deep within Team Δy's SMTP/POP protocols. Britton said that Focus Groups and even n-sized test markets could be assembled abstractly via ANOVAs† on consumers' known patterns, that the TFG vetting was built right in — as in e.g. who showed an interest? who bought the product or related products and from which cybervendor via which link thing? — that not only would there be no voir dire and no archaic per diem expenses but even the unnecessary variable of consumers even *knowing* they were part of any sort of market test was excised, since a consumer's subjective awareness of his identity as a test subject instead of as a true desire-driven consumer had always been one

---

*(venues 1–4 historically comprising TV, Radio, Print, and Outdoor [= mainly billboards])

† = ANalysis Of VAriance model, a hypergeometric multiple regression technique used by Team Δy to establish the statistical relations between dependent and independent variables in market tests.

of the distortions that market research swept under the rug because they had no way of quantifying subjective-identity-awareness on any known ANOVA. Focus Groups would go the way of the dodo and bison and art deco. Alan Britton had already had versions of this conversation with Scott Laleman several times; it was part of Britton's way of pumping himself up. Laleman had a vision of himself at a very large and expensive desk, Chloe Jaswat behind him kneading his trapezius muscles, while an enormous macadamia nut sat in a low chair before the desk and pleaded for a livable severance package. Sometimes, on the rare occasions when he masturbated, Laleman's fantasy involved a view of himself, shirtless and adorned with warpaint, standing with his boot on the chest of various supine men and howling upward at what lay outside the fantasy's frame but was probably the moon. That in other words, gesturing with the great red embrous tip, the exact same wonkish technology that Laleman's boys in Technical Processing now used to run analyses on the TFG paperwork could *replace* the paperwork. No more small-sample testing; no more β-risks or variance-error probabilities or $1-\alpha$ confidence intervals or human elements or entropic noise. Once, in his junior year at Cornell U., Scott R. Laleman had been in an A.C.S. Dept. lab accident and had breathed halon gas, and for several days he went around campus with a rose clamped in his teeth, and tried to tango with anyone he saw, and insisted everybody all call him *The Magnificent Enriqué,* until several of his fraternity brothers finally all ganged up and knocked some sense back into him, but a lot of people thought he was still never quite the same after the halon thing. For now, in Belt and Britton's forward-looking vision, the market becomes its own test. Terrain = Map. Everything encoded. And no more facilitators to muddy the waters by impacting the tests in all the infinite ephemeral unnoticeable infinite ways human beings always kept impacting each other and muddying the waters. Team Δy would become 100% tech-driven, abstract, its own Captured Shop. All they needed was some hard study data showing unequivocally that human facilitators made a difference, that variable elements of their appearance and manner and syntax and/or even small personal tics of individual personality or attitude affected the Focus Groups' findings.

Something on paper, with all the Systat t's crossed and i's dotted and even maybe yes a high-impact full-color graph — for these were professional statisticians, after all, the Field Researchers; they knew the numbers didn't lie; if they saw that the data entailed their own subtraction they'd go quietly, some probably even offering to resign, for the good of the Team. Plus then also Laleman pointed out that the study data'd also come in handy if some of them tried to fight it or squeeze Team Δy for a better severance by threatening some kind of bullshit WT suit. He could almost feel the texture of Mr. B.'s sternum under his heel. Not to mention (said Britton, who sometimes then held the cigar like a dart and jabbed it at the air when stipulating or refining a point) that not all would need to go. The Field men. That some could be kept. Transferred. Retrained to work the machines, to follow the Cookies and run the Systat codes and sit there while it all compiled. The rest would have to go. It was a rough business; Darwin's tagline still fit. Britton sometimes addressed Scott Laleman as Laddie or Boyo, but of course never once as *The Magnificent Enriqué*. Mr. B. had absolutely 0% knowledge of what and who Scott R. Laleman really was inside, as an individual, with a very special and above-average destiny, Laleman felt. He had practiced his smile a great deal, both with and w/o rose. Britton said that the sub rosa experiments' stressors would, as always in nature and hard science, determine survival. Fitness. As in who fit the new pattern. Versus who made too much difference, see, and where, when push came to shove there *in camera*. This was all artful bullshit. Britton poked glowing holes in the air above the desk. To see, he said he meant, how the facilitators reacted to unplanned stimuli, how they responded to their Focus Groups' own reactions. All they needed were the stressors. Nested, high-impact stimuli. Shake them up. Rattle the cage, he said, watch what fell out. This was all really what was known in the game as Giving Someone Enough Rope. The big man leaned back, his smile both warm and expectant. Inviting the Boyo he'd chosen to mentor to brainstorm with him on some possible stressors right here and now. As in with Britton himself, to flesh out the needed tests. No time like now. Scott Laleman felt a kind of vague latent dread as the big man made a show of putting out his Fuente. A chance to step up to the plate with the big dogs, get a taste of real frontlines creative action. Right here and now. A chance for Δy's golden boy to strut his stuff. Impress the boss. Run something up the rampant pole. Anything at all. Spontaneous flow. To brainstorm. The trick was not to think or edit, just let it all fly.* The big man counted down from five and put one hand to his ear and came down with the other hand to point at Scott Laleman as if to signal You're On the Air, his eyes now two nailheads and tiny mouth turned down. The finger had something dark's remains in the rim around its nail. Laleman sat there smiling at it, his mind a great flat blank white screen.

---

*Britton knew all about Laleman trying to jew him out to A.C. Romney–Jaswat; who did the smug puppy think he was dealing with; Alan S. Britton had been contending and surviving when this kid was still playing with his little pink toes.

The Soul Is Not a Smithy

TERENCE VELAN WOULD LATER BE DECORATED IN COMBAT IN THE WAR IN INDOCHINA, AND HAD HIS PHOTOGRAPH AND A DRAMATIC AND FLATTERING STORY ABOUT HIM IN THE *DISPATCH*, ALTHOUGH HIS WHEREABOUTS AFTER DISCHARGE AND RETURNING TO AMERICAN LIFE WERE NEVER ESTABLISHED BY ANYONE MIRANDA OR I EVER KNEW OF.

This is the story of how Frank Caldwell, Chris DeMatteis, Mandy Blemm, and I became, in the city newspaper's words, the *4 Unwitting Hostages,* and of how our strange and special alliance and the trauma surrounding its origin bore on our subsequent lives and careers as adults later on. The repeated thrust of the *Dispatch* articles was that it was we four, all classified as slow or problem pupils, who had not had the presence of mind to flee the Civics classroom along with the other children, thereby creating the *hostage circumstance* that justified the taking of life.

The site of the original trauma was 4th grade Civics class, second period, at R. B. Hayes Primary School here in Columbus. A very long time ago now. The class had a required seating chart, and all of us had assigned desks, which were bolted to the floor in orderly rows. It was

1960, a time of fervent and somewhat unreflective patriotism. It was a time that is now often referred to as a somewhat more innocent time. Civics was a state-mandated class on the Constitution, the U.S. presidents, and the branches of government. In the second quarter, we had actually built papier mâché models of the branches of government, with various tracks and paths between them, to illustrate the balance of powers that the Founding Fathers had built into the federal system. I had fashioned the Doric columns of the Judicial Branch out of the cardboard cylinders inside rolls of Coronet paper towels, which was our mother's preferred brand. It was during the cold and seemingly endless period in March when our regular Civics teacher was absent that we had our Constitution unit and perused the American Constitution and its various drafts and amendments under the supervision of Mr. Richard A. Johnson, a long-term sub. There was no recognized term for maternity leave then, although Mrs. Roseman's pregnancy had been obvious since at least Thanksgiving.

The Civics classroom at R. B. Hayes consisted of six rows of five desks each. The desks and chairs were bolted securely to each other and to the floor and had hinged, liftable desktops, just as all primary classrooms' desks tended to in that era before backpacks and bookbags. Inside your assigned desk was where you stored your No. 2 pencils, theme paper, paste, and other essentials of primary school education. It was also where you were required to place your textbook out of view during in-class tests. I can remember that the theme paper of that era was light grey, soft, and slippery, with very wide rules of dotted blue; all assignments completed on this paper came out looking somewhat blurred.

Up to the 6th grade in Columbus, one had an assigned homeroom. This was a specific classroom where you kept your winter coat and rubbers on a hook and a rectangle of newspaper, respectively, along the wall, a pupil's specific hook designated with a piece of colored construction paper with your first name and last initial printed in Magic Marker. It was under the lid of your homeroom desktop that you kept your central cache of school supplies. At that time, the most grown up thing about Fishinger Secondary School across the street seemed to be that the upperclassmen there had no homeroom but went from room to room for classes and stored their materials in a locker with a combination lock whose combination you had to memorize and then destroy the slip of paper on which the combination was given so that no one could break into your locker. None of this is directly relevant to the story of how the unlikely quartet of myself, Chris DeMatteis, Frankie Caldwell, and the strange and disturbed Mandy Blemm were brought by circumstance to coalesce into what became known more informally as *The 4*, except perhaps for the fact that Art and Civics were the only two classes for which we left our homeroom. Both of these classes used special facilities and materials, so both had their own quarters and specially trained teachers, and the pupils came to them from their respective homerooms at specified periods. This was, in our case, second period. The single-file line in which we proceeded from homeroom to Mrs. Barrie's and Mrs. Roseman's respective Art and Civics rooms was silent, alphabetical, and closely supervised. The very late '50s and early '60s were not a time of lax discipline or disorder, which made what occurred in Civics on the day in question all the more traumatic, and caused several of the class's children (one of whom was Terence Velan, who was perhaps somewhat effete for a boy of that era, and sometimes wore sandals and leather shorts, but was extremely good at soccer, and had a father who was a hydraulic engineer from West Germany who had attained American citizenship, and could also roll his eyelids up in such a way as to disclose the mucous membranes of their insides and then walk around the playground like that, which lent him a certain cachet) to transfer out of Hayes Primary for good, as even just being back in the building caused traumatic, perseverative memories and emotions.

Only much later would I understand that the incident at the chalkboard in Civics was likely to be the most dramatic and exciting event I would ever be involved in in my life. As with the case of my father, I think that I am ultimately grateful not to have been aware of this at the time.

MY SEAT WAS NOW, TO WHAT WOULD HAVE BEEN MRS. ROSEMAN'S
CONSIDERABLE CHAGRIN, NEXT TO THE WINDOW.

Mrs. Roseman's Civics classroom, which had portraits of all 34 U.S. presidents evenly spaced around all four walls just below the ceiling, as well as pulldown relief maps of the thirteen original colonies, the Union and Confederate states circa 1861, and the present United States, including the Hawaiian islands, and steel cabinets filled with additional resources of all kinds, mainly contained a large metal teacher's desk and black slate chalkboard at the front of the room, and 30 total bolted desks and chairs in which we, Miss Vlastos's 4th grade homeroom class, were alphabetically arrayed in six rows of five pupils each. Mr. Johnson being a sub, we had amused ourselves by altering Mrs. Roseman's normal seating chart and reversing our assigned rows' east-west placement in the classroom, placing Rosemary Ahearn and Emily-Ann Barr in the first desks of the row nearest the west wall's coathooks (which were always empty, as Mrs. Roseman's Civics classroom was not anybody's homeroom) and classroom door, and the latter of the Swearingen twins at the front of the easternmost row, next to the first of the east wall's two large windows, whose heavy shades could be lowered for filmstrips and the occasional historical film. I was in the second to last desk in the easternmost row, which was a logistical error that Mrs. Roseman would never have allowed, as I was classified as unsatisfactory in Listening Skills as well as its associated category, Following Directions, and every full-time teacher in the first several grades at R. B. Hayes knew that I was a pupil whose assigned seat should be as far away from windows and other sources of possible distraction as possible. All of the school building's windows had a reticulate wire mesh built directly into the glass in order to make the window harder to break with an errant dodgeball or vandal's hurled stone. Also, the pupil to my immediate left in the next row in the ersatz arrangement was Sanjay Rabindranath, who studied maniacally at all times, and also had exemplary cursive, and was perhaps the single best pupil to sit next to during tests in all of R. B. Hayes. The wire mesh, which divided the window into 84 small squares with an addi-

tional row of 12 slender rectangles where the first vertical line of mesh
nearly abutted the window's right border, was designed in part to make
the windows less diverting and to minimize the chances that a pupil
could become distracted or lost in contemplation of the scene outside,
which in Civics in March consisted mostly of grey skies and bare trees'
chassis and the ravaged edges of the soccer fields and unfenced ball diamond on which Little League was held each May 21 to August 4.
Behind, and much foreshortened — being occluded by Taft Avenue
and occupying only three squares at the window's lower left — was the
fenced and regulation-size Fishinger Secondary ballfield, where the
big boys played American Legion baseball to keep themselves in peak
condition for the high school season. A handful of our school's windows were cracked by vandals each spring; there were several exposed
rocks in the soccer fields, of which at least half or more could be
brought into calibrated view from my seat without any discernible
movement of my head. Nearly all of the empty and forlorn ball
diamond could be seen with one or two subtle adjustments as well, the
infield now mud wherever there wasn't snow. I am someone who has
always possessed good peripheral vision, and for much of Mr. Johnson's
three weeks on the U.S. Constitution, I had primarily attended Civics
in body only, my real attention directed peripherally at the fields and
street outside, which the window mesh's calibration divided into discrete squares that appeared to look quite like the rows of panels comprising cartoon strips, filmic storyboards, Alfred Hitchcock Mystery
Comics, and the like. Obviously, this intense preoccupation was lethal
in terms of my Listening Skills during second period Civics, in that
it led my attention not merely to wander idly, but to actively construct
whole linear, discretely organized narrative fantasies, many of which
unfolded in considerable detail. That is to say that anything in any
way remarkable in the view outside — such as a piece of vivid litter
blowing from one wire square to the next, or a city bus flowing stolidly
from right to left through the lowest three horizontal columns of
squares — became the impetus for privately imagined films' or cartoons' storyboards, in which each of the remaining squares of the
window's wire mesh could be used to continue and deepen the panels'

narrative — the ordinary looking C.P.T. bus in reality commandeered by Batman's then-archnemesis, the Red Commando, who in an interior view in successive squares holds hostage, among others, Miss Vlastos, several blind children from the State School for the Blind and Deaf, and my terrified older brother and his piano teacher, Mrs. Doudna, until the moving bus is penetrated by Batman and (behind his small decorative mask) a markedly familiar looking Robin, through a series of acrobatic rope and grappling hook maneuvers each one of which filled and animated one reticulate square of the window and then was frozen in tableau as my attention moved on to the next panel, and so on. These imagined constructions, which often took up the entire window, were difficult and concentrated work; the truth is that they bore little resemblance to what Mrs. Claymore, Mrs. Taylor, Miss Vlastos, or my parents called daydreaming. At the time of the inciting trauma, I was still nine years old; my tenth birthday would be April 8. Ages seven to nearly ten were also the troubling and upsetting period (particularly for my parents) when I could not, in any strictly accepted sense, read. By which I mean that I could scan a page from *From Sea to Shining Sea: The Story of America in Words and Pictures* (which was the mandated textbook for all primary school Civics classes statewide at that time) and supply a certain amount of specific quantitative information, such as the exact number of words per page, the exact number of words on each line, and often the word and even letter with the most and the fewest occurrences of use on a given page, for example, as well as the number of occurrences of each word, often retaining this information long after the page had been read, and yet I could not, in the majority of cases, internalize or communicate in any very satisfactory way what the words and their various combinations were intended to mean (this is my memory of the period, at any rate), with the result that I performed well below average when tested on homework assimilation and reading comprehension. Much to everyone's relief, the reading problem reversed itself, almost as mysteriously as it had first appeared, somewhere around my tenth birthday.

MR. JOHNSON, ORIGINALLY OF NEARBY URBANCREST, WAS LATER
REVEALED TO HAVE NO RECORD OF MENTAL DISTURBANCE OR
CRIMINAL BEHAVIOR OF ANY KIND, ACCORDING TO PRESS
ACCOUNTS.

It had last snowed in early March. The classroom window's east-
ward view, in other words, was now primarily mud and dirty snow.
What sky there was was colorless and rode somewhat low, like something sodden or quite tired. The ballfield's infield was all mud, with
only a small hyphen of snow atop the pitcher's rubber. Usually,
throughout second period, the window's only real movement was litter
or a vehicle of some sort on Taft, with the day of the trauma's exception being the appearance of the dogs. It had happened only once before, earlier in the Constitution unit, but not again until now. The two
dogs entered the window's upper right grid from a copse of trees to the
northeast and proceeded diagonally down towards the northern goal
area of the soccer fields. They then began moving in gradually diminishing circles around each other, apparently preparing to copulate. A
similar scenario had unfolded once before, but then the dogs had not
reappeared for some weeks. Their actions appeared to be consistent
with those of mating. The larger of the two dogs mounted the other's
back from the rear and wrapped its forelegs around the brindle-
colored dog's body and began to thrust repeatedly, taking a series of tiny
steps with its rear legs as the other dog attempted to escape. This occupied slightly more than one square of the window's wire mesh. The
visual impression was of one large, anatomically complex dog having a
series of convulsions. It was not a pretty sight, but it was vivid and
compelling. One of the animals was larger, and black with a dun chest
element, possibly a rottweiler mix, though it lacked a purebred rottweiler's breadth of head. The breed of the smaller dog beneath it was
unidentifiable. According to my older brother, we had had a dog for a
short period when I would have been too young to remember, which
had chewed on the base of the piano and the legs of a spectacular 16th
century antique Queen Elizabeth dining room table our mother had

discovered at a rummage sale, which was worth over one million dollars when appraised and caused the family dog to have disappeared one day when my brother came home from nursery school and found both the dog and the table missing, adding that my parents had been very upset about the whole business and that if I ever brought the dog up or asked our mother about it and upset her he would put my fingers in the hinge of the foyer closet and lean with all his weight on the door until all my fingers were so mangled they would have to be amputated and I would be even more hopeless at the piano than I already was. Both my brother and I had been involved in intensive piano instruction and recitals at that juncture, though it was only he who had showed true promise, and had continued twice a week with Mrs. Doudna until his own difficulties began to emerge so dramatically in early adolescence. The conjoined dogs were too distant to ascertain whether they had collars or tags, yet close enough that I could make out the expression on the face of the dominant dog above. It was blank and at the same time fervid — the same type of expression as on a human being's face when he is doing something that he feels compulsively driven to do and yet does not understand just why he wants to do it. Rather than mating, it could have been one dog merely asserting its dominance over another, as I later learned was common. It appeared to last a long time, during which the dog on the receiving end underneath took a number of small, unsteady steps which bore both animals across four different panels of the fourth row down, complicating the storyboard activity on either side. A collar and tags comprise a valid sign that the dog has a home and owner rather than being a stray animal, which a guest speaker from the Public Health Department in homeroom had explained could be a concern. This was especially true of the rabies vaccination tag required by Franklin County ordinance, for obvious reasons. The unhappy but stoic expression on the face of the brindle-colored dog beneath was harder to characterize. Perhaps it was less distinct, or obscured by the window's protective mesh. Our mother had once described the expression of our Aunt Tina, who had profound physical problems, as this — *long suffering.*

MARY UNTERBRUNNER, KNOWN ALSO BY OEHMKE AND LLEWELLYN'S GROUP ON THE PLAYGROUND AS BIG BERTHA, WAS THE ONLY OTHER GIRL WHO SOMETIMES EVER PLAYED WITH MANDY BLEMM AFTER SCHOOL HOURS. MY BROTHER, WHO WAS IN THE SAME CLASS AS MANDY BLEMM'S ELDER SISTER, BRANDY, SAID THAT THE BLEMMS WERE WELL KNOWN TO BE A DISTURBED FAMILY, WHOSE FATHER ALWAYS STAYED HOME ALL DAY IN JUST HIS UNDERSHIRT, AND THEIR YARD LOOKED LIKE A JUNKYARD, AND THEIR GERMAN SHEPHERD WOULD TRY TO KILL YOU IF YOU EVEN CAME NEAR THE BLEMMS' FENCE, AND THAT ONCE, WHEN BRANDY DIDN'T CLEAN UP THE DOG'S DROPPINGS, WHICH WAS APPARENTLY HER ASSIGNED CHORE, ALLEGEDLY THE FATHER CAME ANGRILY STAGGERING OUT AND MADE HER LIE DOWN IN THE YARD AND PUT HER FACE IN THE DROPPINGS; MY BROTHER SAID THAT TWO DIFFERENT 7TH GRADERS HAD SEEN THIS, AND IT WAS WHY BRANDY BLEMM (WHO WAS ALSO SOMEWHAT SLOW) WAS KNOWN AROUND FISHINGER SECONDARY AS *THE SHIT GIRL,* WHICH SURELY COULD NOT HAVE FELT GOOD FOR A GIRL IN HER EARLY TEEN YEARS TO BE CALLED, NO MATTER HOW MUCH SHE DID OR DID NOT HAVE ON THE BALL.

The only other time at which Mr. Johnson had substituted for the real teacher in any of my classes had been for two weeks in 2nd grade, when Mrs. Claymore, our homeroom teacher, had been in a traffic accident and came back with a large white metal and canvas brace around her neck which no one was allowed to sign, and could not turn her head to either side for the remainder of the school year, after which time she retired to Florida with independent means. As I remember him, Mr. Johnson was of average height for an adult, with the standard crew cut, suit jacket and necktie, and eyeglasses with scholarly black frames that everyone who wore glasses in that day and age wore. Evidently, he had subbed for several other grades and classes at R. B. Hayes as well. The only time anyone had ever seen him outside school was one time when Denise Kone and her mother saw Mr. Johnson in the A&P, and Denise said his cart had been full of frozen foods, which her mother had associated with the fact that he was unmarried. I do not recall noticing whether Mr. Johnson wore a wedding band or not, but the *Dispatch* articles later made no mention of his being survived by a wife after the authorities stormed the classroom. I also do not remember his face except as it existed in a *Dispatch* photo afterwards, which was evidently taken from one of his own student yearbooks several years prior. Barring some obvious problem or characteristic, most adults' faces were not easy to attend to closely at that age — their very adultness obscured all other characteristics. To the best of my recollection, Mr. Johnson's was a face whose only memorable characteristic was that it appeared slightly tilted or angled upwards in its position on the front of his head. This was not excessive but only a matter of one or two degrees — imagine holding up a mask or portrait so that it was facing you and then tilting it one or two degrees upwards off of normal center. As if, in other words, its eyeholes were now looking slightly upwards. And that this, together with what was either poor posture or a problem involving his neck like Mrs. Claymore, caused Mr. Johnson to look as if he were wincing or slightly recoiling from whatever he was saying. It was not gross or obvious, but both Caldwell and Todd Llewellyn had noticed Mr. Johnson's wincing quality, too, and remarked on it. Llewellyn said the sub looked like he was scared of his own shadow, like Miles O'Keefe or *Gunsmoke*'s Festus (who we all hated — nobody ever wanted to be Festus in re-creations of *Gunsmoke*). On his first day substituting for Mrs. Roseman, he introduced himself to us as Mr. Johnson, writing it on the chalkboard in perfect Palmer cursive as did all teachers of that era; but as his full name recurred so often in the *Dispatch* for several weeks after the incident, he tends to remain now more in my memory as Richard Allen Johnson, Jr., 31, originally of nearby Urbancrest, which is a small bedroom community outside of Columbus proper.

According to my brother's own flights of fancy in childhood, the antique table we had possessed before I was old enough to be aware of anything that was going on had been burled walnut, with a large number of diamonds, sapphires, and rhinestones inset in the top in the likeness of the face of Queen Elizabeth I of England (1533–1603) as seen from the right side, and that the disappointment of its loss was part of the reason our father often looked so dispirited on coming home at the end of the day.

The easternmost row's second to last desk had a deep stick figure with a cowboy hat and much oversized six-shooter gouged deeply into it and colored in with ink from some previous 4th grader, obviously the product of much slow, patient effort over the course of that previous academic year. Directly ahead of me were the thick neck, upper vertebrae, and severely bobbed hairline of Mary Unterbrunner, whose neck's pale and patternless freckles I had studied for almost two years, as Mary Unterbrunner (who would later become an administrative secretary at the large women's detention center in Parma) had also been in my 3rd grade homeroom with Mrs. Taylor, who read the class ghost stories and could play the ukulele and was a great deal of fun as a homeroom teacher so long as you didn't get on the wrong side of her temper. Mrs. Taylor once hit Caldwell on the back of his hand with her ruler, which she carried in the large kangaroo pocket of her smock, so hard that it swelled up almost like a cartoon hand, and Mrs. Caldwell (who knew judo, and who you also did not want to fool around with in terms of her own temper, according to Caldwell) came down to the school to complain to the principal. What teachers and the administration in that era never seemed to see was that the mental work of what they called daydreaming often required more effort and concentration than it would have taken simply to listen in class. Laziness is not the issue. It is just not the work dictated by the administration. For the sake of the visual interest of the narrative that day, I wish that I could say that each panel of the story that the window generated from the view of the two dogs either mating or struggling for dominance remained animated, so that by the end of the class the window's wire mesh squares were all filled with narrative panels like the pictorial stained windows at Riverside Methodist Church, where my brother, mother, and I attended Sunday service each week, along with my father when he felt up to getting up early enough. He often had to work at the office six days a week, and he liked to call Sunday his day to try to glue what was left of his nerves back together. But that was not how it worked. It would have taken some kind of mental marvel to hold each square's illustrated tableau in memory throughout the whole narrative of the window, not unlike the backseat game on trips where you and someone else pretend that you're planning a picnic, and he says one item that will be brought, and you repeat that item and add another, and he repeats the two mentioned previously and adds a third, and you must repeat and then add a fourth which he must remember and repeat, and so on, until each of you is trying to hold a memorized string of 30 or more items in your mind as you each keep adding to it further by turns. This was never a game I excelled at, although my brother could sometimes perform feats of memory that amazed my parents and may even have frightened them a little, given how he eventually turned out (our father often referred to him as the *brains of the outfit*). Each square in the window's mesh filled and recounted its part of the story of the poor unhappy owner of the brindle dog only while that particular square was attended to; it reverted to its natural state of transparency once the entire panel was actuated and filled and the story moved on to the mesh's next square, in which the little girl whose young and unworldly brindle-colored dog, Cuffie, had dug its way out under the shabby back fence and escaped down to the banks of the Scioto River, wearing a lemon-colored pinafore, pink hair ribbon, and shiny black patent leather shoes with polished buckles, was sitting in her 4th grade Art class making a Playdoh statuette of Cuffie, her dog, all by touch, at the State School for the Blind and Deaf on Morse Rd. She was blind, and her name was Ruth, although her mother and father called her Ruthie and her two older sisters, who played the bassoon, called her Ruthie Toothie because they were trying to convince her — we see this in three consecutive panels where the sisters, who are older and have the disagreeable expressions and akimbo postures that cruel people in cartoons always have — of how unfortunately homely she is, due to her terrible overbite, and of how everyone can see it but her, and there is nearly a whole horizontal row of panels of Ruth in dark glasses with her little hands over her face, crying over the older sisters' remarks and chants of *Ruthie Toothie, your dog has gotten loothie,* while the little girl's poor but kindhearted father, who works as a groundskeeper for a wealthy man in a white metal and canvas brace who owns a lavish mansion in Blacklick Estates with a wrought iron gate and a curving driveway over one mile in length out past Amberly, is driving the family's old, battered car slowly up and down the cold streets of their shabby neighborhood, calling Cuffie's name out of the open car window and jingling the brindle dog's collar and tags. A series of panels in the very top row of mesh squares, which is often reserved for flashbacks and backstory elements that help fill in gaps in the window's unfolding action, reveals that Cuffie's collar and vaccination tags have gotten torn off as he wriggles under the Simmons family's yard's fence in excitement over seeing the two stray dogs, one black and dun and the other predominantly piebald, that have loped up to the cheap wire fence and urged Cuffie to come join them in some freely roaming dog adventures, the dark one, who in the panel has angled eyebrows and a sinister pencil mustache, crossing his heart over the promise that they won't go far at all and will be sure and show the trusting Cuffie the way back home again. Much of the specific day's storyboard, which extends like arms or the radial spikes one often sees around a cartoon sun, involves the split narrative of small, pale, blind Ruth Simmons (who is not bucktoothed in the slightest but is, understandably, not a very good Playdoh sculptor) sitting in her Art for the Blind class wishing desperately that she could know whether or not her father has been successful in finding the dog, Cuffie, who is Ruth Simmons' faithful canine companion and never chews on anything or makes any trouble for the household and often sits devotedly under the small, wobbly desk the father had found in the trash of the wealthy manufacturer he works for, and which he had brought home and nailed empty spools onto the drawers of for drawer handles, and Cuffie often sits under there resting his nose on Ruth Simmons' patent leather shoes as she sits in her dark bedroom (it doesn't matter to blind people whether the lights in a room are on or not) at the desk and does her homework in Braille, while her sisters practice the bassoon or lie in the light on their bedroom's plush carpeting talking pointlessly about boys or the Everly Brothers on the princess telephone, often tying up the phone for hours at a time, while the father moonlights at his night job of singlehandedly lifting heavy crates into the rear of delivery trucks, and the family's mother, an Avon Lady who has never successfully sold even one Avon home product, spends every evening lying splayed and semiconscious on the living room couch, which is missing one of its legs and is propped unsteadily up with a phone book while the father tries to scavenge the right kind of wood to replace the leg, Mr. Simmons being the kind of poor but honest father who makes his living with physical labor rather than poring over facts and figures all day. The top row's backstory of the window's large, black and dun dog is somewhat vague, and consists of a few hastily sketched panels involving a low cement building filled with dogs barking in cages, and a back alley in a seedy district in which several garbage cans are overturned and a man in a stained apron is shaking his fist at something we cannot see. Then, in the main row, we see the family's father getting a demanding phone call from the wealthy owner of the mansion telling him to come back and start priming the large, expensive, gas-driven industrial snowblower for the mansion's long driveway with lines of small colored lights all along its length like a runway, because the owner's personal meteorologist has said that it's getting ready to snow again like the absolute dickens. Then we see Ruth Simmons' mother — whom we have already seen take several pills throughout the day from a small brown prescription bottle in her handbag, by way of another upper row's backstory — relieving the father and driving the battered family car aimlessly up and down the seedy neighborhood's streets, very slowly and weaving a bit, as a dense, persistent snow begins to fall and the streetlights begin to glow and the panel's light turns ashy and sad, the way late afternoon in Columbus in winter so often makes the light seem sad.

ESSENTIALLY, I HAD NO IDEA WHAT WAS GOING ON.

Just which specific aspects of the U.S. Bill of Rights were being covered by Mr. Johnson while this story of Ruth Simmons and her lost Cuffie filled in panel after panel of the window I cannot say, as by that point it is fair to say that I was absent in both mind and spirit. This tended to happen throughout this period. To be fair, this was the reason why Mrs. Roseman and the administration were determined to keep me away from distractions of all kinds — prohibiting Caldwell and I from sitting near each other, for instance. I do not remember even noticing just when it was that the exterior's dogs broke off their initial attachment and began moving in circles of somewhat different size, sniffing at the ground and the mud of the ballfield's infield. The temperature outside was an estimated 45 degrees; it was melting that winter's second to last snow. I do remember that it snowed heavily the next day, March 15, and that, as school was closed on the day after the trauma, we were able to go sledding after several interviews with the Ohio State Police and a special Unit 4 psychologist named Dr. Biron-Maint, who had a strangely configured nose and smelled faintly of mildew, and that later on that day Chris DeMatteis' sled had tipped to one side and struck a tree, and his forehead had had blood all over it while we all watched him keep touching his forehead and cry in fear at the reality of his own blood. I do not remember what anyone did to help him; we were all likely still in shock. Ruth Simmons' mother, whose name was Marjorie and had grown up admiring herself in different dresses in the mirror and practicing saying, 'How do you do?' and 'My, what a funny and amusing remark!' and dreaming of marrying a wealthy doctor and hosting elaborate dinner parties of doctors and their wives in diamond tiaras and fox wraps at their mansion's beautiful burled walnut dining room table in which she looked almost like a fairy princess under the chandelier's lights, now, as an adult, looked puffy and dull-eyed and had a perpetually downturned mouth as she drove the battered car. She was smoking a Viceroy and had the windows rolled up and was not even rolling down the window to call, *'Cuffie!'* as the kindly, long suffering father before her had done. There was backstory above, in which the blind infant Ruth Simmons was lying in her bassinet in her tiny dark glasses holding out her arms and crying for her mother while the mother would stand with a glass with an olive with a toothpick in it and a downturned mouth looking down at the blind baby and then turning and looking at herself in the room's ancient, cracked mirror and practicing giving a bitter, sardonic little curtsy without spilling her glass. Usually the baby would give up and stop crying after a while and just make small whimpering noises (this occupied only two or three panels). Meanwhile, unbeknownst to her, Ruth Simmons' Playdoh figurine looked almost disfigured, less like a dog than a satyr or Great Ape which something heavy had run over. Her beautiful little snow white face with its dark glasses and hair ribbon is seen tilted upwards several degrees as she offers innocent, childlike prayers for Cuffie's safe return, praying that her father has perhaps spotted Cuffie huddled inside a tire in one of their seedy neighbors' unkempt yards, or has spotted Cuffie loping innocently along the side of Maryville Road and has stopped the car in the middle of traffic on the busy thoroughfare and knelt down with open arms by the side of the road for the dog to come running joyfully into his arms, her blind fantasies' thought-bubbles occupying several of the panels that had previously been taken up by the actual scene of a frightened and limping Cuffie being harried by the two hardened, feral adult dogs along the seedy east bank of the Scioto River, which even in 1960 was already starting to smell bad above the Griggs Dam and had rusty tin cans and abandoned hubcaps scattered along its east bank by Maryville Road, and which my father said he could remember being able to fish right out of with a string and safety pin circa 1935, in knickers and a straw hat, with his parents in their own straw hats picnicking behind himself and his brother (who was later wounded in Salerno, Italy, in World War II, and had a wooden foot that he could unstrap and take right off with its special enclosing shoe provided by the GI Bill, so the shoe was never empty even when it was in his closet when he went to sleep, and worked for a manufacturer of cardboard dividers for different kinds of shipping containers in Kettering) in the shade of the many beech and buckeye trees that thrived along the Scioto before the University unduly influenced the city fathers into building the Maryville commuter road to more conveniently connect Upper Arlington to the West Side proper. With the faithful dog's lustrous brown eyes now moist with regret at leaving the yard, and with fear, because Cuffie was now far, far away from home, further by far than the young little dog had ever been before. We have already seen that the puppy was only one year old; the father had

brought him home from the A.S.P.C.A. as a surprise on the previous
Good Friday, and had allowed Ruth to bring Cuffie along to Easter
services at St. Anthony's Catholic Church (they were Roman Catholics,
as poor people in Columbus often were) in a small wicker basket covered with a checkered cloth from which only the dog's wet, inquisitive
little nose had shown, and he had been every bit as quiet as Ruth's
mother had said he better be or else they were all going to have to get
up and leave even if it was right in the middle of the services, which
for Roman Catholics would have been a terrible sin, even though one
of Ruth's elder sisters had surreptitiously kept poking at one of the
puppy's paws with a hatpin to try to get it to cry out, which it didn't,
none of which Ruth had had any idea about as she sat on the hard
wooden pew in her dark glasses, holding the basket in her lap and
swinging her little legs with gratitude and joy at having a puppy for a
companion (as a rule, the blind have a natural affinity for dogs, whose
eyesight is not very good either). And the two feral dogs (whose fur
was matted, and their ribcages showed, and the piebald one had a large
greenish sore near the base of its tail) were hard and cruel, and showed
their teeth at Cuffie whenever he faltered, even when they went
through the pools of half-frozen mud and sludge that plashed into the
river out of the mouths of huge cement pipes with curse words written
on them with spraypaint, and even though Cuffie was just a dog and
didn't have thought-bubbles as you or I do, the look in his soft brown
eyes spoke volumes as the piebald dog suddenly leapt up into one of
these huge pipes and its matted head and tail with the big sore disappeared, and the larger, black dog began growling at Cuffie to follow
into the pipe, which was not gushing but had a trickle of something
dark orange and terrible smelling (even to a dog) out of it, and in the
next square Cuffie was forced to put his little forelegs up onto the lip of
the cement pipe and try to pull his hindquarters up into it with the black
dog growling and chewing at his rear tendons. The dog's illustrated
facial expression said it all. It conveyed that Cuffie was very frightened
and unhappy and wishing only to be back in the fenced yard wagging
its brindle tail and waiting for the *tap, tap* sound of Ruth's miniature
white cane coming up the sidewalk to greet Cuffie and bring him in to

rub his stomach and whisper to him over and over how beautiful he was and how wonderful his ears and little soft paws smelled, and how lucky they all were to have him, as the black dog leapt easily up onto the lip of the trickling culvert behind Cuffie and, with an ominous look to either side, disappeared into the round black mouth of the pipe, completing the horizontal row.

Meanwhile, in the inception of the real incident, Mr. Johnson had evidently just written *KILL* on the chalkboard. The most obvious flaw in my memory of the incident as a whole is that much of the trauma's inception unfolded outside my awareness, so intently was I concentrating on the window's mesh squares, which in the narrative I was filling the next row of with panels of the unhappy mother, Mrs. Simmons, weaving the family auto slowly down the snow filled streets of the neighborhood while she plucks at various grey hairs that she is trying to find and get a grip on with tweezers in the rearview mirror, as well as scenes of the father, outdoors in the falling snow, operating a large, gas-operated appliance which looks a little like a power lawnmower but is larger and has twice as many rotating blades, as well as being the distinctive bright orange that sportsmen and hunters normally wear, which is the mansion's wealthy owner's company's trademark color, and is also the color of the special snowpants the owner makes the stoic and uncomplaining father wear, beginning to push the machine through the dense, wet snow of the mansion's driveway. The driveway is so long that by the time the father has finished snowblowing the whole thing he will have to start back at the beginning again, as the snowfall (which you can also see in the background out the mesh window of the State School for the Blind and Deaf classroom, even though little Ruthie obviously is unaware) is becoming heavy and turning into a real snowstorm, with the father's thought-bubble in one panel saying, 'Oh, well! It is not so bad, at least I am lucky to have a job, and I am certain that good old Marjorie will find Cuffie in time to bring our pet home in time for Ruthie's return from school!' with a patient, uncomplaining expression on his face as the loud, heavy appliance (which the mansion's owner had patented and his company manufactures, which is why he makes Mr. Simmons wear the undignified orange pants) erases the driveway's white like a chalkboard being cleaned with damp paper towels by someone serving out an administrative detention. It was thus that I did not literally see or know what began to unfold during the Civics class, although I received the full story so many times from classmates and authorities and the *Dispatch* that in memory it nearly feels as if I were present as a full witness from the beginning. Dr. Biron-Maint, the administrative psychologist, gave his professional opinion that I was a full witness, but had been too traumatized (*shellshocked* was his stated term; each child's parents received a copy of his evaluation) to be able to acknowledge the memory of it. However crude or erroneous, my role in all legal proceedings after the incident was thus limited by Dr. Biron-Maint's diagnosis, which my mother and father assented to in writing. Such is adult memory's strangeness, though, that I can still recall in great detail the sight of Dr. Biron-Maint's nostrils, which were of noticeably different shapes and size, and can remember trying to imagine various things that might have happened to his nose in life or perhaps even in his mother's stomach as a baby to produce such a marked anomaly. The clinician was very tall, even by adult standards, and I spent much of the required interview looking up at his nostrils and lower jaw. He also smelled the way someone's bathmat can smell in the summer, though I did not identify this scent as such at the time. To be frank, the consensus was that Dr. Biron-Maint gave many of us the willies even more than Mr. Johnson, although having to watch something like that would obviously be traumatic for anyone, especially young children.

LATER, MR. DeMATTEIS WAS FORCED OUT OF THE WHOLESALE NEWSPAPER DELIVERY TRADE BY WHAT CHRIS DeMATTEIS SAID WERE ELEMENTS OF ORGANIZED CRIME THAT WERE MOVING DOWN FROM CLEVELAND AND TAKING OVER ALL NEWSPAPER AND COIN OPERATED VENDING MACHINE BUSINESSES IN THE STATE, FORCING MR. DeMATTEIS TO TAKE A JOB AS A TAXI DISPATCHER, BUT AT LEAST CHRIS STOPPED HAVING TO GET UP SO EARLY THAT HE COULD NOT STAY AWAKE IN HIS CLASSES, AND LATER DISCOVERED A NATURAL TALENT FOR MANUAL MACHINE OPERATION IN

MR. VAUGHAN'S INDUSTRIAL ARTS CLASS AT FISHINGER, AND IS
NOW A SHOP STEWARD AT PRECISION TOOL & DIE ONLY A FEW
BLOCKS FROM MY OWN FIRM'S OFFICES.

In the midst of writing on the chalkboard, illustrating that the
phrase *due process of law* appears identically in both the Vth and XIVth
Amendments, Mr. Richard Allen Johnson inadvertently inserted
something else in the phrase, as well — the capital word *KILL*. Ellen
Morrison, Sanjay Rabindranath, and some other of the class's more
diligent pupils, copying down word for word what Mr. Johnson was
putting up on the chalkboard, discovered that they had written *due
process KILL of law* and that that, too, was what was on the chalkboard,
which Mr. Johnson had stepped one or two steps back from and was
looking up in evident puzzlement at what was written there. At least,
many classmates later reported this as puzzlement because of the way,
even though the sub was facing the chalkboard and thus had his back to
the class, his head was now cocked curiously over to the side, not unlike
a dog's when it hears a certain type of high sound, and he remained
that way for a moment before shaking his head slightly as if shaking
off some confusion and, using the board's eraser to erase the *KILL of
law*, replaced it with the correct *of law*. As usual, Chris DeMatteis had
his head on his desk in the second row and was asleep, because his
father and older brothers ran a newspaper delivery service for news-
stands and retail vendors covering over a third of the city early in the
morning, and often they made DeMatteis get up as early as 3:00 in
the morning to pitch in and help, even if it was a school day, and
DeMatteis often fell asleep in his classes, especially if it was a sub.
Mandy Blemm, who most of the other children at R. B. Hayes knew
very little about in terms of the realities of her personal life or history
(both I and Tim Applewhite had been placed in Miss Clennon's slow
readers class with Blemm in 3rd grade, although Applewhite later got
bused to a special school in Minerva Park, as he just could not read at
all — he literally was a slow reader, whereas Blemm and I were not),
rarely ever even took her book or pencils out in class, and always sat
looking at the desktop in a withdrawn or sullen manner, and never

paid attention or completed any of her assignments, until the school authorities reached a point where they became so concerned that they began making plans to have Blemm transferred to Minerva Park as well, at which time she would abruptly begin completing her assignments and being involved in classroom goings on. Then, as soon as the administrative heat was off, she would once more revert to just sitting there staring at her desktop or biting dead skin off of the sides of her thumbnail very slowly for the whole class period. She had also been known to eat paste. Everyone was a little afraid of her. At the same time, Frankie Caldwell, who now works in Dayton as a quality control inspector for Uniroyal, had his head down and was drawing something on his theme paper with great precision and intensity. Alison Standish (who later moved away) was absent again. Meanwhile, the Xth Amendment (the first I–IX are what comprise the familiar Bill of Rights, although the Xth Amendment was adopted simultaneously in 1791) contains the phrase *The powers not delegated to the United States by the Constitution, nor prohibited by it to the States,* and so forth, which Mr. Johnson, while at the board, according to Ellen Morrison and every other pupil taking notes, wrote as *The powers not delegated KILL to the United States THEM by the Constitution, nor prohibited by it KILL THEM to the States,* at which time there was again, evidently, another long classroom silence, during which the pupils all began looking at one another while Mr. Johnson stood with his back to the room at the board with his hand with the yellow chalk hanging at his side and his head again cocked to the side as if he were having trouble hearing or understanding something, without turning around or saying anything, before picking up the board's eraser once again and trying to continue the lesson on Amendments X and XIII as though nothing unusual had taken place. According to Mandy Blemm, by this time the room was deathly quiet, and many of the pupils had an uneasy expression on their face as they dutifully crossed out the *THEM* and *KILL THEM* that Mr. Johnson had initially inserted in the quotation. At this same time, in the window, a terrible series of events was transpiring for Ruth Simmons' father, who in a diagonal series of panels in the protective mesh was stoically and uncomplainingly clearing the long black driveway of snow with the enormous Snow Boy brand device that the owner's company engineers had invented in his R&D laboratories, which was why he was now so wealthy. This was just the beginning of the era of power lawnmowers and snow removers for ordinary consumers. Meanwhile, Mrs. Marjorie Simmons' car was stuck in the street's heavy snow and was idling with the windows so fogged up that the observer had no idea what she might be doing in there, and Cuffie and the hardbitten feral dogs were presumably still traversing the lengthy industrial pipe that ran from the Scioto River to a large industrial-chemical factory on Olentangy River Road, as for several consecutive panels there are depictions of the cement exterior of the pipe but no visible activity or anything exiting the pipe at either end except for the ominous orange trickle into the river. The whole Civics classroom had become very quiet. The total number of words on the chalkboard after the erasures was either 104 or 121, depending on whether one counted Roman numerals as words or not. If asked, I could probably have told you the total number of letters, the most and the least used letters (in the latter case, a tie), as well as a number of different statistical functions by which the relative frequency of different letters' appearance could be quantified, although I would not have put any of these data in this way, nor was I even quite aware that I could. The facts about the words were simply there, much the way a knowledge of how your tummy feels and where your arms are are there regardless of whether you're paying attention to these parts or not. They were simply part of the whole peripheral environment in which I sat. What I was, however, wholly aware of was that I was becoming more and more disturbed by the graphic narrative that was unfolding, square by square, in the window. While compelling and diverting, few of the window's narratives were ever gruesome or unpleasant. Most had upbeat — if somewhat naive and childish — themes. And it was only on days when there was enough time before the bell rang for the end of Civics that I got to see how they ended. Some carried over from the prior day, but as a practical matter this was rare, as it was difficult to hold all the unfolding details in mind for that long.

IN CHILDHOOD, I HAD NO INSIGHT WHATSOEVER INTO MY
FATHER'S CONSCIOUSNESS, NOR ANY AWARENESS OF WHAT IT
MIGHT HAVE FELT LIKE, INSIDE, TO DO WHAT HE HAD TO SIT
THERE AT HIS DESK AND DO EVERY DAY. IN THIS RESPECT, IT
WAS NOT UNTIL MANY YEARS AFTER HIS DEATH THAT I FELT I
TRULY KNEW HIM.

In terms of the precise order of events in the Civics classroom,
something was now evidently wrong with Mr. Johnson's face and its
expression as the lesson moved on to Amendment XIII. In this same
interval, in a series of panels several rows down, the large, orange, gas-
powered Snow Boy device, which removed snow from driveways by
means of a system of rotary blades that chopped the snow into fine
particles and then a powerful blower that enhanced the vacuum of the
blades' rotation to throw the snow five, eight, or twelve feet in a high
arc to the side of the man operating the machine (the distance of the
arc could be controlled by adjusting the angle of the chute by means of
three pre-installed pins and holes, not unlike the Howitzer Mark IV
artillery used in Korea and elsewhere), stalled. The blizzard's snow was
evidently so heavy and wet that it had clogged the rotating system of
eight razor sharp blades, and the Snow Boy's self-protective choke had
stalled the engine (whose turbine was also the blades' rotor) instead of
allowing the engine's cylinders to overheat and melt the pistons, which
would ruin the expensive machine. The Snow Boy was, in this respect,
little more than a modified power lawnmower, which our neighbor
Mr. Snead was proudly the first on our street to get one of, and had
turned it over for the neighborhood children's inspection after dis-
abling the spark plugs — he emphasized several times that one must
disable the lawnmower's spark plugs if you were going to place any
part of your hands near the blades, which he said rotated at over
360 rpm of torque and could slice a man's hand off before he even
knew what was happening — and the window's side panel's schematic
view of the Snow Boy's moving parts was based closely on Mr. Snead's
explanation of how his power lawnmower was put together to mow his

grass with only a featherlight touch on the controls. (Mr. Snead always wore a tan cardigan sweater, and beneath his surface bonhomie seemed palpably sad, and our mother said that the reason he was so friendly to the neighborhood children and even gave each of us a Christmas present for several years was because he and Mrs. Snead couldn't have any children of their own, which was sad, and which my brother said privately was due to Mrs. Snead's back alley abortion as a roundheel teen, which at the time I don't believe I understood enough to feel anything other than sorry for Mr. and Mrs. Snead, both of whom I liked.) As I recall it now, the Sneads' lawnmower had been orange as well, and much larger than its modern descendants. I did not, though, initially recall the window's narrative including any explanation of what fate befell the smaller, subordinate feral dog, with the sore, whose name was Scraps, and had run away from home because of the way its owner mistreated it when the tedium and despair of his lower level administrative job made him come home empty-eyed and angry and drink several highballs without any ice or even a lime, and later always found some excuse to be cruel to Scraps, who had waited alone at home all day and only wanted some petting or affection or to play tug of war with a rag or dog toy in order to take its mind off of its own bored loneliness, and whose life had been so awful that the backstory cut off abruptly after the second time the man kicked Scraps in the stomach so hard that Scraps couldn't stop coughing and yet still tried to lick the man's hand when he picked Scraps up and threw him in the cold garage and locked him in there all night, where Scraps lay alone in a tight ball on the cement floor coughing as quietly as he could. Meanwhile, in the main narrative row, his mind distracted by concern over his blind daughter's sadness and the hope that his wife, Marjorie, was OK driving in the blizzard to look for Cuffie, Mr. Simmons, using his blue collar strength to easily turn the stalled Snow Boy device over onto its side, reached into the system of blades and the intake chute in order to clear them of the wet, packed snow that had gotten compressed in there and jammed the blade. Normally a careful worker who paid good attention and followed directions, this time he was so distracted that he forgot to disable the Snow Boy's spark plugs before reaching in, as the schematic panel with an arrow and dotted line at the intact spark plugs showed. Thus, when enough of the packed snow had been removed to allow the rotor to turn freely, the Snow Boy sprang into life on its side while Ruth Simmons' father had his hand deep inside the intake chute, severing not only Mr. Simmons' hand but much of his forearm, and badly splintering his forearm's bone all the way down to the bone marrow, with a horrifying full color spray of red snow and human matter jetting at full force straight up into the air (the Snow Boy being on its side, its chute was now facing straight upwards) and completely blinding Mr. Simmons, whose face was right over the chute. My shock and alarm over what was happening to Ruth Simmons' father, whom I liked, and felt for, created a sense of shock and numbness that distanced me from the panels' scene somewhat, and I remember being distanced enough to be able to be on some level aware that the Civics classroom seemed unusually quiet, with not even the little sounds of whispering or coughing that usually made up the room's ambient noise when the teacher was writing on the chalkboard. The only sound, except for Chris DeMatteis clicking and grinding his rear molars in his sleep, being that of Richard A. Johnson writing on the chalkboard, ostensibly about the XIIIth Amendment's abolition of Negro slavery, except instead it turned out that he was really writing *KILL THEM KILL THEM ALL* over and over again on the chalkboard (as my own eyes would register just moments later) in capital letters that got bigger and bigger with every letter, and the handwriting less and less like the sub's customary fluid script and more and more frightening and ultimately not even human looking, and not seeming to realize what he was doing or stopping to give any kind of explanation but only cocking his already oddly cocked head further and further over to the side, like somebody struggling might and main against some terrible type of evil or alien force that had ahold of him at the chalkboard and was compelling his hand to write things against his will, and making (I was not conscious of hearing this at the time) a strange, highpitched vocal noise that was something like a scream or moan of effort, except that it was evidently just one note or pitch maintained throughout, and stayed that way, with the sound coming out for much longer than anyone can normally even hold their breath, while he remained facing the chalkboard so that no one yet could see what his expression looked like, and writing *KILL KILL KILL THEM ALL KILL THEM DO IT NOW KILL THEM* over and over again, the chalkboard's handwriting getting more and more jagged and gigantic and spiky, with one part of the board already completely filled with the repetitive phrase. What most credible witnesses seemed to recall most vividly at this point was the classroom's resultant confusion and fear — Emily-Ann Barr and Elizabeth Frazier were both crying out and holding on to each other, and Danny Ellsberg, Raymond Gillies, Yolanda Maldonado, Jan and Erin Swearingen, and several other pupils were whipping themselves back and forth in their bolted seats, and Philip Finkelpearl was preparing to throw up (which was, in those years, his response to any strong stimuli), and Terence Velan was calling for his *Stepmutti,* and Mandy Blemm was sitting up very rigid and straight and staring with an intently concentrated expression at the back of Mr. Johnson's head as it cocked further and further to the side until it was evidently almost touching his shoulder, with his left arm now straight out to the side and his hand forming a kind of almost claw. And while I was not conscious or attentive to any of this directly — except perhaps that the back of Unterbrunner's freckled neck in the seat ahead of me at the left periphery of my vision had gone very white and bloodless and her large head was totally rigid and still — in retrospect, I believe that the atmosphere of the classroom may have subconsciously influenced the unhappy events of the period's window's mesh's narrative fantasy, which was now more like a nightmare, and was now proceeding radially along several rows and diagonals of panels at once, which required tremendous energy and concentration to sustain. Both the Art class's deaf children and the other blind children (the latter of whom could not see the statuette, but whose sense of touch was very acute, and could, in a manner of speaking, see with their hands, and had passed the malformed statuette hand to hand) were ridiculing the statuette of Cuffie and laughing at Ruth Simmons, the cruel blind students laughing in a normal way, while the cruel deaf students' laughter was either an apish hooting (those deaf people who are not mute tend to produce a hooting sound — I do not know why this is, but when I was very small, one of the boys who lived on our street had been deaf, and had played with and sometimes gotten into terrible fistfights with my older brother, until eventually their home caught fire in the middle of the night, and several of the family suffered minor burns and smoke inhalation, and they moved away even though their insurance had covered all expenses and repairs, and this boy had often made the characteristic hooting noises) or the mute and uncanny mime of normal laughter's gestures and expressions, while the school's Art teacher, who was both deaf and blind, smiled idiotically from her desk at the front of the classroom, unaware that Ruth Simmons was at the weeping center of a laughing, mocking, hooting, cane-waving circle of deaf and blind children, one of whom was tossing Ruth's figurine up into the air and swinging his slender white cane at it like an American Legion coach hitting fungoes for outfield practice (though with considerably less success); while, in another series of panels further down, Mrs. Marge Simmons' idling car was now just a large, throbbing, and only vaguely car shaped mound of snow with a peculiar greyish cast to it, as a result of the snowstorm's piling snow having clogged the worn old car's exhaust outlet and diverted the exhaust to the car's interior, where, in an interior view, sat the late Marjorie Simmons, still behind the steering wheel, with her mouth and chin smeared all red as she had been applying Avon Acapulco Sunset lipstick when the carbon monoxide of the vent began to attack, forcing her hand into the shape of a claw that smeared lipstick all over her lower face as she gasped and clawed at herself for air, sitting rigidly upright and blue and staring sightlessly into the auto's rearview mirror while, outside the idling mound, women so bundled up that they could hardly bend over began shoveling easements for their returning husbands into their driveways, and distant sounds of emergency sirens and ambulances began to approach the scene. At the same time, a single, traumatically abrupt panel appeared to depict Scraps, the subordinate, piebald feral dog with the sore, being attacked in the industrial tunnel by swarms of what were either small, tailless rats or gigantic, atomically mutated cockroaches as Cuffie, nearby,

stands frozen with his paws over his eyes in instinctual shock and terror, until the tougher, more experienced and dominant feral rottweiler
mix saves Cuffie's life by dragging him by the scruff of the neck into a
smaller side tunnel that serves as an escape hatch and led more
towards the area of R. B. Hayes Primary and the Fairhaven Knolls golf
course that lay just beyond the copse of trees at the window's rear right
horizon. The tableau, complete with the unfortunate piebald dog's
mouth open in agony and a rat or mutated roach abdomen protruding
from his eyesocket as the predator's anterior half consumed his eye and
inner brain, was so traumatic that this narrative line was immediately
stopped and replaced with a neutral view of the pipe's exterior. As a
result, the lone, nightmarish panel appeared in the window as just a
momentary peripheral snapshot or flash of a horrifying scene, much
the way such single, horrible flashes often appear in bad dreams —
somehow the speed with which they appear and disappear, and the lack
of any time to get any perspective or digest what you are seeing or fit it
into the narrative of the dream as a whole, makes it even worse, and often a rapid, peripheral flash of something contextless and awful could
be the single worst part of a nightmare, and the part that stayed with
you the most vividly and kept popping into your mind's eye at odd
moments while brushing your teeth or getting a box of cereal down
out of the cereal cabinet for a snack, and unsettling you all over again,
perhaps because its very instantaneousness in the dream meant that
your mind had to keep subconsciously returning to it in order to work
it out or incorporate it. As if the fragment were not done with you yet,
in much the same way that now, so very much later, the most persistent memories of early childhood consist of these flashes, peripheral
tableaux — my father slowly shaving as I pass my parents' bathroom
on the way downstairs, our mother on her knees in a kerchief and
gloves by a rosebush out the kitchen's east window as I fill a water
glass, my brother breaking his wrist in a fall off of the jungle gym and
the far-off sound of his cries as I drew in the sand with a stick. The piano's casters in their small protective sleeves; his face in the foyer coming home. Later, when I was in my 20s and courting my wife, the
traumatic film *The Exorcist* came out, a controversial film that both of

us found disturbing — and not disturbing in an artistic or thought-provoking way, but simply offensive — and walked out of together at just the point where the little girl was mutilating her private areas with a crucifix similar in size and design to the one that Miranda's parents had on the wall of their front sitting room. In fact, the first moment of what I would consider true affinity and concord that Miranda and I experienced was, as I recall it, in the car on the way home from walking out of this film, which we had done mutually, with one quick glance between us in the theatre confirming that our distaste and rejection of the film were in perfect concordance, with an odd thrill in that moment of mutuality that was itself not wholly unsexual, although in the context of the film's themes the sexuality of the response was both disturbing and unforgettable. Suffice to say we have not seen it since. And yet the lone moment of *The Exorcist* that has stayed so emphatically with me over the years consisted only of a few frames, and had precisely this rapid, peripheral quality, and has obtruded at odd moments into my mind's eye ever since. In the film, Father Karras' mother has died, and he has drunk a bit too much out of grief and guilt ('I should have been there, I should have been there,' is his refrain to the other Jesuit, Father Dyer, who is removing his shoes and helping him into bed), and has a bad dream, which the film's director depicts with frightening intensity and skill. It was one of our first unaccompanied dates, not long after I had started at the firm where I still work — and yet, even now, the interval of this dream sequence remains vivid to me in nearly every detail. Father Karras' mother, pale and dressed in funereal black, ascends from an urban subway stop while Father Karras waves desperately at her from across the street, trying to get her attention, but she does not see or acknowledge him and instead turns — moving with the terrible, implacable quality that other people in dreams often have — and descends back down the subway station's stairway, sinking implacably from view. There is no sound, despite its being a busy street, and the absence of sound is both frightening and realistic — many people's recollected nightmares are often soundless, with suggestions of thick glass or deep water and these media's effect on sound. Father Karras is an actor seen in no other film of the time, so far as I know, with a brooding, Mediterranean cast to his features, whom another character in the film compares to Sal Mineo. The dream sequence also includes a lengthy, slow motion view of a Roman Catholic medal falling through the air, as if from a great height, with its thin silver chain undulating in complex shapes as the coin rotates as it slowly falls. The iconography of the falling coin is not complicated, as Miranda pointed out when we discussed the film and our reasons for leaving before the exorcism proper. It symbolizes Father Karras' feelings of impotence and guilt at his mother's death (she had died alone in her apartment, and it had been three days before someone found her; this type of scenario would make anyone feel guilty), and the blow to Father Karras' faith in himself as a son and a priest, a blow to his vocation, which must be rooted not only in faith in a god but a belief that the person with the vocation could make some kind of difference and help alleviate suffering and human loneliness, which now, in this case, he has blatantly failed to do with his own mother. Not to mention the classic problem of how a supposedly loving god could permit this terrible outcome, a problem that always arises when people to whom we are connected suffer or die (as well as the secondary backlash of guilt over the buried hostility we often feel towards the memory of parents who have died — an interval of backstory had shown Father Karras' mother forcing some kind of unpleasant medicine down his throat with a steel spoon as a child, as well as berating him in Italian for causing her to worry, and once walking silently past the window when he had fallen on rollerskates and skinned his knees and was crying out for her to come out to the sidewalk and help him). Such reactions are common to the point of being nearly universal, and all of this is symbolized by the dream's slowly falling medallion, which at the sequence's end lands upon a flat stone in either a cemetery or untended garden, full of moss and spiky undergrowth. Despite the bucolic setting, the air through which the coin falls has been airless and black, the extreme black of nothingness, even as the medallion and chain come to rest on the stone; just as there is no sound, there is no background. But spliced very quickly into the sequence is a brief flash of Father Karras' face, terribly transformed.

The face's white, reptilian eyes and extrudent cheekbones and root-white pallor are plainly demonic — it is the face of evil. This flash of face is extremely brief, probably just enough frames to register on the human eye, and devoid of sound or background, and is gone again and immediately replaced with the Catholic medal's continued fall. Its very brevity serves to stamp it on the viewer's consciousness. My wife, it turned out, did not even see the rapid splice of the face — she may have sneezed, or looked away from the screen for a moment. Her interpretation was that even if the rapid, peripheral image truly had been in the film and not my imagination, it too could be readily interpreted as a symbol of Father Karras subconsciously seeing himself as evil or bad for having allowed his mother to (as he saw it) die alone. I have never forgotten these frames, though — and yet, although I privately disagreed with Miranda's quick dismissal, I am still far from being certain of what the rapid flash of the Father's transfigured face was meant to mean, nor why it remains so vivid in my memory of our courtship. I think it can only be the incongruous, near instantaneous quality of its appearance, the utter peripheralness of it. For it is true that the most vivid and enduring occurrences in our lives are often those that occur at the periphery of our awareness. Its significance for the story of how those of us who did not flee the Civics classroom in panic became known as the *4 Unwitting Hostages* is fairly obvious. In testing, many schoolchildren labeled as hyperactive or deficient in attention are observed to be not so much unable to pay attention as to have difficulty exercising control or choice over what it is they pay attention to. And yet much the same thing happens in adult life — as we age, many people notice a shift in the objects of their memories. We often can remember the details and subjective associations far more vividly than the event itself. This explains the frequent tip-of-the-tongue feeling when trying to convey what is important about some memory or occurrence. Similarly, it is often what makes it so difficult to communicate meaningfully with others in later life. Often, the most vividly felt and remembered elements will appear at best tangential to someone else — the scent of Velan's leather shorts as he ran up the aisle, or the very precise double fold at the top of my father's brown bag lunch, for

instance, or even the peripheral tableaux of little Ruth Simmons gazing blindly upwards while a circle of peers castigates her for the Plato
figurine and — contiguously in the window but elsewhere in the actual narrative — in the woods along the driveway of the estate of the
wealthy manufacturer, of Mr. Simmons, her father, staggering blindly
in and out of view while holding the stump of his severed hand, groan-
ing for help as he runs in his vivid snowsuit, and all too often running
blindly into the forest's trees due to his own hurled blood and partic-
ulate matter's having rendered him blind, and the whole highspeed
tableau is grainy and imperfectly seen because of all of the trees and
spiky undergrowth and the driving blizzard and huge drifts of wind
driven snow, which Mr. Simmons finally bounces headfirst off of a tree
and falls headlong into one of, a massive snowdrift, and disappears all
the way up to his boots, one of which is moving spasmodically as he
tries to struggle for stable footing, unaware in his shock, pain, loss of
blood, and blindness that he is even upside down, while, meanwhile,
diagonally down and across, a C.P.D. technician is kneeling on the di-
lapidated front seat of the Simmons family's car, drawing a body outline around the place behind the wheel where the rescue team had
found the bright blue body of Marjorie Simmons, whose frustrations
and disappointments were now all over, and whose body — still holding its lipstick, which made a small, sharp looking lump in the white
blanket that covered it — was being loaded in the blizzard onto a large
ambulance stretcher by two orderlies in white gowns while a C.P.D.
detective with snow on his hat talked to the heavily bundled house-
wives who had been shoveling out their driveways and were now all
leaning tiredly on their snowshovels talking to the detective, who was
taking notes in a small notebook with a very dull pencil, and whose
own fingernails were slightly blue in the cold, and the driving snow
made everyone's eyelashes white, and the two Columbus Public Works
workers in large yellow boots who had shoveled Mrs. Simmons' car
out of the igloo-sized mound stood together next to a towtruck, blowing into their cupped hands and hopping slightly up and down, the
way people who are both cold and bored often do, facing away from
the street and the blanket with the lump over the stretcher with just

two small boots with fake fur fringe at the ankles poking out, and the house that the two bored C.P.W. workers (one of whom has a red and silver Ohio State U. ski cap on with a buckeye fluffball at the top) are facing without even really seeing it is one of the houses whose backyards (this one's has a swingset whose swings each have a large, brick-shaped block of snow on them, that has accumulated) abut the copse of elm and fir trees at the edge of Fairhaven Knolls that separates the neighborhood homes from the R. B. Hayes school ballfield in which even now the dominant rottweiler is again trying to mount the Simmons' lost dog, in the actual field through the classroom window, miming the position and expressions of mating, exhorting the defenseless, long suffering whelp to sit still and endure it or else something really terrible would happen.

IN THE LIGHT OF THE POLITICAL SITUATION OF OUR LATER ADO-LESCENCE, ONE OF THE MOST TROUBLING AND MUCH DISCUSSED ASPECTS OF THE TRAUMA FOR THOSE OF US OF *THE 4* WAS THAT MR. JOHNSON HAD NOT APPEARED TO CONFRONT, RESIST, OR THREATEN THE ARMED OFFICERS WHO CAME FORCIBLY INTO THE ROOM THROUGH BOTH THE DOOR AND THE EAST WALL'S WINDOWS, BUT MERELY CONTINUED TO WRITE *KILL* OVER AND OVER AGAIN ON THE CHALKBOARD, WHICH WAS NOW SO FILLED THAT HIS NEWER *KILL, KILL THEM*'S OVERLAY AND OFTEN OB-SCURED HIS EARLIER EXHORTATIONS, FINALLY RESULTING IN LIT-TLE MORE THAN AN ABSTRACT MASH OF LETTERS ON THE BOARD. WHILE THE JAGGED LENGTH OF CHALK, THE BROAD ARM MO-TIONS, AND THE PROXIMITY OF MR. JOHNSON'S BRIEFCASE ON THE DESK WERE CITED AS THE *PERCEIVED THREAT TO HOSTAGE SAFETY* THAT JUSTIFIED THE SHOOTING IN THE EYES OF THE C.P.D. BOARD OF INQUIRY, THE REAL TRUTH IS THAT IT WAS CLEARLY MR. JOHNSON'S FACIAL EXPRESSION AND SUSTAINED HIGH SOUND, AND HIS COMPLETE OBLIVIOUSNESS TO THE OFFI-CERS' COMMANDS TO DROP THE CHALK AND STEP AWAY WITH BOTH HANDS IN FULL VIEW AS HE COPIED HIMSELF WITH EVER INCREASING INTENSITY ONTO THE BOARD'S VERBAL CHAOS, WHICH

PROMPTED THEM TO OPEN FIRE. THIS WAS THE ONLY REAL
TRUTH — THEY WERE AFRAID.

Of the so-called *4 Hostages*, it was only Mandy Blemm and Frank
Caldwell (who would later, at Fishinger Secondary, attend both Junior
and Senior Prom as a couple, maintaining a steady dating relationship
throughout those years in spite of Blemm's reputation, after which
Caldwell enlisted in the U.S. Navy, eventually also serving overseas)
who were attentive and aware enough throughout the first part of the
incident to recount for DeMatteis and I later how very long it was that
Mr. Johnson remained facing and writing jaggedly on the chalkboard
while emitting the high, atonal sound while the classroom behind
him turned more and more into a bedlam of surreal and nightmarish
terror, with some of the children crying and quite a few (Blemm later
named them) reverting, under the strain, to early childhood coping
mechanisms such as sucking their thumbs, wetting themselves, and
rocking slightly in their seats humming disconnected bars of various
lullabies to themselves, and Finkelpearl leaned forward over his desktop and threw up, which most of the pupils closest to him appeared to
be too mesmerized with fear to even notice. It was in this interval that
my own conscious awareness finally left the window's mesh and returned to the Civics classroom, which to the best of my memory occurred right after the chalk in Mr. Johnson's hand snapped with a loud
sound and he stood rigid with both arms out and his head to the side,
the sound he produced rising higher and higher in pitch as he turned
around very slowly to face the class, his entire body trembling electri-
cally and his face . . . Mr. Johnson's face's character and expression
were indescribable. I will never forget it. This was the first part I fully
saw of the incident the *Dispatch* first called *Deranged Substitute's Classroom Terror — Mentally Unbalanced Instructor Stricken at Blackboard,
Appears 'Possessed,' Threatens Mass Murder, Several Pupils Hospitalized,
Unit 4 Board Calls Emergency Session, Bainbridge Under Gun* (at that
time, Dr. Bainbridge was Superintendent of Schools for Unit 4).
Philip Finkelpearl's throwing up was also a factor. There is something
about someone throwing up anywhere within a child's earshot that

serves to direct and concentrate his attention with an almost instant force, and even when my awareness returned in full to the classroom, it was Finkelpearl's vomitus and the associated sounds and odors of it that I first can recall being struck by. The final frame I remember was when it was revealed in midair, during the ridicule, in a close-up, stop-action view as it rose end over end in the air and the wicked boy prepared to swing his cane, that the true subject of the clay statuette Ruth Simmons had fashioned was, in reality, a human being, who in her distraught distraction she had given four legs instead of two, despite the crude human features, creating a somewhat monstrous or unnatural image as in Greek myth or *The Isle of Dr. Moreau*. The import of this detail in the narrative I do not remember, though I recall the detail itself very clearly. Nor can I remember for just how long the Civics classroom remained like that, with Mr. Johnson in extremis with both arms extended outward at the chalkboard (when you've been intensely preoccupied, coming back to what is actually happening around you is somewhat like coming out of a movie theatre in the afternoon, when the sunlight and sensory press of the street's activity nearly stun you), looking simultaneously electrocuted and demonically possessed (there is no other way to describe the way his upturned face was transformed, with its look of both suffering and ghastly exultation, or rather it may have been that the two different expressions alternated so rapidly on his uptilted face that in the mind's perception they became conjoined), and making that sound, with what Ahearn and Ellsberg and others in the front row said looked like every single hair on Mr. Johnson's head, neck, wrists, and hands standing straight up, and the children in the classroom sitting bolt upright with many of their eyes bulging out and rolling around and around in their heads like cartoon characters' eyes, with sheer terror. It was in the midst of this scene that Chris DeMatteis awoke in the rear of his row with a small plaintive shout — which is how he sometimes woke up when he had fallen unconscious in school. In retrospect, my impression is that Chris's absently panicked cry of awakening is what started the class's other pupils openly screaming and rising from their desks to begin an hysterical mass exodus from the Civics classroom (rather the way one random infantryman's firing his weapon will precipitate the start of a battle when, up to that point, it had been just two tense and ready armies facing each other with weapons drawn but not yet fired), and what wrested my attention from the sight of Philip Finkelpearl's vomit hanging in strings and clots from the side of his bolted desktop was the sudden simultaneous mass movement of the class's pupils as all of them except Chris DeMatteis, Frank Caldwell, Mandy Blemm, and I began running for the door of the classroom, which unfortunately was closed, and the mass of children behind Emily-Ann Barr and the fleet Raymond Gillies (a Negro) and the others who had reached the door first and were clawing hysterically at the knob of the door drove the first children physically into the door with such force that there was a gruesome sound of the impact of someone's face or head against the thick, frosted glass of the door's upper half; and, as the door (like all classroom doors of that era) opened inward and there was a rapidly growing mass of panicked children in the way, it seemed a very long time before the door was forced open by someone bulky enough — in hindsight I believe this to have been Gregory Oehmke, who at age ten was already well over 100 pounds and had a neck the same width as his shoulders, and who would also go on to serve overseas, though I base this belief not on directly seeing Oehmke do it but only from noting the brute savagery with which it was yanked open, hitting and scraping several children with the edge of the heavy door as it was forced open, and causing one of the tall Swearingen sisters in roughly the middle of the herd to lose her footing and disappear and presumably get badly trampled in the subsequent exodus, for when the noise of the screaming children receded north up the hallway and the door was slowly closing on its pneumatic hinge, and two unidentified sets of hands reached quickly in to grasp Jan Swearingen's ankles and pull her from the Civics classroom, she did not move or in any way revive as she slid facedown on the checkered tile, leaving a lengthy smear of either her own blood or someone else's that was already on the floor from some other mishap at the door, the long braids both Swearingen sisters tended to play with and even to chew on when distracted or tense trailing behind and missing by just inches getting trapped in the crack of the slowly closing door.

IN THESE LATER DISCUSSIONS, IT ALSO EMERGED THAT FRANKIE
CALDWELL HAD HYPERVENTILATED FROM TERROR AND BRIEFLY
LOST CONSCIOUSNESS DURING THE MASS EXODUS. OF THE *4 UN-
WITTING HOSTAGES,* IT WAS ONLY WE OTHER THREE WHO WERE
ACTUALLY CLASSIFIED BY THE SCHOOL ADMINISTRATION AS DE-
FICIENT OR SLOW. THAT FRANKIE NEVER PROTESTED AGAINST
THE PRESS'S ERROR IS TESTIMONY TO THE DEEP EMBARRASS-
MENT THAT HE, TOO, MUST HAVE FELT AT BEING SO AFRAID.

For my own part, I had begun having nightmares about the reality
of adult life as early as perhaps age seven. I knew, even then, that the
dreams involved my father's life and job and the way he looked when
he returned home from work at the end of the day. His arrival was always between 5:42 and 5:45, and it was usually I who was the first to
see him come through the front door. What occurred was almost
choreographic in its routine. He came in already turning in order to
press the door closed behind him. He removed his hat and topcoat and
hung the coat in the foyer closet; he clawed his necktie loose with two
fingers, took the green rubber band off of the *Dispatch,* entered the living room, greeted my brother, and sat down with the newspaper to wait
for my mother to bring him a highball. The nightmares themselves
always opened with a wide angle view of a number of men at desks
in rows in a large, brightly lit room or hall. The desks were arranged in
precise rows and columns like the desks of an R. B. Hayes classroom,
but these were all more like the large, grey steel desks that the teachers had at the front of the room, and there were many, many more of
them, perhaps 100 or more, each occupied by a man in suit and tie. If
there were windows, I do not remember noticing them. Some of the
men were older than others, but they were all obviously adults —
people who drove, and applied for insurance coverage, and had high-
balls while they read the paper before dinner. The nightmare's room
was at least the size of a soccer or flag football field; it was utterly silent
and had a large clock on each wall. It was also very bright. In the foyer,
turning from the front door while his left hand rose to remove his hat,
my father's eyes appeared lightless and dead, empty of everything we

associated with his real persona. He was a kind, decent, ordinary look-ing man. His voice was deeply pitched but not resonant. Softspoken, he had a sense of humor that kept his natural reserve from seeming remote or aloof. Even when my brother and I were small, we were aware that he spent more time with us and took the trouble to show us that we were important to him a good deal more than most fathers of that era did. (It was many years before I had any real idea of how our mother felt about him.) The foyer was directly off of the living room, where the piano was, and at that time, I often read or played with my trucks outside of kicking range beneath the piano while my brother practiced his Hanons, and I was often the first to register the sound of my father's key in the front door. It took only four steps and a brief sockslide into the foyer to be able to see him first as he entered on a wave of outside air. I remember the foyer as dim and cold and smelling of the coat closet, the bulk of which was filled with my mother's different coats and matching gloves. The front door was heavy and dif-ficult to open and close, as if the foyer were somehow pressurized. The door had a small, diamond-shaped window in the center, though we later moved before I was ever tall enough to see out of it. He had to put his side into the door somewhat in order to make it close all the way, and I would not see his face until he turned to remove his hat and coat, but I can recall that the angle of his shoulders as he leaned into the door had the same quality as his eyes. I could not convey this quality now and most assuredly couldn't have then, but I know that it helped inform the nightmares. His face was not at all like this on weekends off. It is in hindsight that I believe the dreams to have been about adult life. At the time, I knew only their terror — much of the difficulty they complained of in getting me to lie down and go to sleep at night was due to these dreams. Nor could it always have been dusk at 5:42, though that is what I recall its being, and the inrush of outside air he brought with him as cold, and scented with burnt leaves and the sad way the street smelled at twilight, when all of the houses became the same color and all of their porch lights came on like bulwarks against something without name. His eyes when he turned from the door didn't scare me, but the feeling was somehow related to being scared.

Often I still had a truck in my hand. His hat went on the hatrack, his coat shouldered out of, then the coat was folded over his left arm, the closet opened with his right hand, the coat transferred to that hand while the third wooden coathanger from the left is removed with his left hand. There was something about this routine that cast shadows deep down in parts of me I could not access on my own. I knew something of boredom by then, of course, at Hayes, and Riverside, or on Sunday afternoons when there was nothing to do — the fidgety type of childhood boredom that is more like worry than despair. But I do not believe I consciously connected the way my father looked at night with the far different and deeper, soul-level boredom of his job, which I knew was actuarial because in 2nd grade everyone in Mrs. Claymore's homeroom had had to give a short presentation on what our father's profession was. I knew that insurance was protection that adults applied for in case of risk, and I knew that it had numbers in it because of the documents that were visible in his briefcase when I got to pop its latches and open it for him, and my brother and I had had the building that housed the insurance company's HQ and my father's tiny window in its face pointed out to us by our mother from the car, but the actual specifics of his job were always vague. And they remained so for many years. Looking back, I suspect that there was something of a cover-your-eyes and stop-your-ears quality to my lack of curiosity about just what my father had to do all day. I can remember certain exciting narrative tableaux based around the competitive, almost primitive connotations of the word *breadwinner,* which had been Mrs. Claymore's blanket term for our fathers' occupations. But I do not believe I knew or could even imagine, as a child, that for almost 30 years of 51 weeks a year my father sat all day at a metal desk in a silent, fluorescent lit room, reading forms and making calculations and filling out further forms on the results of those calculations, breaking only occasionally to answer his telephone or meet with other actuaries in other bright, quiet rooms. With only a small and sunless north window that looked out on other small office windows in other grey buildings. The nightmares were vivid and powerful, but they were not the kind from which you wake up crying out and then have to try to explain to your mother when she comes what the dream was about so that she could reassure you that there was nothing like what you just dreamed in the real world. I knew that he liked to have music or a lively radio program on and audible all of the time at home, or to hear my brother practicing while he read the *Dispatch* before dinner, but I am certain I did not then connect this with the overwhelming silence he sat in all day. I did not know that our mother's making his lunch was one of the keystones of their marriage contract, or that in mild weather he took his lunch down in the elevator and ate it sitting on a backless stone bench that faced a small square of grass with two trees and an abstract public sculpture, and that on many mornings he steered by these 30 minutes outdoors the way mariners out of sight of land use stars. My father died of a coronary when I was sixteen, and I can acknowledge, despite the obvious shock and loss, that his passing was less hard to bear than much of what I learned about his life when he was gone. For instance, it was very important to my mother that my father's burial plot be somewhere where there were at least a few trees in view; and given the logistics of the cemetery and the details of the mortuary contract he'd prepared for them both, this caused a great deal of trouble and expense at a difficult time, which neither my brother nor I saw the point of until years later when we learned about his weekdays and the bench where he liked to eat his lunch. At Miranda's suggestion, I made a point, one spring, of visiting the site where his little square of grass and trees had been. The area had been refashioned into one of the small and largely unutilized downtown parks that were characteristic of the New Columbus renewal programs of the early '80s, in which there were no longer grass or beech trees but a small, modern children's play area, with wood chips instead of sand and a jungle gym made entirely of recycled tires. There is also a swingset, whose two empty swings moved back and forth at different rates in the wind the whole time I sat there. For a time in my early adulthood, I had periods of imagining my father sitting on the bench year after year, chewing, and looking at that carved out square of something green, always knowing exactly how much time was left for lunch without taking his watch out. Sadder still was trying to imagine what he thought about as he sat there, imagining him perhaps thinking about us, our faces when he got home or the way we smelled at night after baths when he came in to kiss us on the top of the head — but the truth is that I have no idea what he thought about, what his internal life might have been like. And that were he alive I still would not know. Or trying (which Miranda feels was saddest of all) to imagine what words he might have used to describe his job and the square and two trees to my mother. I knew my father well enough to know it could not have been direct — I am certain he never sat down or lay beside her and spoke as such about lunch on the bench and the twin sickly trees that in the fall drew swarms of migrating starlings, appearing en masse more like bees than birds as they swarmed in and weighed down the elms' or buckeyes' limbs and filled the mind with sound before rising again in a great mass to spread and contract like a great flexing hand against the downtown sky. Trying thus to imagine remarks and attitudes and tiny half anecdotes that over time conveyed enough to her that she would go through hell and back to have his grave site moved to the premium areas nearer the front gate and its little stand of blue pines. It was not quite a nightmare proper, but neither was it a daydream or fancy. It came when I had been in bed for a time and was beginning to fall asleep but only partway there — the part of the featherfall into sleep in which whatever lines of thought you've been pursuing begin now to become surreal around the edges, and then at some point the thoughts themselves are replaced by images and concrete pictures and scenes. You move, gradually, from merely thinking about something to experiencing it as really there, unfolding, a story or world you are part of, although at the same time enough of you remains awake to be able to discern on some level that what you are experiencing does not quite make sense, that you are on some cusp or edge of true dreaming. Even now, as an adult, I still can consciously recognize that I am starting to fall asleep when my abstract thoughts turn into actual pictures and tiny films, ones whose logic and associations are ever so slightly off — and yet I am always aware of this, of the illogic and my reactions to it. The dream was of a large room full of men in suits and ties seated at rows of great grey desks, bent forward over the papers on their desks, motionless, silent, in a monochrome room or hall under long banks of high lumen fluorescents, the men's faces puffy and seamed with adult tension and wear and appearing to hang slightly loose, the way someone's face can go flaccid and loose when he seems to be staring at something without really seeing it. I acknowledge that I could never convey just what was so dreadful about this tableau of a bright, utterly silent room full of men immersed in rote work. It was the type of nightmare whose terror is less about what you see than about the feeling you have in your lower chest about what you're seeing. Some of the men wore glasses; there were a few small, neatly trimmed mustaches. Some had grey or thinning hair or the large, dark, complexly textured bags beneath their eyes that both our father and Uncle Gerald had. Some of the younger men had wider lapels; most did not. Part of the terror of the dream's wide angle perspective was that the men in the room appeared as both individuals and a great anonymous mass. There were at least 20 or 30 rows of a dozen desks each, each with a blotter and desklamp and file folders with papers in them and a man in a straightback chair behind the desk, each man with a subtly different style or pattern of necktie and his own slightly distinctive way of sitting and positioning his arms and inclining his head, some feeling at their jaw or forehead or the crease of their tie, or biting dead skin from around their thumbnail, or tracing along their lower lip with their pencil's eraser or pen's metal cap. You could tell that the particular styles of sitting and the small, absent habits that individualized them had evolved over years or even decades of sitting like this over their job's work every day, moving purposefully only once in a while to turn a stapled page, or to move a loose page from the left side of an open file folder to the right side, or to close one file folder and slide it a few inches away and then pull another file folder to themselves and open it, gazing down into it as if they were at some terrible height and the documents were the ground far below. If my brother dreamed, we certainly never heard about it. The men's expressions were somehow at once stuporous and anxious, enervated and keyed up — not so much fighting the urge to fidget as appearing to have long ago surrendered whatever hope or expectation causes one to fidget. A few of the chairs' seat portions had cushions made of corduroy or serge, one or two of them brightly colored and edged with fringe in such a way that you could tell they had been handmade by a loved one and given as a gift, perhaps for a birthday, and for some reason this detail was the worst of all. The dream's bright room was death, I could feel it — but not in any way you could convey or explain to my mother if I cried out in fear and she hurried in. And the idea of ever trying to tell my father about the dream was — even later, after it had vanished as abruptly as the problem with reading — unthinkable. The feeling of telling him about it would have been like coming to our Aunt Tina, one of my mother's sisters (who, among her other crosses to bear, had been born with a cleft palate that operations had not much been able to help, besides also having a congenital lung condition), and pointing out the cleft palate to Aunt Tina and asking her how she felt about it and how her life had been affected by it, at which even imagining the look that would come into her eyes was unthinkable. The overall feeling was that these colorless, empty-eyed, long suffering faces were the face of some death that awaited me long before I stopped walking around. Then, when real sleep descended, it becomes a real dream, and I lost the perspective of someone merely looking at the scene and am in it — the lens of perspective pulls suddenly back, and I am one of them, one part of the mass of grey faced men stifling coughs and feeling at their teeth with their tongues and folding the edges of papers down into complex accordion creases and then smoothing them carefully out once more before replacing them in their assigned file folders. And the dream's perspective's view slowly moves further and further in until it is primarily me in view, in close-up, with a handful of other desks' men's faces and upper bodies framing me, and the backs of a few photos' frames and either an adding machine or a telephone at the edge of the desk (mine is also one of the chairs with a handmade cushion). As I can recall it now, in the dream

I look neither like my father nor my real self. I have very little hair, and what I do have is wet combed carefully around the sides, and a small Vandyke or maybe goatee, and my face, which is angled downwards at the desktop in concentration, looks as if it has spent the last 20 years pressed hard against something unyielding. And at a certain point in the interval, in the middle of removing a paper clip or opening a desk drawer (there is no sound), I look up and into the lens of the dream's perspective and stare back at myself, but without any sign of recognition on my face, nor of happiness or fright or despair or appeal — the eyes are flat and opaque, and only mine in the way that a very old album's photo of you as a child in a setting you have no memory of is nevertheless you — and in the dream, as our eyes meet, it is impossible to know what the adult me is seeing or how I am reacting or if there is anything in there at all.

STILL LATER, ANOTHER SHARED AND COHESIVE DISCOMFORT AMONG WE WHO CONSTITUTED *THE UNWITTING 4* WOULD CONCERN THE INTENDED MEANING OF THE WORD *THEM* IN THE REPEATED IMPERATIVES THAT MR. JOHNSON HAD FIRST INSERTED AND THEN FINALLY EFFACED AND OBSCURED THE BOARD'S LESSON WITH. THROUGHOUT THE INCIDENT AND ITS AFTERMATH, EVERYONE CONCERNED HAD ASSUMED WITHOUT QUESTION THAT THE CHALKBOARD'S *THEM* REFERRED TO HIS SUBSTITUTE PUPILS, AND THAT THE INVOLUNTARY REPETITIONS WERE SOME DISTURBED PART OF MR. JOHNSON'S PSYCHE EXHORTING HIM TO KILL US EN MASSE. TO THE BEST OF MY RECOLLECTION, IT WAS MY OLDER BROTHER (WHO BY THAT TIME HAD ENLISTED IN THE ARMED FORCES BY TACIT ARRANGEMENT WITH THE FRANKLIN COUNTY COURT OF COMMON PLEAS, AND WENT ON TO SERVE IN THE SAME REGIMENT IN WHICH TERENCE VELAN WOULD DISTINGUISH HIMSELF THREE YEARS LATER) WHO FIRST SUGGESTED THAT THE IMPERATIVES' *THEM* MAY NOT HAVE REFERRED TO US AT ALL, THAT IT MIGHT, RATHER, HAVE BEEN US WHO MR. JOHNSON'S DISTURBED PART WAS EXHORTING, AND THE *THEM* SOME OTHER TYPE OR GROUP OF PEOPLE ALTOGETHER. JUST WHO THIS

THEM COULD HAVE BEEN MEANT TO BE WAS ANYONE'S GUESS —
THE LATE SUB WAS HARDLY IN A POSITION TO ELABORATE, MY
BROTHER'S LETTER OBSERVED.

I have only general, impressionistic memories of Mrs. Roseman's classroom itself, which did not, even when nearly empty after the mass exodus, seem all that large. There were either 30 or 32 desks facing due north, and on the north wall was the chalkboard with its jagged mass of 212 overstruck *KILL THEM*'s and fragmentary portions of same, as well as the teacher's assigned desk and a grey steel cabinet just west of the blackboard in which were kept art supplies and Civics related audiovisual aids. The east wall was partly comprised of two large rectangular windows; the lower half of each was hinged along the sill and could be opened slightly outward in mild weather. In the absence of any imposed tableaux, the reticulate wire mesh gave the windows an institutional quality and contributed to a sense of being encaged. Also, there was the chronological series of U.S. presidents running above the windows' upper sills up near the ceiling. The ceiling itself was an institutional drop unit comprised of white asbestos tile, numbering 96 total plus 12 fractional tiles at the south end (the tiles' dimensions did not divide evenly into the classroom's length, which I would estimate at 25 feet). Two long, fluorescent banks of lights hung a foot or so beneath the false ceiling, supported by struts that I imagine must have been secured to the same metal grillwork on which the drop tiles rested. All acoustic tile of that era was asbestos. The interior walls' composition appeared to be cinderblock thickly overlaid with multiple coats of paint (possibly as many as four or more coats, so that the uneven texture of the cinderblocks underneath was very much smoothed and occluded), which in the classrooms was an emetic green and in the hallways a type of creamy beige or grey. The tile floor's pattern was an irregular checkerboard of off-grey and green as well, though a subtly different shade or hue of green, so that it was not clear whether the flooring had been selected to complement the walls or whether the whole thing was a coincidence. I know nothing about when R. B. Hayes was built, or under what arrangements — it was, however, razed during the Carter and Rhodes administrations and a new, supposedly more energy efficient structure put up in its place. On the Civics classroom's south wall (which no one but the teacher was able to see because of the way the pupils' desks all faced) were the room's clock and attached bell and the P.A. speaker, whose cabinet was wood and its face covered in what appeared to be some kind of synthetic burlap, and was attached to the Public Address system in the principal's office.

The classroom's westernmost wall — on which were arrayed the unused coathooks, and against which just lately all of the terrified pupils had been clambering over one another to flee the room as Richard Allen Johnson stood frozen and transported, holding out the cuspate length of chalk like a toy sword — also featured, towards the back, two more freestanding cabinets containing spare or damaged copies of *From Sea to Shining Sea . . .*, various testing forms and supplies, construction paper and a large jar of blunt scissors, two wide boxes of filmstrips on governmental and legal systems, and several white woolen wigs and velveteen waistcoats in dark red or plum, with white ruffled plastrons safety-pinned to the lapels, together with a stovepipe hat, a lensless pair of wire spectacles, a collapsible wheelchair and lengthy cigarette holder, and over a dozen small, handheld American flags (these latter out of date as they contained only 49 stars in the corner), all for use in the annual Presidents' Day presentation that Mrs. Roseman organized and directed every February, and in which the previous month Chris DeMatteis had portrayed Franklin D. Roosevelt, and Mrs. Roseman had felt ill and faint and had had to direct the entire show sitting down on the little set of steps leading up to the gymnasium's stage, and in which I had had a dual role, playing a flagwaving supporter of democracy in the audiences for Thomas Jefferson's 2nd Inaugural Address and Abraham Lincoln's Gettysburg Address, as well as the thunder in the thunderstorm in which Philip Finkelpearl as Benjamin Franklin held a construction paper kite with a piece of string with a large skeleton key on it while Raymond Gillies and I stood just offstage behind the curtain and rolled a large piece of industrial tin with pieces of green felt taped over the sharp edges back and forth with a motion reminiscent of one snapping out a blanket to make it lie flat on the bed, producing a sound much like thunder if heard from the gymnasium's seats, while Ruth Simmons and Yolanda Maldonado stood with adult supervision on the catwalk above the row of colored lights for the stage and dropped blue and white bolts of construction paper lightning that we had spent an entire class period using rulers to trace the zigzags of and cut out. My father got permission to leave work early in order to attend the presentation, and even though our mother was again not feeling up to par and could not join him, we had a fun time later recounting for her all that went on, with Terence Velan in stovepipe hat and woolen beard having memorized the Gettysburg Address and reciting it perfectly while his long beard's glue detached at one side and began slipping further and further down, until the beard came off altogether at one side and was swinging in the breeze of sixteen furiously waving little flags, and Chris DeMatteis forgetting (or never having had the chance to even study, as he claimed) the bulk of his lines and opting to simply thrust his lower jaw and empty cigarette holder out further and further and to repeat, 'Fear itself, fear itself,' over and over (my father claimed it was dozens of times) while, backlit on the stage behind him, Gregory Oehmke and several other boys who had access to their fathers' helmets and tags charged with broomsticks and aluminum foil bayonets (Llewellyn also brought a sidearm that turned out to be real, even though he claimed the firing pin had been removed, and afterwards he got in trouble, and his father had to come in and talk to Mrs. Roseman) against the papier mâché bulwarks of Iwo Jima.

Incarnations of Burned Children

The Daddy was around the side of the house hanging a door for the tenant when he heard the child's screams and the Mommy's voice gone high between them. He could move fast, and the back porch gave onto the kitchen, and before the screen door had banged shut behind him the Daddy had taken the scene in whole, the overturned pot on the floortile before the stove and the burner's blue jet and the floor's pool of water still steaming as its many arms extended, the toddler in his baggy diaper standing rigid with steam coming off his hair and his chest and shoulders scarlet and his eyes rolled up and mouth open very wide and seeming somehow separate from the sounds that issued, the Mommy down on one knee with the dishrag dabbing pointlessly at him and matching the screams with cries of her own, hysterical so she was almost frozen. Her one knee and the bare little soft feet were still in the steaming pool, and the Daddy's first act was to take the child under the arms and lift him away from it and take him to the sink, where he threw out plates and struck the tap to let cold wellwater run over the boy's feet while with his cupped hand he gathered and poured or flung more cold water over the head and shoulders and chest, wanting first to see the steam stop coming off him, the Mommy over his shoulder invoking God until he sent her for towels and gauze if they had it, the Daddy moving quickly and well and his man's mind empty of everything but purpose, not yet aware of how smoothly he moved or that he'd ceased to hear the high screams because to hear them would freeze him and make impossible what had to be done to help his own child, whose screams were regular as breath and went on so long they'd become already a thing in the kitchen, something else to move quickly around. The tenant side's door outside hung half off its top hinge and moved slightly in the wind, and a bird in the oak across the driveway appeared to observe the door with a cocked head as the cries still came from inside. The worst scalds seemed to be the right arm and shoulder, the chest and stomach's red was fading to pink under the cold water and his feet's soft soles weren't blistered that the Daddy could see, but the toddler still made little fists and screamed except maybe now merely on reflex from fear, the Daddy would know he thought it possible later, small face distended and thready veins standing out at the temples and the Daddy kept saying he was here he was here, adrenaline ebbing and an anger at the Mommy for allowing this thing to happen just starting to gather in wisps at his mind's extreme rear and still hours from expression. When the Mommy returned he wasn't sure whether to wrap the child in a towel or not but he wet the towel down and did, swaddled him tight and lifted his baby out of the sink and set him on the kitchen table's edge to soothe him while the Mommy tried to check the feet's soles with one hand waving around in the area of her mouth and uttering objectless words while the Daddy bent in and was face to face with the child on the table's checked edge repeating the fact that he was here and trying to calm the toddler's cries but still the child breathlessly screamed, a high pure shining sound that could stop his heart and his bitty lips and gums now tinged with the light blue of a low flame the Daddy thought, screaming as if almost still under the tilted pot in pain. A minute, two like this that seemed much longer, with the Mommy at the Daddy's side talking singsong at the child's face and the lark on the limb with its head to the side and the hinge going white in a line from the weight of the canted door until the first seen wisp of steam came lazy from under the wrapped towel's hem and the parents' eyes met and widened — the diaper, which when they opened the towel and leaned their little boy back on the checkered cloth and unfastened the softened tabs and tried to remove it resisted slightly with new high cries and was hot, their baby's diaper burned their hand and they saw where the real water'd fallen and pooled and been burning their baby boy all this time while he screamed for them to help him and they hadn't, hadn't thought and when they got it off and saw the state of what was there the Mommy said their God's first name and grabbed the table to keep her feet while the father turned away and threw a haymaker at the air of the kitchen and cursed both himself and the world for not the last time while his child might now have been sleeping if not for the rate of his breathing and the tiny stricken motions of his hands in the air above where he lay, hands the size of a grown man's thumb that had clutched the Daddy's thumb in the crib while he'd watched the Daddy's mouth move in song, his head cocked and seeming to see way past him into something his eyes made the Daddy lonesome for in a sideways way. If you've never wept and want to, have a child. Break your heart inside and something will a child is the twangy song the Daddy hears again as if the radio's lady was almost there with him looking down at what they've done, though hours later what the Daddy most won't forgive is how badly he wanted a cigarette right then as they diapered the child as best they could in gauze and two crossed handtowels and the Daddy lifted him like a newborn with his skull in one palm and ran him out to the hot truck and burned custom rubber all the way to town and the clinic's ER with the tenant's door hanging open like that all day until the hinge gave but by then it was too late, when it wouldn't stop and they couldn't make it the child had learned to leave himself and watch the whole rest unfold from a point overhead, and whatever was lost never thenceforth mattered, and the child's body expanded and walked about and drew pay and lived its life untenanted, a thing among things, its self's soul so much vapor aloft, falling as rain and then rising, the sun up and down like a yoyo.

ANOTHER PIONEER

Nevertheless gentlemen I fear the lone instance I can recall having heard aloud derived from an acquaintance of a close friend who said that he had himself overheard this *exemplum* aboard a high-altitude commercial flight while on some type of business trip, the fellow evidently holding a commercial position that called for frequent air travel. Certain key contextual details remained obscure. Nor, one hastens to admit, did the variant or *exemplum* contain any formal Annunciation as such, nor any *comme on dit* Period of Trial or Supernatural Aid, Trickster Figures, archetypal Resurrection, nor any of certain other recognized elements of the cycle; nevertheless gentlemen I leave it to you to judge for yourselves as of course you each in turn have left it to us as well. As I understood it the man in question was diverted by weather onto the continuation of a United Airlines flight and overheard its narration as part of a lengthier discourse between two passengers seated in the row just ahead of his own. He was, in other words, forced to sit in steerage. It was a continuation of some much longer flight, perhaps even Transatlantic, and the two passengers had evidently been seated together on the flight's first leg, and were already deep in conversation when he boarded; and the crux here is that the fellow said he missed the first part of whatever larger conversation it was part of. Meaning that there was no enframing context or deictic antecedent as such surrounding the archetypal narrative as of course there is with all of us together here this afternoon. That it appeared to come, as the fellow described it, out of nowhere. Also that he had evidently been seated in the particular medial exit row that is always nearest the wing's large jet engine, the overwing exit often in I believe on this type of aircraft Row 19 or 20, whereat in an evacuation you are required to turn two handles in two separate and opposed directions and supposedly then to somehow pull the entire window apparatus out of the jetliner's fuselage and stow it in some very complicated way all detailed in glyphs on the instructional safety card that on so many commercial airlines is very nearly impossible to interpret with any confidence. With his point being that because of the location's terrific ambient engine noise throughout the flight he was able to overhear the narrative fragment only because one of the prenominate passengers before him seemed to be either hard of hearing or cognitively challenged in some way, for the somewhat younger passenger — the one who appeared to be relating and interpreting the cycle's variant or parable or whatever you may adjudge it to be — seemed to articulate his sentences very slowly and with unusual clarity and distinctness. Which he said come to think of it is also the way people who are not particularly bright or sensitive speak to foreigners, so that perhaps the older passenger was a non-native speaker of English and the narrator was himself not bright. The two never turned round or turned their two heads sufficiently for him to get a real look at them; all there ever was to look at as the narrative unfolded were the rear portions of their heads and necks, which he said appeared average and unremarkable and difficult to extrapolate anything from, which is the way the backs of strangers' heads on airliners nearly always look. Though of course there are exceptions. From the outset, certain parallels were striking. For it concerned a certain child born in a very primitive paleolithic village somewhere. Just where he did not know; this was undoubtedly a part of the narrative's protasis or exposition which he had missed by finding himself forced to fly standby and entering in as it were *medias res*. On the United leg. The sense he got was of a certain extraordinarily primitive, Third World, jungle or rain-forest region of the world, perhaps Asia or South America, and so terrifically long ago as to be literally paleolithic or perhaps mesolithic, as of course the anthropological origins of genres like this nearly always are. The context in which my friend then subsequently had it related to him by his acquaintance was if possible, he said, even more banal and unexpected than a commercial airline flight, as if somehow the quotidian and as it were modern *everydayness* of the narrative circumstances made its archetypal parallels even more remarkable. But he also emphasized extremely primitive and paleolithic, in the variant, as in spears and crude lean-tos and pantheistic shamanism and an extremely primitive hunting-and-gathering mode of subsistence; and in a certain isolated village deep in the region's rain forest apparently a certain child is born who emerges as one of these extraordinarily high-powered, supernaturally advanced human specimens who come along in every culture every once in a great while, as history shows, although he said the younger airline passenger, whom he surmised may have been a corporate or academic scientist, did not use 'supernatural' or 'messianic' or 'prophetic' or any of the other terms the cycle usually reserves for specimens like this, instead using terms such as 'advanced,' 'brilliant,' or 'ingenious' and describing the child's exceptional qualities and career almost exclusively in terms of cognitive ability, raw IQ — because he said apparently at a very young age, an age at which most of the village's children were just beginning to learn the very basic customs and behaviors that the primitive village expected of its citizens, this two- or perhaps three-year-old child was already evincing an ability to answer absolutely any question put to it. To answer correctly, accurately, comprehensively. Even very difficult or even paradoxical questions. Of course the full range and depth of the child's interrogatory intelligence were not manifested for some time; thus their emergence serves as the *comme on dit* Threshold Experience and occupies much of the protasis. That at first the ability seems simply a novelty, something for its parents to so to speak dine out on and amuse the other villagers with, something on the order of, 'Look: our two-year-old knows how many twigs you have if you hold five twigs and then pick up three more twigs'; until of course one of the parents' amused neighbors happens to say or ask something that prompts the child to disclose that it also knows everything culturally important about each different individual twig the man happens to be holding, such as for example the village's official and idiomatic names for the trees the twigs derived from, and the various pantheistic deities and religious significance of each species of relevant tree, as well as which ones had edible leaves or bark that eased fever if boiled, and so on, including which species' grain and tensile flexion were especially good for spear shafts and the small phytotoxic darts the villages of this region used with crude reed blowguns to defend themselves against the tropical rain forest's predacious jaguars, which are apparently the scourge of the paleolithic Third World and the leading statistical cause of death after disease, malnutrition, and intertribal warfare. After which, of course, in short order, after reports of the remarkable twig prelection get about and the parents and other primitive villagers begin regarding the child's intelligence in a wholly different spirit, it emerges that the child is also fully capable of answering all manner of both trivial and also profoundly non-trivial questions, practical questions that bore directly on the village's subsistence-level quality of life, such as for instance where was the best place to find a certain kind of cassava root, and why were the migrations of a certain species of elk or dik-dik — a species which the village depended for its very life on hunting effectively — more predictable in the rainy season than in the dry season, and why were certain types of igneous rock better for fashioning sharp edges or striking together to produce fire than other types of igneous rock, and so on. And then, of course, subsequently, in a rather predictable trial-and-error heuristic evolution, it emerges in the action of the protasis that the child's preternatural brilliance in fact extends even to those questions that are considered by the village supremely important, in other words almost religious-grade questions, questions which — substituting my friend's own terminology for that of the analytical younger man on the United flight — involved not just cerebration or raw IQ but actual sagacity or virtue or wisdom or as Coleridge would have had it *esemplasy,* and soon the child is being called upon to adjudicate very complex and multifaceted conflicts, such as if two gathering-caste villagers both happened on the same breadfruit tree at precisely the same time and both claimed the breadfruit

who should get the breadfruit, or for example if a wife failed to conceive within a certain specified number of lunar or solar cycles did the
husband have the right to banish her altogether or did his rights ex-
tend only to no longer sharing food with her, and so on and so forth —
evidently the passenger up ahead provided any number of exemplary
questions, some of which were very involved and difficult for either my
friend or his acquaintance to reconstruct. The point, however, is that
the exceptional child's answers to these sorts of questions were without fail so ingeniously apposite and simple and comprehensive and fair
that all sides felt justly treated, and often the litigants could not understand why they had not thought of such an obviously equitable solution themselves, and in short order a great many long-standing
conflicts are settled and perennial social conundrums resolved; and by
this time the entire village had come to revere the child and had col-
lectively decided that the child must in fact be a special emissary or
legate or even incarnation of the primitive Dark Spirits on which their
pantheistic religion was primarily based, and some of the village's
shaman and midwife castes — members of what would later become
the new social structure's professional consultant caste — claimed that
the child had in fact come spontaneously into incarnated form deep in
the circumambient rain forest and had been suckled and protected by
divinely mollified jaguars, and that the child's putative mother and father had in fact simply stumbled onto the child while out gathering
cassava roots and were lying about its having been conceived and born
in the usual protomammalian way, and were therefore of course also by
extension lying about their own legal paternity; and after a great deal
of discussion and debate the village exarchs vote to remove the child
from the parents' custody and to make it an as it were ward or dependent *ex officio* of the entire village, and to invest the child with some
sort of unique unprecedented legal status that was neither minor nor
adult nor member of any caste, neither a village exarch nor a thane nor
a shaman per se but something entirely else, and with the nominal
'parents' granted certain special rights and privileges to compensate
them for their supplantation by the village *in loco* — the exarchs apparently having come in secret to none other than the child itself to

help them structure this whole delicate compromise — and they construct for the child a special sort of raised wicker dais or platform in the precise geometric center of the village, and they designate certain extremely rigid and precise intervals and arrangements whereby once every lunar cycle the villagers can all come to the village's center to line up before the dais according to certain arcane hierarchies of caste and familial status and to one by one come before the seated child with questions and disputes for him to resolve via ethical *fatwa* and are in return to compensate the child for its services with an offering of a plantain or dik-dik haunch or some other item of recognized value, which offering was what the primitive but complex legal arrangement provided for the child to live on and support himself instead of being his alleged parents' *comme on dit* 'dependent.' The context in which my own friend then had the narrative related to him by his acquaintance is unknown to me as anything more than 'quotidian' or 'everyday.' They would all line up before the dais to offer the child a yam, an ampoule of blow-dart phytotoxin, et cetera, and in return the child would undertake to answer their question. As *exempla* of this sort of mythopoeic cycle so often go, this arrangement is represented as the origin of something like modern trade in the villagers' culture. Prior to the child's evection, everyone had made their own clothes and lean-tos and spears and gathered all and only their own family's food, and while certain foodstuffs were sometimes shared at equinoctial religious festivals and so forth there was evidently nothing like actual barter or trade until the advent of this child who could and would answer any question put to it. And the small child thereafter lived atop this platform and never left it — the dais had its own lean-to with a pallet of plantain leaves and a small hollowed-out concavity for a fire and primitive cooking pot — and apparently the child's entire childhood was thenceforward spent on the central platform eating and sleeping and sitting for long periods doing nothing, presumably thinking and developing, and waiting out the 29.518 synodic days before the villagers would again line up with their respective questions. And as the village's trade-based economy became more modern and complex, one novel development was that certain especially shrewd and acute members of the shaman and midwife castes began to cultivate the intellectual or as it were rhetorical skill of structuring a monthly question in such a way as to receive a maximally valuable answer from the extraordinary child, and they then began to sell or barter these interrogatory skills to ordinary villagers who wished to extract maximum value for their monthly question, which was the advent of what the narrative apparently terms the village's *consultant caste*. For instance instead of asking the child something narrowly circumscribed such as, 'Where in our village's region of the rain forest should I look for a certain type of edible root?' a professional consultant's suggestion here might be that his client ask the child something more general along the lines for example of, 'How can a man feed his family with less effort than we now expend?' or, 'How might we ensure a store of food that will last our family through periods when available resources are scarce?' Whereas on the other hand, as the whole enterprise became more sophisticated and specialized, the consultant caste also discovered that maximizing the answer's value sometimes entailed making a certain question more specific and practical, as in for instance instead of, 'How can we increase our supply of firewood?' a more efficacious question here might be, 'How might a single man move a whole downed tree close to his home so as to have plentiful firewood?' And evidently some of the village's new consultant caste developed into rather ingenious interlocutors and managed to design questions of historic cultural importance and value such as, 'When my neighbor borrows my spear, how can I make a record of the loan in order to prove that the spear is mine in case my neighbor suddenly turns round and claims that the spear is his and refuses to return it?' or, 'How might I divert water from one of the rain forest's streams so that instead of my wife having to walk miles with a jar balanced on her head in order to haul water from the stream the stream might be made to as it were come to us?' and so forth — here it was not clear whether my friend or his acquaintance were providing their own examples or whether these were actual examples enumerated during the dialogue he overheard on the United flight. He said that certain very general conclusions about the two passengers' different ages and economic status could be deduced from their respective hair's color and cut and their postures and the backs of their necks, but that that was all. That there was no reading material except the seat pocket's customary in-flight catalogue and safety card, and the wing's engine's constant noise would have prevented him from sleeping even had he taken a pill, and that there was literally nothing for him to do but lean ever so subtly forward and try as unobtrusively as possible to make out what the darker-haired young passenger was relating to his less educated seatmate or companion, and to try to interpret it and fit it into some context that would as it were ground the narrative and render it more *comme on dit* illuminating or relevant to his own context. And that but at certain points it became unclear what was part of the cycle's narrative *Ding an sich* and what were the passenger's own editorial interpolations and commentary, such as the fact that it was evidently during the child's decade-long occupancy of the special raised platform that the village's culture evolved from hunting and gathering to a crude form of agriculture and husbandry, and discovered as well the principles of the wheel and rotary displacement, and fashioned their first fully enclosed dwellings of willow and yam-thatch, and developed an ideographic alphabet and primitive written grammar which allowed for more sophisticated divisions of labor and a crude economic system of trade in various goods and services; and in sum the entire village's culture, technology, and standard of living undergo a metastatic evolution that would normally have taken thousands of years and countless paleolithic generations to attain. And, not surprisingly, these quantum leaps arouse a certain degree of fear and jealousy in many of the region's other paleolithic villages, which are all still in the pantheo-shamanistic, hunting-and-gathering, hunch-round-the-fire-when-it's-cold stage of cultural attainment, and the United flight's narrative focuses particularly on the reaction of one large and formidable village, which is ruled by a single autocratic shaman in a kind of totalitarian theocracy, and which has also historically dominated this entire region of the rain forest and exacted tribute from all the other villages, this both because their warriors are so fierce and because their autocratic shaman is extremely ancient and politically astute and merciless and frightening and is universally regarded as

being at the very least in league with the primitive rain forest's dia-
bolical White Spirits — recall that this is an equatorial Third World
region, such that here dark colors are apparently associated with life
and beneficent spiritual forces and light or whitish colors with death,
absence, and pantheism's evil or malignant spirits, and evidently one
reason why the dominant village's warriors are so formidable is that the
shaman forces them to smear themselves with white or light-colored
clay or ground talc or some canescent indigenous substance before
battle such that according to legend they present the appearance of a
regiment of evil spirits or the risen dead coming at one with spears and
phytotoxic blowguns, and the sight always so terrifies all the other villages' warriors that they quail and lose heart before battle is even joined,
and the dominant village has had no serious opposition since the
necromantic shaman took charge many aeons ago. Even so, the more
politically astute upper castes of the dominant village eventually become
concerned, obviously, about this other village with the messianically
brilliant child; they fear that as the child's village continues to evolve
and becomes more and more advanced and sophisticated it will be only
a matter of time before some prescient member of the little village's
warrior caste comes before the child and asks, 'How shall we attack
and defeat the village of —————' (the fellow could not understand
or reproduce the airline passenger's pronunciation of the dominant
village's name, which evidently consisted mostly of glottal clicks and
pops) 'and take their lands and hunting grounds for our own more
advanced and sophisticated culture?' and so on; and a delegation of the
bellicose ————— village's upper-caste citizens finally work up their
nerve and appear *en masse* for an audience with their tyrannical
shaman, who it emerges is not only extremely ancient and powerful
but is in fact an albino — with all that extreme congenital pallor con-
notes in this part of the prehistoric world — and who evidently dwells
in a small, austerely appointed lean-to just outside the dominant village's
city limits, and spends most of his time conducting private necromantic rituals that involve playing crude musical arrangements with human
tibias and femurs on rows of differently sized human skulls like some
sort of ghastly paleolithic marimbas, as well as apparently using skulls

for both his personal stew pot and his commode; and the elite villagers come and make the customary obeisances and offerings and then lay out their concerns about the upstart village's rapid development under the stewardship of this brilliant juvenile *lusus naturae* — who by the way we are informed has by this time been presiding hierophantically from his raised central dais for several solar cycles and is now something more like ten years old — and they respectfully ask their necromantic leader whether he's perhaps had a chance to give any thought to the *über*child issue and/or might see fit to intervene before the child's upstart village becomes so advanced that even the predacious ————— village's albescent warriors are no match for it. There are certain intimations that the dominant ————— village's culture is cannibalistic or else perhaps uses the practice of cannibalizing enemy POWs as a way to further terrify and demoralize rival cultures, but all this is left shadowy and as it were merely suggestive. All he could say for certain was that the flight's highly analytic narrator was darker-haired and — judging from his posture and the distinctively squared-off edge of the haircut against the back of his well-tanned neck — both younger and of a higher social or economic station than was the other passenger, who, again, appeared to have some type of auditory or perhaps cognitive deficit. Structurally, this scene apparently functions as both the climax of the protasis and the as it were engine of the narrative's rising action, because at just this point we are told that the original *exemplum* splits or diverges here into at least three main epitatic variants. All three versions involve the maleficent shaman's hearing out the ————— village's upper-caste citizens' fears and their pleas for counsel and then conducting a lengthy and very intricate pantheistic ritual in which he boils yams in a special ceremonial skull and reads the rising steam, rather the way certain other primitive cultures read tea leaves or the entrails of poultry in order to divine and inform a certain course of action. In one variant of the epitasis, then, the shaman — whose eyes are described as appearing literally red in just the way certain modern albinistic specimens' pupils can appear hemean or red — apparently imbibes some melanistic philter or smears himself with dark clay and disguises himself in a cloak and bushy rabbinical beard and magically transports himself bodily across the region to the upstart village, whereupon he insinuates himself into the long line of villagers waiting to ask their respective questions of the child on the dais, and, upon eventually arriving at the queue's front, the nigrescently disguised shaman presents the child with the offering of a certain mysterious mutant specimen of breadfruit which has a strange excrescent growth resembling the child's village's new crude alphabet's glyph for 'growth,' 'fertility,' 'wisdom,' or 'destiny' (the village's written language still wasn't very advanced or differentiated) on the breadfruit's side, and then instead of asking his question aloud at high volume, publicly, which had gradually evolved into the custom at these lunar Q&A rituals, the malefic shaman instead leans forward in his jaguar-hide mantle and flowing French Fork and whispers something in the child's tiny ear — the natives of this region evidently all have very tiny and close-set ears, rather the way the aborigines of other Third World areas developed racially distinctive eyelids, complexions, and so forth — susurrating some question that is completely inaudible to anyone else in the line but which evidently has a profound effect on the child, because directly after the thanatophilic shaman withdraws and melts back into the rain forest the child on the dais closes its eyes and withdraws its consciousness into some type of meditative catatonic state for weeks or even according to one sub-version of the variant months, refusing to respond to anyone's questions or to react to or even acknowledge the presence of any of the other villagers; and there are apparently all manner of further sub- and sub-sub-versions of the variant which devote a great deal of narrative time to various speculations and allegations about what it was that the dominant ———— village's incognito shaman whispered to the child, although all the sub-versions' theories evidently concur that whatever it was had indeed been in the standard grammatical form of a question and not any sort of declarative statement or apothegm or rhyming mesmeric spell. In the second of the epitasis's three main variants, the autocratic shaman evidently does not disguise or insinuate himself in any way but rather gathers all the upper-caste citizens of the powerful ———— village as well as a phalanx of attendants and palanquin carriers and syces and white-painted security personnel and specialized antijaguar squads and travels with this contingent *en masse* through the rain forest to the puericratic village for a full-scale State Visit or Diplomatic Summit, and in this version the epitatic complication is due not to anything the sibilant shaman asks — because evidently the entire Summit consists of nothing but the endless roundabout courtesies and ritual tropes which intervillage State Visits in that region of the rain forest always entail — but rather to some potion or spell affixed to the mutant glyph-excrescent breadfruit which the shaman presents in a decorative parchment papillote to the seated child as one of the State Visit's countless *de rigueur* ceremonial gifts and tokens of esteem, which potion or spell here then causes the child on the dais to close its eyes and enter the aforementioned oneirically catatonic mystical state, rather like a mainframe compiling, and he refuses to answer or acknowledge the villagers' questions for several lunar cycles. Then in the third, final, and rather more passively modernistic epitatic variant, there is evidently no disguise or State Visit or psychoactive breadfruit; rather in the third version the malefic *angekok* merely consults the yams' evaporate and makes elaborate necromantic calculations and finally tells the ————— village's upper-caste supplicants not to worry, that in fact no action is called for, that the actual threat the *über*child poses is not to them or the ————— village's brutal hegemony over the region, because the child at this point is just on the verge of reaching the sidereal equivalent of eleven years old, which birthday evidently represents the paleolithic Third World's *bar mitzvah* or as it were age of majority; and, the albino shaman tells the delegation, any child this preternaturally gifted and exceptional is itself still growing and developing and learning at a geometric rate and advancing inevitably toward its supernatural entelechy's fulfillment, and that — this is still the shaman, whose role in this third main variant of the epitasis is almost wholly oracular — and that, ironically, it will be the very questions the child is asked by the increasingly modernized and sophisticated villagers that will facilitate the *wunderkind*'s further development into something so supernaturally advanced that it will ultimately prove the upstart village's very undoing, and so the shaman tells his upper-caste subjects not to worry

because before too long the puericratic villagers will all be back hunting
and gathering and worshipping Yam Gods and soiling their loincloths
with fear at the sight of an etiolated regiment and coming across with
their annual tribute of yams and hides to the hegemonic ————
village just as they always have, and so on and so forth; and sure enough
in this moodier and somewhat more contemporary third version of the
epitasis — in which narratively the malevolent shaman is reduced from
a peripeteiac antagonist to a mere vehicle for exposition or foreshad-
owing, this rather anticipating the function which oracles, sorcerers,
Attic choruses, Gaelic *coronach*, Senecan dumbshows, Plautian pro-
logues, and chatty Victorian narrators perform in various later cycles'
exempla — but nevertheless in the variant's next scene sure enough, at
the precise sidereal moment of the paleolithic equivalent of its eleventh
birthday, the child on the central dais spontaneously goes into the
same ptotic autisto-mystical withdrawal as in the more structurally
conventional variants — although according to the highly analytical
younger man on the flight there exist here as well certain even less
conventional sub-versions of the third main variant in which there is
no mention of any regionally dominant village or shaman or cranial
obeah, but rather here it is purportedly the young and extraordinarily
comely daughter of an upper-caste villager, who had just died after a
lengthy death-pallet scene, who — 'who' here meaning the nubile
daughter — leans in and whispers the mysterious *coup de vieux*-type
question in the child's ear; or in another marginal sub-version a mysterious white wasp or possibly trypanosomic bloodsucking fly of genus
Glossina flies through the village straight to the center's raised dais
or platform and stings the child on the forehead in the precise spot
corresponding to the *ajna* or sixth Hindic chakra, with the child immediately thereupon falling into the ptotic and compiling-esque
trance — but the crux nevertheless is that in all the myriad variants
and sub-versions of the rising action the child's trance and its essential
characteristics are the same, and it is at the point of the child's psychic
withdrawal that all three major competing editions of the epitasis
apparently converge again and conclude the as it were Second Act of
the *exemplum;* and what then transpires throughout the catastasis and

various relief scenes and *faux*-reversals and *dal segni* and *scènes à faire* all the way to the narrative's final catastrophe remains the same in all the putative variants and versions, such that the mythopoeic narrative's very structure itself moves from initial unity to epitatic trinity to reconciliation and unity again in the falling action — this observation evidently also inserted by the jetliner's somewhat pedantic young narrator, in or on the back of whose scalp as time passed my friend's acquaintance said he began to think he could discern an unusual patch of gray or prematurely white hair that was of markedly different texture than the surrounding scalp's hair and seemed if gazed at long enough to comprise some sort of strange intaglial glyph or design, though he was quick to admit that the same phenomenon can occur with clouds or configurations of shadows if one looks intently enough for long periods, and on the United flight there was simply very little else to look at — along, of course, with all the iconic resonance that an apparently One-into-Three-into-One dramatic structure will possess for the Western analytical mind. Nevertheless, when the child comes out of the catatonic trance or chrysalis stage, or resurfaces from meditating on the implications of whatever it was that the hegemonic shaman or nubile mourner had whispered, or recovers from the first wash of pubescent testosterone, or whatever precisely it was that was going on on the wickerwork dais while the boy sat motionless and incommunicado for several lunar cycles — afterward it's immediately clear that the child has undergone some significant developmental changes, because when he finally does come out of it and opens his eyes and responds to stimuli and resumes answering the cyclic queue of villagers' questions, evidently he's now answering in a very different way indeed, and his relationship to the questions and to the villagers and to the village's developing culture as a whole now comprises a wholly different *gestalt*. It is the progressively extreme changes in the advanced boy's relation to as it were both Truth and Culture which constitute the *exemplum*'s catastasis or crisis or falling action or Third Act. At first, now, the child will sometimes answer a villager's question just as before, but now will also append to this specific answer additional answers to certain other related or consequent questions which the child apparently believes his initial answer entails, as if he now understands his answers as part of a much larger network or system of questions and answers and further questions instead of being merely discrete self-contained units of information; and whenever the reawakened child breaks with previous convention and extemporizes on an answer's ramifications it evidently sends both cultural and economic shock-waves through the village's community, because the established custom and norm heretofore has of course been that the child on the dais answers only a question that he is explicitly asked, answering in an almost idiotic, cybernetically literal way, such that — as the pedantic younger man reminded his auditor he'd mentioned in passing during the protasis — such that an entire new caste of interrogatory consultants had come into being in the village's economy, consultants whose marketable skill lay in structuring citizens' questions in such a way as to avoid the so-called G.I.G.O. phenomenon to which questions presented to the child before the climactic trance were susceptible, in other words being paid or as it were compensated to ensure that the question posed was not for example something like, 'Can you tell me where my eldest son's lost blowgun might be found?' to which the child would traditionally be wont to answer simply, 'Yes,' the boy intending this answer not to be sarcastic or unhelpful but simply True, operating out of an almost classically binary or *comme on dit* Boolean paradigm, a crude human computer, and as such susceptible to G.I.G.O., being still after all at heart a child no matter how exceptional or even omniscient, and then the unfortunate villager would have to wait an entire lunar cycle before he could re-pose his question in a more efficacious way, an interrogatory syndrome which the consultant caste had gotten more and more successful at preventing, at higher and higher rates of compensation; but now in the epi — pardon me in the catastasis now the powerful new consultant caste's whole stock-in-trade becomes useless or unnecessary, because the child's new incarnation appears now disposed not just to respond to villagers' questions but to as it were *read* them, the questions, with 'read' evidently being either the passenger's or my friend's acquaintance's term for interpreting, contextualizing, and/or anticipating the ramified implications of a given question, the metamorphosed post-trance child in other words now trying to involve his queued interlocutors in actual heuristic exchanges or dialogues, violating custom and upsetting the villagers and rendering the consultant caste's rhetorical or as it were 'computer programming' skills otiose and sowing the seeds of political unrest and ill will simply by having apparently evolved — the exceptional child has — into a new, suppler, more humanistic and less mechanical kind of intelligence or wisdom, which itself is bad enough but then apparently in the next phase of the child's heuristic evolution — as either he pubertally matures and develops or else the hemean shaman's or maiden's or wasp's or tsetse fly's spell takes further hold, depending on the epitatic variant — after a few more lunar cycles the child begins the even more troubling practice of responding to a villager's question with questions of his own, questions which frequently seem to be irrelevant to the issue at hand and are often frankly disturbing, for example in one of what the fellow remembered as the numerous examples proffered on the United liner if the question was along the lines of, for instance, 'My eldest daughter is willful and disobedient; should I follow our local shaman's recommendation to have her clitoridectomy performed early in order to modify her attitude, or should I wait and allow the man she eventually marries to be the one to order the clitoridectomy as custom dictates?' the answer would apparently be something quite off the point or even offensive such as, 'Have you asked your daughter's mother what she thinks?' or, 'What might one suppose to be the equivalent of a clitoridectomy for willful sons?' or — in the case of the example he apparently heard the most clearly because the auditor either did not catch it or was unable to follow the point and asked the pedantic and analytical young United passenger to repeat it more slowly — the question being, 'What method of yam propagation is least apt to offend my family's fields' jealous and temperamental Yam Gods?' the catastatic child apparently launches into an entire protodialectical inquiry into just why exactly the interlocutor believes in jealous and temperamental Yam Gods at all, and whether this villager has ever in quiet moments closed his eyes and sat very still and gazed deep inside himself to see whether in his very heart of hearts he truly believes in these ill-tempered Yam Gods or whether he's merely been as it were culturally conditioned from an early age to ape what he has seen his parents and all the other villagers say and do and appear to believe, and whether it has ever late at night or in the humid quiet of the rain forest's dawn occurred to the questioner that perhaps all these others didn't really, truly believe in petulant Yam Gods either but were themselves merely aping what they in turn saw everyone else behaving as if they believed, and so on, and whether it was possible — just as a thought-experiment if nothing else — that everyone in the entire village had at some quiet point seen into their hearts' hearts and realized that their putative belief in the Yam Gods was mere mimicry and so felt themselves to be a secret hypocrite or fraud; and, if so, that what if just one villager of whatever caste or family suddenly stood up and admitted aloud that he was merely following empty custom and did not in his heart of hearts truly believe in any fearsome set of Yam Gods requiring propitiation to prevent drought or decimation by yam-aphids: would that villager be stoned to death, or banished, or might his admission not just possibly be met with a huge collective sigh of relief because now everyone else could be spared oppressive inner feelings of hypocrisy and self-contempt and admit their own inner disbelief as well; and if, theoretically, all this were to come about, what consequences might this sudden communal admission and relief have for the interlocutor's own inner feelings about the Yam Gods, for instance was it not theoretically possible that this villager might discover, in the absence of any normative cultural requirement to fear and distrust the Yam Gods, that his true religious conception was actually of Yam Gods who were rather kindly and benign and not Yam Gods he had to be fearful of offending or had to try to appease but rather Yam Gods to feel helped, succored, and even *comme on dit* loved by, and to try to love in return, and freely, this of course assuming that the two of them could come to some kind of agreement on what they meant by 'love' in a religious context, in other words *agape* and so on and so forth . . . the child's response appearing to become more and more digressive and pæanistic as the conventionally pious villager and the whole rest of the monthly queue stand there with eyes wide and mouths agape and so on and so forth for quite some time in the example, the more educated passenger's articulation of the child's response here being clear and distinct but evidently also rather prolix, even when slowly repeated, as well as frequently interrupted with pedantic analytical asides and glosses. The important point here being that, from the cultural perspective of the paleolithic village's exarchs and GP shamans, the child has begun to respond to questions not by providing the customary correct answer but now by simply ranting, and no doubt at this point in the *exemplum*'s falling action the child could simply have been discredited and/or dismissed as having gone insane or been possessed by an insane spirit as a result of the dominant ———— village's shaman's whispered question and could — the child could — at this point merely have been as it were deposed, removed from his omphalic dais and divested of his unique legal status and returned to his parents' custody and no longer taken seriously as a hierophantic force . . . were, however, it not for the fact that these more heuristic and less mechanical so-called rants the child inflicts on his interlocutors have such a terribly profound and troubling effect on them — on the villagers who'd continued queuing patiently up every lunar cycle as was the custom, hoping only to receive some clear, comprehensive answer to a developmentally relevant question — the dialogues and exchanges often now sending questioners staggering back to their lean-tos to lie curled foetally on their sides with rolling eyes and high fevers as their primitive CPUs tried frantically to reconfigure themselves. All of which obviously compounds the fear and unrest the villagers feel toward this new metamorphosed catastatic incarnation of the extraordinary child, and many of them might have stopped lining up every lunar cycle with offerings and questions altogether had the sidereal ritual not become such an entrenched social custom that the villagers feel terrific unease and anxiety at the thought of abandoning it; plus we're now told that in addition the villagers also have come more and more to fear offending or provoking the child on its raised dais — a child who according to the glyph-haired passenger is by this point fully pubescent and developing the broad squat torso, protrusive forehead, and hairy extremities of a bona fide paleolithic adult male — and their fear and unease is then further increased in the falling action's third and apparently final stage of the child's development, in which after several more lunar cycles he begins to act increasingly irritable and captious with the villagers' questions and now begins responding not with a sincere answer or a further question or even a digressive chautauqua but now with what often seems a rebuke or complaint, appearing almost to berate them, asking what on earth made them think that theirs are the really important questions, asking rhetorically what the point of all this is, why must he be consigned to life on a wickerwork platform if all he's going to be asked are the sort of dull, small, banal, quotidian, irrelevant questions that these squat hirsute tiny-eared villagers line up under a blazing Third World sun all day with offerings in order to pose, asking what makes them think he can help them when they haven't the slightest idea what they even really *need.* Asking whether the whole thing might not, in fact, be a waste of everyone's time. By which point the village's whole social structure and citizenry, from exarch to *lumpen,* is in an uproar of cultural disorientation and anxiety and antichild sentiment, an hysteria abetted at every turn by the consultant caste, most of whom are now of course out of work because of the metamorphic changes in the child's mode or style of answering questions and now have nothing better to do all day than hold seminars for the angry villagers in which for some type of fee the consultants will advance and debate various theories about what exactly has happened to the child and whom or what the child appears to be metamorphosing into and about what it portends for the village that its central dais's beloved omniscient child has become an agent of disruption and cultural anomie; and in the versions with the disguised malefic shaman or the breathtaking daughter of the deceased exarch there are now also some especially costly elite-caste seminars in which the consultants theorize about just what fatal question the dissimilated magus or *jeune fille dorée* might have whispered into the boy's hypotrophied ear to cause such a ghastly transformation, with various subversions' consultants arguing for every sort of possible question from, 'Why do you put yourself at the service of villagers so much less extraordinary than yourself?' to, 'What sort of Yam Gods and/or Dark

Spirits does someone as supernaturally advanced as yourself believe in, deep inside?' to the deceptively simple but of course all too plausibly disastrous, 'Might there ever be any questions you yourself wish to ask?' — as well as untold other examples which ambient engine and cabin noise obscured, the United flight evidently being filled with weather and turbulence and at least one interval during which it looked as though they were going to be rerouted and forced to land somewhere other than their scheduled destination — but with all the different versions' and sub-versions' seminars' hypothesized questions sharing an essentially recursive quality that bent the child's cognitive powers back in on themselves and transformed him from messianic to monstrous, and whose lethal involution resonates with malignant-self-consciousness themes in everything from Genesis 3:7 to the self-devouring Kirttimukha of the *Skanda Purana* to the *Medousa*'s reflective demise to Gödelian metalogic; and fewer and fewer villagers begin queuing up before the child's platform in the village's center every 29.52 days, although they never make so bold as to stop coming altogether because the villagers are still deeply afraid of offending the child or making him angry, especially after one incident in a recent lunar cycle in which apparently one of the brighter, more ambitious warrior-caste villagers had positioned himself in the very rear of the line and waited until everyone else had had their Q&A exchanges and dispersed and then had — which is to say the warrior-caste villager waited until everyone else had left and then had — had then leaned in and very quietly asked the child what the best strategy might be for attacking and defeating the dominant ———— village's spectral troops and necromantic shaman and seizing the ———— village's lands and exacting tribute from them and from all the rain forest's other primitive villages and establishing their own paleolithic empire over the region, and the child's answer — which no one hears because the rest of the queue has dispersed, which in retrospect raises questions about how the young, vigorous, essentially dark-haired and patriciate narrator on the United flight justifies including it in the catastasis — but in any event the child's answer, which the boy evidently leans way far forward off the edge of the platform to whisper in the warrior's tiny close-set ear, instantly destroys the warrior's higher faculties or spirit or soul and drives him hopelessly insane, and the man reels from the dais with his hands over his ears and staggers off into the rain forest and wanders senselessly about making distressed noises until he's eventually set upon and devoured by the area's predacious jaguars. This incident sends the first wave of open terror through the village; and, with the demotic fomentation of the *lumpen*-consultants, the village's citizens begin truly to hate and fear the child, and there is now more or less a consensus that this preternatural child whom they'd so stupidly revered and depended on and based all their advances and developments on the counsel of is, in fact, either one of the thanatotic White Spirits or a duly authorized agent of same, and that it is only a matter of time before someone catches the child in the wrong mood or asks the wrong question and the child says something which destroys the whole village or perhaps even the entire universe (the two being scarcely distinguished in the paleolithic mind); and a quorum of the exarchs officially decides that the child needs to be assassinated A.S.A.P., but they cannot persuade any of the village's warrior caste to get close enough to the central raised platform or dais or plinth to kill the child, even spear- and/or phytotoxic dart–distance obviously being well within range of the child's voice and the memory of their late comrade's fate — namely that of the ambitious warrior who had been driven insane with a single whisper — remaining still quite vivid in the braves' minds. And thus then there is apparently a brief interval during which a type of Taoist or *comme on dit 'dolce far niente'* or Zenlike constructive-nonaction movement gains ascendancy in the exarchs' counsels, some in the warrior and consultant castes arguing that if the villagers simply all stop lining up with provisions once every lunar cycle then the child, who has not moved from the central dais in years and has never had occasion to learn even rudimentary hunting-and-gathering skills, will inevitably starve to death and so to speak solve their problem for them . . . except it turns out that the child had in fact been farsighted enough to break off and stash a certain portion of all the months and years of offerings under his pallet of plantain leaves — note here please gentlemen that in the catastasis of the first epitatic variant in which the dominant —————— village's theocratic shaman functions as an antagonist it is at this point revealed via flashback or interpolation that what the disguised sorcerer had in fact whispered into the child's tiny close-set ear when he reached the front of the queue had been something along the lines of, 'You, child, who are so gifted and sagacious and wise: Is it possible that you have not realized the extent to which these primitive villagers have exaggerated your gifts, have transformed you into something you know too well you are not? Surely you have seen that they so revere you precisely because they themselves are too unwise to see your limitations? How long before they, too, see what you have seen when gazing deep inside yourself? Surely it has occurred to you. Surely one such as yourself must know already how terribly fickle the affections of a primitive Third World village can be. But tell me, child: Have you begun yet to be afraid? Have you begun yet then to plan for the day when they wake to a truth you already know: that you are not half so complete as they believe? That the illusion these children have made of you cannot be sustained? Have you, for example, thought yet to break off and secrete a portion of their lavish offerings against the day they awaken to what you already know you are, and turn fickly against you, and then because of their own turning become disoriented and anxious and blame you further for it, see you as the thief of their peace and begin to fear you and hate you in earnest and before long perhaps even cease to bring you offerings in the hope that you will starve or slink off like the thief they now believe you to be?' and so forth, which monologue now in a rather oracle-to-Laius-type irony of fate appears in retrospect to have been both sound and fatal advice, although we should note that in certain sub-versions of the other two epitatic variants' catastases there is no mention whatever of irony or hoarding: the child simply endures the catastrophe of the queues' and offerings' end and of his own utter isolation and in effect perverse banishment at the precise center of a village whose center everyone now goes way far out of their way to avoid, the child here enduring alone on the dais for months and months, surviving on nothing but his own saliva and the occasional nibble of plantain leaf from his pallet — here evidently echoing the way certain medieval hagiographies depict their own extraordinarily high-powered, supernaturally advanced subjects as being capable of fasting for months and even years without discomfort — and by this point in the falling action as well the weather had cleared and the fellow said even the noise of the engine seemed to have abated, perhaps because of the United airliner's initial descent in preparation to touch down, which made it possible to hear at least some of the archetypal catastrophe over the rustling noises of the passengers all gathering their personal effects together and beginning to as it were assemble themselves for disembarkation. Because eventually they left. The village did. When the child failed to starve or leave the dais but merely continued to sit there atop it. That at some point the entire community simply gave up and abandoned the village and their tilled fields and centrally heated shelters and chose to strike off *en masse* into the rain forest and to return to hunting and gathering and sleeping beneath trees and fending off the predacious indigenous jaguars as best they could, such was their fear of what they decided the child had grown to become. The exarchs had organized and assembled them and the exodus was extremely quiet, and the boy was not at first aware of the mass departure because evidently for some time now all commerce and social intercourse among the citizens had been conducted only on the extreme perimeters of the village, well out of earshot of the center's dais; the boy had not seen a living soul in the center for months. In the humid quiet of dawn, however, the child could detect a difference in the center's dead stillness: the village had emptied in the night, they were all now spread out and moving, the papoose-laden women keeping sharp eyes out for edible roots and the hunters searching for dik-dik spoor the consultants cast spells to summon, following the herd as they had before the dawn of time. Only a small detachment of elite and lavishly compensated warriors remained behind, and as the sun rose they prepared crude torches and fired the village, the huts' yam-thatch catching easily and the morning breeze spreading the blaze in a great phlogistive hiss as from a dissatisfied crowd; and when they had judged the fire unstoppable the warriors launched their torches like javelins at the village's center and lit out for the jungle to catch up to the migrating tribe. The hindmost of these warriors, looking back as they ran, claimed to have seen the motionless boy still seated, surrounded by glassy daylight flames, although apparently a separate variant's catastrophe follows only the tribe's main body and its forced march into the tropical wilderness and includes only silence and primitive sounds of exertion until one keen-eyed child, hanging extrorse in its sling on a mother's back, saw blue hanging smoke in the dense fronds behind them, and low-caste stragglers, turning round at the long column's rear, could make out the red lace of a fire seen through many layers of trees' moving leaves, a great rapacious fire that grew and gained ground no matter how hard the high castes drove them.

GOOD OLD NEON

My whole life I've been a fraud. I'm not exaggerating. Pretty much all I've ever done all the time is try to create a certain impression of me in other people. Mostly to be liked or admired. It's a little more complicated than that, maybe. But when you come right down to it it's to be liked, loved. Admired, approved of, applauded, whatever. You get the idea. I did well in school, but deep down the whole thing's motive wasn't to learn or improve myself but just to do well, to get good grades and make sports teams and perform well. To have a good transcript or varsity letters to show people. I didn't enjoy it much because I was always scared I wouldn't do well enough. The fear made me work really hard, so I'd always do well and end up getting what I wanted. But then, once I got the best grade or made All City or got Angela Mead to let me put my hand on her breast, I wouldn't feel much of anything except maybe fear that I wouldn't be able to get it again. The next time or next thing I wanted. I remember being down in the rec room in Angela Mead's basement on the couch and having her let me get my hand up under her blouse and not even really feeling the soft aliveness or whatever of her breast because all I was doing was thinking, 'Now I'm the guy that Mead let get to second with her.' Later that seemed so sad. This was in middle school. She was a very big-hearted, quiet, self-contained, thoughtful girl — she's a veterinarian now, with her own practice — and I never even really saw her, I couldn't see anything except who I might be in her eyes, this cheerleader and probably number two or three among the most desirable girls in middle school that year. She was much more than that, she was beyond all that adolescent ranking and popularity crap, but I never really let her be or saw her as more, although I put up a very good front as somebody who could have deep conversations and really wanted to know and understand who she was inside.

Later I was in analysis, I tried analysis like almost everybody else then in their late twenties who'd made some money or had a family or whatever they thought they wanted and still didn't feel that they were happy. A lot of people I knew tried it. It didn't really work, although it did make everyone sound more aware of their own problems and added some useful vocabulary and concepts to the way we all had to talk to each other to fit in and sound a certain way. You know what I mean. I was in regional advertising at the time in Chicago, having made the jump from media buyer for a large consulting firm, and at only twenty-nine I'd made creative associate, and verily as they say I was a fair-haired boy and on the fast track but wasn't happy at all, whatever *happy* means, but of course I didn't say this to anybody because it was such a cliché — 'Tears of a Clown,' 'Richard Cory,' etc. — and the circle of people who seemed important to me seemed much more dry, oblique and contemptuous of clichés than that, and so of course I spent all my time trying to get them to think I was dry and jaded as well, doing things like yawning and looking at my nails and saying things like, '*Am I happy?* is one of those questions that, if it has got to be asked, more or less dictates its own answer,' etc. Putting in all this time and energy to create a certain impression and get approval or acceptance that then I felt nothing about because it didn't have anything to do with who I really was inside, and I was disgusted with myself for always being such a fraud, but I couldn't seem to help it. Here are some of the various things I tried: EST, riding a ten-speed to Nova Scotia and back, hypnosis, cocaine, sacro-cervical chiropractic, joining a charismatic church, jogging, pro bono work for the Ad Council, meditation classes, the Masons, analysis, the Landmark Forum, the

Course in Miracles, a right-brain drawing workshop, celibacy, collecting and restoring vintage Corvettes, and trying to sleep with a different girl every night for two straight months (I racked up a total of thirty-six for sixty-one and also got chlamydia, which I told friends about, acting like I was embarrassed but secretly expecting most of them to be impressed — which, under the cover of making a lot of jokes at my expense, I think they were — but for the most part the two months just made me feel shallow and predatory, plus I missed a great deal of sleep and was a wreck at work — that was also the period I tried cocaine). I know this part is boring and probably boring you, by the way, but it gets a lot more interesting when I get to the part where I kill myself and discover what happens immediately after a person dies. In terms of the list, psychoanalysis was pretty much the last thing I tried.

The analyst I saw was OK, a big soft older guy with a big ginger mustache and a pleasant, sort of informal manner. I'm not sure I remember him alive too well. He was a fairly good listener, and seemed interested and sympathetic in a slightly distant way. At first I suspected he didn't like me or was uneasy around me. I don't think he was used to patients who were already aware of what their real problem was. He was also a bit of a pill-pusher. I balked at trying antidepressants, I just couldn't see myself taking pills to try to be less of a fraud. I said that even if they worked, how would I know if it was me or the pills? By that time I already knew I was a fraud. I knew what my problem was. I just couldn't seem to stop. I remember I spent maybe the first twenty times or so in analysis acting all open and candid but in reality sort of fencing with him or leading him around by the nose, basically showing him that I wasn't just another one of those patients who stumbled in with no clue what their real problem was or who were totally out of touch with the truth about themselves. When you come right down to it, I was trying to show him that I was at least as smart as he was and that there wasn't much of anything he was going to see about me that I hadn't already seen and figured out. And yet I wanted help and really was there to try to get help. I didn't even tell him how unhappy I was until five or six months into the analysis, mostly because

I didn't want to seem like just another whining, self-absorbed yuppie, even though I think even then I was on some level conscious that that's all I really was, deep down.

Right from the start, what I liked best about the analyst was that his office was a mess. There were books and papers everyplace, and usually he had to clear things off the chair so I could sit down. There was no couch, I sat in an easy chair and he sat facing me in his beat-up old desk chair whose back part had one of those big rectangles or capes of back-massage beads attached to it the same way cabbies often put them on their seat in the cab. This was another thing I liked, the desk chair and the fact that it was a little too small for him (he was not a small guy) so that he had to sit sort of almost hunched with his feet flat on the floor, or else sometimes he'd put his hands behind his head and lean way back in the chair in a way that made the back portion squeak terribly when it leaned back. There always seems to be something patronizing or a little condescending about somebody crossing their legs when they talk to you, and the desk chair didn't allow him to do this — if he ever crossed his legs his knee would have been up around his chin. And yet he had apparently never gone out and gotten himself a bigger or nicer desk chair, or even bothered to oil the medial joint's springs to keep the back from squeaking, a noise that I know would have driven me up the wall if it had been my chair and I had to spend all day in it. I noticed all this almost right away. The little office also reeked of pipe tobacco, which is a pleasant smell, plus Dr. Gustafson never took notes or answered everything with a question or any of the cliché analyst things that would have made the whole thing too horrible to keep going back whether it even helped or not. The whole effect was of a sort of likable, disorganized, laid-back guy, and things in there actually did get better after I realized that he probably wasn't going to do anything to make me quit fencing with him and trying to anticipate all his questions so I could show that I already knew the answer — he was going to get his $65 either way — and finally came out and told him about being a fraud and feeling alienated (I had to use the uptown word of course, but it was still the truth) and starting to see myself ending up living this way for the rest of my life and being completely unhappy. I told him I wasn't blaming anybody for my being a fraud. I had been adopted, but it was as a baby, and the stepparents who adopted me were better and nicer than most of the biological parents I knew anything about, and I was never yelled at or abused or pressured to hit .400 in Legion ball or anything, and they took out a second mortgage to send me to an elite college when I could have gone scholarship to U.W.–Eau Claire, etc. Nobody'd ever done anything bad to me, every problem I ever had I'd been the cause of. I was a fraud, and the fact that I was lonely was my own fault (of course his ears pricked up at *fault*, which is a loaded term) because I seemed to be so totally self-centered and fraudulent that I experienced everything in terms of how it affected people's view of me and what I needed to do to create the impression of me I wanted them to have. I said I knew what my problem was, what I couldn't do was stop it. I also admitted to Dr. Gustafson some of the ways I'd been jerking him around early on and trying to make sure he saw me as smart and self-aware, and said I'd known early on that playing around and showing off in analysis were a waste of time and money but that I couldn't seem to help myself, it just happened automatically. He smiled at all this, which was the first time I remember seeing him smile. I don't mean he was sour or humorless, he had a big red friendly face and a pleasant enough manner, but this was the first time he'd smiled like a human being having an actual conversation. And yet at the same time I already saw what I'd left myself open for — and sure enough he says it. 'If I understand you right,' he says, 'you're saying that you're basically a calculating, manipulative person who always says what you think will get somebody to approve of you or form some impression of you you think you want.' I told him that was maybe a little simplistic but basically accurate, and he said further that as he understood it I was saying that I felt as if I was trapped in this false way of being and unable ever to be totally open and tell the truth irregardless of whether it'd make me look good in others' eyes or not. And I somewhat resignedly said yes, and that I seemed always to have had this fraudulent, calculating part of my brain firing away all the time, as if I were constantly playing chess with everybody and figuring out that if I wanted them to move a certain way I had to move in such a way as to induce them to move that way. He asked if I ever played chess, and I told him I used to in middle school but quit because I couldn't be as good as I eventually wanted to be, how frustrating it was to get just good enough to know what getting really good at it would be like but not being able to get that good, etc. I was laying it on sort of thick in hopes of distracting him from the big insight and question I realized I'd set myself up for. But it didn't work. He leaned back in his loud chair and paused as if he were thinking hard, for effect — he was thinking that he was going to get to feel like he'd really earned his $65 today. Part of the pause always involved stroking his mustache in an unconscious way. I was reasonably sure that he was going to say something like, 'So then how were you able to do what you just did a moment ago?,' in other words meaning how was I able to be honest about the fraudulence if I was really a fraud, meaning he thought he'd caught me in some kind of logical contradiction or paradox. And I went ahead and played a little dumb, probably, to get him to go ahead and say it, partly because I still held out some hope that what he'd say might be more discerning or incisive than I had predicted. But it was also partly because I liked him, and liked the way he seemed genuinely pleased and excited at the idea of being helpful but was trying to exercise professional control over his facial expression in order to make the excitement look more like simple pleasantness and clinical interest in my case or whatever. He was hard not to like, he had what is known as an engaging manner. By way of decor, the office wall behind his chair had two framed prints, one being that Wyeth one of the little girl in the wheat field crawling uphill toward the farmhouse, the other a still life of two apples in a bowl on a table by Cézanne. (To be honest, I only knew it was Cézanne because it was an Art Institute poster and had a banner with info on a Cézanne show underneath the painting, which was a still life, and which was weirdly discomfiting because there was something slightly off about the perspective or style that made the table look crooked and the apples look almost square.) The prints were obviously there to give the analyst's patients something to look at, since many people like to look around or look at things on the wall while they talk. I didn't have any trouble looking right at him most of the time I was in there, though. He did have a talent for putting you at ease, there was no question about it. But I had no illusions that this was the same as having enough insight or firepower to find some way to really help me, though.

There was a basic logical paradox that I called the 'fraudulence paradox' that I had discovered more or less on my own while taking a mathematical logic course in school. I remember this as being a huge undergrad lecture course that met twice a week in an auditorium with the professor up on stage and on Fridays in smaller discussion sections led by a graduate assistant whose whole life seemed to be mathematical logic. (Plus all you had to do to ace the class was sit down with the assigned textbook that the prof was the editor of and memorize the different modes of argument and normal forms and axioms of first-order quantification, meaning the course was as clean and mechanical as logic itself in that if you put in the time and effort, out popped the good grade at the other end. We only got to paradoxes like the Berry and Russell Paradoxes and the incompleteness theorem at the very end of the term, they weren't on the final.) The fraudulence paradox was that the more time and effort you put into trying to appear impressive or attractive to other people, the less impressive or attractive you felt inside — you were a fraud. And the more of a fraud you felt like, the harder you tried to convey an impressive or likable image of yourself so that other people wouldn't find out what a hollow, fraudulent person you really were. Logically, you would think that the moment a supposedly intelligent nineteen-year-old became aware of this paradox, he'd stop being a fraud and just settle for being himself (whatever that was) because he'd figured out that being a fraud was a vicious infinite regress that ultimately resulted in being frightened, lonely, alienated, etc. But here was the other, higher-order paradox, which didn't even have a form or name — I didn't, I couldn't. Discovering the first paradox at age nineteen just brought home to me in spades what an empty, fraudulent person I'd basically been ever since at least the time I was four and lied to my stepdad because I'd realized somehow right in the middle of his asking me if I'd broken the bowl that if I said I did it but 'confessed' it in a sort of clumsy, implausible way, then he wouldn't believe me and would instead believe that my sister Fern, who's my stepparents' biological daughter, was the one who'd actually broken the antique Moser glass bowl that my stepmom had inherited from her biological grandmother and totally loved, plus it would lead or induce him to see me as a kind, good stepbrother who was so anxious to keep Fern (whom I really did like) from getting in trouble that I'd be willing to lie and take the punishment for it for her. I'm not explaining this very well. I was only four, for one thing, and the realization didn't hit me in words the way I just now put it, but rather more in terms of feelings and associations and certain mental flashes of my stepparents' faces with various expressions on them. But it happened that fast, at only four, that I figured out how to create a certain impression by knowing what effect I'd produce in my stepdad by implausibly 'confessing' that I'd punched Fern in the arm and stolen her Hula Hoop and had run all the way downstairs with it and started Hula-Hooping in the dining room right by the sideboard with all my stepmom's antique glassware and figurines on it, while Fern, forgetting all about her arm and hoop because of her concern over the bowl and other glassware, came running downstairs shouting after me, reminding me about how important the rule was that we weren't supposed to play in the dining room. . . . Meaning that by lying in such a deliberately unconvincing way I could actually get everything that a direct lie would supposedly get me, plus look noble and self-sacrificing, plus also make my stepparents feel good because they always tended to feel good when one of their kids did something that showed character, because it's the sort of thing they couldn't really help but see as reflecting favorably on them as shapers of their kids' character. I'm putting all this in such a long, rushing, clumsy way to try to convey the way I remember it suddenly hit me, looking up at my stepfather's big kindly face as he held two of the larger pieces of the Moser bowl and tried to look angrier than he really felt. (He had always thought the more expensive pieces ought to be kept secure in storage somewhere, whereas my stepmom's view was more like what was the point of having nice things if you didn't have them out where people could enjoy them.) How to appear a certain way and get him to think a certain thing hit me just that fast. Keep in mind I was only around four. And I can't pretend it felt bad, realizing it — the truth is it felt great. I felt powerful, smart. It felt a little like looking at part of a puzzle you're doing and you've got a piece in your hand and you can't see where in the larger puzzle it's supposed to go or how to make it fit, looking at all the holes, and then all of a sudden in a flash you see, for no reason right then you could point to or explain to anyone, that if you turn the piece this one certain way it will fit, and it does, and maybe the best way to put it is that in that one tiny instant you feel suddenly connected to something larger and much more of the complete picture the same way the piece is. The only part I'd neglected to anticipate was Fern's reaction to getting blamed for the bowl, and punished, and then punished even worse when she continued to deny that she'd been the one playing around in the dining room, and my stepparents' position was that they were even more upset and disappointed about her lying than they were about the bowl, which they said was just a material object and not ultimately important in the larger scheme of things. (My stepparents spoke this way, they were people of high ideals and values, humanists. Their big ideal was total honesty in all the family's relationships, and lying was the worst, most disappointing infraction you could commit, in their view as parents. They tended to discipline Fern a little more firmly than they did me, by the way, but this too was an extension of their values. They were concerned about being fair and having me be able to feel that I was just as much their real child as Fern was, so that I'd feel maximally secure and loved, and sometimes this concern with fairness caused them to bend a little too far over backward when it came to discipline.) So that Fern, then, got regarded as being a liar when she was not, and that must have hurt her way more than the actual punishment did. She was only five at the time. It's horrible to be regarded as a fraud or to believe that people think you're a fraud or liar. It's possibly one of the worst feelings in the world. And even though I haven't really had any direct experience with it, I'm sure it must be doubly horrible when you were actually telling the truth and they didn't believe you. I don't think Fern ever quite got over that episode, although the two of us never talked about it afterward except for one sort of cryptic remark she made over her shoulder once when we were both in high school and having an argument about something and Fern was storming out of the house. She was sort of a classically troubled adolescent — smoking, makeup, mediocre grades, dating older guys, etc. — whereas I was the family's fair-haired boy and had a killer G.P.A. and played varsity ball, etc. One way to put it is that I looked and acted much better on the surface then than Fern did, although she eventually settled down and ended up going on to college and is now doing OK. She's also one of the funniest people on earth, with a very dry, subtle sense of humor — I like her a lot. The point being that that was the start of my being a fraud, although it's not as if the broken-bowl episode was somehow the origin or cause of my fraudulence or some kind of childhood trauma that I'd never gotten over and had to go into analysis to work out. The fraud part of me was always there, just as the puzzle piece, objectively speaking, is a true piece of the puzzle even before you see how it fits. For a while I thought that possibly one or the other of my biological parents had been frauds or had carried some type of fraud gene or something and that I had inherited it, but that was a dead end, there was no way to know. And even if I did, what difference would it make? I was still a fraud, it was still my own unhappiness that I had to deal with.

Once again, I'm aware that it's clumsy to put it all this way, but the point is that all of this and more was flashing through my head just in the interval of the small, dramatic pause Dr. Gustafson allowed himself before delivering his big reductio ad absurdum argument that I couldn't be a total fraud if I had just come out and admitted my fraudulence to him just now. I know that you know as well as I do how fast thoughts and associations can fly through your head. You can be in the middle of a creative meeting at your job or something, and enough material can rush through your head just in the little silences when people are looking over their notes and waiting for the next presentation that it would take exponentially longer than the whole meeting just to try to put a few seconds' silence's flood of thoughts into words. This is another paradox, that many of the most important impressions and thoughts in a person's life are ones that flash through your head so fast that *fast* isn't even the right word, they seem totally different from or outside of the regular sequential clock time we all live by, and they have so little relation to the sort of linear, one-word-after-another-word English we all communicate with each other with that it could easily take a whole lifetime just to spell out the contents of one split-second's flash of thoughts and connections, etc. — and yet we all seem to go around trying to use English (or whatever language our native country happens to use, it goes without saying) to try to convey to other people what we're thinking and to find out what they're thinking, when in fact deep down everybody knows it's a charade and they're just going through the motions. What goes on inside is just too fast and huge and all interconnected for words to do more than barely sketch the outlines of at most one tiny little part of it at any given instant. The internal head-speed or whatever of these ideas, memories, realizations, emotions and so on is even faster, by the way — exponentially faster, unimaginably faster — when you're dying, meaning during that vanishingly tiny nanosecond between when you technically die and when the next thing happens, so that in reality the cliché about people's whole life flashing before their eyes as they're dying isn't all that far off — although the *whole life* here isn't really a sequential thing where first you're born and then you're in the crib and then you're up at the plate in Legion ball, etc., which it turns out that that's what people usually mean when they say 'my whole life,' meaning a discrete, chronological series of moments that they add up and call their life-time. It's not really like that. The best way I can think of to try to say it is that it all happens at once, but that *at once* doesn't really mean a finite moment of sequential time the way we think of time while we're alive, plus that what turns out to be the meaning of the term *my life* isn't even close to what we think we're talking about when we say 'my life.' Words and chronological time create all these total misunderstandings of what's really going on at the most basic level. And yet at the same time English is all we have to try to understand it and try to form anything larger or more meaningful and true with anybody else, which is yet another paradox. Dr. Gustafson — whom I would meet again later and find out that he had almost nothing to do with the big doughy repressed guy sitting back against his chair's beads in his River Forest office with colon cancer in him already at that time and him knowing nothing yet except that he didn't feel quite right down there in the bathroom lately and if it kept on he'd make an appointment to go in and ask his internist about it — Dr. G. would later say that the whole *my whole life flashed before me* phenomenon at the end is more like being a whitecap on the surface of the ocean, meaning that it's only at the moment you subside and start sliding back in that you're really even aware there's an ocean at all. When you're up and out there as a whitecap you might talk and act as if you know you're just a white-cap on the ocean, but deep down you don't think there's really an ocean at all. It's almost impossible to. Or like a leaf that doesn't believe in the tree it's part of, etc. There are all sorts of ways to try to express it.

And of course all this time you've probably been noticing what seems like the really central, overarching paradox, which is that this whole thing where I'm saying words can't really do it and time doesn't really go in a straight line is something that you're hearing as words that you have to start listening to the first word and then each succes-sive word after that in chronological time to understand, so if I'm say-ing that words and sequential time have nothing to do with it you're wondering why we're sitting here in this car using words and taking up your increasingly precious time, meaning aren't I sort of logically con-tradicting myself right at the start. Not to mention am I maybe full of B.S. about knowing what happens — if I really did kill myself, how can you even be hearing this? Meaning am I a fraud. That's OK, it doesn't really matter what you think. I mean it probably matters to you, or you think it does — that isn't what I meant by *doesn't matter*. What I mean is that it doesn't really matter what you think about me, because despite appearances this isn't even really about me. All I'm try-ing to do is sketch out one little part of what it was like before I died and why I at least thought I did it, so that you'll have at least some idea of why what happened afterward happened and why it had the impact it did on who this is really about. Meaning it's like an abstract or sort of intro, meant to be very brief and sketchy . . . and yet of course look how much time and English it's seeming to take even to say it. It's interesting if you really think about it, how clumsy and laborious it seems to be to convey even the smallest thing. How much time would you even say has passed, so far?

One reason why Dr. Gustafson would have made a terrible poker player or fraud is that whenever he thought it was a big moment in the analysis he would always make a production of leaning back in his desk chair, which made that loud sound as the back tilted back and his feet went back on their heels so the soles showed, although he was good at making the position look comfortable and very familiar to his body, like it felt good doing that when he had to think. The whole thing was both slightly overdramatic and yet still likable for some reason. Fern, by the way, has reddish hair and slightly asymmetrical green eyes — the kind of green people buy tinted contact lenses to get — and is attractive in a sort of witchy way. I think she's attractive, anyway. She's grown up to be a very poised, witty, self-sufficient person, with maybe just the slightest whiff of the perfume of loneliness that hangs around unmarried women around age thirty. The fact is that we're all lonely, of course. Everyone knows this, it's almost a cliché. So yet another layer of my essential fraudulence is that I pretended to myself that my loneliness was special, that it was uniquely my fault because I was somehow especially fraudulent and hollow. It's not special at all, we've all got it. In spades. Dead or not, Dr. Gustafson knew more about all this than I, so that he spoke with what came off as genuine authority and pleasure when he said (maybe a little superciliously, given how obvious it was), 'But if you're constitutionally false and manipulative and unable to be honest about who you really are, Neal' (Neal being my given name, it was on my birth certificate when I got adopted), 'how is it that you were able to drop the sparring and manipulation and be honest with me a moment ago' (for that's all it had been, in spite of all the English that's been expended on just my head's partial contents in the tiny interval between then and now) 'about who you really are?' So it turned out I'd been right in predicting what his big logical insight was going to be. And although I played along with him for a while so as not to prick his bubble, inside I felt pretty bleak indeed, because now I knew that he was going to be just as pliable and credulous as everyone else, he didn't appear to have anything close to the firepower I'd need to give me any hope of getting helped out of the trap of fraudulence and unhappiness I'd constructed for myself. Because the real truth was that my confession of being a fraud and of having wasted time sparring with him over the previous weeks in order to manipulate him into seeing me as exceptional and insightful had itself been kind of manipulative. It was pretty clear that Dr. Gustafson, in order to survive in private practice, could not be totally stupid or obtuse about people, so it seemed reasonable to assume that he'd noticed the massive amount of fencing and general showing off I'd been doing during the first weeks of the analysis, and thus had come to some conclusions about my apparently desperate need to make a certain kind of impression on him, and though it wasn't totally certain it was thus at least a decent possibility that he'd sized me up as a basically empty, insecure person whose whole life involved trying to impress people and manipulate their view of me in order to compensate for the inner emptiness. It's not as if this is an incredibly rare or obscure type of personality, after all. So the fact that I had chosen to be supposedly 'honest' and to diagnose myself aloud was in fact just one more move in my campaign to make sure Dr. Gustafson understood that as a patient I was uniquely acute and self-aware, and that there was very little chance he was going to see or diagnose anything about me that I wasn't already aware of and able to turn to my own tactical advantage in terms of creating whatever image or impression of myself I wanted him to see at that moment. His big supposed insight, then — which had as its ostensible, first-order point that my fraudulence could not possibly be as thoroughgoing and hopeless as I claimed it was, since my ability to be honest with him about it logically contradicted my claim of being incapable of honesty — actually had as its larger, unspoken point the claim that he could discern things about my basic character that I myself could not see or interpret correctly, and thus that he could help me out of the trap by pointing out inconsistencies in my view of myself as totally fraudulent. The fact that this insight that he appeared so coyly pleased and excited about was not only obvious and superficial but also wrong — this was depressing, much the way discovering that somebody is easy to manipulate is always a little depressing. A corollary to the fraudulence paradox is that you simultaneously want to fool everyone you meet and yet also somehow always hope that you'll come across someone who is your match or equal and can't be fooled. But this was sort of the last straw, I mentioned I'd tried a whole number of different things that hadn't worked already. So *depressing* is a gross understatement, actually. Plus of course the obvious fact that I was paying this guy for help in getting out of the trap and he'd now showed that he didn't have the mental firepower to do it. So I was now thinking about the prospect of spending time and money driving in to River Forest twice a week just to yank the analyst around in ways he couldn't see so that he'd think that I was actually less fraudulent than I thought I was and that analysis with him was gradually helping me see this. Meaning that he'd probably be getting more out of it than I would, for me it would just be fraudulence as usual.

However tedious and sketchy all this is, you're at least getting an idea, I think, of what it was like inside my head. If nothing else, you're seeing how exhausting and solipsistic it is to be like this. And I had been this way my whole life, at least from age four onward, as far as I could recall. Of course, it's also a really stupid and egotistical way to be, of course you can see that. This is why the ultimate and most deeply unspoken point of the analyst's insight — namely, that who and what I believed I was was not what I really was at all — which I thought was false, was in fact true, although not for the reasons that Dr. Gustafson, who was leaning back in his chair and smoothing his big mustache with his thumb and forefinger while I played dumb and let him feel like he was explaining to me a contradiction I couldn't understand without his help, believed.

One of my other ways of playing dumb for the next several sessions after that was to protest his upbeat diagnosis (irrelevantly, since by this time I'd pretty much given up on Dr. Gustafson and was starting to think of various ways to kill myself without causing pain or making a mess that would disgust whoever found me) by means of listing the various ways I'd been fraudulent even in my pursuit of ways to achieve genuine and uncalculating integrity. I'll spare giving you the whole list again. I basically went all the way back to childhood (which analysts always like you to do) and laid it on. Partly I was curious to see how much he'd put up with. For example, I told him about going from genuinely loving ball, loving the smell of the grass and distant sprinklers, or the feel of pounding my fist into the glove over and over and yelling 'Hey, batterbatter,' and the big low red tumid sun at the game's start versus the arc lights coming on with a clank in the glowing twilight of the late innings, and of the steam and clean burned smell of ironing my Legion uniform, or the feel of sliding and watching all the dust it raised settle around me, or all the parents in shorts and rubber flip-flops setting up lawn chairs with Styrofoam coolers, little kids hooking their fingers around the backstop fence or running off after fouls. The smell of the ump's aftershave and sweat, the little whisk-broom he'd bend down and tidy the plate with. Mostly the feel of stepping up to the plate knowing anything was possible, a feeling like a sun flaring somewhere high up in my chest. And about how by only maybe fourteen all that had disappeared and turned into worrying about averages and if I could make All City again, or being so worried I'd screw up that I didn't even like ironing the uniform anymore before games because it gave me too much time to think, standing there so nerved up about doing well that night that I couldn't even notice the little chuckling sighs the iron made anymore or the singular smell of the steam when I hit the little button for steam. How I'd basically ruined all the best parts of everything like that. How sometimes it felt like I was actually asleep and none of this was even real and someday out of nowhere I was maybe going to suddenly wake up in midstride. That was part of the idea behind things like joining the charismatic church up in Naperville, to try to wake up spiritually instead of living in this fog of fraudulence. 'The truth shall set you free' — the Bible. This was what Beverly-Elizabeth Slane liked to call my holy roller phase. And the charismatic church really did seem to help a lot of the parishioners and congregants I met. They were humble and devoted and charitable, and gave tirelessly without thought of personal reward in active service to the church and in donating resources and time to the church's campaign to build a new altar with an enormous cross of thick glass whose crossbeam was lit up and filled with aerated water and was to have various kinds of beautiful fish swimming in it. (Fish being a prominent Christ-symbol for charismatics. In fact, most of us who were the most devoted and active in the church had bumper stickers on our cars with no words or anything except a plain line drawing of the outline of a fish — this lack of ostentation impressed me as classy and genuine.) But with the real truth here being how quickly I went from being someone who was there because he wanted to wake up and stop being a fraud to being somebody who was so anxious to impress the congregation with how devoted and active I was that I volunteered to help take the collection, and never missed one study group the whole time, and was on two different committees for coordinating fund-raising for the new aquarial altar and deciding exactly what kind of equipment and fish would be used for the crossbeam. Plus often being the one in the front row whose voice in the responses was loudest and who waved both hands in the air the most enthusiastically to show that the Spirit had entered me, and speaking in tongues — mostly consisting of d's and g's — except not really, of course, because in fact I was really just pretending to speak in tongues because all the parishioners around me were speaking in tongues and had the Spirit, and so in a kind of fever of excitement I was able to hoodwink even myself into thinking that I really had the Spirit moving through me and was speaking in tongues when in reality I was just shouting 'Dugga muggle ergle dergle' over and over. (In other words, so anxious to see myself as truly born-again that I actually convinced myself that the tongues' babble was real language and somehow less false than plain English at expressing the feeling of the Holy Spirit rolling like a juggernaut right through me.) This went on for about four months. Not to mention falling over backward whenever Pastor Steve came down the row popping people and popped me in the forehead with the heel of his hand, but falling over backward on purpose, not genuinely being struck down by the Spirit like the other people on either side of me (one of whom actually fainted and had to be brought around with salts). It was only when I was walking out to the parking lot one night after Wednesday Night

Praise that I suddenly experienced a flash of self-awareness or clarity or whatever in which I suddenly stopped conning myself and realized that I'd been a fraud all these months in the church, too, and was really only saying and doing these things because all the real parishioners were doing them and I wanted everyone to think I was sincere. It just about knocked me over, that was how vividly I saw how I'd deceived myself. The revealed truth was that I was an even bigger fraud in church about being a newly reborn authentic person than I'd been before Deacon and Mrs. Halberstadt first rang my doorbell out of nowhere as part of their missionary service and talked me into giving it a shot. Because at least before the church thing I wasn't conning myself — I'd known that I was a fraud since at least age nineteen, but at least I'd been able to admit and face the fraudulence directly instead of B.S.ing myself that I was something I wasn't.

All this was presented in the context of a very long pseudo-argument about fraudulence with Dr. Gustafson that would take way too much time to relate to you in detail, so I'm just telling you about some of the more garish examples. With Dr. G. it was more in the form of a prolonged, multi-session back-and-forth on whether or not I was a total fraud, during which I got more and more disgusted with myself for even playing along. By this point in the analysis I'd pretty much decided he was an idiot, or at least very limited in his insights into what was really going on with people. (There was also the blatant issue of the mustache and of him always playing with it.) Essentially he saw what he wanted to see, which was just the sort of person I could practically eat for lunch in terms of creating whatever ideas or impressions of me I wanted. For instance, I told him about the period of trying jogging, during which I seemed never to fail to have to increase my pace and pump my arms more vigorously whenever someone drove by or looked up from his yard, so that I ended up with bone spurs and eventually had to quit altogether. Or spending at least two or three sessions recounting the example of the introductory meditation class at the Downers Grove Community Center that Melissa Betts of Settleman, Dorn got me to take, at which through sheer force of will I'd always force myself to remain totally still with my legs crossed and back per-

fectly straight long after the other students had all given up and fallen
back on their mats shuddering and holding their heads. Right from
the first class meeting, even though the small, brown instructor had
told us to shoot for only ten minutes of stillness at the outset because
most Westerners' minds could not maintain more than a few minutes
of stillness and mindful concentration without feeling so restless and
ill at ease that they couldn't stand it, I always remained absolutely still
and focused on breathing my prana with the lower diaphragm longer
than any of them, sometimes for up to thirty minutes, even though my
knees and lower back were on fire and I had what felt like swarms of
insects crawling all over my arms and shooting out of the top of my
head — and Master Gurpreet, although he kept his facial expression
inscrutable, gave me a deep and seemingly respectful bow and said that
I sat almost like a living statue of mindful repose, and that he was impressed. The problem was that we were also all supposed to continue
practicing our meditation on our own at home between classes, and
when I tried to do it alone I couldn't seem to sit still and follow my
breath for more than even a few minutes before I felt like crawling out
of my skin and had to stop. I could only sit and appear quiet and mindful and withstand the unbelievably restless and horrible feelings when
all of us were doing it together in the class — meaning only when
there were other people to make an impression on. And even in class,
the truth was that I was often concentrating not so much on following
my prana as on keeping totally still and in the correct posture and having a deeply peaceful and meditative expression on my face in case
anyone was cheating and had their eyes open and was looking around,
plus also to ensure that Master Gurpreet would continue to see me as
exceptional and keep addressing me by what became sort of his class
nickname for me, which was 'the statue.'

Finally, in the final few class meetings, when Master Gurpreet told
us to sit still and focused for only as long as we comfortably could and
then waited almost an hour before finally hitting his small bell with
the little silver thing to signal the period of meditation's end, only I
and an extremely thin, pale girl who had her own meditation bench
that she brought to class with her were able to sit still and focused for

the whole hour, although at several different points I'd get so cramped and restless, with what felt like bright blue fire going up my spine and shooting invisibly out of the top of my head as blobs of color exploded over and over again behind my eyelids, that I thought I was going to jump up screaming and take a header right out the window. And at the end of the course, when there was also an opportunity to sign up for the next session, which was called Deepening the Practice, Master Gurpreet presented several of us with different honorary certificates, and mine had my name and the date and was inscribed in black calligraphy, CHAMPION MEDITATOR, MOST IMPRESSIVE WESTERN STUDENT, THE STATUE. It was only after I fell asleep that night (I'd finally sort of compromised and told myself I was practicing the meditative discipline at home at night by lying down and focusing on following my breathing very closely as I fell asleep, and it did turn out to be a phenomenal sleep aid) that while I was asleep I had the dream about the statue in the commons and realized that Master Gurpreet had actually in all likelihood seen right through me the whole time, and that the certificate was in reality a subtle rebuke or joke at my expense. Meaning he was letting me know that he knew I was a fraud and not even coming close to actually quieting my mind's ceaseless conniving about how to impress people in order to achieve mindfulness and honor my true inner self. (Of course, what he seemed not to have divined was that in reality I actually seemed to have no true inner self, and that the more I tried to be genuine the more empty and fraudulent I ended up feeling inside, which I told nobody about until my stab at analysis with Dr. Gustafson.) In the dream, I was in the town commons in Aurora, over near the Pershing tank memorial by the clock tower, and what I'm doing in the dream is sculpting an enormous marble or granite statue of myself, using a huge iron chisel and a hammer the size of those ones they give you to try to hit the bell at the top of the big thermometer-like thing at carnivals, and when the statue's finally done I put it up on a big bandstand or platform and spend all my time polishing it and keeping birds from sitting on it or doing their business on it, and cleaning up litter and keeping the grass neat all around the bandstand. And in the dream my whole life flashes by like that, the sun and moon go back and forth across the sky like windshield wipers over and over, and I never seem to sleep or eat or take a shower (the dream takes place in dream time as opposed to waking, chronological time), meaning I'm condemned to a whole life of being nothing but a sort of custodian to the statue. I'm not saying it was subtle or hard to figure out. Everybody from Fern, Master Gurpreet, the anorexic girl with her own bench, and Ginger Manley, to people from the firm and some of the media reps we bought time from (I was still a media buyer at this time) all walk by, some several times — at one point Melissa Betts and her new fiancé even spread out a blanket and have a sort of little picnic in the shade of the statue — but none of them ever look over or say anything. It's obviously another dream about fraudulence, like the dream where I'm supposedly a big pop star on-stage but all I really do is lip-synch to one of my stepparents' old Mamas and Papas records that's on a record player just off-stage, and somebody whose face I can't ever look over long enough to make out keeps putting his hand in the area of the record as if he's going to make it skip or scratch, and the whole dream makes my skin crawl. These dreams were obvious, they were warnings from my subconscious that I was hollow and a fraud and it was only a matter of time before the whole charade fell apart. Another of my stepmother's treasured antiques was a silver pocketwatch of her maternal grandfather's with the Latin RESPICE FINEM inscribed on the inside of the case. It wasn't until after she passed away and my stepfather said she'd wanted me to have it that I bothered to look up the term, after which I'd gotten the same sort of crawly feeling as with Master Gurpreet's certificate. Much of the nightmarish quality of the dream about the statue was due to the way the sun raced back and forth across the sky and the speed with which my whole life blew by like that, in the commons. It was obviously also my subconscious enlightening me as to the meditation instructor's having seen through me the whole time, after which I was too embarrassed even to go try to get a refund for the Deepening the Practice class, which there was now no way I felt like I could show up for, even though at the same time I also still had fantasies about Master Gurpreet becoming my mentor or guru and using all kinds of inscrutable Eastern techniques to show me the way to meditate myself into having a true self . . .

. . . Etc., etc. I'll spare you any more examples, for instance I'll spare you the literally countless examples of my fraudulence with girls — with the ladies as they say — in just about every dating relationship I ever had, or the almost unbelievable amount of fraudulence and calculation involved in my career — not just in terms of manipulating the consumer and manipulating the client into trusting that your agency's ideas are the best way to manipulate the consumer, but in the inter-office politics of the agency itself, like for example in sizing up what sorts of things your superiors want to believe (including the belief that they're smarter than you and that that's why they're your superior) and then giving them what they want but doing it just subtly enough that they never get a chance to view you as a sycophant or yes-man (which they want to believe they do not really want) but instead see you as a tough-minded independent thinker who from time to time bows to the weight of their superior intelligence and creative firepower, etc. The whole agency was one big ballet of fraudulence and of manipulating people's images of your ability to manipulate images, a virtual hall of mirrors. And I was good at it, remember, I thrived there.

It was the sheer amount of time Dr. Gustafson spent touching and smoothing his mustache that indicated he wasn't aware of doing it and in fact was subconsciously reassuring himself that it was still there. Which is not an especially subtle habit, in terms of insecurity, since after all facial hair is known as a secondary sex characteristic, meaning what he was really doing was subconsciously reassuring himself that something *else* was still there, if you know what I mean. This was some of why it was no real surprise when it turned out that the overall direction he wanted the analysis to proceed in involved issues of masculinity and how I understood my masculinity (my 'manhood' in other words). This also helped explain everything from the lost-female-crawling and two-testicle-shaped-objects-that-looked-deformed prints on the wall to the little African or Indian drum things and little figurines with (sometimes) exaggerated sex characteristics on the shelf over his desk, plus the pipe, the unnecessary size of his wedding band, even the somewhat overdone little-boy clutter of the office itself. It was pretty clear that there were some major sexual insecurities and maybe even homosexual-type ambiguities that Dr. Gustafson was subconsciously trying to hide from himself and reassure himself about, and one obvious way he did this was to sort of project his insecurities onto his patients and get them to believe that America's culture had a uniquely brutal and alienating way of brainwashing its males from an early age into all kinds of damaging beliefs and superstitions about what being a so-called 'real man' was, such as competitiveness instead of concert, winning at all costs, dominating others through intelligence or will, being strong, not showing your true emotions, depending on others seeing you as a real man in order to reassure yourself of your manhood, seeing your own value solely in terms of accomplishments, being obsessed with your career or income, feeling as if you were constantly being judged or on display, etc. This was later in the analysis, after the seemingly endless period where after every example of fraudulence I gave him he'd make a show of congratulating me on being able to reveal what I felt were shameful fraudulent examples, and said that this was proof that I had much more of an ability to be genuine than I (apparently because of my insecurities or male fears) seemed able to give myself credit for. Plus it didn't exactly seem like a coincidence that the cancer he was even then harboring was in his colon — that shameful, dirty, secret place right near the rectum — with the idea being that using your rectum or colon to secretly *harbor an alien growth* was a blatant symbol both of homosexuality and of the repressive belief that its open acknowledgment would equal disease and death. Dr. Gustafson and I both had a good laugh over this one after we'd both died and were outside linear time and in the process of dramatic change, you can bet on that. (*Outside time* is not just an expression or manner of speaking, by the way.) By this time in the analysis I was playing with him the way a cat does with a hurt bird. If I'd had an ounce of real self-respect I would have stopped and gone back to the Downers Grove Community Center and thrown myself on Master Gurpreet's mercy, since except for maybe one or two girls I'd dated he was the only one who'd appeared to see all the way through to the core of my fraudulence, plus his oblique, very dry way of indicating this to me betrayed a sort of serene indifference to whether I even understood that he saw right through me that I found incredibly impressive and genuine — here in Master Gurpreet was a man with, as they say, nothing to prove. But I didn't, instead I more or less conned myself into sticking with going in to see Dr. G. twice a week for almost nine months (toward the end it was only once a week because by then the cancer had been diagnosed and he was getting radiation treatments every Tuesday and Thursday), telling myself that at least I was trying to find some venue in which I could get help finding a way to be genuine and stop manipulating everybody around me to see 'the statue' as erect and impressive, etc.

Nor however is it strictly true that the analyst had nothing interesting to say or that he didn't sometimes provide helpful models or angles for looking at the basic problem. For instance, it turned out that one of his basic operating premises was the claim that there were really only two basic, fundamental orientations a person could have toward the world, (1) love and (2) fear, and that they couldn't coexist (or, in logical terms, that their domains were exhaustive and mutually exclusive, or that their two sets had no intersection but their union comprised all possible elements, or that:

$(\forall x) ((Fx \rightarrow \sim (Lx)) \& (Lx \rightarrow \sim (Fx))) \& \sim ((\exists x) (\sim (Fx) \& \sim (Lx)))$),

meaning in other words that each day of your life was spent in service to one of these masters or the other, and 'One cannot serve two masters' — the Bible again — and that one of the worst things about the conception of competitive, achievement-oriented masculinity that America supposedly hardwired into its males was that it caused a more or less constant state of fear that made genuine love next to impossible. That is, that what passed for love in American men was usually just the need to be regarded in a certain way, meaning that today's males were so constantly afraid of 'not measuring up' (Dr. G.'s phrase, with evidently no pun intended) that they had to spend all their time convincing others of their masculine 'validity' (which happens to also be a term from formal logic) in order to ease their own insecurity, making genuine love next to impossible. Although it seemed a little bit simplistic to see this fear as just a male problem (try watching a girl stand on a scale sometime), it turns out that Dr. Gustafson was very nearly right in this concept of the two masters — though not in the way that he, when alive and confused about his own real identity, believed — and even while I played along by pretending to argue or not quite understand what he was driving at, the idea struck me that maybe the real root of my problem was not fraudulence but a basic inability to really love, even to genuinely love my stepparents, or Fern, or Melissa Betts, or Ginger Manley of Aurora West High in 1979, whom I'd often thought of as the only girl I'd ever truly loved, though Dr. G.'s bromide about men being brainwashed to equate love with accomplishment or conquest also applied here. The plain truth was that Ginger Manley was just the first girl I ever went all the way with, and most of my tender feelings about her were really just nostalgia for the feeling of immense cosmic validation I'd felt when she finally let me take her jeans all the way off and put my so-called 'manhood' inside her, etc. There's really no bigger cliché than losing your virginity and later having all kinds of retrospective tenderness for the girl involved. Or what Beverly-Elizabeth Slane, a research technician I used to see outside of work when I was a media buyer, and had a lot of conflict with toward the end, said, which I don't think I ever told Dr. G. about, fraudulence-wise, probably because it cut a little too close to the bone. Toward the end she had compared me to some piece of ultra-expensive new medical or diagnostic equipment that can discern more about you in one quick scan than you could ever know about yourself — but the equipment doesn't care about you, you're just a sequence of processes and codes. What the machine understands about you doesn't actually *mean* anything to it. Even though it's really good at what it does. Beverly had a bad temper combined with some serious firepower, she was not someone you wanted to have pissed off at you. She said she'd never felt the gaze of someone so penetrating, discerning, and yet totally empty of care, like she was a puzzle or problem I was figuring out. She said it was thanks to me that she'd discovered the difference between being penetrated and really known versus penetrated and just violated — needless to say, these thanks were sarcastic. Some of this was just her emotional makeup — she found it impossible to really end a relationship unless all bridges were burned and things got said that were so devastating that there could be no possibility of a rapprochement to haunt her or prevent her moving on. Nevertheless it penetrated, I never did forget what she said in that letter.

Even if being fraudulent and being unable to love were in fact ultimately the same thing (a possibility that Dr. Gustafson never seemed to consider no matter how many times I set him up to see it), being unable to really love was at least a different model or lens through which to see the problem, plus initially it seemed like a promising way of attacking the fraudulence paradox in terms of reducing the self-hatred part that reinforced the fear and the consequent drive to try to manipulate people into providing the very approval I'd denied myself. (Dr. G.'s term for approval was *validation*.) This period was pretty much the zenith of my career in analysis, and for a few weeks (during a couple of which I actually didn't see Dr. Gustafson at all, because some sort of complication in his illness required him to go into the hospital, and when he came back he appeared to have lost not only weight but some kind of essential part of his total mass, and no longer seemed too large for his old desk chair, which still squeaked but now not as loudly, plus a lot of the clutter and papers had been straightened up and put in several brown cardboard banker's boxes against the wall under the two sad prints, and when I came back in to see him the absence of mess was especially disturbing and sad, for some reason) it was true that I felt some of the first genuine hope I'd had since the early, self-deluded part of the experiment with Naperville's Church of the Flaming Sword of the Redeemer. And yet at the same time these weeks also led more or less directly to my decision to kill myself, although I'm going to have to simplify and linearize a great deal of interior stuff in order to convey to you what actually happened. Otherwise it would take an almost literal eternity to recount it, we already agreed about that. It's not that words or human language stop having any meaning or relevance after you die, by the way. It's more the specific, one-after-the-other temporal ordering of them that does. Or doesn't.

It's hard to explain. In logical terms, something expressed in words will still have the same 'cardinality' but no longer the same 'ordinality.' All the different words are still there, in other words, but it's no longer a question of which one comes first. Or you could say it's no longer the series of words but now more like some limit toward which the series converges. It's hard not to want to put it in logical terms, since they're the most abstract and universal. Meaning they have no connotation, you don't feel anything about them. Or maybe imagine everything anybody on earth ever said or even thought to themselves all getting collapsed and exploding into one large, combined, instantaneous sound — although *instantaneous* is a little misleading, since it implies other instants before and after, and it isn't really like that. It's more like the sudden internal flash when you see or realize something — a sudden flash or whatever of epiphany or insight. It's not just that it happens way faster than you could break the process down and arrange it into English, but that it happens on a scale in which there isn't even time to be aware of any sort of time at all in which it's happening, the flash — all you know is that there's a before and an after, and afterward you're different. I don't know if that makes sense. I'm just trying to give it to you from several different angles, it's all the same thing. Or you could think of it as being more a certain configuration of light than a word-sum or series of sounds, too, afterward. Which is in fact true. Or as a theorem's proof — because if a proof is true then it's true everywhere and all the time, not just when you happen to say it. The thing is that it turns out that logical symbolism really would be the best way to express it, because logic is totally abstract and outside what we think of as time. It's the closest thing to what it's really like. That's why it's the logical paradoxes that really drive people nuts. A lot of history's great logicians have ended up killing themselves, that is a fact.

And keep in mind this flash can happen anywhere, at any time.

Here's the basic Berry paradox, by the way, if you might want an example of why logicians with incredible firepower can devote their whole lives to solving these things and still end up beating their heads against the wall. This one has to do with big numbers — meaning really big, past a trillion, past ten to the trillion to the trillion, way up there. When you get way up there, it takes a while even to describe numbers this big in words. 'The quantity one trillion, four hundred and three billion to the trillionth power' takes twenty syllables to describe, for example. You get the idea. Now, even higher up there in these huge, cosmic-scale numbers, imagine now the very smallest number that can't be described in under twenty-two syllables. The paradox is that *the very smallest number that can't be described in under twenty-two syllables,* which of course is itself a description of this number, only has twenty-one syllables in it, which of course is under twenty-two syllables. So now what are you supposed to do?

At the same time, what actually led to it in causal terms, though, occurred during maybe the third or fourth week that Dr. G. was back seeing patients after his hospitalization. Although I'm not going to pretend that the specific incident wouldn't strike most people as absurd or even sort of insipid, as causes go. The truth is just that late at night one night in August after Dr. G.'s return, when I couldn't sleep (which happened a lot ever since the cocaine period) and was sitting up drinking a glass of milk or something and watching television, flipping the remote almost at random between different cable stations the way you do when it's late, I happened on part of an old *Cheers* episode from late in the series' run where the analyst character, Frasier (who went on to have his own show), and Lilith, his fiancée and also an analyst, are just entering the stage set of the underground tavern, and Frasier is asking her how her workday at her office went, and Lilith says, 'If I have one more yuppie come in and start whining to me about how he can't love, I'm going to throw up.' This line got a huge laugh from the show's studio audience, which indicated that they — and so by demographic extension the whole national audience at home as well — recognized what a cliché and melodramatic type of complaint the inability-to-love concept was. And, sitting there, when I suddenly realized that once again I'd managed to con myself, this time into thinking that this was a truer or more promising way to conceive of the problem of fraudulence — and, by extension, that I'd also somehow deluded myself into almost believing that poor old Dr. Gustafson had anything in his mental arsenal that could actually help me, and that the real truth was probably more that I was continuing to see him partly out of pity and partly so that I could pretend to myself that I was taking steps to becoming more authentic when in fact all I was doing was jerking a gravely ill shell of a guy around and feeling superior to him because I was able to analyze his own psychological makeup so much more accurately than he could analyze mine — the flash of realizing all this at the very same time that the huge audience-laugh showed that nearly everybody in the United States had probably already seen through the complaint's inauthenticity as long ago as whenever the episode had originally run — all this flashed through my head in the tiny interval it took to realize what I was watching and to remember who the characters of Frasier and Lilith even were, meaning maybe half a second at most, and it more or less destroyed me, that's the only way I can describe it, as if whatever hope of any way out of the trap I'd made for myself had been blasted out of midair or laughed off the stage, as if I were one of those stock comic characters who is always both the butt of the joke and the only person not to get the joke — and in sum I went to bed feeling as fraudulent, befogged, hopeless and full of self-contempt as I'd ever felt, and it was the next morning after that that I woke up having decided I was going to kill myself and end the whole farce. (As you probably recall, *Cheers* was an incredibly popular series, and even in syndication its metro numbers were so high that if a local advertiser wanted to buy time on it the slots cost so much that you pretty much had to build his whole local strategy around those slots.) I'm compressing a huge amount of what took place in my psyche that next-to-last night, all the different realizations and conclusions I reached as I lay there in bed unable to sleep or even move (no single series' line or audience-laugh is in and of itself going to constitute a reason for suicide, of course) — although to you I imagine it probably doesn't seem all that compressed at all, you're thinking here's this guy going on and on and why doesn't he get to the part where he kills himself and explain or account for the fact that he's sitting here next to me in a piece of high-powered machinery telling me all this if he died in 1991. Which in fact I knew I would from the moment I first woke up. It was over, I'd decided to end the charade.

After breakfast I called in sick to work and stayed home the whole day by myself. I knew that if I was around anyone I'd automatically lapse into fraudulence. I had decided to take a whole lot of Benadryl and then just as I got really sleepy and relaxed I'd get the car up to top speed on a rural road way out in the extreme west suburbs and drive it head-on into a concrete bridge abutment. Benadryl makes me extremely foggy and sleepy, it always has. I spent most of the morning on letters to my lawyer and C.P.A., and brief notes to the creative head and managing partner who had originally brought me aboard at Samieti and Cheyne. Our creative group was in the middle of some very ticklish campaign preparations, and I wanted to apologize for in any way leaving them in the lurch. Of course I didn't really feel all that sorry — Samieti and Cheyne was a ballet of fraudulence, and I was well out of it. The note was probably ultimately just so that the people who really mattered at S. & C. would be more apt to remember me as a decent, conscientious guy who it turned out was maybe just a little too sensitive and tormented by his personal demons — 'Almost too good for this world' is what I seemed to be unable to keep from fantasizing a lot of them saying after news of it came through. I did not write Dr. Gustafson a note. He had his own share of problems, and I knew that in the note I'd spend a lot of time trying to seem as if I was being honest but really just dancing around the truth, which was that he was a deeply repressed homosexual or androgyne and had no real business charging patients to let him project his own maladjustments onto them, and that the truth was that he'd be doing himself and everybody else a favor if he'd just go over to Garfield Park and blow somebody in the bushes and try honestly to decide if he liked it or not, and that I was a total fraud for continuing to drive all the way in to River Forest to see him and bat him around like a catnip toy while telling myself there was some possible nonfraudulent point to it. (All of which, of course, even if they weren't dying of colon cancer right in front of you you still could never actually come out and say to somebody, since certain truths might well destroy them — and who has that right?)

I did spend almost two hours before taking the first of the Benadryl composing a handwritten note to my sister Fern. In the note I apologized for whatever pain my suicide and the fraudulence and/or inability to love that had precipitated it might cause her and my stepdad (who was still alive and well and now lived in Marin County, California, where he taught part-time and did community outreach with Marin County's homeless). I also used the occasion of the letter and all the sort of last-testament urgency associated with it to license apologizing to Fern about manipulating my stepparents into believing that she'd lied about the antique glass bowl in 1967, as well as for half a dozen other incidents and spiteful or fraudulent actions that I knew had caused her pain and that I had felt bad about ever since, but had never really seen any way to broach with her or express my honest regret for. (It turns out there are things that you can discuss in a suicide note that would just be too bizarre if expressed in any other kind of venue.) Just one example of such an incident was during a period in the mid-'70s, when Fern, as part of puberty, underwent some physical changes that made her look chunky for a year or two — not fat, but wide-hipped and bosomy and sort of much more broad than she'd been as a pre-teen — and of course she was very, very sensitive about it (puberty also being a time of terrible self-consciousness and sensitivity about one's body image, obviously), so much so that my stepparents took great pains never to say anything about Fern's new breadth or even ever to bring up any topics related to eating habits, diet and exercise, etc. And I for my own part never said anything about it either, not directly, but I had worked out all kinds of very subtle and indirect ways to torment Fern about her size in such a way that my stepparents never saw anything and I could never really be accused of anything that I couldn't then look all around myself with a shocked, incredulous facial expression as if I had no idea what she was talking about, such as just a quick raise of my eyebrow when her eyes met mine as she was having a second helping at dinner, or a quick little quiet, 'You sure you can fit into that?' when she came home from the store with a new skirt. The one I still remembered the most vividly involved the second-floor hall of our house, which was in Aurora and was a three-story home (including the basement) but not all that spacious or large, meaning a skinny three-decker like so many you always see all crammed together along residential streets in Naperville and Aurora. The second-floor hallway, which ran between Fern's room and the top of the stairway on one end and my room and the second-floor bathroom on the other, was cramped and somewhat narrow, but not anywhere close to as narrow as I would pretend that it was whenever Fern and I passed each other in it, with me squashing my back against the hallway wall and splaying my arms out and wincing as if there would barely be enough room for somebody of her unbelievable breadth to squeeze past me, and she would never say anything or even look at me when I did it but would just go on past me into the bathroom and close the door. But I knew it must have hurt her. A little while later, she entered an adolescent period where she hardly ate anything at all, and smoked cigarettes and chewed several packs of gum a day, and used a lot of makeup, and for a while she got so thin that she looked angular and a bit like an insect (although of course I never said that), and I once, through their bedroom's keyhole, overheard a brief conversation in which my stepmother said she was worried because she didn't think Fern was having her normal time of the month anymore because she had gotten so underweight, and she and my stepfather discussed the possibility of taking her to see some kind of specialist. That period passed on its own, but in the letter I told Fern that I'd always remembered this and certain other periods when I'd been cruel or tried to make her feel bad, and that I regretted them very much, although I said I wouldn't want to seem so egotistical as to think that a simple apology could erase any of the hurt I'd caused her when we were growing up. On the other hand, I also assured her that it wasn't as if I had gone around for years carrying excessive guilt or blowing these incidents out of all proportion. They were not life-altering traumas or anything like that, and in many ways they were probably all too typical of the sorts of cruelties that kids tend to inflict on each other growing up. I also assured her that neither these incidents nor my remorse about them had anything to do with my killing myself. I simply said, without going into anything like the level of detail I've given you (because my purpose in the letter was of course very different), that I was killing myself because I was an essentially fraudulent person who seemed to lack either the character or the firepower to find a way to stop even after I'd realized my fraudulence and the terrible toll it exacted (I told her nothing about the various different realizations or paradoxes, what would be the point?). I also inserted that there was also a good possibility that, when all was said and done, I was nothing but just another fast-track yuppie who couldn't love, and that I found the banality of this unendurable, largely because I was evidently so hollow and insecure that I had a pathological need to see myself as somehow exceptional or outstanding at all times. Without going into much explanation or argument, I also told Fern that if her initial reaction to these reasons for my killing myself was to think that I was being much, much too hard on myself, then she should know that I was already aware that that was the most likely reaction my note would produce in her, and had probably deliberately constructed the note to at least in part prompt just that reaction, just the way my whole life I'd often said and done things designed to prompt certain people to believe that I was a genuinely outstanding person whose personal standards were so high that he was far too hard on himself, which in turn made me appear attractively modest and unsmug, and was a big reason for my popularity with so many people in all different avenues of my life — what Beverly-Elizabeth Slane had termed my 'talent for ingratiation' — but was nevertheless basically calculated and fraudulent. I also told Fern that I loved her very much, and asked her to relay these same sentiments to Marin County for me.

Now we're getting to the part where I actually kill myself. This occurred at 9:17 PM on August 19, 1991, if you want the time fixed precisely. Plus I'll spare you most of the last couple hours' preparations and back-and-forth conflict and dithering, which there was a lot of. Suicide runs so counter to so many hardwired instincts and drives that nobody in his right mind goes through with it without going through a great deal of internal back-and-forth, intervals of almost changing your mind, etc. The German logician Kant was right in this respect, human beings are all pretty much identical in terms of our hardwiring. Although we are seldom conscious of it, we are all basically just instruments or expressions of our evolutionary drives, which are themselves the expressions of forces that are infinitely larger and more important than we are. (Although actually being conscious of this is a whole different matter.) So I won't really even try to describe the several different times that day when I sat in my living room and had a furious mental back-and-forth about whether to actually go through with it. For one thing, it was intensely mental and would take an enormous amount of time to put into words, plus it would come off as somewhat cliché or banal in the sense that many of the thoughts and associations were basically the same sorts of generic things that almost anyone who's confronting imminent death will end up thinking. As in, 'This is the last time I will ever tie my shoe,' 'This is the last time I will look at this rubber tree on top of the stereo cabinet,' 'How delicious this lungful of air right here tastes,' 'This is the last glass of milk I'll ever drink,' 'What a totally priceless gift this totally ordinary sight of the wind picking trees' branches up and moving them around is.' Or, 'I will never again hear the plaintive sound of the fridge going on in the kitchen' (the kitchen and breakfast nook are right off my living room), etc. Or, 'I won't see the sun come up tomorrow or watch the bedroom gradually undim and resolve, etc.,' and at the same time trying to summon the memory of the exact way the sun comes up over the humid fields and the wet-looking I-55 ramp that lay due east of my bedroom's sliding glass door in the morning. It had been a hot, wet August, and if I went through with killing myself I wouldn't ever get to feel the incremental cooling and drying that starts here around mid-September, or to see the leaves turn or hear them rustle along the edge of the courtyard outside S. & C.'s floor of the building on S. Dearborn, or see snow or put a shovel and bag of sand in the trunk, or bite into a perfectly ripe, ungrainy pear, or put a piece of toilet paper on a shaving cut. Etc. If I went in and went to the bathroom and brushed my teeth it would be the last time I did those things. I sat there and thought about that, looking at the rubber tree. Everything seemed to tremble a little, the way things reflected in water will tremble. I watched the sun begin to drop down over the townhouse developments going up south of Darien's corporation limit on Lily Cache Rd. and realized that I would never see the newest homes' construction and landscaping completed, or that the homes' white insulation wrap with the trade name TYVEK all over it flapping in all the wind out here would one day have vinyl siding or plate brick and color-coordinated shutters over it and I wouldn't see this happen or be able to drive by and know what was actually written there under all the nice exteriors. Or the breakfast nook window's view of the big farms' fields next to my development, with the plowed furrows all parallel so that if I lean and line their lines up just right they seem to all rush together toward the horizon as if shot out of something huge. You get the idea. Basically I was in that state in which a man realizes that everything he sees will outlast him. As a verbal construction I know that's a cliché. As a state in which to actually be, though, it's something else, believe me. Where now every movement takes on a kind of ceremonial aspect. The very sacredness of the world as seen (the same kind of state Dr. G. will try to describe with analogies to oceans and whitecaps and trees, you might recall I mentioned this already). This is literally about one one-trillionth of the various thoughts and internal experiences I underwent in those last few hours, and I'll spare both of us recounting any more, since I'm aware it ends up seeming somewhat lame. Which in fact it wasn't, but I won't pretend it was fully authentic or genuine, either. A part of me was still calculating, performing — and this was part of the ceremonial quality of that last afternoon. Even as I wrote my note to Fern, for instance, expressing sentiments and regrets that were real, a part of me was noticing what a fine and sincere note it was, and anticipating the effect on Fern of this or that heartfelt phrase, while yet another part was observing the whole scene of a man in a dress shirt and no tie sitting at his breakfast nook writing a heartfelt note on his last afternoon alive, the blondwood table's surface trembling with sunlight and the man's hand steady and face both haunted by regret and ennobled by resolve, this part of me sort of hovering above and just to the left of myself, evaluating the scene, and thinking what a fine and genuine-seeming performance in a drama it would make if only we all had not already been subject to countless scenes just like it in dramas ever since we first saw a movie or read a book, which somehow entailed that real scenes like the one of my suicide note were now compelling and genuine only to their participants, and to anyone else would come off as banal and even somewhat cheesy or maudlin, which is somewhat paradoxical when you consider — as I did, sitting there at the breakfast nook — that the reason scenes like this will seem stale or manipulative to an audience is that we've already seen so many of them in dramas, and yet the reason we've seen so many of them in dramas is that the scenes really are dramatic and compelling and let people communicate very deep, complicated emotional realities that are almost impossible to articulate in any other way, and at the same time still another facet or part of me realizing that from this perspective my own basic problem was that at an early age I'd somehow chosen to cast my lot with my life's drama's supposed audience instead of with the drama itself, and that I even now was watching and gauging my supposed performance's quality and probable effects, and thus was in the final analysis the very same manipulative fraud writing the note to Fern that I had been throughout the life that had brought me to this climactic scene of writing and signing it and addressing the envelope and affixing postage and putting the envelope in my shirt pocket (totally conscious of the resonance of its resting there, next to my heart, in the scene), planning to drop it in a mailbox on the way out to Lily Cache Rd. and the bridge abutment into which I planned to drive my car at speeds sufficient to displace the whole front end and impale me on the steering wheel and instantly kill me. Self-loathing is not the same thing as being into pain or a lingering death, if I was going to do it I wanted it instant.

On Lily Cache, the bridge abutments and sides' steep banks support State Route 4 (also known as the Braidwood Highway) as it crosses overhead on a cement overpass so covered with graffiti that most of it you can't even read. (Which sort of defeats the purpose of graffiti, in my opinion.) The abutments themselves are just off the road and about as wide as this car. Plus the intersection is isolated way out in the country-side around Romeoville, ten or so miles south of the southwest suburbs' limits. It is the true boonies. The only homes are farms set way back from the road and embellished with silos and barns, etc. At night in the summer the dew-point is high and there's always fog. It's farm country. I've never once passed under 4 here without seeming to be the only thing on either road. The corn high and the fields like a green ocean all around, insects the only real noise. Driving alone under creamy stars and a little cocked scythe of moon, etc. The idea was to have the accident and whatever explosion and fire was involved occur someplace isolated enough that no one else would see it, so that there would be as little an aspect of performance to the thing as I could manage and no temptation to spend my last few seconds trying to imagine what impression the sight and sound of the impact might make on someone watching. I was partly concerned that it might be spectacular and dramatic and might look as if the driver was trying to go out in as dramatic a way as possible. This is the sort of shit we waste our lives thinking about.

The ground fog tends to get more intense by the second until it seems that the whole world is just what's in your headlights' reach. High beams don't work in fog, they only make things worse. You can go ahead and try them but you'll see what happens, all they do is light up the fog so it seems even denser. That's kind of a minor paradox, that sometimes you can actually see farther with low beams than high. All right — and there's the construction and all the flapping TYVEK wrap on houses that if you really do do it you'll never see anyone live in. Although it won't hurt, it really will be instant, I can tell you that much. The fields' insects are almost deafening. If the corn's high like this and you watch as the sun sets you can practically watch them rise up out of the fields like some great figure's shadow rising. Mostly mos-quitoes, I don't know what all they are. It's a whole insect universe in there that none of us will ever see or know anything about. Plus you'll notice the Benadryl doesn't help all that much once you're under way. That whole idea was probably ill-conceived.

All right, now we're coming to what I promised and led you through the whole dull synopsis of what led up to this in hopes of. Meaning what it's like to die, what happens. Right? This is what everyone wants to know. And you do, trust me. Whether you decide to go through with it or not, whether I somehow talk you out of it the way you think I'm going to try to do or not. It's not what anyone thinks, for one thing. The truth is you already know what it's like. You already know the difference between the size and speed of everything that flashes through you and the tiny inadequate bit of it all you can ever let anyone know. As though inside you is this enormous room full of what seems like everything in the whole universe at one time or another and yet the only parts that get out have to somehow squeeze out through one of those tiny keyholes you see under the knob in older doors. As if we are all trying to see each other through these tiny keyholes.

But it does have a knob, the door can open. But not in the way you think. But what if you could? Think for a second — what if all the infinitely dense and shifting worlds of stuff inside you every moment of your life turned out now to be somehow fully open and expressible afterward, after what you think of as *you* has died, because what if afterward now each moment itself is an infinite sea or span or passage of time in which to express it or convey it, and you don't even need any organized English, you can as they say open the door and be in anyone else's room in all your own multiform forms and ideas and facets? Because listen — we don't have much time, here's where Lily Cache slopes slightly down and the banks start getting steep, and you can just make out the outlines of the unlit sign for the farmstand that's never open anymore, the last sign before the bridge — so listen: What exactly do you think you are? The millions and trillions of thoughts, memories, juxtapositions — even crazy ones like this, you're thinking — that flash through your head and disappear? Some sum or remainder of these? Your *history?* Do you know how long it's been since I told you I was a fraud? Do you remember you were looking at the RESPICEM watch hanging from the rearview and seeing the time, 9:17? What are you

looking at right now? Coincidence? What if no time has passed at all?*
The truth is you've already heard this. That this is what it's like. That
it's what makes room for the universes inside you, all the endless inbent fractals of connection and symphonies of different voices, the in-
finities you can never show another soul. And you think it makes you
a fraud, the tiny fraction anyone else ever sees? Of course you're a
fraud, of course what people see is never you. And of course you know
this, and of course you try to manage what part they see if you know
it's only a part. Who wouldn't? It's called free will, Sherlock. But at the
same time it's why it feels so good to break down and cry in front of
others, or to laugh, or speak in tongues, or chant in Bengali — it's not
English anymore, it's not getting squeezed through any hole.

---

*One clue that there's something not quite real about sequential time the way you ex-
perience it is the various paradoxes of time supposedly passing and of a so-called 'present' that's always unrolling into the future and creating more and more past behind
it. As if the present were this car — nice car by the way — and the past is the road
we've just gone over, and the future is the headlit road up ahead we haven't yet gotten
to, and time is the car's forward movement, and the precise present is the car's front
bumper as it cuts through the fog of the future, so that it's *now* and then a tiny bit later
a whole different *now*, etc. Except if time is really passing, how fast does it go? At what
rate does the present change? See? Meaning if we use time to measure motion or
rate — which we do, it's the only way you can — 95 miles per hour, 70 heartbeats a
minute, etc. — how are you supposed to measure the rate at which time moves? One
second per second? It makes no sense. You can't even talk about time flowing or moving without hitting up against paradox right away. So think for a second: What if
there's really no movement at all? What if this is all unfolding in the one flash you call
the present, this first, infinitely tiny split-second of impact when the speeding car's
front bumper's just starting to touch the abutment, just before the bumper crumples
and displaces the front end and you go violently forward and the steering column
comes back at your chest as if shot out of something enormous? Meaning that what if
in fact this *now* is infinite and never really passes in the way your mind is supposedly
wired to understand *pass*, so that not only your whole life but every single humanly
conceivable way to describe and account for that life has time to flash like neon shaped
into those connected cursive letters that businesses' signs and windows love so much
to use through your mind all at once in the literally immeasurable instant between impact and death, just as you start forward to meet the wheel at a rate no belt ever made
could restrain — THE END.

So cry all you want, I won't tell anybody.

But it wouldn't have made you a fraud to change your mind. It would be sad to do it because you think you somehow have to.

It won't hurt, though. It will be loud, and you'll feel things, but they'll go through you so fast that you won't even realize you're feeling them (which is sort of like the paradox I used to bounce off Gustafson — is it possible to be a fraud if you aren't aware you're a fraud?). And the very brief moment of fire you'll feel will be almost good, like when your hands are cold and there's a fire and you hold your hands out toward it.

The reality is that dying isn't bad, but it takes forever. And that forever is no time at all. I know that sounds like a contradiction, or maybe just wordplay. What it really is, it turns out, is a matter of perspective. The big picture, as they say, in which the fact is that this whole seemingly endless back-and-forth between us has come and gone and come again in the very same instant that Fern stirs a boiling pot for dinner, and your stepfather packs some pipe tobacco down with his thumb, and Angela Mead uses an ingenious little catalogue tool to roll cat hair off her blouse, and Melissa Betts inhales to respond to something she thinks her husband just said, and David Wallace blinks in the midst of idly scanning class photos from his 1980 Aurora West H.S. yearbook and seeing my photo and trying, through the tiny little keyhole of himself, to imagine what all must have happened to lead up to my death in the fiery single-car accident he'd read about in 1991, like what sorts of pain or problems might have driven the guy to get in his electric-blue Corvette and try to drive with all that O.T.C. medication in his bloodstream — David Wallace happening to have a huge and totally unorganizable set of inner thoughts, feelings, memories and impressions of this little photo's guy a year ahead of him in school with the seemingly almost neon aura around him all the time of scholastic and athletic excellence and popularity and success with the ladies, as well as of every last cutting remark or even tiny disgusted gesture or expression on this guy's part whenever David Wallace struck out looking in Legion ball or said something dumb at a party, and of how impressive and authentically at ease in the world the guy always seemed, like an actual living person instead of the dithering, pathetically self-conscious outline or ghost of a person David Wallace knew himself back then to be. Verily a fair-haired, fast-track guy, whom in the very best human tradition David Wallace had back then imagined as happy and unreflective and wholly unhaunted by voices telling him that there was something deeply wrong with him that wasn't wrong with anybody else and that he had to spend all of his time and energy trying to figure out what to do and say in order to impersonate an even marginally normal or acceptable U.S. male, all this stuff clanging around in David Wallace '81's head every second and moving so fast that he never got a chance to catch hold and try to fight or argue against it or even really even feel it except as a knot in his stomach as he stood in his real parents' kitchen ironing his uniform and thinking of all the ways he could screw up and strike out looking or drop balls out in right and reveal his true pathetic essence in front of this .418 hitter and his witchily pretty sister and everyone else in the audience in lawn chairs in the grass along the sides of the Legion field (all of whom already probably saw through the sham from the outset anyway, he was pretty sure) — in other words David Wallace trying, if only in the second his lids are down, to somehow reconcile what this luminous guy had seemed like from the outside with whatever on the interior must have driven him to kill himself in such a dramatic and doubtlessly painful way — with David Wallace also fully aware that the cliché that you can't ever truly know what's going on inside somebody else is hoary and insipid and yet at the same time trying very consciously to prohibit that awareness from mocking the attempt or sending the whole line of thought into the sort of inbent spiral that keeps you from ever getting anywhere (considerable time having passed since 1981, of course, and David Wallace having emerged from years of literally indescribable war against himself with quite a bit more firepower than he'd had at Aurora West), the realer, more enduring and sentimental part of him commanding that other part to be silent as if looking it levelly in the eye and saying, almost aloud, 'Not another word.'

[→NMN.80.418]

PHILOSOPHY AND THE MIRROR OF NATURE

Then just as I was being released in late 1996 Mother won a small product liability settlement and used the money to promptly go get cosmetic surgery on the crow's feet around her eyes. However the cosmetic surgeon botched it and did something to the musculature of her face which caused her to look *insanely frightened* at all times. No doubt you know the way an individual's face can look in the split second before they start to scream. That was now Mother. It turns out that it only takes a minuscule slip of the knife one way or the other in this procedure and now you look like someone in the shower scene of Hitchcock. So then she went and had more cosmetic surgery to try and correct it. But the second surgeon also botched it and the appearance of fright became even worse. Especially around the mouth this time. She asked for my candid reaction and I felt our relation demanded nothing less. Her crow's feet indeed were things of the past but now her face was a *chronic mask of insane terror*. Now she looked more like Elsa Lanchester when Elsa Lanchester first lays eyes on her prospective mate in the 1935 classic of the studio system *Bride of Frankenstein*. Now after the second botched procedure even dark glasses were no longer of much help as there was still the matter of the gaping mouth and mandibular distention and protrudant tendons and so forth. So now she was involved in still another lawsuit and when she regularly took the bus to the attorney she had chosen's office I would *escort her.* We rode at the bus's front in one of the two longer seat areas which are aligned sideways instead of frontally. We had learned through experimental method to not sit further back in the rows of more regular seats which face frontally because of the way certain fellow passengers would visibly react when they board and perform the seemingly reflexive action as they start moving down the aisle to a seat of briefly scanning the faces facing them from the narrow rows of seats extended backward through the bus and would suddenly see Mother's distended and soundlessly screaming face appearing to gaze back at them in *mindless terror.* And there were a smattering of such cases and interactions before I applied myself to the problem and evolved a more workable right-angle habitat. Nothing in sources sufficiently explains why people perform the scan of faces when they first board though anecdotally it appears to be a defensive reflex species-wide. Nor am I even a good specimen to sit with if she wanted to be inconspicuous because of the way my head physically *towers over* all others in the crowd. Physically I am a large specimen and have distinctive coloration, to look at me you would never know I have such a studious bend. There also are the goggles worn and specially constructed gloves for field work, it is far from impossible to find specimens on a public bus even though surveys as yet have yielded no fruit. No it is not as if actively speaking I could be said *to enjoy* riding with her while she exerts all her effort trying to not allow the embarrassment of the chronic expression to make it even more frightened-looking. Or that I can truthfully *look forward* to sitting in a would-be reception area reading Rotary newsletters two times per week. It is not as if I do not have other things and studies to occupy my time. But what is one to do, the terms of my probation involve Mother's sworn statement to assume liability as my custodian. Yet anyone observing the reality of life together since the second procedure would agree the reality was the other way around because due to despondency and fear of others' reactions to it she is all but incapable of leaving the house and can answer the attorney's wheedling summonses to his office only with my presence and protection throughout the long ride. Also I have never liked direct sunlight and burn with great ease. This time the attorney smells a windfall profit if and when he can get Mother in a courtroom and let a jury see for itself the consequence of the cosmetic surgeons' negligence. I also carry a briefcase at all times since my own case. One today would call a briefcase a *sematic accessory* to warn off potential predators. Since the original negligence I have primarily immunized myself to Mother's chronic expression of horror but am even so capable of being made uncomfortable by some's reaction to us visually, it takes some getting use to. A bus's circular steering wheel is not only larger but is set at an *angle of incidence* more horizontal than any taxi, private car or police cruiser's wheel I have seen and the driver turns the wheel with a broad all-body motion which is resemblant of someone's arm sweeping all the material off a table or surface in a sudden fit of emotion. And the special perpendicular seats in the bus's anterior segment comprise a good vantage from which to watch the driver wrestle with the bus. Nor did I have anything against the boy in any way. Nor is there anything in any state, county or local ordinance restricting what varieties you can study or stipulating in any way that cultivating more than a certain number thereof constitutes reckless endangerment or a hazard to the community at large. If the appointment is AM then the driver sometimes keeps a newspaper folded in a hutch by the automatic coin or token box which he tries to peruse while idling at stoplights although it is not as if he will get much of his daily reading done in this way. He was only nine which was repeatedly stressed as if his age in any way strengthened any charge of negligence on my part. A common Asian species not only has the sematic ventral insignia but a red line straight down the back, leading to its indigenous name, *Red line on back*. Standardized testing has confirmed that I have both a studious bend and outstanding retention in study which she would not even deny. I have evolved the theory that the driver peruses his newspaper and reluctantly refolds it and replaces it in the hutch on green to signal the paralyzed dislike he feels about his paid job and a court-appointed psychologist might diagnose the newspaper as *a cry for help*. Our customary habitat now is the lateral seat that is on the same side as the bus's door minimizing any likelihood that someone boarding will have a sudden frontal view of her expression. This too being a lesson learned the *old-fashioned way*. The only lighthearted interlude was that when they brought her the mirror and the first surgery's bandages came off then one could at first not ascertain whether the face's expression was a reaction to what she saw in the mirror or if it itself was what she saw and this was the stimulus causing the noises. Mother herself who is a decent-hearted if vain, bitter and timid female specimen but who is not a colossus of the roads of the human intellect, to put it frankly, could herself not ascertain at first if the look of insane terror was the response or the stimulus and if it was a response then a response to what in the mirror if the response itself was the expression. Causing no end of confusion before they got her sedated. The surgeon was leaning forward against the wall with his face to the wall a behavioral reaction which signaled, *Yes* there was an objective problem in the surgery's results. The bus is because we have no car, a situation this new attorney says he can now remedy in spades. The whole thing was carefully contained and screened off and even the state conceded that if he had not been up fiddling around on the roof of someone else's garage there is no way he could have come in contact with them in any form. This factoring into the terms of probation. At the outset too it was of interest on the bus to see the way passengers upon catching any glimpse of her expression will by reflex turn to look out whichever of the bus windows Mother appears to them to be responding to with such facial alarm. Her fear of the phylum *arthropodae* is long-standing which is why she never ventured in the garage and could contend *ignorantia facti excusat*, a point of law. Ironically also hence her constant spraying of R - - d© despite my repeatedly advising her that these species are long-resistant to resmethrin and trans-d allethrin. The active ingredients in R - - d©. Granted widow bites are a bad way to go because of the potent neurotoxin involved prompting one physician all the way in 1935 to comment, *I do not recall having seen more abject pain manifested in any other medical or surgical condition* whereas the painless loxoceles or *recluse* toxin only causes necrosis and severe sloughing of the area. Recluses however exhibiting *a native aggression* which widow species never share unless actively disturbed. Which he did. The bus's interior is flesh-colored plastic with promotions for legal and medical services arrayed above the windows. Many *par Español*. The ventilation varies according to such criteria as fullness. The phobia becomes so extreme she will carry a can in her bag of knitting until I always find it before leaving and say firmly, *No*. In one or two regrettable moments of insensitivity also I have joked about taking the bus all the way through into Studio City and environs and auditioning Mother as an extra in one of the many films nowadays in which crowds of extras are paid to look upwards in terror of a *special effect* which is only later inserted into the film through computer-aided design. Which I sincerely regret, after all I'm all the support she has. To my mind however it is quite a stretch to say that an area of weakness in a twenty-year-old garage roof equals failing to exercise due diligence or care. Whereas Hitchcock and other classics used only primitive *special effects* but to more terrifying results. To say nothing of him trespassing and having no business up there anyhow. In the deposition. To say nothing of claiming that not foreseeing a trespasser falling through a portion of a garage roof and wholesale wrecking a complex and expensive tempered-glass container complex and crushing or otherwise disturbing a great many specimens and inevitably, due to the mishap, leading to some partial decontainment and penetration of the surrounding neighborhood amounts to my failing due exercise of caution. This then being my argument for preferring the classics of older film terror. Declining to ever place the briefcase under the seat I keep it on my lap throughout the frequent rides. My position throughout the proceedings was a natural deep regret for the kid and his family but that the misfortune of what happened as a result did not justify hysterical or trumped-up charges of any kind. Quality counsel would have been able to translate this reasoning into effective legal language in legal briefs and arguments *in camera*. But the reality is counsel proves to be abundant if you are the aggressor but not if you are merely prey, they're parasites, daytime TV is infested with their commercials urging the viewer to wait patiently for the opportunity to attack, *handled on a percentage basis, no fee of any kind if you are the aggressor!* One could see them come right out of the woodwork after Mother's original product liability. Objectively no one even knows how the widow's neurotoxin works to produce such abject pain and suffering in larger mammals, science is baffled as to evolutionarily what advantage there is for a venom well in excess of required for this unique but common specimen to subdue its prey. Science is often confounded by both the luminous widow and the more average-looking recluse. Plus the ones who say they will really get down in the dirt of the trench and really fight for you are *sleazeballs* such as this supposed Van Nuys negligence specialist Mother has lined up. From another context the hysteria would have almost been humorous as any environs as unkempt as our surrounding neighborhood will already be naturally infested with them in all the clutter and run-down homes. Clutter's abundant shelter being their *native element.* Specimens of widely varied size and aggression are to be found in basement corners, beneath shelves of sheds, garages and linen closets, behind large appliances and in the innumerable crevices of cast-away litter and unkempt weeds. Widows in particular favoring ill-lit right angles for their web's construction. In the right angles of most structures' shaded sides up under the eaves for example in summer months. If you know what to look for. Hence the clear goggles and polyurethane gloves are indispensable even in the shower stall whose right angles can be infested in just so many few absent hours. Widows being long noted as industrious weavers. Or outside the moving bus in the palm trees they stand so naively beneath in the shade to await their buses, *Rent a ladder and carefully examine the undersides of those fronds sometime!* one is tempted to shout through the window. Once conditioned to know what to look for they are often observable everywhere *hiding in plain sight.* Patience being another hallmark. This habitat and also further inland both contain the more exotic variety of *red widow* whose ventral hourglass is brown or tan as well as one of the hemisphere's two smaller *brown* or *gray* species in the further-inland desert regions which prefer arid climes. The red widow's red lacking however the spellbinding lustre of the familiar household black variety, it is more a dull or dullish red, and they are rare and both specimens escaped in his mishap and have not been reacquired. Here as so often in the arthropod realm the female dominates as well. To be frank Mother's *pain and suffering* appeared somewhat inflated in the original product liability claim and in reality she coughs less than during her own deposition. Far be it from me to deny her however due to the *thickness of blood.* Sitting at home in dark glasses as ever knitting while monitoring my activities her *mouth parts working idly.* Scientifically however a large mammal would have to inhale a great deal of trans-d allethrin for permanent damage to result which as predicted did impact the modesty of her settlement. The true facts are less than a centimeter either way is the difference between smooth youthful eyes and the chronic expression of Vivian Leigh in the shower in the 1960 classic of that name. The briefcase is aerated at select tiny points in each corner and 2.5 dozen polystyrene chocks distributed throughout the interior can protect the contents from jostling or trauma. Her new case's complexity is exactly how to distribute the liability claim between the original surgeon whose negligence gave her the frightened eyes and forehead and the second whose *repair's callous butchery* left her with a chronic mask of crazed suffering and terror that now can fortunately only possibly cause incidents in the case of someone in the opposing lateral seat. Directly behind the driver. Because the sole exposure to liability of Mother's placement here is that any such individual in the opposing seat hence will have the vantage of gazing frontally at us throughout the ride. And on select occasions such a specimen will, if predisposed by environmental conditioning or instinctive temperament, appear to assume that the stimulus causing her expression is me. That with my size and distinctive mark that I have kidnapped this horror-stricken middle-aged female or behaved in a somehow threatening manner toward her saying, *Ma'am is there some problem* or, *Why don't you just leave the lady alone* as she sinks lower in her knitted scarf in self-discomfort over their reaction but my own evolved response is to calmly smile and raise my gloves in puzzled bemusement as if to say, *Why who knows for certain why anyone wears the face they do my good fellow let us not leap to conclusions based on incomplete data!* Her original liability was that a worker at the assembly plant actually glued a can's nozzle on facing backward, I submit a clear-cut case of failing to exercise due care. The fifth condition of the settlement being to never under any circumstances mention the trade name of the common household spray in any connection to the liability suit which I am resolved to honor on her behalf, the law is the law. Respecting mating I have been on dates but there was insufficient chemistry, Mother is blackly cynical in matters of the heart referring to the entire spectrum of mating rituals as a *disaster waiting to happen.* Recently as the bus crossed Victory Boulevard as I looked down to check the status I saw accidentally protruding from one of the ventilation holes at the case's corner the slender tip of a black jointed foreleg, it was moving about slightly and possessed the same luminous coloration as the rest of the specimens, moving tentatively in an exploratory way. Unseen against the more inorganic black of the briefcase's side. Unseen by Mother whose reaction's expression I must lightheartedly say would not change in the least, once you get accustomed it is like *a poker face.* Even if I opened up the entire case right here on my lap and tipped it out into the central aisle allowing rapid spreading out and penetration of the contained environs. The worse-case scenario only occurring if one confronts some young duo of *punks* or hostile organisms in the opposing seat whose reaction to Mother might be an aggressive challenging stare or aggressive, *What the f--k are you looking at.* It is for such a case that I am her sematic accessory or escort, with my imposing size and goggles one can tell beneath the gaping rictus she believes I can protect her which is good.

OBLIVION

Fortunately, Hope's stepfather and myself had just completed the 'front' nine and were washing our balls in the Tenth tee's device when the thunderstorm broke, and I was able to get him into the Club-house before the worst of the wind and the rain of the storm commenced, and to get the cart checked back in while my stepfather-in-law dried off, changed clothes and telephoned his wife about another adjustment in his morning schedule due to our having gotten 'in' only nine holes. The old fellow had originally wanted to tee off at almost dawn, and I had found myself unable to explain why this could represent a possibly untenable hardship without opening the whole 'can of worms' of the conflict in front of Hope, who was there at the prior evening's restaurant's table as we finalized arrangements; and now, in the Club-house vestibule, there was an air of, as it were, 'triumphant' grievance in the retired M.D.'s posture at the bank of phones when I found him there, freshly changed except for his visor and spikes, which he had also worn when driving us to the Raritan Club at 7:40 A.M., insisting on our taking his red Saab coupe *pace* the fact that it was my own vehicle which had the 'Member' parking sticker, resulting in administrative delays in parking which caused us to miss our scheduled 'Tee time,' adding to the incompleteness of our round.

Then we were seated together, Hope's stepfather and myself, at a window-side table in the club's 19th Hole Room, picking small salty things out of the table's bowl as we waited for Jack Bogen's youngest daughter to bring the draft lagers which 'Father' (which is what Hope, together with all of her 'true' and 'step-' siblings and their respective spouses, addressed him as, though I myself had my own Father in Wilkes Barre, and, in actual practice, made a point of attempting to avoid addressing Dr. Sipe directly whenever possible) had ordered. The old septuagenarian had again made a point of referring to a draft Feigenspan lager as '[a] P.O.N.,' and I had therefore had to explain the slang term's origins to Audrey Bogen while 'Father' examined his German wrist watch and held it to one ear, expressing concern over the rainstorm's moisture damage and referring once more to the watch's retail price. Heavy, torrential rain struck the 19th Hole Room's large 'bay window' and ran down the leaded panes in lustrous sheets which overlapped complexly, and the sound on the glass and canvas awnings was much like a mechanized or 'automated' Car wash; and, with all of the fine, imported wood and dim light and scents of beverages and after shave and hair oil and fine, imported tobaccos and men's damp sports wear, the 19th Hole felt both warm and cozy and 'snug' and yet also somewhat over-confined, not unlike the lap of a dominant adult. It was approximately then that a fresh wave of disorientation and, in a manner of speaking, distorted or 'altered' sensory perception from nearly seven months of severe sleep disturbance struck once more, as it had on the Fourth fairway with such embarrassing results, the symptoms and sensations of which were nearly impossible to describe, except perhaps to say that when these periods hit they were not unlike a cerebral earthquake or 'tsunami,' an, as it were, 'neural protest' or '-revolt' against the conditions of emotional stress and chronic sleep deprivation which they had been forced to function under. At the present time, everything in the 19th Hole's respective colors seemed suddenly to brighten uncontrollably and become over-saturant, the visual environment appeared to faintly pulse or throb, and individual objects appeared, paradoxically, both to recede and become far-away and at the same time to come into an unnatural visual focus and become very, very precisely configured and lined, not unlike scenes in a Victorian oil. (Hope and her younger stepsister, Meredith, had once co-managed a Gallery together in Colts Neck.) The Raritan Club's distinctive escutcheon and motto, for instance, appeared both to recede and come into an almost excruciant focus on 'the Hole''s opposite wall, beneath a perceptually tiny stuffed tarpon whose every imbricate scale seemed outlined or limned in an almost 'Photo realist' detail. There was the more quotidian dizziness and nausea, also. I gripped the small maple table's 'burled' or beveled sides in a show of distress as 'Father' pored over the contents of the snack bowl, touching the contents of the bowl with his finger as he stirred them about. It was then at which I tried to bring up in conversation to Dr. Sipe (Sipe being my wife's original or 'maiden' name), in some kind of 'male-' or 'familial' confidence, the strange and absurdly frustrating marital conflict between Hope and myself over the issue of my so-called 'snoring.'

Whereupon: 'Do not even take up my time in mentioning this, as any man knows what an absurd and trivial issue it is compared to many other marital conflicts and problems. In other words, *"de minimis non curat,"* or, *the whole matter is, ultimately, beneath my notice'* — for such was the gist or 'thrust' of the dismissive hand gesture which Hope's stepfather made in response to my broaching of this delicate subject, making the derisive gesture which all of my wife's other siblings still associate with him from throughout their youths, and which her eldest stepbrother, Paul, a successful entrepreneur in automated, out-sourced Medical and Dental billing, can imitate so uncannily to this day when our families all get together over the Holiday season at Paul and his wife Theresa's extraordinary vacation home in Sea Girt, where the Winter surf booms against the rocks of the light-house tower which the Coast Guard closed once G.P.S. or 'satellite' navigation rendered its functions redundant, and where all of the both 'true' and 'step-' siblings and their spouses and families will gather in Norwegian sweaters with insulated thermi of hot cider on the basalt outcroppings amid gulls' pulsing cries to watch the booming surf and the distant lights of the Point Pleasant ferry moving north-ward up the Inter Coastal Waterway towards Staten Island, the vistas all iron greys and profound maroons and, privately to myself, desolate in the extreme. Consciously or otherwise, it is a hand gesture ideally designed to make its recipient feel like an otiose moron or bore, and 'Father''s feelings about myself and my place in the overall 'family dynamic' had never been what one would call well disguised. Audrey Bogen, whom our own Audrey had played closely with as small children before Jack Bogen's affairs had unraveled and their lives took such dramatically different paths, and was now already an 'unwed' mother and a career beverage waitress at the Raritan Club's 19th Hole (she was, to many of the nubile adolescents in our own Audrey's peer circle, a kind of cautionary tale, one of her children being plainly inter-racial), now appeared with our Feigenspan lagers on a small, oaken blonde-wood tray, and Hope's stepfather exercised a prerogative exclusive to men of advanced age with young women, which was to look frankly and speculatively at the young, voluptuous waitress's face, uniform and physical body as she set down the frosted steins and stated her intentions to bring us more snack mix. 'Father''s advanced age and physical senescence, in other words, making the frankness of his gaze — which, in Wilkes Barre during my own youth, was termed 'Look[ing] her over' — appear ingenuous, child-like and apparently almost 'innocent' or harmless to young women instead of salacious or lewd. This was a quality (or, as it were, lack of it) which I myself was, of course, all too conscious or aware of, since, as our own Audrey had entered the adolescence whose onset, in contemporary times' girls, seems to become earlier all the time, and had physically 'matured' or (in my wife's phrase) 'fill[ed] out,' so also, of course, had the other members of the peer group whom she 'hung' around with or brought to the house or along on seaside vacations and\or inland canoe trips in June, July or early August; and, in the case of some of the more prematurely 'mature' or voluptuous of these peers, the conflict between the natural urge or instinctual drive to look at them as would any adult, 'red-blooded' man, $v.$ the obvious social restrictions erected by my role as their friend's adoptive father, became, in some cases, so awkward or painful that I could scarcely bring myself to look at or scarcely even to acknowledge them at all, a phenomenon which our Audrey, not surprisingly, rarely even noticed, but which sometimes vexed Hope to the point that once or twice, during marital arguments, she would mock my pained confusion, and would aver that she'd prefer it — or the term she used might more aptly have been that she would 'respect' it more — if I would simply, openly ogle or leer rather than the stricken, affectedly casual avoidance which I feigned as if I expected it to fool anyone with eyes in their head as they watched my sad pantomime with pity and disgust. Because of the severe sleep disturbance, discord with Hope and trouble in my Dept. of the company for which I served as Assistant Systems Supervisor (which provided out-sourced data and document storage facilities and systems for a number of small- and mid-sized insurance providers in the Mid-Atlantic region), my chronic distress had reached the point at which sometimes I felt near tears, which, of course, in the 19th Hole with Hope's stepfather, would be an unthinkable happen-stance. Sometimes, often while driving, I feared that I was going to have an infarction. Next, in a predictable yet far more disturbing stage of the wave of disorientation, came the appearance of a strange, static, hallucinatory tableau or mental 'shot,' 'scene,' *Fata morgana* or 'vision' of a public telephone in an airport or commuter rail terminal's linear row or 'bank' of public phones, ringing. Travelers are hurrying laterally past the row of phones, some bearing or pulling 'carry on' luggage and other personal possessions, walking or hurrying past while the telephone, which remains at the center of the view of the scene or tableau, rings on and on, persistently, but is unanswered, with none of the 'bank' of phones' other phones in use and none of the air travelers or commuters acknowledging or even so much as glancing at the ringing phone, about which there is suddenly something terribly 'moving' or poignant, forlorn, melancholic or even foreboding, an endlessly ringing and unanswered public phone, all of which appears or seems to occur both endlessly and in, as it were, 'no-time,' and is accompanied by an incongruous odor of saffron.

Hope's stepfather, a career Medical executive for Prudential Insurance, Inc. — or, 'The Rock,' as it is often popularly known — as his own father before him evidently was, as well, as well as being a 'Fourth Ward' historical district native born and bred, knew Feigenspan lager by its original trademark, 'Pride of Newark' (or, 'P.O.N.'), and made rather a point of referring to it in no other way, also affecting to brush across his upper lip with a knuckle after drinking, in the way of the

city's 'working-'men, reaching then into a pocket of his vest and producing his cigar case and clip, as well as his slim, modernistic gold
lighter, a gift from his wife (and accordingly inscribed), and commencing the ritual of preparing to smoke an expensive Cohiba cigar with
his draft lager, gesturing peremptorily in the direction of the bar for an
ash-tray, at which juncture I noted once more how exceedingly thin,
sallow and, as it were, escharotic or flaky the flesh of his left wrist and
hand in the air appeared. His ears, which had always been quite large
or protrusive, were flushed from recent exertion. When asked if, upon
reflection, he thought a cigar this early in the day was perhaps such a
good idea, Dr. Sipe, who was due to turn age 76 this coming July 6th
(his birth stone was known to be 'the Ruby'), responded that the sole
indicator of his desiring my input on his personal habits would consist
in his explicitly coming to me and requesting it, at which I cleared my
throat slightly and shrugged or smiled, avoiding Audrey Bogen's dark
(our own Audrey's being grey-green or, in certain lights, 'Hazel') eyes
as she placed on the table a small bowl of very shiny nuts and an ash-
tray of clear glass on whose bottom was reproduced the Raritan Club's
escutcheon, which Dr. Sipe pulled closer and rotated slightly to satisfy
some obscure criteria in his ritual for enjoying a cigar. Twice already, I
had yawned so violently that a popping noise and sudden, as it were,
'stabbing' pain manifested just beneath my left ear. 'Father,' whose
physical health's minutiae were a topic of endless colloquy among his
different children, had apparently suffered a number of tiny, highly
localized strokes over the previous several years — or, in the language
of Health Plan underwriting, 'Transient ischemic accidents' — which
Hope's younger brother, 'Chip' (whose actual given name is Chester)
had confirmed, in the bland, almost affectless or subdued way evidently
characteristic of practicing Neurologists everywhere, were almost 'Par'
for the 'course' for a septuagenarian male of Dr. Sipe's history and condition, and were, evidently, individually of little account, producing
little more in the way of symptomology than transient dizziness or
perceptual distortion. Empirically, the evident result of this was that
'Father' was now one of the particular sort of well to do elderly (or, as
some prefer, 'Senior') men who appear well preserved and even still

somewhat distinguished from a certain distance away, but whose eyes, on closer proximity, reveal a subtle lack of focus, and whose facial expression or affect appears to be, in some subtle but unmistakable way, 'off,' resulting in a perpetual 'queer look' or mien which sometimes frightened his younger grandchildren. (This notwithstanding the fact that our own Audrey, now 19 and Dr. Sipe's second oldest grandchild, had, on the other hand, never once reported being frightened of or by her 'Greatfather [a childhood sobriquet which had stuck],' who had, in turn, addressed Audrey as — sans any detectable trace of irony or awareness — 'My little Princess,' and had, together with his wife, 'spoiled' Audrey with such lavish and excessive indulgence as to sometimes arouse tensions between Hope and this latest Mrs. Sipe, the two of whom were not [as Hope would have it] the 'closest of friends' to begin with. [By mutual and unspoken consensus, our Audrey customarily addressed Hope as 'Mother' or 'Mom' and myself as 'Randall,' 'Randy,' or, when angry or trying to make some ironic point in the perennial struggle for youthful control v. independence, as 'Mr. Napier,' 'Mr. and Mrs. Napier' or (with decided sarcasm) as 'the Dynamic Duo.']) Besides his forehead's four distracting, pre-cancerous spots, or lesions or 'keratonesis,' it was only in recent years, too, that Hope's stepfather's mouth had developed the habit of continuing to move slightly after he had ceased speaking, either as if savoring the words' taste or silently reprising them, and these movements sometimes reminded one of some type of small animal which has been struck or run over and continues to writhe wetly in the road-way, which was, to say the least, disconcerting. There is also the issue or matter of 'Father''s bowed upper back and consequent jutting head, which causes him to appear to be thrusting his face and mouth forward directly at one in an aggressive, almost predatory fashion, which is also disconcerting, which may be a matter of geriatric posture or disc compression or else the beginning of an actual 'hunch-back' or 'hump,' which he is evidently very vain and sensitive about and which no one in the 'family' is ever under any circumstances permitted to mention except his wife, who will suddenly touch or push at his jutting head impatiently and tell him, 'For God's sake, Edmund, straighten up,' in a tone which makes everyone at the table uncomfortable. Then an extremely brief and almost 'strobe'-like associative tableau in which Hope's stepfather and herself, at some past or distantly prior point in time, are seated together in an unfamiliar coupe or sports car which is speeding along a rural or markedly under-maintained inland State route in the sultry light of August or late July, and an interior scene of a somewhat younger and unescharotic 'Father,' with his iron grey hair, small, cruel mustache and thin, calf-skin gauntlets or 'driving' gloves, driving the vehicle, as well as views of the exterior vistas and divided center or median line distending and rushing past at an unnatural rate of speed, as if the vehicle were traveling far too fast for extant road conditions, and of a younger and noticeably more lissome and voluptuous Hope applying facial products in the small, inset mirror of the sun shade or visor as 'Father,' posture erect and distinguished and gazing stolidly ahead at the road, assures her that it isn't so much dislike or 'disapproval' of the fellow *per se,* while the powerful vehicle recedes up ahead in the radiant late Summer haze, the whole brief tableau or interior 'vision' or shot so rapid and incongruous that it can only be truly, as it were, 'seen' in retrospect.

According to my own pocket watch, no more than five or six minutes had passed since we had first entered the 19th Hole. The rain against the window's convex and mullioned and glass window came in what now appeared to be vascular or peristaltic 'pulses' or 'waves,' and during the brief, rhythmic lulls or troughs of these, one could make out the Eighteenth fairway's 'dog leg''s copse of trees being bent and wrung by the storm's violent winds, as well as tiny and fore-shortened golfing foursomes running hard for their carts or the Pro-shop's shelter, their shoes' spikes producing the exaggeratedly high stride of men almost running in place. Those wearing hats held them down with one hand. The 19th Hole's long, mahogany bar and tables began gradually to fill as more and more men chased in off various parts of the course by the storm came in to get warm and wait out the rain before going home to whatever was left of their families. 'Father''s hand trembled as he manipulated the clip, which supposedly required great precision. Much of the more recent entrants' conversation appeared to concern lightning and inquiring whether anyone had seen or heard lightning on the course, as well as whom among the Raritan Club's regular members might still be 'out there.' Many of the men's faces appeared unusually smooth and pinkened, their color high from the adrenaline of sudden flight. Actuarially speaking, lightning kills an average of over 300 denizens of Western industrialized nations *per annum*, more than the average number of accidental deaths due either to recreational boating or insect stings combined, and a substantial number of these electro-cutions occur on the nation's golf courses.

Since our Audrey had graduated as Salutatorian of her class and left the 'nest' of home for her freshman collegiate year at out-of-State Bryn Mawr (although she calls home faithfully once or twice a week) the previous Autumn, my wife and myself's marriage's single major conflict has now been over the fact that she now suddenly claims that I 'snore,' and that this alleged 'snoring' was preventing or depriving her of much needed sleep. I will, for instance, be lying quietly supine upon my back with my forearms and hands arranged across my chest (which is the customary way I prepare to gradually relax and fall asleep), and our bedroom upstairs will be pleasantly dark and quiet, with refracted lights from the light traffic on the quiet or 'tree muffled' residential intersection below running slowly across the bedroom walls and elon-gating, distending or collapsing interestingly at the north and east walls' angles, myself gradually relaxing and descending in peaceful increments towards a good night's sleep, until Hope suddenly cries out angrily in the darkness, claiming that my 'snoring' is making it impos-sible for her to fall asleep, and insisting that I either turn on to my side or else leave and go sleep in the 'Guest' bedroom (which is what, by unspoken agreement, Audrey's former childhood bedroom is now referred to by us as) and to 'for God's sake' grant her some 'peace.' This now occurs almost nightly — more than once on certain nights — and is intensely frustrating and upsetting. In my relaxed state, the sudden vehemence of her crying out floods my nervous system with adrena-line, cortisol or other stress related hormones, and the violence with which she thrashes up to a seated position in her bed — as well as a note of deep vexation or even hostility in her voice, as if this were an issue which had been silently aggravating her for years and she had finally come to the end of her 'rope' or 'last straw' with it — produces in myself a set of natural, physiological 'stress' responses which, subsequently, make it nearly impossible for me to fall asleep, sometimes for hours or even more.

In the past, particularly during head colds, or in some calendar years' Summer months when the 'pollen count' is high and my hay fever is active or severe (I suffer from hay fever, and as a boy, in Wilkes Barre, my sister [whose allergies were even more severe than my own, as well as suffering from congenital asthma] and myself had to be brought by our mother twice a week to the local pediatrician for allergy shots for several years), I have, admittedly, suffered occasional bouts of snoring which have disturbed or awakened Hope in the course of our marriage. But these past bouts or episodes had always been easily resolved by her gently suggesting that I roll on to my side, which I always, immediately and without objection, did, often resolving the problem without either of us even coming fully awake — the whole exchange was friendly, and so unexceptionable that Hope could often compel me to roll over without awakening me or getting either of us 'worked up' or aggravated.

Thus it was not, I had originally planned to aver either during the 'back' nine or in the 19th Hole, that I claimed, as do some husbands, never to 'snore,' nor that I am unwilling to roll to one side or the other or to take reasonable steps to accommodate Hope when something has caused me every once in a great while to rasp, cough, gurgle, wheeze or breathe in any way obstructedly in sleep. Rather, that the true, more vexing or 'paradoxical' source of the present marital conflict is that I, in reality, am not yet truly even asleep at the times my wife cries out suddenly now about my 'snoring' and disturbing her nearly every night since our Audrey's departure from home. It is very nearly always within no more than roughly an hour of our retiring (after reading in our beds for approximately one half hour, which is something of a marital 'ritual' or custom), at which time I am still lying in bed on my back with my arms arranged and my eyes either closed or relaxedly watching the walls' and ceiling's angles and distending exterior lights through the blinds, continuing to be aware of every sound but slowly relaxing and 'unwinding' and descending gradually towards falling asleep, but not yet in fact asleep. When she now cries out.

The real issue, in other words, is that it is Hope (who is well known for falling asleep the moment she has closed her current *'livre de chevet,'* replaced it on her night-stand and struck the light in the brushed steel sconce above her bed — as opposed to myself, who have been a difficult and somewhat, as it were, 'fragile' or 'delicate' sleeper from childhood onwards) who is, in point of fact, asleep at these junctures, and dreaming, said dreams evidently consisting, at least in part, of the somewhat paradoxical belief and perception that I myself am asleep and am 'snoring' loudly enough to — as she puts it — 'wake the dead.'

I do, of course, have my personal faults, as do all or most husbands; but 'snoring' during the year's cold weather months (like most, my hay fever is seasonal or, more technically, an 'Auto-immune system' response to certain classes of pollen) is not one of them. Not, of course, that it would even necessarily constitute an actual 'fault' as such, as it would not be an action which I was performing 'consciously' or had any voluntary control over. But I do not. Nor am I in the habit of being incorrect or confused about whether I myself am asleep or not — and it is an established fact in our marriage that it takes me far longer to truly fall asleep than it does Hope or my erstwhile first wife (we had joked about it together many times), as well as longer to fully awaken. Hope, in particular, moves quickly and easily between states of consciousness which, for me, are — due, perhaps, to professional stress — somewhat of a struggle. One could point to, for instance, the fact that it is nearly always myself who drives when driving any appreciable distance as a couple, or that it is frequently I who must rouse or shake her gently awake at the shore, or in front of the Home entertainment room's television, or often at the end of a long piece of music or theater.

Since the prior Autumn, however, there simply has been no reasoning with her on this point. She steadfastly avows, in other words, that my putative 'snoring' is a waking reality instead of her own dream. And in the dark of our bedroom, when she suddenly wakes and cries out in such a way that I am myself jolted up-right, with adrenaline coursing through my system (just as when the telephone rings at night, its signal or 'ring' now piercing in a way which daylight never makes it), there is in her 'snoring' complaint a note of near hysteria which makes it perfectly evident that she has been asleep, or else has been in the type of semi-waking, oneiric state in which some people '"talk" in their sleep,' confabulating past and present and truth and dream, and 'believing' it all in such a way that there is simply no reasoning with someone in such a state.

And yet I have largely refused to patronize or placate her about something which simply was not true. There are, even in marriage, limits. After an initial period last Autumn in which I would attempt to argue or reason with Hope *'in situ'* in the darkened bedroom, informing her that I was in reality not yet asleep and to simply go back to sleep and forget all about it, that she was only dreaming (a response which so irked and provoked her, however, that her voice would begin to rise sharply in such a 'tone' as to so upset me that any chance of real sleep would then be impossible for the next several hours), I then, subsequently, attempted or tried refusing to respond *'in situ'* or to in any way acknowledge her complaints that I was keeping her awake, instead waiting for the morning of the next day to remonstrate that I had not yet even been asleep, and to mildly observe that her agitated dreams of my 'snoring' were becoming worse and more frequent, and to urge her to make some sort of appointment and perhaps inquire about a prescription. And yet Hope has been wholly obdurate and unyielding on this point, insisting that it was I who was 'the one who's asleep,' and that if I could or would not acknowledge this, my refusal to 'trust' her indicated that I must be 'angry at [her]' over something, or perhaps unconsciously wished to 'hurt' her, and that if anyone around here needed to 'make an appointment' it was myself, which according to Hope I would not hesitate to do if my respect and concern for her even slightly outweighed my own selfish insistence on being 'right.' Worse, on certain mornings, was when she, as it were, 'took a page' from her 'true' or biological sibling, Vivian (a twice divorced 'halogen' blonde and devotee of numerous so-called 'Support' or 'self help' groups and movements, to whom Hope was extremely close be-fore their 'falling out')'s lexicon and accused me of being 'in denial,' an accusation any denial of which was held, of course, to be evidence in its own favor, maddeningly. Once or twice, however, in the early Winter months, I admittedly yielded and did, with a frustrated groan or sigh, take my own bed's bedding down the hall to the 'Guest' bedroom and attempt to 'drop off' or sleep there amidst all of the frilled pastels, saf-fron joss and boxed detritus of our Audrey's recent adolescence, lying perfectly still and motionless and scarcely breathing, and straining to hear, down the hall, any sounds of Hope perhaps once again sitting up-right and accusing a now empty or unoccupied bed of 'snoring' and 'keeping [her] awake' — which would be indisputable proof of just who was asleep and who merely the innocent subject of someone else's dream of being kept awake. Lying there alone, I envisioned something like myself hearing the vexed cries and complaints and arising in-stantly to quickly traverse the hallway, bursting through our bedroom door with something resembling a triumphant *'Aha!'* — so filled with frustrated and aggrieved hormones, however, and devoting so much effort and close concentration to vigilantly listening for any sound or movement from our bedroom, that I got scarcely one iota or 'wink' of sleep the entire night in Audrey's former bed, and yet had, neverthe-less, to still arise and go forth to attempt to stagger through my pro-fessional responsibilities at work and both sides of the lengthy commute the following day with my entire body, mind and psyche on the edge of what felt to be nearly complete collapse. It was, I was, of course, aware, perhaps petty to be so fixated on vindication or 'proof,' but, by this point of the conflict, I was often nearly 'not' or 'beside' myself with frustration, choler or anger and fatigue. One must understand (as it was my original intention to attempt to explain to her stepfather) that though, as in any marriage, Hope and I had had our fair share of conflicts and difficult marital periods, the evident vehemence, anger and persecution with which she now dismissed my protests of being awake at the crucial junctures of alleged 'snoring' were unprecedented, and, for the first several weeks of the dreams and accusations, I was concerned primarily for Hope herself, and feared that she was having a more difficult time of it adjusting to our Audrey's 'leav[ing] the nest' than it had at first appeared (*pace* that it had been Hope, even more than Audrey herself, who had insisted or 'lobbied' for an out-of-State college, the relatively nearby Bryn Mawr and Sarah Lawrence Colleges having been Audrey and myself's tacitly agreed upon choices as a compromise or [in the language of insurance regulation] 'Technical compliance' with this priority), and that this difficulty or grief was manifesting itself as sleep disruptions and unconscious or misdirected anger or 'blame' at myself. (Audrey is Hope's child by her first, short lived marriage, but was no more than a toddler when Naomi and myself's own divorce was declared 'Final, *a mensa et thoro*' and Hope and myself were free to marry, which occurred sixteen years ago this coming August 9th. For all practical purposes, she is, essentially, 'my' daughter as well, and I too found her physical absence and the house's strange new silence and schedules and the gamut of readjustments difficult, as well, as I tried to repeatedly reassure Hope.) After some further time had passed, however, and all attempts to discuss the conflict rationally or induce Hope to consider even the mere possibility that it was she, not myself, who was in reality asleep when the alleged 'snoring' problem manifested itself led only to a further entrenchment or 'hardening' in her own position — the essence of her position being that I myself was being irrationally 'stubborn' and 'untrusting' of what she could plainly hear with her own two ears — I essentially ceased, then, to say or do anything in the way of '*in situ*' response or objection when she would suddenly sit violently up in bed across the room (her face often inhuman and spectral in the bedroom's faint light because of the white emollient cream she wore to bed during the cold, dry months of the year, and distorted unpleasantly by vexation and choler) to accuse me of 'snoring horribly' and demanding that I roll over at once or be exiled again to Audrey's former bed. Instead, I would now lie perfectly still, silent and motionless, my eyes closed, pantomiming a deeply sleeping man who could not hear or in any way acknowledge her, until eventually her pleas and vituperations trailed drowsily off and she would settle back with a deep and pointed sigh. Then I would continue to lie supine and motionless in my pale blue flannel or acetate sleep wear, still and silent as a 'tomb,' waiting silently for Hope's breathing to change and for the slight, small chewing or grinding sounds she produced in sleep to indicate that she had once more fallen back to sleep. Even then, however, sometimes she now once again bolts awake only moments later, once again sitting up to accuse me of 'snoring' and angrily demanding that I do something to halt or impede it so that she might finally have some 'peace' and be able to sleep.

By this point in time, the Spring thunderstorm's downpour had receded or ebbed to the point that individual droplets' impacts' sounds were individually countable against the striped canvas awnings of the 19th Hole's large bay windows — meaning being discretely audible, but in sum arrhythmic and not what one would term pleasant or soothing; the larger drops sounded almost eerie or, as it were, almost 'brutal' in their impact's force. Inside, Hope's father was leaning back and slightly to the side in his heavy 'captain's' chair, running the fine cigar over his upper lip in order to savor the aroma as he searched in a side pocket (this is what is making him lean; it is not a distortion) for his clip's special monogrammed case. Without informing Hope (an omission which was, I confess, petty, and that I was in all likelihood unwilling, by that point in the conflict, to give her the 'satisfaction' of it), I, during my annual Physical exam, requested a referral from our P.P.O.'s Health Plan's 'Primary care' physician to one of the Plan's designated 'Ear, Nose and Throat' specialists, who then subsequently examined my nasal passages, sinus cavities, trachea, adenoids and 'soft' palate, and pronounced that he saw no evidence of anything unusual or out of the ordinary. I later, however, made the mistake of 'throwing' this clean bill of health 'up' in Hope's 'face' during one of the increasingly heated and upsetting arguments (these often occurring over the following morning's breakfast) respecting the so-called 'snoring' issue, whereupon Hope seized on my failure to have told her about the 'E., N. & T.' referral as evidence that I '. . . kn[e]w the snoring [was] real,' and was secretly concerned about it, and that I had been unwilling to tell her about the appointment in advance for fear that the specialist's diagnosis would identify something amiss in my 'soft' palate or nasal passages and that I would have to admit openly to her that the

'snoring [was] real' and that all of my accusations that she was asleep
and simply dreaming that I was snoring had been merely so much self
serving 'denial' and 'projection' of the problem on to the 'victim' of
it (referring to, of course, herself). These brief, bitter arguments —
which came in waves or clusters throughout the Winter- and early
Spring months, and most often tended to occur or 'erupt' at breakfast,
fueled by a sleepless night and anxiety about facing the demands of the
coming day on insufficient sleep, and were often so bitter and upsetting that I would then go through the subsequent commute and the
first several hours of work in some type of emotional daze, mentally
're-playing' the argument and conceiving of new ways to present or
arrange evidence or catch Hope in a logical contradiction, sometimes
going so far as to interrupt work in order to jot these ideas or cutting
rejoinders down in the margins of my professional Day-planner for
possible future use — were terrifying in their sudden heat and the
speed with which they escalated in intensity and 'spleen,' as well as
in the way Hope's dry, dark, narrow, increasingly haggard face across
the breakfast nook sometimes becomes nearly unrecognizable to me,
twisted, distorted and even somewhat repellent in its anger and stony
suspicion; and, for my part, I must confess that, at least once or twice,
I had felt an actual urge to strike or shove her or up-end the nook's
breakfast hutch or table with rage, so 'beside myself' with irrational
rage had I been 'driven' by the strange, stony, bitter and irrational ob-
durance with which she would flatly refuse to consider — to acknowledge even the bare possibility, despite all of the reasonable rebuttals,
rejoinders, reasoned arguments, evidence, facts not in dispute and cita-
tions of precedent (there had, in the course of our marriage, been other
conflicts in which Hope had been utterly convinced of the validity
of her position, but had had to acquiesce in the face of subsequent
proof that she had, in point of fact, been wrong, and had then had to
apologize) which I advanced — that it was I who was awake and she
who was — 'just possibly' — asleep, and that the 'snoring' issue was in
point of fact in reality '[her] issue' and was in fact capable of real resolution only by her 'making [some kind of Medical, or even psychiatric]
appointment.' My hands sometimes literally trembled or shook with

frustration and fatigue related disorientation as I started my vehicle, with a series of rapid, indistinct and unwelcome 'images' or hallucinatory distortions often also moving in rapid, arrhythmic succession across my 'mind's eye' as I undertook my commute north up the Garden State Parkway. (In one of the most heated and upsetting of these arguments, I had only brought up the Ear, Nose and Throat examination as evidence that at least I, unlike Hope, was willing to entertain at least the possibility that I was somehow wrong and might in reality be somehow truly 'snoring,' and thus that any workable compromise or resolution was going to be impossible unless there was at least some slight mutuality about our willingness to concede, *pace* the information of our senses, at least the 'theoretical possibility' that we might be wrong about just who was asleep and dreaming and\or 'snoring' and who was not.)

Also, by this point in time, our routine (or, 'ritual') for preparing to retire and go to sleep in the bedroom had also often become almost indescribably tense and unpleasant. Hope often would not acknowledge or speak to me, and when, from my side of the room, I 'caught her eye' as she was emerging from her clothes closet or the washroom or applying emollient at her beige enamel 'Vanity' ensemble's lighted mirrors, her expression was often that of someone regarding a distasteful stranger. (Hope's stepfather and stepsisters, Meredith and Denise [or, more familiarily, 'Donni'], are also accomplished at this expression, as I first noted upon my first or initial introduction to her family, which occurred at a dinner at Dr. Sipe and his wife's large, Victorian style home in the historical 'Fourth Ward' district of West Newark, in the course of which, at two different points, 'Father' asked me some type of personal or biographical question and then, in the midst of my attempt to reply, interrupted in order to publicly indicate that he was becoming impatient or wished that I would 'Cut to the chase' in a blunter or apparently more time efficient way.) Often, by the time the bedroom's lights are now extinguished, I will have become so overwrought and tense that any likely prospect of falling asleep in the near future vanished altogether, despite the fact that I was often now so exhausted as to literally tremble and my vision, as mentioned, regularly went in and out of different states of exaggerated focus, depth and abstract flux or *'retroussage'* — for instance, the way Audrey Bogen's once fresh, voluptuous and innocent face seemed to tremble or shudder on the edge of exploding into abstract shards when she brought Dr. Sipe's ash-tray, which was formed of heavy, black glass and emblazoned with the Raritan Club's heraldic crest and Latin motto — **'Resurgam!'** — in virid red.

As well, of course, as the fact that the absurd ephemeracy, triviality and obvious displacement or projection of the whole 'snoring' conflict — of which, between Hope and myself, only I seemed truly aware or frustrated at the absurdity and irrelevance of the whole conflict — made it that much worse. I myself simply could not believe that Hope and myself's relationship at this crucial, 'Empty nest' point in our marriage could founder on such a trivial issue, one which, even in far less happy or viable unions than our own, must, for the most part, be resolved or 'worked through' rather early on. Like conflicts concerning, for instance, partners' differing communicative 'styles,' amounts of time spent together as opposed to physically apart, division of responsibilities for household tasks and so forth, mutual compatibility of sleeping 'styles' and arrangements is simply part of the domestic compromise of living with a spouse, as, of course, almost every man of any worldly experience knows. I could not, for several weeks or even months, even bring myself to raise the issue of the conflict with personal friends or family. It simply seemed too silly to credit. I even went so far as to try consulting or 'seeing' a professional Couple counselor — again, an action undertaken on my own and, as it were, *'sub-rosa,'* as I knew quite well Hope's, her stepfather's, and the bulk of her true and adoptive family's (with the exception of Vivian, whose allegedly 'Recovered' memories and hysterical public accusations at the extended family's Holiday get-together at Paul and Theresa's extraordinary vacation home off the Manasquan inlet had led to herself and Hope's 'falling out' and to the entire extended family's unspoken prohibition of any mention of the entire subject, besides which were

Dr. Sipe's own sentiments respecting the issue of 'therapy''s eligibility as a Medical expense for the purposes of Health Care plans and 'Managed Care,' which were well known and vociferous) feelings *vis à vis* the 'therapy' issue, and knew also, by that point, that Hope's flat, tight-mouthed refusal, were I to broach the issue, even to consider 'seeing' the counselor with me as a 'couple' would frustrate and aggravate me all over again, and simply escalate or further the scope of the marital conflict — only, there-upon, to my considerable chagrin, to repeatedly have, suffer or endure a series of 'therapeutic' exchanges such as, in substance, the following:

'But snoring is not really the issue, Randall, is it?'

'But I never for one moment suggested that it was the real issue.'

'After all, hay fever or no, lots of men snore.'

'And were I one of them [meaning someone who 'snored' even during seasons when hay fever was not a factor], I would submit [meaning to Hope's accusations] without hesitation.'

'Why is it so important to you whether you snore or not?'

'The whole point is that it is not important to me. That is my entire point. If I were, in point of actual fact, "snoring," I'd have no trouble admitting it, assuming responsibility and taking any reasonable steps necessary in order to address the alleged problem.'

'I'm afraid I still don't understand. How can you even know for certain whether you snore or not? If you are snoring, then by definition you're asleep.'

'But [attempting to respond] . . .'

'I mean, who can know?'

'But [becoming more and more frustrated by this point in time] that's the whole point, which I have tried here to explain I don't even know how many times already: it is precisely when I am *not* in fact yet even asleep that she accuses me.'

'Why are you getting so upset? Do you have some special stake in the issue of whether you snore?'

'If I am, as you put it, getting "upset," it is perhaps because I am somewhat irked, impatient or frustrated with these types of exchanges.

The whole point is that I emphatically do not have a stake in the so-called "snoring" issue. The point is that if I were in fact "snoring," I would admit it and simply roll over on to my side or even offer to go sleep in Audrey's bed and not think twice about the issue beyond a certain natural regret that I had in any way disturbed or "compromised" Hope's rest. But I do, however, know that one must be asleep to "snore," and that I know when I am truly asleep and when I am not, and that what I do have a "stake" in is refusing to placate someone who is being not just irrational but blindly stubborn and obtuse in accusing me of something which I must be asleep in order to be guilty of when in fact I am not yet asleep, due largely to how tense and exhausted I am from the whole absurd conflict in the first place.'

The P.P.O.'s counselor, who appeared to be in, at most, his mid- or late 30s, and wore spectacles, had a large forehead which was domed in such a way as to suggest deep thoughtfulness, an appearance which was, it increasingly emerged, misleading.

'And is there no chance — just for the sake, Randall, of argument — no chance or possibility, however remote, that you yourself might be being, as you put it, in any way stubborn or blind about this conflict in you and Mrs. Napier's relationship?'

'Now I must confess to becoming frustrated or even, if I might say so, somewhat annoyed or exasperated, as the whole point, the entire root of the unfairness and my frustration or even anger with Hope, is that I myself *am* willing to examine this possibility. That it is myself who am here, examining it, as you can plainly see. Do you see my wife here? Is she willing to come "lay [the problem] out" and look at it with a disinterested party?'

'And can I ask why the thing with the fingers?'

'But no, Ed [the P.P.O.'s counselor all but insisting on being addressed by his first name], if I may, the fact is that Hope is even now returning home from Exercise class or the cosmetician and is very probably in the tub stewing privately over the conflict and fortifying her position and preparing for another endless round of the conflict whenever she next dreams that I am keeping her awake and robbing her of her youth, vivacity and daughterly charms, while at the same moment I myself sit here in an unventilated office being asked whether I might be "blind."'

'So, if I am hearing you accurately, the real issue is fairness. Your wife is not being fair.'

'The real issue is that it's bizarre, surreal, an almost literal "waking nightmare." My wife is now no one I know. She's claiming to know better than I myself whether I'm even awake. It's less unfair than seemingly almost totally insane. I know whether I'm sitting here having these exchanges. I know I am not dreaming this. To doubt this is insane. But this, to all appearances, is what she's doing.'

'Mrs. Napier might deny that you are really even here right now, you feel.'

'That isn't the point. The issue of my actually being here or not is merely an analogy intended to high-light the fact of my knowing whether or not I am asleep, just as you do. To doubt this would be the road to insanity, would it not? Might we agree on that much?'

'Randall, here let me reassure you once again that I am not in any way disagreeing with you, but simply trying to make certain I understand this. When you are asleep, can you really actually *know* that you are asleep?' . . . And so on and so forth. My hands often ached from gripping the vehicle's steering wheel as I then resumed or continued the commute home along the Garden State Parkway from the Couple counselor's office in a small collection (or, 'complex') of Medical and Dental buildings in suburban Red Bank. More generally, I began often to worry or fear that I would succumb to sleep deprivation or fatigue and might fall asleep at the wheel and drift across or 'jump' the median into on-coming traffic, as I had all too often seen the tragic aftermath of in my many years of commuting.

Then, while seated with Dr. Sipe at the table in what Raritan Club members often refer to as simply '19' or 'the Hole,' another unwilled or involuntary interior tableau or, as it were, hallucinatory 'shot' or scene of myself standing, as a boy or small child, on a precarious or slanted surface at the foot of something resembling a ladder or rope ladder or rope, looking upward in child-like fear, the stairway, ladder or rope trailing down from some point in the gloom above, beyond or atop the great, stone icon or statue or 'bust' of someone too massively huge and ill lit for the face to be seen overhead (or, 'made out'), I myself standing precariously on a rise in the statue's great granite lap with one or both hands clutching or grasping the end of the rope, peering up, as well as with someone far larger behind me's hand heavy upon my shoulder and back and a dominant or 'booming' voice from the darkness of the great stone head overhead repeatedly commanding *'Up,'* and the hand pushing or shaking and saying *'For God . . .'* and \or *'. . . Hope'* several times. 'Father' — whose area of professional expertise at The Prudential is (or, rather, was) something called 'Demographic Medicine,' which involved his evidently not ever once, during his entire career, physically touching a patient — had always regarded me as a bit of a bore and \or ninny, someone at once obtrusive and irrelevant, the human equivalent of a house fly or pinched nerve, and has made precious little effort to disguise this, although as a 'Greatfather' he has always been exceptionally doting and kind to our Audrey, which with Hope and myself goes a long way. When he concentrates on the clipped end to get it alight, he appears briefly strabismic or 'cross eyed,' and the hand holding the lighter shakes badly, and in that instant he appears every bit his age or more. The excised tip was nowhere in view. The whole room seemed somehow menacingly coiled. He and I both looked at the red end as he held the silver Ronson to it and drew and exhaled, trying to light it in a durable way. His wrists and hands were yellowish and somewhat freckled, not unlike a corn- or 'tortilla'-chip, and the size of the flame and Cohiba made his very dry, narrow, furrowed, hunched and outthrust face appear smaller and more distant than in reality it was; and this effect was not a visual distortion or hallucination but a common and simple 'Illusion of perspective,' not unlike a Renaissance horizon. The true flame was the one in the middle. Feigenspan's slight tannic bitterness being also traditional. (The following, as well, being also typical of the exchanges with the second Couple counselor in his sterile, generic office in suburban Red Bank:

'And it is not possible that some of these hallucinations you feel as though you are experiencing might be auditory? That you are sometimes rasping or snoring and do not realize it because you are, as you put it, hallucinating?'

'But I know when I am hallucinating. The photograph of your wife and daughter or perhaps conceivably stepdaughter or niece here on your desk — the daughter's face is beginning ever so slightly to whirl and distend. That is a hallucination. I mean "hallucination" in the very broadest sense. These are not hallucinations which mimic reality or can be confused with it. Sometimes, for instance, trying to shave in the mirror, my visage will appear to have an extra eye in the center of my forehead, whose pupil is sometimes rotated or "set" on its "side" like a cat or nocturnal predator's, or occasionally our Audrey's chest on Parents' Weekend at Bryn Mawr's two breasts will go up and down in her sweater like pistons and her head is surrounded by a halo or, as it were, "nimbus" of animated Disney characters. When these hallucinations occur, I am able to say to myself, "Randall, you are hallucinating slightly due to chronic sleep deprivation compounded by discord and chronic stress."'

'But they must still be frightening. I know they would certainly frighten me.'

'The point is that I know when I'm hallucinating and when I'm not, just as I also quite obviously know when I'm asleep or not.') At which juncture an additional momentary, hallucinatory 'flash' or vision of our Audrey supine in a beached canoe and myself straining piston-like above her, my face whirling and beginning to distend as the tableau or *Fata morgana* shifts almost immediately back to the present day's 19th Hole or 'the Hole,' with our Audrey — now 19 and burgeoned into full woman-hood or the 'Age of consent' — in her familiar saffron bustier, 'Capri' style pants and white, elbow length gloves now moving smoothly or languidly among the tables, stools and chairs, languidly serving high-balls to wet men. Nor should one omit to add that Jack Vivien was now there, as well, at the window-side table in the 19th Hole with myself and Dr. Sipe, also with a beverage and seated on 'Father''s right or 'off' side. Jack Vivien wore none of the customary golfer's jacket or visor, as well as appearing dry, unhurried and, as always, collected or unflustered, although he nevertheless still wore his spikes or

'Golf shoes' (the traditional shoe's sole's 0.5 inch steel or iron spikes being the culprit or component which conducts electricity with such 'hair raising' efficacy. The public course's resident 'Pro' in Wilkes Barre, in my boyhood, for instance, was once struck and killed instantly by lightning, and my own Father had been in the trio of other golfers who had bravely remained in the open with the stricken lightning victim until a physician could be summoned and arrive, the 'Pro' lying prone and blackened and still holding the Twelfth hole's flag [whose pole, or 'pin,' like traditional golfers' spikes, was, in that era, still comprised of conductive metal] in his smoking fist.), and here the logistics of his entrance or 'logic' of the 'coincidence' which brought him, dry and, as it were, 'bright eyed' (Jack Vivien having bright or 'expressive' eyes in a markedly large, broad, if somewhat flat or immobile or 'expressionless' [with the exception of the animated, 'thoughtful' eyes] face, as well as a sharp, dark 'Van Dyke' style beard which served to compensate or de-emphasize the somewhat unusual qualities of his mouth's size and position), to our table in 'the Hole' at this precise point in time is somewhat unclear and, in retrospect, contrived or, as it were, 'suspicious.' It is, for example, unlikely that Jack Vivien and Hope's stepfather knew one another, as not only was 'Father' not a member of the Raritan Club and had played as a 'Guest' only once or twice prior to this time, but in reality Jack (or, more formally, 'Chester') Vivien served as a high ranking Employee Assistance executive at my own company (whose physical plant, or, 'Nerve center' was located in Elizabeth), a company which 'Father' had made rather a point, numerous times, of implying or characterizing as so ephemeral or unimportant to the region's insurance industry as to have caused him never once to have encountered or 'heard one word about' it throughout his entire tenure at 'The Rock.' Nor did Hope's stepfather appear to speak to, look at or in any way to acknowledge the presence of Jack Vivien (whom, through his role in the recent 'snoring' issue's attempted resolution, I had gotten acquainted with rather well) as he got the thing finally alight and leaned back at a slight smoker's angle in his 'captain's' chair, smoking slowly and joining Jack Vivien (whose circumoral balbo or 'Van Dyke' was, admittedly, frankly and incongruously 'merkin-esque' or pudendal in appearance, I myself being far from the only person in Systems to remark this) in looking appraisingly at me as I covered first one eye and then the other (a well known 'home-remedy' for common optical illusions). It was clearly evident that 'Father' did not 'approve of' or like what he currently saw: an, as it were, 'second string' son-in-law with a mediocre Handicap and background in addition to a trivial or undistinguished career, one whose personal affairs were in disarray and appeared potentially 'on the rocks' over a conflict this trivial and absurd with a wife who was, herself, clearly merely suffering from either the 'Empty nest' syndrome, early symptoms of the climacteric or mere incubi or bad dreams (more clinically known as 'Night terrors'), and yet could not manage to be assertive, assuasive or 'man' enough to convince her that these natural and *de minimis* causes were at their so-called 'impasse"s core, and who now seemed all too obviously to be working up the courage or 'nerve' to ask 'Father' himself to use his paternal influence or authority over Hope (*pace* that he was, of course, when convenient, merely or 'just' her step-father, and in his pale eyes was what sometimes looked or appeared to be the terrible stepfatherly knowledge of what our Audrey could have been to me, perhaps as Hope — as well as Vivian [as she had 'hysterically' claimed to have later been professionally helped to 'Recover' unconscious memories of] — had once served as or been to himself; and it was not at all difficult to conceive almost at will a low angle image or vision or nightmarish 'shot' of his prone face just above, engorged and straining, one well freckled right hand clamped tight over Hope or Vivian [the two of whom appear almost 'interchangeably' alike in childhood photos] beneath him's open mouth, and his crushing weight thoroughly and terribly adult) to intercede in the conflict, though it was neither the old man's 'place' nor remote intention to do so, as anyone with any discernment or 'eyes with which to see' should be capable of seeing.

More specifically, it had been Chester A. (or, 'Jack') Vivien — age: 'Mid 50s,' Handicap: '11,' marital status: 'Unknown,' and the Director of Employee Assistance Programs for Advanced Data Capture (our company's legal name)'s Elizabeth operations — to whose coveted,

corner office I'd finally gone with my 'hat in hand' in order to confide
the entire absurd, seemingly quotidian or banal, conjugal 'snoring' impasse, and its escalating impact on my marriage, health and ability to
function productively in my Dept. within Systems. This had been the
prior March. Though his *résumé* included an 'advanced' or Graduate
degree in the field of industrial psychology from Cornell University
(which is located in northern or 'up-State' New York), Jack Vivien was
no mere counselor or 'front line' staff for Advanced Data Capture's
'E.A.P.' (as it is often known) program, but rather had been deliberately hired away from Weyerhauser Paper, Inc.'s Brunswick operation
several years prior in order to specifically manage and oversee the entire 'E.A.P.' program, and now served also as 'Administrative liaison'
for the company's P.P.O. Group Health Plan program, which evidently required considerable managerial and accounting expertise, as
well. Jack Vivien and I had always gotten 'on' and enjoyed a mutual
regard. We were frequently (when his chronic lower back condition
permitted) in the same flight at company tournaments during warm
weather months, and sometimes enjoyed light conversation together
in the cart on Par 4s and\or 5s while waiting for other members of our
foursome to locate an errant ball or 'hole out' on the hole's green. More
importantly, it was Jack Vivien who, in late March, had subsequently
suggested or 'Throw[n] out [the] idea [of]' the reportedly highly respected Edmund R. and Meredith R. Darling Memorial Sleep Clinic,
which, he said, was affiliated or ensconced within the teaching hospital affiliated with Rutgers University in 'in-State' Brunswick, as a
possible option. It had also been Jack — as opposed to either of the
supposedly 'expert,' professional Couple counselors I had gone to
some lengths to consult or 'see,' in desperation, some months prior —
who had made an almost immediate 'impression' by quickly 'Cut[ting]
to the chase' and inquiring — somewhat 'leadingly' or 'rhetorically,'
but without condescension or a sense of being patronized — whether
I myself, on balance, would prefer to prevail or 'win' in the conflict and
be vindicated as 'innocent' or 'right,' on one hand, or would rather instead have Hope and myself's marriage back on track and to once
more derive pleasure in one another's company and affections and to

resume its being possible to get enough uninterrupted sleep at night to be able to function effectively and feel more like '[my]self again.'

The specific proposal, respecting which Hope agreed to at least 'hear [me] out' on a morning of low skies and light mist which made the small, decorative, 'bay window''s light in our breakfast nook appear shadowless and unreal and appeared to exaggerate the haggardness of our exhausted faces, was as follows: that if Hope would consent to attend Rutgers' Edmund R. and Meredith R. Darling Sleep Clinic with me and place ourselves in the trained and respected Clinic's Sleep researchers' experienced hands, then, if the results of the Sleep Clinic's study of our sleep patterns served, in any substantive way, form or manner to confirm her perceptions and beliefs in the dispute over my 'snoring,' then I myself would move immediately back into our Audrey's former *agapemone* or 'Guest' room down the hall and consent to follow the Medical staff's recommendations about treating my then presumably bona fide 'snoring.' (It is true, as a child, that I myself had evidently sucked or 'nursed at' my own thumb while asleep for such an extended period of time during my childhood that our family's pediatrician in Wilkes Barre had finally directed my parents to coat or paint the nail of my thumb with an aversive tasting prescription lacquer or, as it were, 'nail' polish each night before retiring — at least, such was my Father's stated recollection of anything unusual or out of the ordinary in my childhood sleep habits. [The Darling Sleep Clinic staff had required Hope and myself to fill out exhaustive, preliminary or 'Intake' reports on our present and past sleep patterns, including data as far back as possible, including, if possible, childhood.])

On his own, 'personal' time, over the course of several appointments and interchanges in his comfortably appointed 'E.A.P.' program office, Jack Vivien, despite his own ponderous work load, had helped me to prepare carefully for the presentation of this 'last ditch' proposal, during which I made certain to keep my facial expression and vocal tone non-accusatory and neutral other than a certain level of undisguised exhaustion (the previous night had been a particularly difficult or 'bad' one, with numerous awakenings and accusations). The suggestion of last ditch exhaustion or 'giving up' in the way I presented it in the

breakfast nook, which, no doubt (as Jack Vivien predicted), made the
proposal more impactful, was, in most respects, sincere or 'heart-felt,'
although not, obviously, in the way Hope (who, too, appeared to have
aged several whole years over the preceding Winter along with myself
[though I would never have given voice to this observation aloud —
be 'Father''s opinions on our marriage as they may, I do know enough
about the dynamics of a solid marriage to discern the difference between honesty and mere brutality, and that tact and circumspection
play as large a part in an intimate relation as candor and 'soul baring,'
if not more], and who often complained that chronic lack of sleep [al-
though she often was asleep; what she was, in reality, actually feeling
the effects and complaining of were traumatic dreams or 'Night terrors,' though I, of course, once again kept my own counsel on these
matters] produced a distracting 'sound' [or, rather, a mild aural hallucination — I literally bit my tongue in restraint when she discussed
this putative 'sound'] which mimicked the tone of a 'Tuning fork' or
well rung bell) appeared to believe, her face, over the table's center-
piece, grapefruit and dry toast, flirting at times with vortical abstraction and pulses of virid color but managing to retain or 'hang on' to its
visual or optical integrity or cohesion in the drained grey morning
light in a way which seemed almost stubborn. Small framed and sharp
featured, with a swart or tanned complexion and high-lighted hair in
a tall 'Bouffante' which stood aloof and unchanging above the shifting
tides of coiffure fashion, Hope's strong will and refusal to be anyone
other than 'who' and 'what' she was had been one of the original
attractions between her and myself; and at this point, even during
my exhausted presentation of the 'last resort' of the Edmund R. and
Meredith R. Darling Sleep Clinic, I can even now remember remem-
bering that I had never forgotten this, or been unmoved by her 'inner
fire,' or ceased to (in my 'way') 'love' and find her desirable despite the
fact that, even prior to the enervating dissolution of the present conflict, the intervening recent years had not been, as the saying goes,
'kind' with respect to Hope's gynecic or womanly charms or appeal, although, in her own case, the spoliations of time have not resulted in
the swelling, puddling, thickening or bloated effects of the aging

process in both her stepsisters and (to a somewhat lesser extent) myself. Once voluptuous to the point of being nearly 'Ruben-esque,' Hope's own aging or anility's type has established itself as being primarily one now consisting of 'weazening' or desiccation, her skin toughening and becoming in places leathery in appearance, her dark tan permanent and her teeth, neck's tendons and extremities' joints appearing protrusive in a way they once never did. In brief, her over-all mien has taken on a lupine or predatory aspect, and what was once her eyes' well known 'twinkle' has become a mere avidity. (None of this is, of course, in any way surprising or 'unnatural' — air and time have simply done to my wife what they also 'do' to bread and hung laundry. Indeed, we must all come to terms with our own actuarial plight, so to speak, of which the 'Empty nest' is such a vivid mile post along the way of.) The natural but nevertheless terrible reality — albeit unspoken of in any viable union, over time — is that, by this point in our marriage, Hope was already *de facto* or practically speaking unsexed, an, as the saying goes withered vine or bloom, and this somehow all the worse or 'more so' for all of her scrupulous devotion to self care and youthful *desiderata,* just as so many of her own other bloated or desiccant circle of friends and Book and Horticulture clubs' middle aged wives and divorcées who habitually congregate together around the Raritan Club's pool throughout the Summer season are obsessed by, as well: the Exercise classes and caloric regimes, emollients and toners, Yoga, supplements, tanning or (albeit rarely mentioned) Surgical 'work' or procedures — all the willful clinging to the same nubile or *'virgo intacta'* vivacity which their own daughters unknowingly serve to mock as they latterly blossom. (In fact, *pace* her natural verve and *'esprit fort,'* it was often all too easy a matter to remark the pain in Hope's eyes and her mouth's crimped or 'pinched' set when watching or within the purview of our Audrey's later, increasingly mature and comely peer circle, an anile grief so easily then transferred or 'projected' as anger onto myself for merely owning eyes with which to see and be naturally affected by.) One is, in fact, hard pressed to regard it as coincidental that all of these blossoming girls and daughters were, almost without exception, all dispatched to 'out-of-State' colleges, as with each passing year the mere physical sight of them became for their mothers a living rebuke.

The actual 'beds' for the sleep patients and their cases' accrued data at the Darling Sleep Clinic were directly side by side, but were also markedly narrow, and possessed of thin, extremely firmly reinforced mattresses, as well as only one sheet and 'medium weight' acrylic blanket despite the sterile chill of the Sleep chamber. The diagnostic regimen — which took no little time and negotiations with our P.P.O. to secure coverage or 'authorization' concerning which — consisted of Hope and myself's making the slightly over 90 mile (with myself, as usual, at the wheel while Hope dozed with her Travel pillow against the passenger side door) drive, via 'I'-195 and State routes 9 and 18, one Wednesday evening per week, to Rutgers-Brunswick Memorial Hospital, and there 'checking in' at the institution's Fourth floor's Neurology\Somnology Dept., which contained the Edmund R. and Meredith R. Darling Memorial Sleep Clinic, whose reputation in the industry truly was, according to both Jack Vivien and other sources, 'top-flight.' The Sleep specialist (or, 'Somnologist') in charge of our case, a large, mild mannered, burly, heavily set fellow with a lead colored crew cut and what appeared to be an extraordinary number of keys on a promotional 'Parke Davis, Inc.' key ring — his manner pleasant in the neutral, subdued and punctilious way of morticians and certain types of Horticulture lecturers — appeared also to have what Hope later remarked was little or no discernible neck or throat *per se*, his head appearing to sit or, as it were, 'rest' directly upon his shoulders, which I pointed out may have only been an illusion or effect caused by the high collar of the Somnologist's white Medical or 'lab' coat, which most of the other Darling Memorial Sleep Clinic's staff on duty wore, as well, with laminated and 'photo-' Identification cards clipped (or, in A.D.C.'s Systems Dept.'s more familiar argot or parlance, 'gator clipped') to the breast pocket. Select members of the Somnologist's technical staff (or, 'Sleep team') conducted our formal 'Intake interview,' with the M.D. himself then acting as docent or guide in briefly showing Hope and myself around the Darling Sleep Clinic facility, which appeared to consist of four or more small, self contained 'Sleep chambers' which were surrounded on all sides by soundless, clear, thick or 'Plexi-'glass walls, sophisticated audio- and video recording devices, and neurological monitoring equipment. Dr. Paphian's office itself was adjoined to the Clinic's centrally located 'Nerve-' or 'Command center,' in which professional Somnologists, Neurologists, aides, technicians and attendants could observe the occupants of the different Sleep chambers on a wide variety of 'Infrared' monitors and 'brain' wave measurement and display equipment. Every staff and 'Sleep team' member also wore white, noiseless shoes with gum or rubber soles, and the insubstantial blankets on each chamber's bed were also either spotlessly white or else pastel or 'sky-' (or, 'electric-') blue. Also, the Darling Sleep Clinic's system of 'halogen' based, track- or cove style, overhead lighting was white and completely shadowless (which is to say, no one in the facility appeared to cast any shadow, which, together with the funereal quiet, Hope felt, she said, lent a somewhat 'dreamy' or dream-like aspect to the atmosphere of the place) and made everyone appear sallow or ill, as well as its being markedly chilly in the Sleep chamber. The Somnologist explained that relatively cool temperatures conduced to both human sleep and to the complex measurements of brain wave activity which the Clinic's sophisticated equipment was designed to monitor, explaining that different types and levels of 'E.E.G.' (or, 'brain') waves corresponded to several unique and distinct different levels or 'stages' of wakefulness and sleep, including the popularly known 'R.E.M.-' or 'Paradoxical stage' in which the voluntary muscles were paralyzed and dreams occurred. Each of the majority of his many keys was encased around the 'head' with a rubber or plastic casement, which, I hypothesized, cut down on the overall noise factor of the huge ring of keys when the Somnologist walked or stood holding the keys in his slightly moving palm in a way suggesting heft or the gauging of weight while he spoke, which was evidently his primary 'nervous' or unconscious habit. (Later, at the outset of the initial drive back home [before beginning, as was her usual wont, to doze or 'nod' against her side's door], Hope posited that there seemed to her to be something re-

assuring, trustworthy or [in Hope's own term] 'substantial' about a fellow with this many keys [with myself, for my own part, keeping to myself the fact that my own associations *anent* the keys were somewhat
more janitorial].)

By arrangement, Hope and myself were to attend the Sleep Clinic
once per week, on Wednesdays, for a total duration of from four to six
weeks, sleeping over-night in the Sleep chamber under close observation. Much of the Intake data collection process concerned Hope and
myself's nocturnal routines or 'rituals' surrounding retiring and preparing for sleep (these said 'rituals' being both common to and unique or
distinctive of most married couples, the Sleep specialist explained), in
order that these logistics and practices might be 're-created' — with
the obvious exception of any physically intimate or sexual routines, the
Somnologist inserted, clinically evincing no discernible embarrassment or 'shyness' as Hope avoided my glance — as closely as possible
on these 'over-nights,' as we prepared to sleep under observation. In
separate Dressing rooms, we first changed in to light green hospital
gowns and disposable slippers, then proceeded in tandem to our assigned Sleep chamber, Hope using one hand to keep the long vertical
'slit' or incision or 'cleft' at the rear of her gown clenched shut over her
bottom. Neither the gowns nor the high intensity lighting were what
anyone would term 'flattering' or 'modest' — and Hope, as a woman,
later remonstrated to me that she had felt somewhat demeaned or
'violated' to be sleeping under thin coverlets with nameless persons
observing her through a glass partition. (Frequent remarks or complaints like this were argumentative 'bait' to which I refused to respond or engage on the long, return rides home so early the following
morning, where I would hurriedly shave, change clothes and prepare
for the by now torturous, 'peak hour' commute up to Elizabeth for a
full day of work. A frequent habit of Hope's was sometimes to seemingly agree or acquiesce to a proposal and wait to give voice to her ob-
jections until the 'agreed upon' course of action was under way, at
which time what would have been reasonable caveats and reservations
now emerged as being merely pointless carping. I had, however, by this

point in the conflict, learned to suppress frustration, indignation or even pointing out that the time for such complaints being productive had long passed, as pointing this out inevitably leads to the sort of conjugal argument or 'clash of wills' in which there can be no winner. One should also insert, as I had done to Chester [or (*"For God's sake"*), 'Jack'] Vivien, that our respective make-ups were such that conflict or argument was more difficult or 'harder' on myself than on either Hope, Naomi or Audrey, all of whom seemed to have a comparatively easy time of 'shaking off' the adrenaline and upset of a heated exchange.) We were instructed or encouraged to bring our personal hygiene or grooming products from home, and to use (first Hope doing so, then myself, just as at home) a private washroom and to undergo our personal hygiene 'rituals' in preparation for sleep (with, however, Hope eschewing her facial emollient, hair net, moisturizer and gloves due to the observers and panoply of 'low light' cameras, despite instructions to mimic, as closely as possible, our at home routines). Aides or attendants subsequently affixed white, circular 'E.E.G.' patches or 'leads' — whose conductive gels were extremely chilly and 'queer' feeling, Hope observed — to our heads' temples, foreheads, upper chests and arms, whereupon we then lay carefully or 'gingerly' down along the lengths of the Sleep chamber's parallel beds, careful to avoid tangling the complex nests of wires which led from the leads to a grey chassised 'relay' or 'induction' monitor which hummed quietly in the Sleep chamber's north-east corner. The 'Sleep team' technicians — some of whom, it emerged, were enrolled Medical students at nearby Rutgers University — wore the customary noiseless, white foot wear and 'lab' coats unbuttoned over casual or 'mufti' clothing. Somewhat surprisingly, three of our Sleep chamber's apparently 'glass' walls were, upon being inside them, revealed to be, in reality, mirrored, such that we could not, from inside, see any of the technicians or recording equipment, while the fourth or final wall's interior comprised a sophisticated, 'Wall sized' video screen or 'projection' of various commonly relaxing or soporific vistas, 'scenes' or tableaux: fields of nodding wheat, trickling streams, Winter spruces trimmed in fresh snow, small forest animals nibbling at deciduous ground fall, a sea-side sunset and so forth in this vein. The twin beds' mattress and lone pillows were also revealed to be layered in a plastic compound which crinkled audibly under any movement, which I personally found distracting and somewhat unsanitary. The beds also contained metal railings along the sides which appeared rather higher and more substantial than the rails or sides one is accustomed to associating with a more typical 'Hospital' bed. Our case's assigned Somnologist — Dr. Paphian, with his aforementioned subdued countenance and short, 'salt and pepper' hair-cut and sessile head — explained that some patients' particular sleep dysfunctions involved somnambulism or certain frenetic or even potentially violent movements in the midst of sleep, and that the 24.5 inch brushed steel railings affixed to the chambers' beds' sides had been mandated by the Sleep Clinic's insurance underwriter.

Also — as light reading for an average of 20 to 30 minutes before Hope customarily struck the elevated sconce's light above her bed at home was a fairly firmly established part of our marriage's routine for preparing to retire — Hope and myself spent, for three consecutive Wednesdays in a row, 20 or more minutes sitting awkwardly up in the narrow and 'crib'-like (because of the high lateral railings) beds with only a crinkling institutional pillow for back support, ostensibly 'reading' in our respective beds in the Sleep chamber as we did at home, each holding our current 'livre de chevets' of choice, which Hope had brought in her Book club bag from home, but which were here, in this artificial setting, mere 'props,' and I did little more than absently turn the pages of Kurt Eichenwald's *Serpent on the Rock,* as the idea of relaxing or 'winding down' while covered in E.E.G. leads and extrudent wires and fully reflected in three of the small room's walls was somewhat farcical or absurd; but I was — in what remained close if *sub-rosa* 'consultation' with Jack Vivien — determined now to go through the experiment in full technical compliance, and not to complain, demur or give Hope any cause to suspect or think that I was not fully prepared to go through with my side of the 'bargain.' (Sometimes, nevertheless, admittedly, for instance when driving — particularly along the daily commute via the Garden State Parkway, or west-ward via I95, the 'Jersey' Turnpike, and 'I'-276 around metropolitan Philadelphia's northern border to the campus of out-of-State Bryn Mawr, to there-upon park the vehicle along Montgomery Avenue and upwardly observe the lights of our Audrey's Freshman dormitory [or, more for-mally, 'Ardmore House,' in honor of a Nineteenth century college benefactor, and designed or 'done up' in the steep, grey, vertiginous, crenellated tower or 'Martello' style of a medieval era fortress] room on the tower or 'keep''s Fourth floor's north-east corner come on or off as she moved about the room with her room-mate or prepared to retire or undress — I become so distraught, melancholic or consumed with over-whelming anguish or 'dread' for no apparent or discernible reason [the feeling, unrelated to the sleep deprivation whose symptoms I knew so well by that point in time, seems to come 'out of nowhere' and arise, as it were, out of some profound, unconscious, psychic void or 'hole'] that I consider intentionally 'jumping' the median into on-coming traffic. This fear, on average, will last just a moment or two.)

Despite, however, my nervousness or excitement at the prospect of objective verification of my 'side' of the dispute, my life-long custom or habit of lying supine on my back with my elbows bent and hands atop one another upon my chest made relaxing as the Sleep chamber's soothing vistas and harsh lights were extinguished from somewhere outside the chamber somewhat more straightforward for myself as op-posed to Hope, whose habit (unlike our Audrey, who tends to curl somewhat 'foetally' on her right side, and often appears to awaken in precisely the same position in which she had originally lost conscious-ness) is to fall asleep procumbent or 'prone,' with her arms splayed and her head rotated or, as it were, almost 'twisted' violently to the side, as though some great, unwelcome weight were pressing her down from behind and above (a position which most adults would find noticeably uncomfortable), and she complained to the 'Sleep team' that it would be nearly impossible for her to fall truly asleep when supine and fac-ing, as it were, 'up' as the E.E.G. leads and wires seemed to dictate. Nevertheless, she subsequently did (as usual) fall promptly asleep; and, on our second Wednesday 'over-night' in the Sleep chamber, neither she nor 'Dr. Paphian' (the Sleep specialist's cognomen or sur-name) ever again referred to her vehement protests of the week prior.

As previously mentioned, our diagnostic protocol dictated our traveling to and 'checking in' to sleep together at the Darling Memorial Sleep Clinic once per week for a possible time frame of up to six weeks, with Hope and myself's brains' respective wave patterns monitored and any untoward movements, sounds or awakenings recorded on state of the art Infra-red or 'low light' videotape (Hope often made a point of verifying the audio's quality, as well, while I gazed neutrally at the Fourth wall's screen's relaxing tableaux), which would be analyzed by our Somnologist and eventually form the basis for a medical diagnosis and recommended course of treatment. I myself, of course, as previously mentioned, was looking forward with some anticipation to the recordings' empirical verification of the fact that, when Hope cried out in vexation to accuse me once again of 'snoring,' my E.E.G. waves would indicate that, not only was I myself not truly asleep, but that, on the contrary, Hope's own brain 'reading' would prove conclusively that it was, in reality, she herself who at that time was actually asleep and had dreamt, hallucinated or otherwise 'fantasized' the unpleasant noises which she so steadfastly believed were 'robbing' her of her sleep, health, youth and ability to trust that she and myself were 'on the same wave length' enough anymore to make our marriage anything more than a sexless sham, especially now that Audrey was no longer at home to 'preoccupy' me or serve as the 'focus of [my] affections' (this among the charges which Hope had levied in the vindictive heat of the very worst morning arguments respecting the conflict and our whole viability as a marriage and putative 'family').

As it eventuated, however, it only took the P.P.O.'s authorized minimum (or, 'Floor') of three weeks for an administrative aide or factotum at the Darling Clinic to page me in my small Systems Dept. office at the work-place (he had apparently called our home phone number, as well, but Hope had been either [as was more and more frequently the case] 'out' or else asleep [she openly napped, despite the Clinic's informational material at the outset's clear instructions against diurnal napping for patients with any type of sleep related condition]) to inform me that the Darling Memorial Sleep Clinic's administration, in conjunction with Dr. Paphian and the rest of the 'Sleep team' in charge

of Hope and myself's case, now felt that they had enough accrued data
to offer a firm diagnosis and a recommended course of any 'treatments
or procedures [deemed] indicated.' This official diagnosis was to be
proffered the following week (on, for scheduling reasons, a Monday
morning) in a small Conference room off the 'main' or central corridor
or hallway of the hospital's Fourth floor's unusual, stelliform or 'diamond' shaped floor plan or 'lay-out,' a small, brightly lit room with one
all too familiar 'Goya' among the more generic or commercial Impres-
sionist prints on the wall, and a round, maple or wood grain table with
matching 'captain's' chairs whose seats' and arm rests' padding was a
dark and somewhat over-saturant red in color. Like so much of the rest
of the Darling Memorial Clinic, this room was also markedly chilly (the
more so as we had driven down, amidst peak morning traffic, in a severe
storm, with high winds and heavy precipitation, only then to find that
Rutgers-Brunswick Hospital's indoor parking garage's vehicle entrance
was emblazoned with a sign reading, **'LOT FULL.'** Both our over-
coats were, as a result, sodden, and dripped on the Conference room's
floor, as well as the fact that Hope — whose morbid, long-standing
fear of 'violent' storms had prevented her from sleeping or napping
throughout the stressful commute — was, as a result, in a particularly
foul, obdurate temper), and was equipped or outfitted with an illuminated wall mount appliance or device for reading X-rays and 'M.R.I.'
images, as well as a large video- and\or audio Monitor on a rolling
'stand' or cart of reinforced aluminum or iron, painted an institutional
brown and with each leg terminating in a small 'caster' or wheel for mo-
bility. Everyone in the Conference room appeared to have disposable,
styrofoam cups of coffee or tea which sat on the table at our respective
places, and steamed. Having, due to anticipation or 'nerves,' gotten little or no sleep the prior night, both my glasses and vest felt too tight
once again, and all sounds appeared to amplify or 'ramify' somewhat,
but with the room only moving slightly in and out of exaggerant visual
focus and hue. Each time I yawned, however, produced a sharp bloom
or flower of pain in my ear. My trouser cuffs and garters being wet, as
well, and Hope's tall coiffure being somewhat canted to the right, and
her shadowless face resembling something De Kooning himself might

have torn from the easel and discarded in *medias res,* as well. Also around the table, a small, dark, unfamiliar, 'saucer' eyed, Hispanic man with chloasmatic or pre-cancerous lesions on the backs of his hands, his 'business attire' or suit of fine, dark grey wool, the knot of his tie the size of a toddler's head. The sound of a hand-held hammer. The sound of a Driving range. The sound of a nail gun and portable air compressor. Of one or more rotary or 'power' saws. The sound of a Saab with mild turbo lag. The sound of impacting rain and wipers on High. The sound of a blender making frozen drinks, of coins in a Prudential 'Executive-' or 'Senior Management' lounge's vending machine. Of a lengthy putt being 'made' or 'drained' in the cup's shallow hole. The sound of struggles and muffled breathing and a male- or 'Father' figure's whispered grunts and shushing. Some type of construction, maintenance or related activity was under way some distance along the central corridor or hallway, in the evident direction of the actual Darling Clinic's Sleep chambers and observational 'Nerve' center, and the emphatic sounds of a hammer started and stopped without discernible rhythm. I suffered or experienced a rapid and terrible flash or 'strobe-'lit interior vision of a prone female figure wrapped in clear plastic industrial sheeting, which cleared almost instantly. Around the table with Hope and myself were seated or 'arrayed' the Somnologist with his ever present array of keys and white, 'lab' soutane or coat, two somewhat younger technicians or aides who were also members of our case's 'Sleep team,' and a finely arrayed, male, Hispanic or, perhaps, ethnically Cuban, Medical administrative professional, who was explained to be present representing Rutgers-Brunswick Memorial Hospital's periodic 'Review' or evaluation of the Darling Memorial Clinic's diagnostic procedures and activities. The cart's Monitor — attended by a young, female 'Sleep team' technician with no discernible wedding band and a severely pulled back brunette hair-style, who also carried a collection of various tapes and files associated with Hope and myself's case, one of which she apparently activated via a hand-held or 'remote' device — now displayed my own name, date, and personal eight digit 'P.P.O. Number' (as well as a specially assigned 'D.S.C.' [for 'Darling Sleep Clinic'] Number) beneath a template of four evenly spaced, horizontal lines, not unlike a musical score's, between which moved a jagged or erratic line of white light which signified my own 'brain' waves, which had evidently been recorded through the conductive E.E.G. leads throughout our nights in the Sleep chamber. The waves' white 'line' was discomfiting, being palsied, bumpy and arrhythmic rather than regular or consistent, as well as being trended with dramatic troughs and spikes or 'nodes' suggestive in appearance of an arrhythmic heart or financially troubled or erratic 'Cash flow' graph. Also, not unlike a series of Hewlett-Packard HP9400B mainframes arrayed in sequence for co-sequential (or, in A.D.C.'s nomenclature, 'Sysplex') data processing, a digital display in the monitor's upper left corner displayed the elapsed time along several minutely calibrated temporal gradients.

As the entire 'Sleep team' knew from our Intake data, my wife's own morbid fear of insomnia or sleep deprivation was long-standing. When, for instance, our Audrey was, as a child, ill or anxious respecting bad dreams or phantasms, it was often I who 'sat' up with her so that Hope could, as she would have it, 'try to' sleep.

Meanwhile, the initial 'result' or 'diagnosis' proffered by the Sleep specialist was, in a word, shocking and wholly unexpected. On each of the five or six occasions when special, 'low light' video equipment had recorded Hope sitting suddenly up-right and accusing me of 'snoring,' as well as on the evidently at least two of these recorded instances when I had audibly rejoined that I was not even yet asleep and thus could not logically be 'guilty' of the accusation, the Sleep specialist — aided in his presentation by the youthfully severe technician's laser pointer and her 'remote' device's ability to halt or 'freeze' the Monitor's display in order to draw the table's attention to a certain time specific interval in the E.E.G. — averred or affirmed *ipse dixit* that in fact I had, indeed, been, clinically speaking — despite my belief or perception of being fully conscious — 'technically asleep,' predominantly in the Second or Third of the four well known levels or 'stages' of sleep, which the Somnologist once again outlined or glossed. As the rest of the table and 'Sleep team' looked on, the Somnologist (who, as usual, held and unconsciously 'toyed with' his ponderous, Parke-Davis key ring) delivered this verdict with all the clinical objectivity of modern science, and took pains to make it clear once again that he was empirically neutral in the marital discord and took neither one 'side' in the dispute nor the other. Nevertheless, I felt, upon the putative 'diagnosis''s initial delivery, a spasm or 'wave' of both anger and disbelief, which caused one of my first unconscious or 'reflexive' thoughts to be that Dr. Paphian *et alia* were in fact on Hope's 'side,' and that she had somehow induced the Darling Clinic to alter the testing data to somehow indicate that I was asleep when I knew very well (meaning, every bit as well as I knew I was seated there in that Conference room, gripping the blood colored arms of the chair in disbelief) I was not. Meanwhile, my physical demeanor betrayed none of this admittedly irrational suspicion, but rather only shock and surprise — my jaw quite literally 'dropped,' and for a brief interval of time I was so non-plussed that I did not think or have the 'presence of mind' to ask about any parallel results indicated by the study and E.E.G.'s aural or audio portion — meaning, in other words, whether or not it was also confirmed that my being 'technically asleep' was or was not accompanied by audible 'snoring.' (Here I also, it should be inserted, had an erection or 'Boner' at this time [my first in several months], the origins and associations of which were, in my disoriented state, wholly unknown; the indirect cause may have been the sudden surge of adrenal- or stress-related hormones caused by the findings' sudden shock.)

There were, following this alleged 'diagnosis,' approximately two to four seconds of collective silence, punctuated by the noise of construction activities, rain striking the Conference room's west window, and a ringing telephone somewhere deeper within the administrative offices of the Darling Memorial Sleep Clinic. My *quondam* or former first wife, Naomi, never accepted the fact that I did not want children with her; I was afraid of 'repeating the cycle.' Also, my pager was vibrating. Hope's own facial expression or mien, upon the Sleep specialist's news, was the somewhat exaggeratedly 'bland' or 'unreactive' one which I knew so well from other marital embarrassments, an affect which signified that she was experiencing a sense of bitter vindication or triumph, but was disguising or effacing her pleasure in order to appear to be taking the 'high-road' in the conflict, as well as to avoid my possibly accusing her of vindictive triumph, as well as to show a lack of any surprise and to attempt to make clear that she had 'never' had or entertained the 'slightest doubt' that she was in the right in the dispute over the conflict, and that the Somnologist was now merely confirming what she had in reality 'kn[own] all along.' Only a certain slight gleam or avidity in Hope's pale eyes betrayed her surprise and triumph at my stunned disbelief at the Sleep team's apparent Medical diagnosis or 'ruling.' The sound of the ringing telephone, seemingly unanswered, continued on in this brief, silent interval prior to the young, forbiddingly nubile or 'paphian' technician's there-upon ejecting, inserting and manually adjusting or 're-setting' the Monitor's display as the bland, phlegmatic Somnologist's diagnosis now shifted its focus to my wife's own E.E.G. measurement's recorded 'brain' waves, which, on the Monitor, to Hope and myself's inexpert or 'lay' eyes, appeared indistinguishable from my own display, except, of course, for the difference of its now being Hope's own name and P.P.O. and Darling Clinic 'Patient code' numbers displayed beneath the template whose palsied, erratic line now signified Hope's brain's electrical activity during this calibrated time frame. These particular areas, Dr. Paphian averred between several sudden, conspicuous, screaming or 'shrieking' sounds from a 'power' saw or router somewhere down the corridor (there was also the ambient smell of freshly cut wood, as well as industrial plastic, in addition to the Hispanic's pungent cologne and Hope's customary brand of 'JOY'), pointing out with the salacious technician's hand-held pointer distinctive spikes or 'nodes' in the erratic line of Hope's 'brain' waves, indicated — to (as it, so to speak, 'goes,' quite obviously, 'without saying') both of our further surprise — that not merely myself but Hope, as well, had herself evidently *also* been verifiably or empirically asleep during the recorded time periods when she allegedly 'heard' my 'snoring' (while, in addition or concurrently, due possibly either to extreme fatigue or adrenaline, I myself was also experiencing at the same time a radically compressed or seemingly accelerated sensuous mnemonic tableau [or, as it were, interior 'clip'] of my memories of teaching Audrey to operate 'her' [although registered, for insurance purposes, in Dr. and Mrs. Sipe's legal name] new Mazda coupe's five speed 'stick' transmission in a Lower Squankum parking lot filled with myriad parallel angled lines, Audrey's fulgent auburn hair untied or 'down' and chewing some type of bright blue gum, the compartment awash in sunlight and her yearly Christmas saffron bath gel's scent, the noisome sound of her breathing and shapes of her leg as she worked the relevant pedals up and down, the *sotto voce* profanities when we lugged, bucked or stalled with soft squeals and bit lip and — [*'Do stop'*] — and thus, in the renewed, brief, 'stunned' silence after the M.D.'s second diagnosis, I myself forgot to feel triumph, 'vindication' or even any confusion at the apparent or paradoxical sleep 'verdict''s reversal. My heart had, as it were, 'sunk' several inches; I missed our Audrey terribly; I wanted now to go alone to help her pack and Withdraw and be borne back home [notwithstanding my foot's by now being almost numb or 'asleep,' I could and would not uncross my legs], to drive at rates well in excess of the posted limit and to storm the out-of-State dormitory or 'castle' or *'enceinte'* or machicolated banishment's *donjon*'s fortifications and to pound, smite or ring its massive, oaken front door's bell in the middle or wee hours of the night and loudly say, avow or cry aloud what may and must never even be remotely thought or 'dreamt of' [unlike, it went without saying, 'Father']. I felt very nearly over-whelmingly fatigued, melancholy, worn down and desolate or 'alone,' and my wet bottom or prostate throbbed, as well, gripping the burled arms' sides in order to sit up erect), with the more pronounced or 'acute' E.E.G. spiking, verifiably associated with each time interval just prior to her sitting bolt up-right and crying out, clearly indicating — 'almost textbook' being the Sleep specialist's term of professional admiration for Hope's E.E.G.'s distinctive 'Theta' wave's spikes or 'nodes' — Hope's being, at each crucial, accusatory juncture, in 'stage Four,' the well known 'Paradoxical' stage of sleep associated with muscular paralysis, rapid eye movement and oneiric dreaming. From the inner construction area, two distinct hammers' rapid sounds of impact overlapped or 'mated' briefly for a moment, one then ceasing and the other seeming to grow more vehement in compensation. I then either imagined, hallucinated or witnessed

Dr. 'Desmondo-Ruiz''s — the large eyed Latin administrator's or *compère's* — mouth mouth, very distinctly, the word *'Su-i-cide,'* sans any emergent sound. Hope, meanwhile, leaning slightly and somewhat aggressively forward over tightly crossed legs in her chair, was asking the Sleep specialist, Dr. Paphian, in her familiarily brittle or affectedly composed and unreactive way, to please allow her to 'get [her] facts straight here': was the Sleep team saying that it was her husband Mr. Napier here who was, in point of fact, asleep and truly snoring, or that in reality it was '[Hope]' who was asleep and dreaming (or, 'fantasizing' or, 'making up') the whole snoring issue 'out,' as it were, of 'thin air'? I myself remaining seated erect (or, ". . . *up!*") with my legs tightly crossed and neutrally covering first one eye and then the other, meanwhile.

At this juncture, the Somnologist — knowing, as he did, only the bare outline or 'skeleton' of the unprecedented marital discord which the alleged 'snoring' issue which had brought us to his Memorial Clinic had precipitated between Hope and myself, and evidently mis-apprehending my somnolent or dolorous cast of countenance as am-bivalence or an insouciant passivity or 'apathy' (Hope's own mien, meanwhile, had gone ominously rigid or 'hard' in the face of this sud-den apparent diagnostic *'volte face'* or reversal and the M.D.'s evident vindication of my own long held claims that the specific episodes of 'snoring' which had so aggrieved her were, strictly speaking, in fact the 'unreal' products of either a dream or the 'loosened associations' of nocturnal or oneiric 'Night terrors,' precisely as I had claimed repeti-tively throughout the previous cold weather months' traumatic and devitalizing conflict, the vessels and tendons in her neck flaring invol-untarily and her narrow, somewhat lupine and leathery face's every line, fissure, wrinkle, seam, pleat, lesion, pouch or 'flaw' standing out as if starkly high-lighted in the muscular rigidity of her expression; she looked, for a moment, literally decades above and beyond her true age, and I could well imagine the oblivious or unwilled affront which our Audrey's own 'dewy' or epithelial complexion must have presented to Hope before her banishment out-of-State, Audrey comprising an, as it were, walking compendium of all the daughterly charms Hope so feared acknowledging were now 'behind' her. [See, for instance, the prior early Spring's 'Elective' or 'non-essential' and hence uncovered out-patient procedure to have the Varicose veins removed or erased from the rear of her bottom and legs' upper portion, her convalescence from which was plainly so rebarbative and, frankly, sad or pathetic in its impotent vanity and, as it were, 'denial' of what had, in fact, long ceased to make any substantive difference. (*"not start this again my"*)]), now felt absently or 'unconsciously' at his forehead's keratoses, and — in yet still another apparent, confusing or 'paradoxical' diagnostic reversal (*pace* his phlegmatic or sanguine demeanor, the Somnologist's 'bed side manner' left something to be desired, Hope and I had both agreed) — averred (meaning, the Sleep specialist now averred) that, yes, technically speaking, my wife's accusations as to 'snoring,' while based on (in his terms) 'interior, dreamed experience' as opposed to 'exterior sensory input,' nonetheless were, in a Medical or scientific sense, 'technically' correct. With the large collection or 'ring' of insulated keys now in his left hand, and addressing some type of facial signal or 'cue' to the nubile technician, the neutrally objective Somnologist stated that the 'low' or Infra-red light videotape of two such 'Fourth-' or 'Paradoxical' sleep stage intervals immediately prior to Hope's loud accusations of my 'snoring' would, he said, confirm that I myself had indeed, within these intervals, been engaged in the 'occluded' or, more formally, 'nasopharyngeal' respiration commonly referred to among the lay populace as 'snoring,' this being a transient or recurrent phenomenon or condition often common to males over 40 or more, Dr. Paphian explained — particularly in those whose nocturnal posture was, by habit (like myself's), supine as opposed to prone, lateral or 'foetal' — and occurring predominantly in human sleep's medial or 'deep' stages Two and Three of sleep. Apparently, however, the 'Fourth-' or 'Paradoxical' stage's paralysis of certain key laryngeal muscle groups rendered actual 'snoring' as or while one actively dreamt during R.E.M.- or 'dream' sleep physiologically impossible. All the Sleep specialist's information was concise and bore directly on the matter at hand. My wife, meanwhile, was massaging her temples in order to signify stress or impatience. The Conference room's somewhat subordinate or 'junior' aide to the Somnologist's Sleep team — a roughly college age young man (or, in today's more popular nomenclature, 'Dude') who wore, beneath his unbuttoned and not altogether spotless or sterile 'lab' coat, a pink, faded, red or fuchsia cotton 'tee' shirt on whose front appeared the line drawing or caricature of a nameless but somehow 'naggingly' familiar or famous person's stymied or confused looking face, below which, on the garment's fabric, appeared the statement or caption, 'MY WIFE SAYS I'M INDECISIVE, BUT I'M NOT SO SURE,' which was almost certainly not meant to be taken seriously or at 'face' value but was, rather, some form of droll or ironic sally — now returned from his brief hiatus from the Conference room with a small, boxed set of ordinary or 'commercial' VHS type videotapes, which were labeled in black, felt tip ink, 'R.N.' and 'H.S.-N.,' along with Hope and myself's respective P.P.O. and D.M.C. 'Patient codes' and the dates of the relevant Wednesday nights during which the actual filmed sleep 'experiments' had been held or conducted; and this youth and the ("only hurt a tiny") Somnologist conferred together over a brushed steel or aluminum Medical chart holder respecting precisely which tape to 'load' and\or 'cue' in order to empirically verify the Somnologist's diagnosis of Hope's accusations' ultimately unreal, oneiric or 'Paradoxical' content. Hope, at this point, leaning once more slightly forward and furiously twitching or 'joggling' one high heeled shoe of her crossed legs, posited or inquired whether, from the sum total of the Clinic's diagnostic data, it might be thus possible that 'he' (meaning, I myself) could somehow be deeply asleep and 'snoring' in the Sleep chamber's bed and yet could simultaneously be dreaming the precise 'sensation' or 'experience' of being still somehow, as it were, still fully 'awake' in the narrow, firmly reinforced Clinic bed, a possibility which (Hope suggested) would account for my sincere or heartfelt 'denials' of having been asleep whenever she finally '[couldn't] stand it' and cried aloud in order to wake me — to which, interjecting somewhat irritatedly in response, I myself pointed out the obvious 'hole' or logical flaw in Hope's theory's scenario, and asked the Somnologist to stipulate once again, for, as it were, the 'record,' that, according to his explanations respecting the well known stages of human sleep, I physically could not be 'snoring' when ("dreaming") dreaming, since, by basic logic, if I were, *a.*, literally 'dreaming' that I was awake, I would, *b.*, be, by definition, in the 'Fourth-' or 'Paradoxical' stage of sleep, and thus, *c.*, due to the 'Paradoxical' stage's well known laryngeal paralysis, I could, *d.*, not be producing the rasping, gurgling or 'nasopharyngeal' snoring sounds which in fact Hope had herself in reality only dreamt that she'd heard me producing *in situ*. Both Hope's shoes, gloves and expensive purse or hand bag matched perfectly in regards to color and constituent leather texture; she also always smelled quite fine. It was in or around this point that the lissome, mature, voluptuous but some-what severe or 'forbidding' technician began to insert or 'load' a given, selected videotape in to a receptacle or 'slot' or 'hole' in the Monitor's rear, and — utilizing a sheet of coded (*"Please!"*) Somnological data and the hand-held remote — to begin to 'cue' the 'low' light recording to the relevant stage Four or 'Paradoxical' interval just prior to (one would presume, based on the Sleep specialist's *prolegomenon* or gloss [physio-logically, I myself still remained 'At attention,' one might say]) a sudden, aggrieved and high volume accusation of 'snoring' on my wife's part.

Whether seemingly somewhat forebodingly or not, both all exterior or extraneous noise and my own neglected pager itself — as well as the swart, handsomely dressed Medical administrator's audible imbiba-tion or 'slurping' of his hot tea (a personal pet peeve of mine since childhood, followed as it was by the somewhat affected knuckle across the upper lip) — appeared at this point in time to cease, producing a sudden and somewhat dramatic or unsettling silence or distended 'pause.' Meanwhile, on the room's Monitor, the video recording, which formed or comprised a diptych or 'Split screen' image, showed Hope and myself's darkened Sleep chamber in a low amber light which was evidently distinctive of the appearance of low light film, the screen's upper left and right corners displaying both the relevant date and '0204' (or, 2:04 A.M. in scientific or 'Zulu time') along with each suc-cessive second and decimal increments of same, with the (from our perspective) dextral or right hand side of the video display being com-prised of a sustained, Infra-red close up (or, 'tight shot') of myself in the bed, deeply asleep, supine on my back with my hands on my chest, and — far more unsettlingly — of my own face, asleep. I myself had, not, of course, surprisingly, never seen or observed my own 'unconscious' face prior to this time; and, in the Monitor's diptych's *recto* or, as it were, right or 'starboard' portion's unblinking close up, it was now revealed as being not a face I in any way recognized or 'knew,' with its slack jaw and protrusive jowls, hands on my chest spiderishly twitching, lips fishily loose or agape; and, although there was (to the Sleep team's consternation and whispered colloquy among the aides and technicians at the Monitor's rear, with which there was evidently some technical 'glitch' or malfunction) no audible sound (Hope, gazing in rigid fascination or horror at the dextral display right along-side myself, herself was silently 'frozen' [or, 'paralyzed' (*"or hurt you if"*)] in mid gesture, her pupils quite large and liquidly black), the flaccid mien, gaping mouth, slack jaw and puddled and quivering jowls I'd never 'envisioned' lying down (for, as with most husbands, I had, of course, only seen my face when seated or standing erect at the mirror, as in shaving, removing unwanted nasal or auricular hairs, masturbating with a saffron scented under-garment, tightening the knot of my tie and so forth), as well as, despite the recording's defective audio portion's absence of sound, the variably changing shapes and contortions of my unconsciously open mouth in the close up sleeping shot or wee hour 'scene,' as Hope and myself watched in rigid fascination (as when passing the wreckage and prone, twisted figures of a vehicular accident or 'Crime scene'), signifying or 'meaning,' in other words, that the distinctive, alternating shapes of my image's mouth's slack lips, as well as the small bubbles of saliva or spit which alternately formed and dissolved at my open mouth's corners (there was labial 'film' or paste in those corners, as well, gummy and sepia colored, distending slightly as my mouth changed shape), signified undeniably that sounds and noises of which I had no conscious or 'voluntary' awareness were in fact escaping my throat and mouth — no one with eyes could deny it — and, as the video camera's focus 'tightened' or closed further in on my wholly unfamiliar, inhuman, unconscious visage, I either saw, hallucinated, 'imagined' (Hope at this juncture still rigidly or foetally 'frozen,' open mouthed and saucer eyed, as both the forbidding technician and Latin executive began to peel their respective faces off in a 'top down' fashion or manner, beginning at each temple and pulling downwards with sharp, emphatic, peeling or 'tugging' motions, the Cuban's foreign wrist watch and hands a mass of amber lesions) or actually watched or literally 'witnessed' one sleeping eyelid open just a crack, ever so slightly, allowing a minuscule sliver or ray or 'blade' of light — as in, for instance, under a dark bedroom's closed door when the hallway light outside is illuminated or 'turned on' as a heavy, familiar nocturnal tread slowly ascends the Victorian staircase to the bedroom door — from the rapidly moving and unconscious eye below, seeing as well in the Split screen's right- or 'off' side's shot my own wet mouth and slack, soft and spreading cheeks now begin to distend in a 'grinningly' familiar and sensual or even predatory facial ex

"*up.* Wake up, for the love of."

"God. My God I was having."

"Wake up."

"Having the worst dream."

"I should certainly say you were."

"It was awful. It just went on and on."

"I shook you and shook you and."

"Time is it."

"It's nearly — almost 2:04. I was afraid I might hurt you if I prodded or shook any harder. I couldn't seem to rouse you."

"Is that thunder? Did it rain?"

"I was beginning to really worry. Hope, this cannot go on. When are we going to make that appointment?"

"Wait — am I even married?"

"Please don't start all this again."

"And who's this Audrey?"

"Just go on back to sleep now."

"And what's that — Daddy?"

"Just lie back down."

"What's wrong with your mouth?"

"You are my wife."

"None of this is real."

"It's all all right."

THE SUFFERING CHANNEL

1.

'But they're shit.'

'And yet at the same time they're art. Exquisite pieces of art. They're literally incredible.'

'No, they're literally shit is literally what they are.'

Atwater was speaking to his associate editor at *Style*. He was at the little twin set of payphones in the hallway off the Holiday Inn restaurant where he'd taken the Moltkes out to eat and expand their side of the whole pitch. The hallway led to the first floor's elevators and restrooms and to the restaurant's kitchen and rear area.

At *Style*, editor was more of an executive title. Those who did actual editing were usually called associate editors. This was a convention throughout the BSG subindustry.

'If you could just see them.'

'I don't want to see them,' the associate editor responded. 'I don't want to look at shit. Nobody wants to look at shit. Skip, this is the point: people do not want to look at shit.'

'And yet if you —'

'Even shit shaped into various likenesses or miniatures or whatever it is they're alleging they are.'

Skip Atwater's intern, Laurel Manderley, was listening in on the whole two way conversation. It was she whom Atwater'd originally dialed, since there was simply no way he was going to call the associate editor's head intern's extension on a Sunday and ask her to accept a collect call. *Style*'s whole editorial staff was in over the weekend because the magazine's Summer Entertainment double issue was booked to close on 2 July. It was a busy and extremely high stress time, as Laurel Manderley would point out to Skip more than once in the subsequent debriefing.

'No, no, but *not* shaped into, is the thing. You aren't — they come out that way. Already fully formed. Hence the term incredible.' Atwater was a plump diminutive boy faced man who sometimes unconsciously made a waist level fist and moved it up and down in time to his stressed syllables. A small and bell shaped *Style* salaryman, energetic and competent, a team player, unfailingly polite. Sometimes a bit overfastidious in presentation — for example, it was extremely warm and close in the little Holiday Inn hallway, and yet Atwater had not removed his blazer or even loosened his tie. The word among some of *Style*'s snarkier interns was that Skip Atwater resembled a jockey who had retired young and broken training in a big way. There was doubt in some quarters about whether he even shaved. Sensitive about the whole baby face issue, as well as about the size and floridity of his ears, Atwater was unaware of his reputation for wearing nearly identical navy blazer and catalogue slacks ensembles all the time, which happened to be the number one thing that betrayed his Midwest origins to those interns who knew anything about cultural geography.

The associate editor wore a headset telephone and was engaged in certain other editorial tasks at the same time he was talking to Atwater. He was a large bluff bearish man, extremely cynical and fun to be around, as magazine editors often tend to be, and known particularly for being able to type two totally different things at the same time, a keyboard under each hand, and to have them both come out more or less error free. *Style*'s editorial interns found this bimanual talent fascinating, and they often pressed the associate editor's head intern to get him to do it during the short but very intense celebrations that took place after certain issues had closed and everyone had had some drinks and the normal constraints of rank and deportment were relaxed a bit. The associate editor had a daughter at Rye Country Day School, where a number of *Style*'s editorial interns had also gone, as adolescents. The typing talent thing was also interesting because the associate editor had never actually written for *Style* or anyone else — he had come up through Factchecking, which was technically a division of Legal and answered to a whole different section of *Style*'s parent company. In any event, the doubletime typing explained the surfeit of clicking sounds in the background as the associate editor responded to a pitch he found irksome and out of character for Atwater, who was normally a consummate pro, and knew quite well the shape of the terrain that *Style*'s WHAT IN THE WORLD feature covered, and had no history of instability or substance issues, and rarely even needed much rewriting.

The editorial exchange between the two men was actually very rapid and clipped and terse. The associate editor was saying: 'Which think about it, you're going to represent how? You're going to propose we get photos of the man on the throne, producing? You're going to describe it?'

'Everything you're saying is valid and understandable and yet all I'm saying is if you could see the results. The pieces themselves.' The two payphones had a woodgrain frame with a kind of stiff steel umbilicus for the phone book. Atwater had claimed that he could not use his own phone because once you got far enough south of Indianapolis and Richmond there were not enough cellular relays to produce a reliable signal. Due to the glass doors and no direct AC, it was probably close to 100 degrees in the little passage, and also loud — the kitchen was clearly on the other side of the wall, because there was a great deal of audible clatter and shouting. Atwater had worked in a 24 hour restaurant attached to a Union 76 Truck 'n Travel Plaza while majoring in journalism at Ball State, and he knew the sounds of a short order kitchen. The name of the restaurant in Muncie had been simply: *EAT.* Atwater was facing away from everything and more or less concave, hunched into himself and the space of the phone, as people on payphones in public spaces so often are. His fist moved just below the

little shelf where the slim GTE directory for Whitcomb–Mount
Carmel–Scipio and surrounding communities rested. The technical
name of the Holiday Inn's restaurant, according to the sign and
menus, was Ye Olde Country Buffet. Hard to his left, an older couple
was trying to get a great deal of luggage through the hallway's glass
doors. It was only a matter of time before they figured out that one
should just go through and hold the doors open for the other. It was
early in the afternoon of 1 July 2001. You could also hear the associate
editor sometimes talking to someone else in his office, which wasn't
necessarily his fault or a way to marginalize Atwater, because other
people were always coming in and asking him things.

A short time later, after splashing some cold water on his ears and
face in the men's room, Atwater reemerged through the hallway's
smeared doors and made his way through the crowds around the
restaurant's buffet table. He had also used the sink's mirror to pump
himself up a little — periods of self exhortation at mirrors were usually
the only time he was fully conscious of the thing that he did with his
fist. There were red heat lamps over many of the buffet's entrees, and a
man in a partly crumpled chef's hat was slicing prime rib to people's
individual specs. The large room smelled powerfully of bodies and hot
food. Everyone's face shone in the humidity. Atwater had a short man's
emphatic, shoulder inflected walk. Many of the Sunday diners were
elderly and wore special sunglasses with side flaps, the inventor of
whom was possibly ripe for a WITW profile. Nor does one hardly ever
see actual flypaper anymore. Their table was almost all the way in
front. Even across the crowded dining room it was not hard to spot
them seated there, due to the artist's wife, Mrs. Moltke, whose great
blond head's crown was nearly even with the hostess's lectern. Atwater
used the head as a salient to navigate the room, his own ears and forehead flushed with high speed thought. Back at *Style*'s editorial offices
on the sixteenth floor of 1 World Trade Center in New York, meanwhile, the associate editor was speaking with his head intern on the intercom while he typed internal emails. Mr. Brint Moltke, the proposed
piece's subject, was smiling fixedly at his spouse, possibly in response
to some remark. His entree was virtually untouched. Mrs. Moltke was

removing mayo or dressing from the corner of her mouth with a pinkie and met Atwater's eye as he raised both arms:

'They're very excited.'

←

Part of the reason Atwater had had to splash and self exhort in the airless little men's room off the Holiday Inn restaurant was that the toll call had actually continued for several more minutes after the journalist had said '. . . pieces themselves,' and had become almost heated at the same time that it didn't really go anywhere or modify either side of the argument, except that the associate editor subsequently observed to his head intern that Skip seemed to be taking the whole strange thing more to heart than was normal in such a consummate pro.

'I do good work. I find it and I do it.'

'This is not about you or whether you could bring it in well,' the associate editor had said. 'This is simply me delivering news to you about what can happen and what can't.'

'I seem to recollect somebody once saying no way the parrot could ever happen.' Here Atwater was referring to a prior piece he'd done for *Style*.

'You're construing this as an argument about me and you. What this is really about is shit. Excrement. Human shit. It's very simple: *Style* does not run items about human shit.'

'But it's also art.'

'But it's also shit. And you're already tasked to Chicago for something else we're letting you look at because you pitched me, that's already dubious in terms of the sorts of things we can do. Correct me if I'm mistaken here.'

'I'm on that already. It's Sunday. Laurel's got me in for tomorrow all day. It's a two hour toot up the interstate. The two are a hundred and ten percent compatible.' Atwater sniffed and swallowed hard. 'You know I know this area.'

The other *Style* piece the associate editor had referred to concerned The Suffering Channel, a wide grid cable venture that Atwater had gotten Laurel Manderley to do an end run and pitch directly to the editor's head intern for WHAT IN THE WORLD. Atwater was one of three full time salarymen tasked to the WITW feature, which received .75 editorial pages per week, and was the closest any of the BSG weeklies got to freakshow or tabloid, and was a bone of contention at the very highest levels of *Style*. The staff size and large font specs meant that Skip Atwater was officially contracted for one 400 word piece every three weeks, except the juniormost of the WITW salarymen had been on half time ever since Eckleschafft-Böd had forced Mrs. Anger to cut the editorial budget for everything except celebrity news, so in reality it was more like three finished pieces every eight weeks.

'I'll overnight photos.'

'You will not.'

As mentioned, Atwater was rarely aware of the up and down fist thing, which as far as he could recall had first started in the pressure cooker environs of the Indianapolis *Star*. When he became aware he was doing it, he sometimes looked down at the moving fist without recognition, as if it were somebody else's. It was one of several lacunae or blind spots in Atwater's self concept, which in turn were part of why he inspired both affection and mild contempt around the offices of *Style*. Those he worked closely with, such as Laurel Manderley, saw him as without much protective edge or shell, and there were clearly some maternal elements in Laurel's regard for him. His interns' tendency to fierce devotion, in further turn, caused some at *Style* to see him as a manipulator, someone who complicitly leaned on people instead of developing his own inner resources. The former associate editor in charge of the magazine's SOCIETY PAGES feature had once referred to Skip Atwater as an emotional tampon, though there were plenty of people who could verify that she had been a person with all kinds of personal baggage of her own. As with institutional politics everywhere, the whole thing got very involved.

Also as mentioned, the editorial exchange on the telephone was in fact very rapid and compressed, with the exception of one sustained pause while the associate editor conferred with someone from Design about the shape of a pull quote, which Atwater could overhear clearly. The several beats of silence after that, however, could have meant almost anything.

'See if you get this,' the associate editor said finally. 'How about if I say to you what Mrs. Anger would say to me were I hypothetically as enthused as you are, and gave you the OK, and went up to the ed meeting and pitched it for let's say 10 September. Are you out of your mind. People are not interested in shit. People are disgusted and repelled by shit. That's why they call it shit. Not even to mention the high percentage of fall ad pages that are food or beauty based. Are you insane. Unquote.' Mrs. Anger was the Executive Editor of *Style* and the magazine's point man with respect to its parent company, which was the US division of Eckleschafft-Böd Medien.

'Although the inverse of that reasoning is that it's also wholly common and universal,' Atwater had said. 'Everyone has personal experience with shit.'

'But personal *private* experience.' Though technically included in the same toll call, this last rejoinder was part of a separate, subsequent conversation with Laurel Manderley, the intern who currently manned Atwater's phone and fax when he was on the road, and winnowed and vetted research items forwarded by the shades in Research for WHAT IN THE WORLD, and interfaced for him with the editorial interns. 'It's done in private, in a special private place, and flushed. People flush so it will go away. It's one of the things people don't want to be reminded of. That's why nobody talks about it.'

Laurel Manderley, who like most of the magazine's high level interns wore exquisitely chosen and coordinated professional attire, permitted herself a small diamond stud in one nostril that Atwater found slightly distracting in face to face exchanges, but she was extremely shrewd and pragmatic — she had actually been voted Most Rational by the Class of '96 at Miss Porter's School. She was also all but incapable of writing a simple declarative sentence and thus could not, by any dark stretch of the imagination, ever be any kind of rival for Atwater's salaryman position at *Style*. As he had with perhaps only one or two previous interns, Atwater relied on Laurel Manderley, and sounded her out, and welcomed her input so long as it was requested, and often spent large blocks of time on the phone with her, and had shared with her certain elements of his personal history, including pictures of the four year old schipperke mixes who were his pride and joy. Laurel Manderley, whose father controlled a large number of Blockbuster Video franchises throughout western Connecticut, and whose mother was in the final push toward certification as a Master Gardener, was herself destined to survive, through either coincidence or premonition, the tragedy by which *Style* would enter history two months hence.

Atwater rubbed his nose vertically with two fingers. 'Well, some people talk about it. You should hear little boys. Or men, in a locker room setting: "Boy, you wouldn't believe the dump I took last night." That sort of thing.'

'I don't want to hear that. I don't want to imagine that's what men talk to each other about.'

'It's not as if it comes up all that often,' Atwater conceded. He did feel a little uneasy talking about this with a female. 'My point is that the whole embarrassment and distaste of the issue is the point, if it's done right. The transfiguration of disgust. This is the UBA.' UBA was their industry's shorthand for upbeat angle, what hard news organs would call a story's hook. 'The let's say unexpected reversal of embarrassment and distaste. The triumph of creative achievement in even the unlikeliest places.'

Laurel Manderley sat with her feet up on an open file drawer of Atwater's desk, holding her phone's headset instead of wearing it. Slender almost to the point of clinical intervention, she had a prominent forehead and surprised eyebrows and a tortoiseshell barrette and was, like Atwater, extremely earnest and serious at all times. She had interned at *Style* for almost a year, and knew that Skip's only real weakness as a BSG journalist was a tendency to grand abstraction that was usually not hard to bring him back to earth on and get him to tone down. She knew further that this tendency was a form of compensation for what Skip himself believed was his chief flaw, an insufficient sense of the tragic which an editor at the *Indiana Star* had accused him of at an age when that sort of thing sank deep out of sight in the psyche and became part of your core understanding of who you are. One of Laurel Manderley's profs at Wellesley had once criticized her freshman essays for what he'd called their tin ear and cozening tone of unearned confidence, which had immediately become dark parts of her own self concept.

'So go write a Ph.D. thesis on the guy,' she had responded. 'But do not ask me to go to Miss Flick and make a case for making *Style* readers hear about somebody pooping little pieces of sculpture out of their butt. Because it's not going to happen.' Laurel Manderley now nearly always spoke her mind; her cozening days were behind her. 'I'd be spending credibility and asking Ellen to spend hers on something that's a lost cause.

'You have to be careful what you ask people to do,' she had said. Sometimes privately a.k.a. Miss Flick, Ellen Bactrian was the WHAT IN THE WORLD section's head intern, a personage who was not only the associate editor's right hand but who was known to have the ear of someone high on Mrs. Anger's own staff on the 82nd floor, because Ellen Bactrian and this executive intern often biked down to work together from the Flatiron district on the extraordinary bicycle paths that ran all the way along the Hudson to almost Battery Park. It was said that they even had matching helmets.

For complicated personal and political reasons, Skip Atwater was uncomfortable around Ellen Bactrian and tried to avoid her whenever possible.

There were a couple moments of nothing but background clatter on his end of the phone.

'Who is this guy, anyhow?' Laurel Manderley had asked. 'What sort of person goes around displaying his own poo?'

2.

Indiana storms surprise no one. You can see them coming from half a state away, like a train on a very straight track, even as you stand in the sun and try to breathe. Atwater had what his mother'd always called a weather eye.

Seated together in the standard Midwest attitude of besotted amia-
bility, the three of them had passed the midday hours in the Moltkes'
sitting room with the curtains drawn and two rotating fans that picked
Atwater's hair up and laid it down and made the little racks' magazines
riffle. Laurel Manderley, who was something of a whiz at the cold call,
had set this initial meeting up by phone the previous evening. The
home was half a rented duplex, and you could hear its aluminum siding tick and pop in the assembling heat. A window AC chugged
gamely in one of the interior rooms. The off white Roto Rooter van in
the driveway had signified the Moltkes' side of the ranch style twin;
Laurel's Internet directions to the address had been flawless as usual.
The cul de sac was a newer development with abrasive cement and engineering specs still spraypainted on the curbs. Only the very western
horizon showed piling clouds when Atwater pulled up in the rented
Cavalier. Some of the homes' yards had not yet been fully sodded.
There were almost no porches as such. The Moltkes' side's front door
had had a US flag in an angled holder and an anodized cameo of perhaps a huge black ladybug or some kind of beetle attached to the
storm door's frame, which one had to back slightly off the concrete
slab in order to open. The slab's mat bid literal welcome.

The sitting room was narrow and airless and done mostly in green
and a tawny type of maple syrup brown. It was thickly carpeted
throughout. The davenport, chairs, and end tables had plainly been acquired as a set. A bird emerged at intervals from a catalogue clock; a
knit sampler over the mantel expressed conventional wishes for the
home and its occupants. The iced tea was kneebucklingly sweet. An
odd stain or watermark marred the room's east wall, which Atwater
educed was the load bearing wall that the Moltkes shared with the duplex's other side.

'I think I speak for a lot of folks when I want to know how it works.
Just how you do it.' Atwater was in a padded rocker next to the television console and thus faced the artist and his wife, who were seated
together on the davenport. The reporter had his legs crossed comfortably but was not actually rocking. He had spent a great deal of preliminary time chatting about the area and his memories of regional features

and establishing a rapport and putting the Moltkes at ease. The recorder was out and on, but he was also going with a stenographer's notebook because it made him look a little more like the popular stereotype of someone from the press.

You could tell almost immediately that something was off about the artist and/or the marriage's dynamics. Brint Moltke sat hunched or slumped with his toes in and his hands in his lap, a posture reminiscent of a scolded child, but at the same time smiling at Atwater. As in smiling the entire time. It was not an empty professional corporate smile, but the soul effects were similar. Moltke was a thickset man with sideburns and graying hair combed back in what appeared to be a lopsided ducktail. He wore Sansabelt slacks and a dark blue knit shirt with his employer's name on the breast. You could tell from the dents in his nose that he sometimes wore glasses. A further idiosyncrasy that Atwater noted in Gregg shorthand was the arrangement of the artist's hands: their thumbs and forefingers formed a perfect lap level circle, which Moltke held or rather somehow directed before him like an aperture or target. He appeared to be unaware of this habit. It was a gesture both unsubtle and somewhat obscure in terms of what it signified. Combined with the rigid smile, it was almost the stuff of nightmares. Atwater's own hands were controlled and well behaved — his tic with the fist was entirely a private thing. The journalist's childhood hay fever was back with a vengeance, but even so he could not help detecting the Old Spice scent which Mr. Moltke emitted in great shimmering waves. Old Spice had been Skip's own father's scent and, reportedly, his father's father's before him.

The pattern of the davenport's upholstery, Skip Atwater also knew firsthand, was called Forest Floral.

↓

The WITW associate editor's typing feats were just one example of the various leveling traditions and shticks and reversals of protocol that made *Style*'s parties and corporate celebrations the envy of publishing interns throughout Manhattan. These fetes took place on the six-

teenth floor and were usually open bar; some were even catered. The
normally dry and insufferable head of Copyediting did impressions of
various US presidents smoking dope that had to be seen to be believed. Given the right kinds of vodka and flame source, a senior re-
ceptionist from Haiti could be prevailed upon to breathe fire. A very
odd senior paralegal in Permissions, who showed up to the office in
foul weather gear nearly every day no matter what the forecast, turned
out to have been in the original Broadway cast of *Jesus Christ Superstar*,
and organized revues that could get kind of risqué. Some of the interns
got bizarrely dressed up; nails were occasionally done in White Out.
Mrs. Anger's executive intern had once worn a white leather suit with
outrageous fringe and a set of cap pistols in a hiphugger belt and hol-
ster accessory. A longtime supervisor of shades used Crystal Light,
Everclear, skinned fruit, and an ordinary office paper shredder to produce a libation she called Last Mango in Paris. The interns' annual ersatz awards show at the climax of Oscars Week often had people on
the floor — one year they'd gotten Gene Shalit to appear. And so on
and so forth.

Of arresting and demotic party traditions, however, none was so
prized as Mrs. Anger's annual essay at self parody for the combination
New Year's and closing of the Year's Most Stylish People double issue
bash. Bedecked in costume jewelry, mincing and fluttering, affecting a
falsetto and lorgnette, holding her head in such a way as to produce a
double chin, tottering about with a champagne cocktail like one of
those anserine dowagers in Marx Brothers films. It would be difficult
to convey this routine's effect on morale and esprit. The rest of the
publishing year, Mrs. Anger was a figure of near testamental awe and
dread, serious as a heart attack. A veteran of Fleet Street and two separate R. Murdoch startups, wooed over from *Us* in 1994 under terms
that were industry myth, Mrs. Anger had managed to put *Style* in the
black for the first time in its history, and was said to enjoy influence at
the very highest levels of Eckleschafft-Böd, and had worn one of the
first Versace pantsuits ever seen in New York, and was nobody's fool
whatsoever.

↓

Mrs. Amber Moltke, the artist's young spouse, wore a great billowing pastel housedress and flattened espadrilles and was, for better or worse, the sexiest morbidly obese woman Atwater had ever seen. Eastern Indiana was not short on big pretty girls, but this was less a person than a vista, a quarter ton of sheer Midwest pulchritude, and Atwater had already filled several narrow pages of his notebook with descriptions and analogies and abstract encomia to Mrs. Moltke, none of which could be used in the compressed piece he was even then conceiving how to pitch and submit. Some of the allure was atavistic, he acknowledged. Some was simply contrast, a relief from the sucking cheeks and starved eyes of Manhattan's women. He had personally seen *Style* interns weighing their food on small pharmaceutical scales before they consumed it. In one of the more abstract notebook entries, Atwater had theorized that Mrs. Moltke's was perhaps a sort of negative beauty that consisted mainly in her failure to be repellent. In another, he had compared her face and throat to whatever canids see in the full moon that makes them howl. The associate editor would never see one jot of material like this, obviously. Some BSG salarymen built their pieces gradually from the ground up. Atwater, trained originally as a background man for news dailies, constructed his own WITW pieces by pouring into his notebooks and word processor an enormous waterfall of prose which was then filtered more and more closely down to 400 words of commercial sediment. It was labor intensive, but it was his way. Atwater had colleagues who were unable even to start without a Roman numeral outline. *Style*'s daytime television specialist could compose his pieces only on public transport. So long as salarymen's personal quotas were filled and deadlines met, the BSG weeklies tended to be respectful of people's processes.

When as a child he had misbehaved or sassed her, Mrs. Atwater had made little Virgil go and cut from the fields' edge's copse the very switch with which she'd whip him. For most of the 1970s she had belonged to a splinter denomination that met in an Airstream trailer on the outskirts of Anderson, and she did spareth not the rod. His father had been a barber, the real kind, w/ smock and pole and rat tail combs in huge jars of Barbicide. Save the odd payroll data processor at Eckleschafft-Böd US, no one east of Muncie had access to Skip's true given name.

Mrs. Moltke sat with her spine straight and ankles crossed, her huge smooth calves cream white and unmarred by veins and the overall size and hue of what Atwater wrote were museum grade vases and funereal urns of the same antiquity in which the dead wore bronze masks and whole households were interred together. Her platter sized face was expressive and her eyes, though rendered small by the encasing folds of fat, were intelligent and alive. An Anne Rice paperback lay face down on the end table beside her fauxfrosted beverage tumbler and a stack of Butterick clothing patterns in their distinctive bilingual sleeves. Atwater, who held his pen rather high on the shaft, had already noted that her husband's eyes were flat and immured despite his constant smile. The lone time that Atwater had believed he was seeing his own father smile, it turned out to have been a grimace which presaged the massive infarction that had sent the man forward to lie prone in the sand of the horseshoe pit as the shoe itself sailed over the stake, the half finished apiary, a section of the simulation combat target range, a tire swing's supporting limb, and the backyard's pineboard fence, never to be recovered or even ever seen again, while Virgil and his twin brother had stood there wide eyed and red eared, looking back and forth from the sprawled form to the kitchen window's screen, their inability to move or cry out feeling, in later recall, much like the paralysis of bad dreams.

The Moltkes had already shown him the storm cellar and its literally incredible display, but Atwater decided to wait until he truly needed to visit the bathroom to see where the actual creative transfigurations took place. He felt that asking to be shown the bathroom as such, and then examining it while they watched him do so, would be awkward and unseemly. In her lap, the artist's wife had some kind of garment or bolt of orange cloth in which she was placing pins in a complicated way. A large red felt apple on the end table held the supply of pins for this purpose. She filled her whole side of the davenport

and then some. One could feel the walls and curtains warming as the
viscous heat outside beset the home. After one of the lengthy and uncomfortable attacks of what felt like aphasia that sometimes afflicted
him with incidentals, Atwater was able to remember that the correct
term for the apple was simply: pin cushion. One reason it was so discomfiting was that the detail was irrelevant. Likewise the twinge of
abandonment he noticed that he felt whenever the near fan rotated
back away from him. On the whole, though, the journalist's spirits
were good. Part of it was actual art. But there was also something that
felt solid and kind of invulnerable about returning to one's native area
for legitimate professional reasons. He was unaware that the cadences
of his speech had already changed.

After one or two awkward recrossings of his leg, Atwater had found
a way to sit, with his weight on his left hip and the padded rocker held
still against that weight, so that his right thigh formed a stable surface
for taking notes. His iced tea, pebbled with condensation, was on a
plastic coaster beside the cable converter box atop the television console. Atwater was particularly drawn to two framed prints on the wall
above the davenport, matched renderings of retrievers, human eyed
and much ennobled by the artist, each with some kind of dead bird in
its mouth.

'I think I speak for a lot of folks when I say how curious I am to
know how you do it,' Atwater said. 'Just how the whole thing works.'

There was a three beat pause in which no one moved or spoke and
the fans' whines harmonized briefly and then diverged once more.

'I realize it's a delicate subject,' Atwater said.

Another stilted pause, only slightly longer, and then Mrs. Moltke
signaled the artist to answer the man by swinging her great dimpled
arm out and around and striking him someplace about the left breast
or shoulder, producing a meaty sound. It was a gesture both practiced
and without heat, and Moltke's only visible reaction, after angling
hard to starboard and then righting himself, was to search within and
answer as honestly as he could.

The artist said, 'I'm not sure.'

↓

The fliptop stenographer's notebook was partly for effect, but it was also what Skip Atwater had gotten in the habit of using out in the field for background at the start of his career, and its personal semiotics and mojo were profound; he was comfortable with it. He was, as a matter of professional persona, old school and low tech. Today's was a very different journalistic era, however, and in the Moltkes' sitting room his tiny professional tape recorder was also out and activated and resting atop a stack of recent magazines on the coffee table before the davenport. Its technology was foreign and featured a very sensitive built in microphone, though the unit also gobbled AAA cells, and the miniature cassettes for it had to be special ordered. BSG magazines as a whole being litigation conscious in the extreme, a *Style* salaryman had to submit all relevant notes and tapes to Legal before his piece could even be typeset, which was one more reason why the day of an issue's closing was so fraught and stressful, and why editorial staff and interns rarely got a whole weekend off.

Moltke's fingers' and thumbs' unconscious ring had naturally come apart when Amber had smacked him and he'd gone over hard against the davenport's right armrest, but now it was back as they all sat in the dim green curtainlight and smiled at one another. What might have sounded at first like isolated gunshots or firecrackers were actually new homes' carapaces expanding in the heat all up and down the Willkie development. No analogy for the digital waist level circle or aperture or lens or target or orifice or void seemed quite right, but it struck Atwater as definitely the sort of tic or gesture that meant something — the way in dreams and certain kinds of art things were never merely things but always seemed to stand for something else that you couldn't quite put a finger on — and the journalist had already shorthanded several reminders to himself to consider whether the gesture was some kind of unconscious visible code or might be a key to the question of how to represent the artist's conflicted response to his extraordinary but also undeniably controversial and perhaps even repulsive talent.

The recorder's battery indicator showed a strong clear red. Amber occasionally leaned forward over her sewing materials to check the amount of audiotape remaining. Once more, Atwater thanked the artist and his wife for opening their home to him on a Sunday, explaining that he had to head on up to Chicago for a day or two but then would be back to start in on deep background if the Moltkes decided to give their consent. He had explained that the type of personality driven article that *Style* was interested in running would be impossible without the artist's cooperation, and that there would be no point in his taking up any more of their time after today if Mr. and Mrs. Moltke weren't totally on board and as excited about the piece as everyone over at *Style* was. He had addressed this statement to the artist, but it had been Amber Moltke's reaction he noted.

On the same coffee table between them, beside the magazines and tape recorder and a small vase of synthetic marigolds, were three artworks allegedly produced through ordinary elimination by Mr. Brint F. Moltke. The pieces varied slightly in size, but all were arresting in their extraordinary realism and the detail of their craftsmanship — although one of Atwater's notes was a reminder to himself to consider whether a word like craftsmanship really applied in such a case. The sample pieces were the very earliest examples that Mrs. Moltke said she'd been able to lay hands on; they had been out on the table when Atwater arrived. There were literally scores more of the artworks arranged in vaguely familiar looking glass cases in the unattached storm cellar out back, an environment that seemed strangely perfect, though Atwater had seen immediately how difficult the storm cellar would be for any of *Style*'s photographers to light and shoot properly. By 11:00 AM, he was mouthbreathing due to hay fever.

Mrs. Moltke periodically fanned at herself in a delicate way and said she did believe it might rain.

When Atwater and his brother had been in the eighth grade, the father of a family just up the road in Anderson had run a length of garden hose from his vehicle's exhaust pipe to the interior and killed himself in the home's garage, after which the son in their class and everyone else in the family had gone around with a strange fixed smile that had seemed both creepy and courageous; and something in the hydraulics of Brint Moltke's smile on the davenport reminded Skip Atwater of the Haas family's smile.

↓

Omitted through oversight above: Nearly every Indiana community has some street, lane, drive, or easement named for Wendell L. Willkie, b. 1892, GOP, favorite son.

↓

The recorder's tiny tape's first side had been almost entirely filled by Skip Atwater answering Mrs. Moltke's initial questions. It had become evident pretty quickly whose show this was, in terms of any sort of piece, on their end. Chewing a piece of gum with tiny motions of her front teeth in the distinctive Indiana style, Mrs. Moltke had requested information on how any potential article would be positioned and when it was likely to run. She had asked about word counts, column inches, boxes, leader quotes, and shared templates. Hers was the type of infantly milky skin on which even the lightest contact would leave some type of blotch. She had used terms like conferral, serial rights, and *sic vos non vobis*, which latter Skip did not even know. She had high quality photographs of some of the more spectacular artworks in a leatherette portfolio with the Moltkes' name and address embossed on the cover, and Atwater was asked to provide a receipt for the portfolio's loan.

The tape's second side, however, contained Mr. Brint Moltke's own first person account of how his strange and ambivalent gift had first come to light, which emerged — the account did — after Atwater had phrased his query several different ways and Amber Moltke had finally asked the journalist to excuse them and removed her husband into one of the home's rear rooms, where they took inaudible counsel together while Atwater circumspectly chewed the remainder of his ice. The result was what Atwater later, in his second floor room at the Holiday Inn, after showering, applying crude first aid to his left knee, and struggling unsuccessfully to move or reverse the room's excruciating painting, had copied into his steno as certainly usable in some part or form for deep background/UBA, particularly if Mr. Moltke, who had appeared to warm to the task or at least to come somewhat alive, could be induced to repeat its substance on record in a sanitized way:

'It was on a field exercise in basic [training in the US Army, in which Moltke later saw action in Kuwait as part of a maintenance crew in Operation Desert Storm], and the fellows on shitter [latrine, hygienic] detail — [latrine] detail is they soak the [military unit's solid wastes] in gas and burn it with a [flamethrower] — and up the [material] goes and in the fire one of the fellows saw something peculiar there in amongst the [waste material] and calls the sergeant over and they kick up a [fuss] because at first they're thinking somebody tossed something in the [latrine] for a joke, which is against regs, and the sergeant said when he found out who it was he was going to crawl up inside the [responsible party's] skull and look out his eyeholes, and they made the [latrine] detail [douse] the fire and get it [the artwork] out and come to find it weren't a[n illicit or unpatriotic object], and they didn't know whose [solid waste] it was, but I was pretty sure it was mine [because subj. then reports having had prior experiences of roughly same kind, which renders entire anecdote more or less pointless, but could foreseeably be edited out or massaged].'

3.

The Mount Carmel Holiday Inn regretfully had neither scanner nor fax for guests' outgoing use, Atwater had been informed at the desk by a man whose blazer was nearly identical to his own.

Temperatures had fallen and the sodium streetlights come on by themselves as Skip Atwater drove the artist and his spouse home from Ye Olde Country Buffet with a styrofoam box of leavings for a dog he'd seen no sign of; and the great elms and locusts were beginning to yaw and two thirds of the sky to be stacked with enormous muttering masses of clouds that moved in and out of themselves as if stirred by a

great unseen hand. Mrs. Moltke was in the back seat, and there was a
terrible noise as the car hit the driveway's grade. Blinds that had been
open on the duplex's other side were now closed, though there was still
no vehicle in that side's drive. The other side's door had a US flag as
well. As was also typical of severe weather conditions in the area, a
gray luminescence to the light made everything appear greasy and unreal. The rear of the artist's company van listed a toll free number to
dial if one had any concerns about the employee's driving.

It had emerged that the nearest Kinko's was in the nearby community
of Scipio, which was only a dozen miles east on SR 252 but could be
somewhat confusing to get around in because of indifferent signage.
Scipio evidently also had a Wal Mart. It was Amber Moltke who suggested that they leave the artist to watch his Sunday Reds game in
peace the way he liked to and proceed together in Atwater's rented
Chevrolet to that Kinko's, and decide together which photos to scan in
and forward, and to also go on and talk turkey in more depth respecting Skip's article on the Moltkes for *Style*. Atwater, whose fear of the
region's weather was amply justified by childhood experience, was un-
sure about either driving or using the Moltke's land line to call Laurel
Manderley during an impending storm that he was pretty sure would
show up at least yellow on Doppler radar — though on the other hand
he was not all that keen about returning to his room at the Holiday
Inn, whose wall had an immovable painting of a clown that he found
almost impossible to look at — and the journalist ended up watching
half an inning of the first Cincinnati Reds game he had seen in a decade
while sitting paralyzed with indecision on the Moltkes' davenport.

↓

Besides the facts that she walked without moving her arms and in general reminded him unpleasantly of the girl in *Election*, the core reason
why Atwater feared and avoided Ellen Bactrian was that Laurel Manderley had once confided to Atwater that Ellen Bactrian — who had
been in madrigals with Laurel Manderley for a year of their overlap at
Wellesley, and at the outset of Laurel's internship more or less took the
younger woman under her wing — had told her that in her opinion

Skip Atwater was not really quite as spontaneous a person as he liked to seem. Nor was Atwater stupid, and he was aware that his being so disturbed over what Ellen Bactrian apparently thought of him was possible evidence that she might actually have him pegged, that he might be not only shallow but at root a kind of poseur. It was not exactly the nicest thing Laurel Manderley had ever done, and part of the fallout was that she was now in a position where she had to act as a sort of human shield between Atwater and Ellen Bactrian, who was responsible for a lot of the day to day administration of WHAT IN THE WORLD; and to be honest, it was a situation that Atwater sometimes exploited, and used Laurel's guilt over her indiscretion to get her to do things or to use her personal connections with Ellen Bactrian in ways that weren't altogether right or appropriate. The whole thing could sometimes get extremely complicated and awkward, but Laurel Manderley for the most part simply bowed to the reality of a situation she had helped create, and accepted it as a painful lesson in respecting certain personal lines and boundaries that turned out to be there for a reason and couldn't be crossed without inevitable consequences. Her father, who was the sort of person who had favorite little apothegms that could sometimes get under one's skin with constant repetition, liked to say, 'Education is expensive,' and Laurel Manderley felt she was now starting to understand how little this saying had really to do with tuition or petty complaint.

↓

Because of some sort of hassle between *Style* and its imaging tech vendor over the terms of the service agreement, the fax machine that Skip Atwater shared with one other full time salaryman had had both a defunct ringer and a missing tray for over a month. Laurel Manderley was in stocking feet at Atwater's console formatting additional background on The Suffering Channel when the fax machine's red incoming light began blinking behind her. The Kinko's franchise in Scipio IN had no scanner, but it did have a digital faxing option that was vastly better than an ordinary low pixel fax. The images Atwater was forwarding to Laurel Manderley began to emerge from the unit's

feeder, coiled slightly, detached, and floated in a back and forth fashion to the antistatic carpet. It would be almost 6:00 before she broke
for a raisin and even saw them.

↓

The first great grape sized drops were striking the windshield as the
severely canted car left Scipio's commercial district, made two left
turns in rapid succession, and proceeded out of town on a numbered
county road whose gravel was so fresh it fairly gleamed in the gathering stormlight. Mrs. Moltke was navigating. Atwater now wore a
mushroom colored Robert Talbott raincoat over his blazer. As was
SOP for Indiana storms, there were several minutes of high winds and
tentative spatters, followed by a brief eerie stillness that had the quality of an immense inhalation as gravel clattered beneath their chassis.
Then fields and trees and cornrows' furrows all vanished in a sheet of
sideways rain that sent vague tumbling things across the road ahead
and behind. It was like nothing anyone east of Cleveland has ever
seen. Atwater, whose father had been a Civil Defense volunteer during
the F4 tornado that struck parts of Anderson in 1977, enjoined Amber
to try to find something on the AM band that wasn't just concussive
static. With the car's front seat unit moved all the way back to accommodate her, Atwater had to strain way out to reach the pedals, which
made it difficult to lean forward anxiously and scan upward for assembling funnels. The odd hailstone made a musical sound against the
rental's hood. The great myth is that the bad ones don't last long.

Amber Moltke directed Atwater through a murine succession of
rural roads and even smaller roads off those roads until they were on
little more than the ghost of a two track lane that cut through great
whipping tracts of Rorschach shrubbery. Her instructions came primarily in the form of slight motions of her head and left hand, which
were all she could move within the confines of her safety belt and harness, against which latter her body strained in several different places
with resultant depressions and folds. Atwater's face was the same color
as his raincoat by the time they reached their destination, some gap or
terminus in the foliage which Amber explained was actually a kind of

crude mesa whose vantage overlooked a large nitrogen fixative factory, whose complex and emberous lights at night were an attraction countywide. All that was visible at present was the storm working against the Cavalier's windshield like some sort of berserk car wash, but Atwater told Mrs. Moltke that he certainly appreciated her taking time out to let him absorb some of the local flavor. He watched her begin trying to disengage her seat's restraint system. The ambient noise was roughly equivalent to midcabin on a jetliner. There was, he could detect, a slight ammonial tang to the area's air.

Atwater had, by this point, helped Amber Moltke into the vehicle three separate times and out of it twice. Though technically fat, she presented more as simply huge, extrudent in all three dimensions. At least a half foot taller than the journalist, she managed to seem both towering and squat. Her release of the seat belt produced an effect not unlike an impact's airbag. Atwater's notebook already contained a description of Mrs. Moltke's fatness as being the smooth solid kind as opposed to the soft plumpness or billowing aspect or loose flapping fat of some obese people. There was no cellulite, no quivery or pendent or freehanging parts — she was enormous and firm, and fair the same way babies are. A head the size of a motorcycle tire was topped by a massive blond pageboy whose bangs were thick and not wholly even, receding into a complexly textured bale of curls in the rear areas. In the light of the storm she seemed to glow; the umbrella she carried was not for rain. 'I so much as get downwind of the sun and I burn,' had been Amber's explanation to Skip as the artist/husband held the great flowered thing out at arms' length to spread it in the driveway and then angle it up over the car's rear door just so.

→

Many of *Style*'s upper echelon interns convened for a working lunch at Chambers Street's Tutti Mangia restaurant twice a week, to discuss issues of concern and transact any editorial or other business that was pending, after which each returned to her respective mentor and relayed whatever was germane. It was an efficient practice that saved the magazine's paid staffers a great deal of time and emotional energy. Many of the interns at Monday's lunches traditionally had the Niçoise salad, which was outrageously good here.

They often liked to get two large tables squunched up together near the door, so that those who smoked could take turns darting out front to do so in the striped awning's shade. Which management was happy to do — conjoin the tables. It was an interesting station to serve or sit near. The *Style* interns all still possessed the lilting inflections and vaguely outraged facial expressions of adolescence, which were in sharp contrast to their extraordinary table manners and to the brisk clipped manner of their gestures and speech, as well as to the fact that their outfits' elements were nearly always members of the same color family, a very adult type of coordination that worked to convey a formal and businesslike tone to each ensemble. For reasons with origins much farther back in history than anyone at the table could have speculated about, a majority of the editorial interns at *Style* traditionally come from Seven Sisters colleges. Also at the table was one very plain but self possessed intern who worked with the design director up in *Style*'s executive offices on the 82nd floor. The two least conservatively dressed interns were senior shades from Research and also always wore, unless the day was really overcast, dark glasses to cover the red rings their jobs' goggles left around their eyes, which were slow to fade. It was also true that no fewer than five of the interns at the working lunch on 2 July were named either Laurel or Tara, although it's not as if people can help what their names are.

Laurel Manderley, who tended to favor very soft simple lines in business attire, wore a black Armani skirt and jacket ensemble with sheer hose and an objectively stunning pair of Miu Miu pumps that she'd picked up for next to nothing at a flea market in Milan the previous summer. Her hair was up and had a lacquer chopstick through the chignon. Ellen Bactrian often took a noon dance class on Mondays and was not at today's working lunch, though four of the other associate editors' head interns were there, one sporting a square cut engagement ring so large and garish that she made an ironic display of having to support her wrist with the other hand in order to show it around the table, which occasioned some snarky little internal emails back at *Style* over the course of the rest of the day.

Skip Atwater's bizarre and quixotic pitch for a WITW piece on some sort of handyman who purportedly excreted pieces of fine art out of his bottom in Indiana, while not the most pressing issue on this closing day for what was known as SE2, was certainly the most arresting and controversial. The interns ended up hashing out what came to be called the miraculous poo story in some detail, and the discussion was lively and far ranging, with passions aroused and a good deal of personal background information laid on the table, some of which would alter various power constellations in subtle ways that would not even emerge until preliminary work on the 10 September issue commenced later in the month.

At one point during the lunch, an editorial intern in a charcoal gray Yamamoto pantsuit related an anecdote of her fiancé's, with whom she had apparently exchanged every detail of their sexual histories as a condition for maximal openness and trust in their upcoming marriage. The anecdote, which the intern amused everyone by trying at first to phrase very delicately, involved her fiancé, as an undergraduate, performing cunnilingus on what was at that time one of Swarthmore's most beautiful and widely desired girls, with zero percent body fat and those great pillowy lips that were just then coming into vogue, when evidently she had, suddenly and without any warning . . . well, farted — the girl being gone down on had — and not at all in the sort of way you could minimize or blow off, according to the fiancé later, but rather 'one of those strange horrible hot ones that are so totally awful and rank.' The anecdote appeared to strike some kind of common chord or nerve: most of the interns at the table were laughing so hard they had to put their forks down, and some held their napkins to their mouths as if to bite them or hold down digestive matter. After the laughter tailed off, there was a brief inbent communal silence while the interns — most of whom were quite intelligent and had had exceptionally high board scores, particularly on the analytical component — tried to suss out just why they had all laughed and what was so funny about the conjunction of oral sex and flatus. There was also something just perfect about the editorial intern's jacket's asymmetrical cut, both incongruous and yet somehow inevitable, which was why Yamamoto was generally felt to be worth every penny. At the same time, it was common knowledge that there was something in the process or chemicals used in commercial dry cleaning that was unfriendly to Yamamotos' particular fabrics, and that they never lay or hung or felt quite so perfect after they'd been dry cleaned a couple times; so there was always a kernel of tragedy to the pleasure of wearing Yamamoto, which may have been a deeper part of its value. A more recent tradition was that the more senior of the interns usually enjoyed a glass of pinot grigio. The intern said that her fiancé tended to date his sexual adulthood as commencing with that incident, and liked to say that he had 'lost literally about twenty pounds of illusions in that one second,' and was now exceptionally, almost unnaturally comfortable with his body and bodies in general and their private functions, rarely even closing the bathroom door now when he went in there for what the intern referred to as big potty.

A fellow WITW staff intern, who also roomed with Laurel Manderley and three other Wellesleyites in a basement sublet near the Williamsburg Bridge, related a vignette that her therapist had once shared with her about dating his wife, whom the therapist had originally met when both of them were going through horrible divorces, and of their going out to dinner on one of their early dates and coming back and sitting with glasses of wine on her sofa, and of she all of a sudden saying, 'You have to leave,' and he not understanding, not knowing whether she was kicking him out or whether he'd said something inappropriate or what, and she finally explaining, 'I have to take a dump and I can't do it with you here, it's too stressful,' using the actual word dump, and of so how the therapist had gone down and stood on the corner smoking a cigarette and looking up at her apartment, watching the light in the bathroom's frosted window go on, and simultaneously, one, feeling like a bit of an idiot for standing out there waiting for her to finish so he could go back up, and, two, realizing that he loved and respected this woman for baring to him so nakedly the insecurity she had been feeling. He had told the intern that standing on that corner was the first time in quite a long time he had not felt deeply and painfully alone, he had realized.

Laurel Manderley's caloric regimen included very precise rules on what parts of her Niçoise salad she was allowed to eat and what she had to do to earn them. At today's lunch she was somewhat preoccupied. She had as yet told no one about any photos, to say nothing of any unannounced overnight package; and Atwater, who had spent the morning commuting to Chicago, made it a principle never to take cellular calls while he drove.

The longtime girl Friday for the associate editor of SURFACES, which was the section of *Style* that focused on health and beauty, had also been among the first of the magazine's interns not to bother changing into pumps on arrival but instead to wear, normally with a high end Chanel or DKBL suit, the same crosstrainers she had commuted in, which somehow for some strange reason worked, and had for a time split the editorial interns into two opposed camps regarding office footwear. She had also at some point spent a trimester at Cambridge, and still spoke with a slight British accent, and asked generally now whether anyone else who traveled abroad much had noticed that in German toilets the hole into which the poop is supposed to disappear when you flush is positioned way in front, so that the poop just sort of *lies* there in full view and there's almost no way you can avoid looking at it when you get up and turn around to flush. Which she observed was so almost stereotypically German, almost as if you were supposed to study and analyze your poop and make sure it passed muster before you flushed it down. Here a senior shade who seemed always to make it a point to wear something garishly retro on Mondays inserted a reminiscence about first seeing the word FAHRT in great block letters on signs all over Swiss and German rail stations, on childhood trips, and how she and her stepsisters had spent whole long Eurail rides cracking one another up by making childish jokes about travelers' various FAHRTS. Whereas, the SURFACES head intern continued with a slight cold smile at the shade's interruption, whereas in French toilets, though, the hole tended to be way in the back so that the poop vanished ASAP, meaning the whole thing was set up to be as elegant and tasteful as possible . . . although in France there was also the whole bidet issue, which many of the interns agreed always struck them as weird and kind of unhygienic. There was then a quick anecdote about someone's once having asked a French concierge about the really low drinking fountain in the salle de bains, which also struck a nerve of risibility at the table.

At different intervals, two or three of the interns who smoked would excuse themselves briefly and step out to smoke and then return — Tutti Mangia's management had made it clear that they didn't really want like eight people at a time out there under the awning.

'So then what about the US toilets here, with the hole in the middle and all this water so it all floats and goes around and around in a little dance before it goes down — what's up with that?'

The design director's intern wore a very simple severe Prada jacket over a black silk tee. 'They don't always go around and around. Some toilets are really fast and powerful and it's gone right away.'

'Maybe up on eighty-two it is!' Two of the newer staff interns leaned slightly toward each other as they laughed.

Laurel Manderley's roommate, who at Wellesley had played both field hockey and basketball and was a national finalist for a Marshall, asked how many of those at the table had had to read those ghastly pieces of Swift's in Post Liz Lit where he went on and on about women taking a crap and how supposedly traumatic it was for the swain when he found out that his beloved went to the bathroom like a normal human being instead of whatever sick mommy figure Swift liked to make women into, quoting the actual lines, '"Send up an excremental Smell/ To taint the Parts from whence they fell/the Pettycoats and Gown perfume/And waft a Stink round every Room,"' which a few people hazarded to say that it was maybe a little bit *disturbing* that Siobhan had seemingly memorized this . . . and thereupon the latter part of the discussion turned more toward intergender bathroom habits and the various small traumas of cohabitation with a male partner, or even just when you reached the stage where one or the other of you were staying over a lot, and the table conversation broke up into a certain number of overlapping smaller exchanges while some people ordered different kinds of coffee and Laurel Manderley sucked abstractedly on an olive pit.

'If you ask me, there's something sketchy about a guy whose bathroom is all full of those little deodorizers and scented candles. I always tend to think, here's somebody who kind of denies his own humanity.'

'It's bad news if it's a big deal either way. It's never a good sign.'

'But you don't want him totally uninhibited, don't get me wrong.'

'Because if he's going around farting in front of you or something, it means on some level he's thinking you're just one of the guys, and that's always bad news.'

'Because then how long before he's sitting there on the couch all day farting and telling you to go get him a beer?'

'If I'm out in the kitchen and Pankaj wants a beer or something, he *knows* he better say please.'

The shade who wore Pucci and two other research interns were evidently going with three guys from *Forbes* to some kind of infamous annual *Forbes* house party on Fire Island over the holiday weekend, which, since the Fourth was on Wednesday this year, meant the following weekend.

'I don't know,' THE THUMB's head intern said. 'My parents pass gas in front of each other. There's something sweet about it, like it's just another part of life together. They'll keep right on talking or whatever as if nothing happened.' THE THUMB was the name of the section of *Style* that contained mini reviews of film and television, as well as certain types of commercial music and books, each review accompanied by a special thumb icon whose angle conveyed visually how positive the assessment was.

'Although that in itself shows there's something different about it. If you sneeze or yawn, there's something said. A fart, though, is always ignored, even though everybody knows what's just happened.'

Some interns were laughing; some were not.

'The silence communicates some kind of unease about it.'

'A conspiracy of silence.'

'Shannon was on some friend of a friend thing at the Hat with some awful guy in she said an XMI Platinum sweater, with that awful

Haverford type of jaunty misogyny, that was going on and on about why do girls always go to the bathroom together, like what's up with that, and Shannon looks at the guy like what planet did you just land from, and says well it should be obvious we're doing *cocaine* in there, is why.'

'One of those guys where you're like, hello, my eyes are *up here*.'

'Carlos says in some cultures the etiquette actually calls for passing gas in some situations.'

'The well known Korean thing about you burp to say thank you.'

'My parents had this running joke — they called a fart an intruder. They'd look at each other over the paper and be, like, "I do believe there's an intruder present."'

Laurel Manderley, who had had an idea, was rooting through her Fendi for her personal cell.

'My mom would just about drop over dead if anybody ever cut one in front of her. It's just not even imaginable.'

A circulation intern named Laurel Rodde, who as a rule favored DKNY, and who wasn't exactly unpopular but no one felt like they knew her very well despite all the time they all spent with one another, and who usually barely said a word at the working lunches, suddenly said: 'You know, did anybody when they were little ever have this thing where you think of your shit as sort of like your baby and sometimes want to hold it and talk to it and almost cry or feel guilty about flushing it and dream sometimes of your shit in a little sort of little stroller with a bonnet and bottle and still sometimes in the bathroom look at it and give a little wave like, bye bye, as it goes down, and then feel a void?' There was an uncomfortable silence. Some of the interns looked at one another out of the corner of their eye. They were at a stage where they were now too adult and socially refined to respond with a drawn out semicruel 'Oooo-kaaaay,' but you could tell that a few of them were thinking it. The circulation intern, who'd gone a bit pink, was bent to her salad once more.

←

Citing bridgework, Atwater again declined the half piece of gum that Mrs. Moltke offered. All the parked car's windows ran in a way that would have been pretty had there been more overall light. The rain had steadied to the point where he could just barely discern the outline of a large sign in the distance below, which Amber had told him marked the nitrogen fixative factory's entrance.

'The man's conflicted, is all,' Mrs. Moltke said. 'He's about the most private man you'd ever like to see. In the privy I mean.' She chewed her gum well, without extraneous noises. She had to be at least 6'1". 'It surely weren't like that at my house growing up, I can tell you. It's a matter of how folks grow up, wouldn't you say?'

'This is fascinating,' Atwater said. They had been parked at the little road's terminus for perhaps ten minutes. The tape recorder was placed on his knee, and the subject's wife now reached over across herself and turned it off. Her hand was large enough to cover the recorder and also make liberal contact with his knee on either side. Atwater still had the same pants size he'd had in college, though these slacks were obviously a great deal newer. In the low barometric pressure of the storm, he was now entirely stuffed up, and was mouth breathing, which caused his lower lip to hang outward and made him look even more childlike. He was breathing rather more rapidly than he was aware of.

It was not clear whether Amber's small smile was for him or herself or just what. 'I'm going to tell you some background facts that you can't write about, but it'll help you understand our situation here. Skip — can I call you Skip?'

'Please do.'

Rain beat musically on the Cavalier's roof and hood. 'Skip, between just us two now, what we've got here is a boy whose folks beat him witless all through growing up. That whipped on him with electric cords and burnt on him with cigarettes and made him eat out in the shed when his mother thought his manners weren't up to snuff for her high and mighty table. His daddy was all right, it was more his mother. One of this churchy kind that's so upright and proper in church but back at home she's crazy evil, whipped her own children with cords and I don't know what all.' At the mention of church, Atwater's facial expression had become momentarily inward and difficult to read. Amber

Moltke's voice was low in register but still wholly feminine, with a quality that cut through the rain's sound even at low volume. It reminded Atwater somewhat of Lauren Bacall at the end of her career, when the aged actress had begun to look more and more like a scalded cat but still possessed of a voice that affected one's nervous system in profound ways, as a child.

The artist's wife said: 'I know that one time when he was a boy that she came in and I think caught Brint playing with himself maybe, and made him come down in the sitting room and do it in front of them, the family, that she made them all sit there and watch him. Do you follow what I'm saying, Skip?'

The most significant sign of an approaching tornado would be a greenish cast to the ambient light and a sudden drop in pressure that made one's ears pop.

'His daddy didn't outright abuse him, but he was half crazy,' Amber said, 'a deacon. A man under great pressure from his own demons that he wrestled with. And I know one time Brint saw her take and beat a little baby kittycat to death with a skillet for messing on the kitchen floor. When he was in his high chair, watching. A little kittycat. Well,' she said. 'What do you suppose a little boy's toilet training is going to be like with folks like that?'

Nodding vigorously being one of his tactics for drawing people out in interviews, Atwater was nodding at almost everything the subject's wife was saying. This, together with the fact that his arms were still out straight before him, lent him a somnambulist aspect. Wind gusts caused the car to shimmy slightly in the clearing's mud.

By this time, Amber Moltke had shifted her mass onto her left haunch and brought her great right leg up and was curled kittenishly in such a way as to incline herself toward Atwater, gazing at the side of his face. She smelled of talcum powder and Big Red. Her leg was like something you could slide down into some kind of unimaginable chasm. The chief outward sign that Atwater was affected one way or the other by the immense sexual force field around Mrs. Moltke was that he continued to grip the Cavalier's steering wheel tightly with both hands and to face directly ahead as though still driving. There was very little air in the car. He had an odd subtle sense of ascent, as if the car were slightly rising. There was no real sign of any type of overhead view, or even of the tiny road's dropoff to SR 252 and the nitrogen works that commenced just ahead — he was going almost entirely on Mrs. Moltke's report of where they were.

'This is a man, now, that will leave the premises to break wind. That closes the privy door and locks it and turns on the exhaust fan and this little radio he's got, and runs water, and sometimes puts a rolled up towel in the crack of the door when he's in there doing his business. Brint I mean.'

'I think I understand what you're saying.'

'Most times he can't do his business if there's somebody even there. In the house. The man thinks I believe him when he says he's going to just go driving around.' She sighed. 'So Skip, this is a very very shy individual in this department. He's wounded inside. He wouldn't hardly say boo when I first met him.'

Following college, Skip Atwater had done a year at IU-Indianapolis's prestigious grad journalism program, then landed a cub spot at the Indianapolis *Star*, and there had made no secret of his dream of someday writing a syndication grade human interest column for a major urban daily, until the assistant city editor who'd hired him told Skip in his first annual performance review, among other things, that as a journalist Atwater struck him as being polished but about two inches deep. After which performance review Atwater had literally run for the privacy of the men's room and there had struck his own chest with his fist several times because he knew that at heart it was true: his fatal flaw was an ineluctably light, airy prose sensibility. He had no innate sense of tragedy or preterition or complex binds or any of the things that made human beings' misfortunes significant to one another. He was all upbeat angle. The editor's blunt but kindly manner had made it worse. Atwater could write a sweet commercial line, he'd acknowledged. He had compassion, of a certain frothy sort, and drive. The editor, who always wore a white dress shirt and tie but never a jacket, had actually put his arm around Atwater's shoulders. He said he liked

Skip enough to tell him the truth, because he was a good kid and just needed to find his niche. There were all different kinds of reporting. The editor said he had acquaintances at *USA Today* and offered to make a call.

Atwater, who also possessed an outstanding verbal memory, retained almost verbatim the questions Laurel Manderley had left him with on the phone at Ye Olde Country Buffet after he'd summarized the morning's confab and characterized the artist as catatonically inhibited, terribly shy, scared of his shadow, and so forth. What Laurel had said didn't yet add up for her in the story was how the stuff got seen in the first place: 'What, he gives it to somebody? This catatonically shy guy calls somebody into the bathroom and says, Hey, look at this extraordinary thing I just pooped out of me? I can't see anybody over age six doing that, much less somebody that shy. Whether it's a hoax or not, the guy's got to be some kind of closet exhibitionist,' she'd opined. Every instinct Atwater possessed had since been crying out that this was the piece's fulcrum and UBA, the universalizing element that made great soft news go: the conflict between Moltke's extreme personal shyness and need for privacy on the one hand versus his involuntary need to express what lay inside him through some type of personal expression or art. Everyone experienced this conflict on some level. Though lurid and potentially disgusting, the mode of production in this case simply heightened the conflict's voltage, underlined the stakes in bold, made it at once deep and accessible for *Style* readers, many of whom scanned the magazine in the bathroom anyway, all the salarymen knew.

Atwater, however, was, since the end of a serious involvement some years prior, also all but celibate, and tended to be extremely keyed up and ambivalent in any type of sexually charged situation, which unless he was off base this increasingly was — which in retrospect was partly why, in the stormy enclosure of the rental car with the pulverizingly attractive Amber Moltke, he had committed one of the fundamental errors in soft news journalism: asking a centrally important question before he was certain just what answer would advance the interests of the piece.

↓

Only the third shift attendant knew that R. Vaughn Corliss slept so terribly, twining in and out of the sheets with bleatings of the purest woe, foodlessly chewing, sitting up and looking wildly about, feeling at himself and moaning, crying out that no he wouldn't go there, not there not again no please. The high concept mogul was always up with the sun, and his first act after stripping the bed and placing his breakfast order was to erase the disk of the bedroom's monitor. A selected few nights' worth of these disks the attendant had slipped in during deep sleep and copied, however, as a de facto form of unemployment insurance, since Corliss's temper and caprice were well known; and the existence of these pirate disks was also known to certain representatives of Eckleschafft-Böd whose business it was to know such things.

It was only if, after sheep, controlled breathing, visualizing IV pentothal drips, and mentally reviewing in close detail a special collector's series of photographs of people on fire entitled *People on Fire,* Corliss still could not fall or fall back asleep that he'd resort to the failsafe: imagining the faces of everyone he had loved, hated, feared, known, or even ever seen all assembling and accreting as pixels into a pointillist image of a single great all devouring eye whose pupil was Corliss's own.

In the morning, the reinvented high concept cable entrepreneur's routine was invariant and always featured a half hour of pretend rowing on a machine that could simulate both resistance and crosscurrent, a scrupulously Fletcherized breakfast, and a session of the 28 lead facial biofeedback in which microelectric sensors were affixed to individual muscle groups and exhaustive daily practice yielded the ability to form, at will, any of the 216 facial expressions common to all known cultures. Corliss was in constant contact via headset cellular throughout this regimen.

Unlike most driven business visionaries he was not, when all was said and done, an unhappy man. He felt sometimes an odd complex emotion that, when broken down and examined in quiet reflection, revealed itself to be self envy, which appears near the top of certain Maslovian fulfillment pyramids as a rare and culturally specific form of

joy. The sense Skip Atwater had gotten, after a brief and highly structured interface with Corliss for a WITW piece on the All Ads cable
channel in 1999, was that the producer's reclusive, eccentric persona
was a conscious performance or imitation, and that Corliss (whom
Atwater had personally liked and not found all that intimidating) was
in reality a gregarious, backslapping, people type person who affected
an hermetic torment for reasons which Atwater's notebooks contained
several multipage theories on, none of which appeared in the article
published in *Style*.

↓

Atwater and Mrs. Moltke were now unquestionably breathing each
other's air; the Cavalier's glass surfaces were almost entirely steamed
over. At the same time, an imperfection in its gasket's seal was allowing rain droplets to enter and move in a complex system of paths down
his window. These branching paths and tributaries were in the left periphery of the journalist's vision; Amber Moltke's face loomed vividly
in the right. Unlike Mrs. Atwater, the artist's wife had a good firm
chin with no wattles, though her throat's girth was extraordinary —
Atwater could not have gotten around it with both hands.

'The shyness and woundedness must be complex, though,' the journalist said. 'Given that the pieces are public. Publicly displayed.' He
had already amassed a certain amount of technical detail about the
preparation of the displays, back at the Moltkes' duplex. The pieces
were not varnished or in any way chemically treated. They were, however, sprayed lightly with a fixative when fresh or new, to help preserve
their shape and intricate detail — evidently some of the man's early
work had become cracked or distorted when allowed to dry completely. Atwater knew that freshly produced pieces of art were placed
on a special silver finish tray, an heirloom of some sort from Mrs.
Moltke's own family, then covered in common kitchen plastic wrap
and allowed to cool to room temperature before the fixative was applied. Skip could imagine the steam from a fresh new piece fogging
the Saran's interior and making it difficult to see the thing itself until
the wrap was removed and discarded. Only later, in the midst of all the

editorial wrangling over his piece's typeset version, would Atwater learn that the fixative in question was a common brand of aerosol styling spray whose manufacturer advertised in *Style*.

Amber gave a brief laugh. 'We're not exactly talking the big time. Two bean festivals and the DAR craft show.'

'Well, and of course the fair.' Atwater was referring to the Franklin County Fair, which like most county fairs in eastern Indiana was held in June, quite a bit earlier than the national average. The reasons for this were complicated, agricultural, and historically bound up with Indiana's refusal to participate in Daylight Savings Time, which caused no end of hassles for certain commodities markets at the Chicago Board of Trade. Atwater's own childhood experiences had been of the Madison County Fair, held during the third week of each June on the outskirts of Mounds State Park, but he assumed that all county fairs were roughly similar. He had unconsciously begun to do the thing with his fist again.

'Well, although the fair ain't exactly your big time either.'

Also from childhood experience, Skip Atwater knew that the slight squeaks and pops one could hear when Amber laughed were from different parts of her complex foundation garment as they strained and moved against one another. Her kneesized left elbow now rested on the seat back between them, leaving her left hand free to play and make tiny languid motions in the space between her head and his. A head nearly twice the size of Atwater's own. Her hair was wiglike in overall configuration, but it had a high protein luster no real wig could ever duplicate.

His right arm still rigidly out against the Cavalier's wheel, Atwater turned his head a few more degrees toward her. 'This, though, will be very public. *Style* is about as public as you can get.'

'Well, except for TV.'

Atwater inclined his head slightly to signify concession. 'Except for TV.'

Mrs. Moltke's hand, with its multiple different rings, was now within just inches of the journalist's large red right ear. She said: 'Well, I look at *Style*. I've been looking at *Style* for years. I don't bet there's a body in town that hasn't looked at *Style* or *People* or one of you all.' The hand moved as if it were under water. 'Sometimes it's hard keeping you all straight. After your girl there called, I said to Brint it was a man coming over from *People* when I was telling him to go on and get cleaned up for company.'

Atwater cleared his throat. 'So you see my point, then, which in no way forms any sort of argument against the piece or Mr. Moltke's —'

'Brint.'

'Against Brint's consenting to the piece.' Atwater would also every so often give a small but vigorous all body shiver, involuntary, rather like a wet dog shaking itself, which neither party commented on. Bits of windblown foliage hit the front and rear windshields and remained for a moment or two before they were washed away. The sky could really have been any color at all and there would be no way to know. Atwater now tried to rotate his entire upper body toward Mrs. Moltke: 'But he will need to know what he's in for. If my editors give the go ahead, which I should again stress I have every confidence they ultimately will, one condition is likely to be the presence of some sort of medical authority to authenticate the . . . circumstances of creation.'

'You're saying in there with him?' The gusts of her breath seemed to strike every little cilium on Atwater's cheek and temple. Her right hand still covered the recorder and several inches of Atwater's knee on either side. Her largo pulse was visible in the trembling of her bust, which was understandably prodigious and also now pointed Atwater's way. Probably no more than four inches separated the bust from his right arm, which was still held out stiffly and attached to the steering wheel. Atwater's other fist was pumping like mad down beside the driver's door.

'No, no, not necessarily, but probably right outside, and ready to perform various tests and procedures on the . . . on it the minute Mr. Moltke, Brint, is finished. Comes out with it.' Another intense little shiver.

Amber gave another small mirthless laugh.

'I'm sure you know what I mean,' Atwater said. 'Temperature and constitution and the lack of any sort of sign of any human hand or tool or anything employed in the . . . process of the . . .'

'And then it'll come out.'

'The piece, you mean,' Atwater said. She nodded. In a way that made no physical sense given their respective sizes, Atwater's eyes seemed now to be exactly level with hers, and without being aware of it he blinked whenever she did, though her hand's small circles often supervened.

Atwater said: 'As I've said, I have every confidence that yes, it will.'

At the same time, the journalist was also trying not to indulge himself by imagining Laurel Manderley's reaction to the faxed reproductions of the artist's pieces as they slowly emerged from the machine. He felt that he knew almost all the different permutations her face would go through.

Nor was it clear whether Mrs. Moltke was looking at his ear or at the underwater movements of her own hand up next to the ear. 'And what you're saying is then, why, to get ready, because once it comes out nothing will be the same. Because there'll be attention.'

'I would think so, yes.' He tried to turn a little further. 'Of various different kinds.'

'You're saying other magazines. Or TV, the Internet.'

'It's often difficult to predict the forms of public attention or to know in advance what —'

'But after this kind of amount of attention you're saying there might be art galleries wanting to handle it. For sale. Do art galleries do auctions, or they just put it out with a price sticker on it and folks come and shop, or what all?'

Atwater was aware that this was a very different type and level of exchange than the morning's confab in the Moltkes' home. It was hard for him not to feel that Amber might be patronizing him a bit, playing up to a certain stereotype of provincial naiveté — he did this himself in certain situations at *Style*. At the same time, he felt that to some extent she was sincere in deferring to him because he lived and worked in New York City, the cultural heart of the nation — Atwater was absurdly gratified by this kind of thing. The whole geographical deference issue could get very complicated and abstract. At the right periphery, he could see that a certain delicate pattern Amber was tracing in the air near his ear was actually the cartography of that ear, its spirals and intending whorls. Sensitive from childhood about his ears' size and hue, Atwater had worn either baseball caps or knit caps all the way through college.

Ultimately, the journalist's failure to think the whole thing through and decide just how to respond was itself a form of decision. 'I think they do both,' he told her. 'Sometimes there are auctions. Sometimes a special exhibit, and potential buyers will come for a large party on the first day, to meet the artist. Often called an art opening.' He was facing the windshield again. The rain came no less hard but the sky looked perhaps to be lightening — although, on the other hand, the steam of their exhalations against the window was itself whitish and might act as some type of optical filter. At any rate, Atwater knew that it was often at the trailing end of a storm front that funnels developed. 'The initial key,' he said, 'will be arranging for the right photographer.'

'Some professional type shots, you mean.'

'The magazine has both staff photographers and freelancers the photo people like to use for various situations. The politics of influencing them as to which particular photographer they might send all gets pretty involved, I'm afraid.' Atwater could taste his own carbon dioxide in the car's air. 'The key will be producing some images that are carefully lit and indirect and tasteful and yet at the same time emphatic in being able to show what he's able to . . . just what he's achieved.'

'Already. You mean the doodads he's come out with already.'

'There will be no way to even pitch it at the executive level without real photos, I don't think,' Atwater said.

For a moment there was only the wind and rain and a whisking sound of microfiber, due to Atwater's fist.

'You know what's peculiar? Is sometimes I can hear it and then other times not,' Amber said quietly. 'That you said up to home you were from back here, and sometimes I can hear it and then other times you sound more . . . all business, and I can't hear it in you at all.'

'I'm originally from Anderson.'

'Up by Muncie you mean. Where all the big mounds are.'

'Anderson's got the mounds, technically. Though I went to school in Muncie, at Ball State.'

'There's some more right here, up to Mixerville off the lake. They still say they don't know who all made those mounds. They just know they're old.'

'The sense I get is there are still competing theories.'

'Dave Letterman on the TV talks about Ball State all the time, that he was at. He's from here someplace.'

'He graduated long before I got there, though.'

She did touch his ear now, though her finger was too large to fit inside or trace the auricle's whorls and succeeded only in occluding Atwater's hearing on that side, so that he could hear his own heartbeat and his voice seemed newly loud to him over the rain:

'But with the operative question being whether he'll do it.'

'Brint,' she said.

'Respecting the subject of the piece.'

'If he'll sit still for it you mean.'

The finger kept Atwater from turning his head, so that he could not see whether Mrs. Moltke was smiling or had made a deliberate sally or just what. 'Since he's so agonizingly shy, as you've explained. You must — he's got to be able to see already that it will be, to some extent, a bit invasive.' Atwater was in no way acknowledging the finger in his ear, which did not move or turn but simply stayed there. The feeling of queer levitation persisted, however. 'Invasive of his privacy, of your privacy. And I don't exactly get the sense, which I respect, that Mr. Moltke burns to share his art with the world, or necessarily to get a lot of personal exposure.'

'He'll do it,' Amber said. The finger withdrew slightly but was still in contact with his ear. The very oldest she could possibly be was 28.

The journalist said: 'Because I'll be honest with you, I think it's an extraordinary thing and an extraordinary story, but Laurel and I are going to have to go right to the mat with the Executive Editor to secure a commitment to this piece, and it would make things really awkward if Mr. Moltke suddenly demurred or deferred or got cold feet or decided it was all just too private and invasive a process.'

She did not ask who Laurel was. She was wholly on her left flank now, her luminous knee up next to her hand on the Daewoo unit, and only the bunched hem of his raincoat separating her knee and his, her great bosom crushed and jutting and its heartbeat's quiver bringing one breast within inches of the Talbott's shawl collar. He kept envisioning her having to strike or swat the artist before he'd respond to the simplest query. And the strange fixed grin, which probably would not photograph well at all.

Again the artist's wife said: 'He'll do it.'

Unbeknownst to Atwater, the Cavalier's right hand tires were now sunk in mud almost to the valves. What he felt as an occult force rotating him up and over toward Mrs. Moltke in clear contravention of the most basic journalistic ethics was in fact simple gravity: the compartment was now at a 20 degree angle. Wind gusts shook the car like a maraca, and the journalist could hear the sounds of thrashing foliage and windblown debris doing God knew what to the rental's paint.

'I have no doubt,' the journalist said. 'I think I'm just trying to determine for myself why you're so sure, although obviously I'm going to defer to your judgment because he is your husband and if anyone knows another's heart it's obviously —'

What he felt in the first instant to be Mrs. Moltke's hand over his mouth turned out to be her forefinger held to his lips, chin, and lower jaw in an intimate shush. Atwater could not help wondering whether it was the same finger that had just been in his ear. Its tip was almost the width of both of his nostrils together.

'He will because he'll do it for me, Skip. Because I say.'

'Mn srtny gld t—'

'But go on and ask it.' Mrs. Moltke backed the finger off a bit. 'We should get it out here up front between us. Why I'd want my husband known for his shit.'

'Though of course the pieces are so much more than that,' Atwater said, his eyes appearing to cross slightly as he gazed at the finger. Another compact shiver, a whisking sound of fabric and his forehead running with sweat. The cinnamon heat and force of her exhalations like one of the heating grates along Columbus Circle where coteries of homeless sat in the winter in fingerless gloves and balaklava hoods, their eyes flat and pitiless as Atwater hurried past. He had to engage the car's battery in order to crack his window, and a burst of noise from the radio made him jump.

Amber Moltke appeared very still and intent. 'Still and all, though,' she said. 'To have your TV reporters or Dave Letterman or that skinny one real late at night making their jokes about it, and folks reading in *Style* and thinking about Brint's bowel, about him sitting there in the privy moving his bowel in some kind of special way to make something like that come out. Because that's his whole hook, Skip, isn't it. Why you're here in the first place. That it's his shit.'

→

It turned out that a certain Richmond IN firm did a type of specialty shipping where they poured liquid styrene around fragile items, producing a very light form fitting insulation. The Federal Express outlet named on the box's receipt, however, was in Scipio IN, which was also featured in the address on the Kinko's cover sheet that had accompanied Sunday's faxed photos, which faxes the next morning's Fed Ex rendered more or less moot or superfluous, so that Laurel Manderley couldn't quite see why Atwater'd gone to the trouble.

At Monday's working lunch, Laurel Manderley's deceptively simple idea with respect to the package's contents had been to hurry back and place them out on Ellen Bactrian's desk before she returned from her dance class, so that they would be sitting there waiting for her, and not to say a word or try to prevail on Ellen in any way, but simply to let the pieces speak for themselves. This was, after all, what her own salaryman appeared to have done, giving Laurel no warning whatsoever that art was on the way.

→

The following was actually part of a lengthy telephone conversation on the afternoon of 3 July between Laurel Manderley and Skip Atwater, the latter having literally limped back to the Mount Carmel Holiday

Inn after negotiating an exhaustive and nerve wracking series of in situ authenticity tests at the artist's home.

'And what's with that address, by the way?'

'Willkie's an Indiana politician. The name is ubiquitous here. I think he may have run against Truman. Remember the photo of Truman holding up the headline?'

'No, I mean the half. What, fourteen and a half Willkie?'

'It's a duplex,' Atwater said.

'Oh.'

There had been a brief silence, one whose strangeness might have been only in retrospect.

'Who lives on the other side?'

There had been another pause. It was true that both salaryman and intern were extremely tired and discombobulated by this point.

The journalist said: 'I don't know yet. Why?'

To which Laurel Manderley had no good answer.

←

In the listing Cavalier, at or about the height of the thunderstorm, Atwater shook his head. 'It's more than that,' he said. He was, to all appearances, sincere. He appeared genuinely concerned that the artist's wife not think his motives exploitative or sleazy. Amber's finger was still right near his mouth. He told her it was not yet entirely clear to him how she viewed her husband's pieces or understood the extraordinary power they exerted. Rain and debris notwithstanding, the windshield was too steamed over for Atwater to see that the view of SR 252 and the fixative works was now tilted 30 or more degrees, like a faulty altimeter. Still facing forward with his eyes rotated way over to the right, Atwater told the artist's wife that his journalistic motives had been mixed at first, maybe, but that verily he did now believe. When they'd taken him through Mrs. Moltke's sewing room and out back and pulled open the angled green door and led him down the raw pine steps into the storm cellar and he'd seen the pieces all lined up in graduated tiers that way, something had happened. The truth was he'd been moved, and he said he'd understood then for the first time, despite some prior exposure to the world of art through a course or two in college, how people of discernment could say they felt moved and redeemed by serious art. And he believed this was serious, real, bona fide art, he told her. At the same time, it was also true that Skip Atwater had not been in a sexually charged situation since the previous New Year's annual YMSP2 party's bout of drunken fanny photocopying, when he'd gotten a glimpse of one of the circulation interns' pudenda as she settled on the Canon's plexiglass sheet, which afterward was unnaturally warm.

↓

Registered motto of Chicago IL's O Verily Productions, which for complicated business reasons appeared on its colophon in Portuguese:

CONSCIOUSNESS IS NATURE'S NIGHTMARE

↓

Amber Moltke, however, pointed out that if conventionally produced, the pieces would really be just small reproductions that showed a great deal of expression and technical detail, that what made them special in the first place was what they were and how they came out fully formed from her husband's behind, and she again asked rhetorically why on earth she would want these essential facts highlighted and talked about, that they were his shit — pronouncing the word shit in a very flat and matter of fact way — and Atwater admitted that he did wonder about this, and that the whole question of the pieces' production and how this rendered them somehow simultaneously both more and less natural than conventional artworks seemed dizzyingly abstract and complex, and that but in any event there would almost inevitably be some elements that some *Style* readers would find distasteful or invasive in an ad hominem way, and confessed that he did wonder, both personally and professionally, whether it wasn't possible that Mr. or at least Mrs. Moltke wasn't perhaps more ambivalent about the terms of public exposure than she was allowing herself to realize.

And Amber inclined even closer to Skip Atwater and said to him that she was not. That she'd thought on the whole business long and hard at the first soybean festival, long before *Style* even knew that Mr. and Mrs. B. F. Moltke of Mount Carmel even existed. She turned slightly to push at her mass of occipital curls, which had tightened shinily in the storm's moist air. Her voice was a dulcet alto with something almost hypnotic in the timbre. There were tiny random fragments of spindrift rain through the window's opened crack, and a planar flow of air that felt blessed, and the front seat's starboard list became more severe, which as he rose so very slowly gave Atwater the sensation that either he was physically enlarging or Mrs. Moltke was diminishing somewhat in relative size, or at any rate that the physical disparity between them was becoming less marked. It occurred to Atwater that he could not recall when he had eaten last. He could not feel his right leg anymore, and his ear's outer flange felt nearly aflame.

Mrs. Moltke said how she'd thought about it and realized that most people didn't even get such a chance, and that this here was hers, and Brint's. To somehow stand out. To distinguish themselves from the great huge faceless mass of folks that watched the folks that did stand out. On the TV and in venues like *Style.* In retrospect, none of this turned out to be true. To be known, to matter, she said. To have church or Ye Olde Buffet or the new Bennigan's at the Whitcomb Outlet Mall get quiet when her and Brint came in, and to feel people's eyes, the weight of their gaze. That it made a difference someplace when they came in. To pick up a copy of *People* or *Style* at the beautician's and see herself and Brint looking back out at her. To be on TV. That this was it. That surely Skip could understand. That yes, despite the overall dimness of Brint Moltke's bulb and a lack of personal verve that almost approached death in life, when she'd met the drain technician at a church dance in 1997 she'd somehow known that he was her chance. His hair had been slicked down with aftershave and he'd worn white socks with his good suit, and had missed a belt loop, and yet she'd known. Call it a gift, this power — she was different and marked to someday stand out and she'd known it. Atwater himself had worn white socks with dress slacks until college, when his fraternity brothers had finally addressed the issue in Mock Court. His right hand still gripping the steering wheel, Atwater's head was now rotated just as far as it would go in order to look more or less directly into Amber's great right eye, whose lashes ruffled his hair when she fluttered them. No more than a quarter moon of tire now showed above the mud on each of the right side's wheels.

What Amber appeared now to be confiding to him in the rented Cavalier struck Atwater as extremely open and ingenuous and naked. The sheer preterite ugliness of it made its admission almost beautiful, Atwater felt. Bizarrely, it did not occur to him that Amber might be speaking to him as a reporter instead of a fellow person. He knew that there was an artlessness about him that helped people open up, and that he possessed a measure of true empathy. It's why he considered himself fortunate to be tasked to WHAT IN THE WORLD rather than entertainment or beauty/fashion, budgets and prestige notwithstanding. The truth is that what Amber Moltke was confiding seemed to Atwater very close to the core of the American experience he wanted to capture in his journalism. It was also the tragic conflict at the heart of *Style* and all soft organs like it. The paradoxical intercourse of audience and celebrity. The suppressed awareness that the whole reason ordinary people found celebrity fascinating was that they were not, themselves, celebrities. That wasn't quite it. An odd thing was that his fist often stopped altogether when he thought abstractly. It was more the deeper, more tragic and universal conflict of which the celebrity paradox was a part. The conflict between the subjective centrality of our own lives versus our awareness of its objective insignificance. Atwater knew — as did everyone at *Style*, though by some strange unspoken consensus it was never said aloud — that this was the single great informing conflict of the American psyche. The management of insignificance. It was the great syncretic bond of US monoculture. It was everywhere, at the root of everything — of impatience in long lines, of cheating on taxes, of movements in fashion and music and art, of marketing. In particular, he thought it was alive in the paradoxes of audience. It was the feeling that celebrities were your intimate friends, coupled with the inchoate awareness that untold millions of people felt the same way — and that the celebrities themselves did not. Atwater had had contact with a certain number of celebrities (there was no way to avoid it at a BSG), and they were not, in his experience, very friendly or considerate people. Which made sense when one considered that celebrities were not actually functioning as real people at all, but as something more like symbols of themselves.

There had been eye contact between the journalist and Amber Moltke this whole time, and by now Atwater could also look down, as it were, to see the complex whorls and parts in the young wife's hair and the numerous clips and plastic clamps that were buried in its lustrous mass. There was still the occasional ping of hail. And it was also the world altering pain of accepting one's individual flaws and limitations and the tautological unattainability of our dreams and the dim indifference in the eyes of the circulation intern one tries, at the stroke of the true millennium, to share one's ambivalence and pain with. Most of these latter considerations occurred during a brief diversion from the exchange's main thread into something having to do with professional sewing and tatting and customized alterations, which evidently was what Amber did out of her home to help supplement her husband's income from TriCounty Roto Rooter: 'There's not a fiber swatch or pattern in this world I cannot work with, that's another gift it pleased God to bestow and I'm thankful, it's restful and creative and keeps me out of trouble, these hands are not ever idle' — she holding up for one moment an actual hand, which could likely have gone all the way around Atwater's head and still been able to touch finger to thumb.

Skip Atwater's one and only serious involvement ever had been with a medical illustrator for the Anatomical Monograph Company, which was located off the Pendleton Pike just outside Indianapolis proper, specializing in intricate exploded views of the human brain and upper spine, as well as in lower order ganglia for neurological comparison. She had been only 5'0", and toward the relationship's end Atwater hadn't cared one bit for the way she had looked at him when he undressed or got out of the shower. One evening he'd taken her to a Ruth's Chris and had almost a hallucination or out of body experience in which he'd viewed himself écorché style from her imagined perspective as he ate, his jaw muscles working redly and esophagus contracting to move bits of bolus down. Only days later had come the shattering performance review from the *Star*'s assistant city editor, and Skip's life had changed forever.

→

Early Tuesday morning was the second time ever that Laurel Manderley had ascended to the executive offices of *Style* magazine, which required getting out and transferring to a whole different elevator at the 70th floor. By prior arrangement, Ellen Bactrian had gone up first and verified that the coast was clear. The sun was barely up yet. Laurel Manderley was alone in the elevator, wearing dark wool slacks, very plain Chinese slippers, and a matte black Issey Miyake shirt that was actually made of paper but looked more like some type of very fine opaque tulle. She looked pale and a little unwell; she was not wearing her facial stud. Through some principle of physics she didn't understand, the box in her arms felt slightly heavier when the elevator was in motion. Its total weight was only a few pounds at most. Apparently Ellen Bactrian's commuting routine with the executive intern was a purely informal one whereby they always met up at some certain spot just north of the Holland Tunnel to bike down together, but if either one wasn't at the spot at the designated time, the other just rode on ahead. The whole thing was very laid back. The interior of the first elevator was brushed steel; the one up from 70 had inlaid paneling and a console with tiny directories next to each floor's button. The entire trip took over five minutes, although the elevators themselves were so fast that some of the executive staff wore special earplugs for the rapid ascent.

Her only other time up had been with two other new interns and the WITW associate editor, as part of general orientation, and in the elevator the associate editor had put his arms up over his head and made his hands sharp like a diver's and said: 'Up, up, and away.'

←

Ever since he was a little boy, a deep perfusive flush to Atwater's ears and surrounding tissues was the chief outward sign that his mind was working to process disparate thoughts and impressions much faster than its normal rate. At these times one could actually feel heat coming off the ear itself, which may have accounted for the rapid self fanning motions that the immense, creamily etiolated seamstress made as she came back on topic and shared the following personal experience. The daytime television celebrity Phillip Spaulding of *Guiding Light* had, at some past point that Amber didn't specify, made a live promotional appearance at the opening of a Famous Barr store at Richmond's Galleria Mall, and she and a girlfriend had gone to see him, and Amber said she had realized then that her deepest and most life informing wish, she realized, was to someday have strangers feel about her mere appearance someplace the way she had felt, inside, about getting to stand near enough to Phillip Spaulding (who was evidently a serious hottie indeed, despite something strange or strangely formed about the cartilage of his nose so that it looked like the tip almost had a little dimple or cleft like you'd more normally see on a human chin, which Amber and her girlfriend had decided they ultimately found cute, and made Phillip Spaulding even more of a hottie because it made him look more like a real human being instead of the almost too perfect mannequins these serials sometimes thought folks wanted to see all the time) to reach out between all the other people there and actually touch him if she'd wanted to.

Skip Atwater, in the course of an involved argument with himself later about whether he had more accurately *engaged in* or *been subject to* an act of fraternization with a journalistic subject, would identify this moment as the crucial fulcrum or tipping point of the whole exchange. Already tremendously keyed up and abstracted by Mrs. Moltke's confidences, he found himself nearly overcome by the ingenuous populism of the Phillip Spaulding anecdote, and wished to activate his tiny tape recorder and, if Amber wouldn't repeat the vignette, to at least get her to allow him to repeat and record its gist on tape, along with the date and approximate time — not that he would ever use it for this or any other piece, but just for his own record of a completely perfect representative statement of what it was like to be one of the people to and for whom he wished his work in *Style* to try to speak, as something to help provide objective dignification of his work and to so to speak hold up shieldlike against the voices in his head that mocked him and said all he really did was write fluff pieces for a magazine most people read in the bathroom. What happened was that Atwater's attempts to subtly work his fingers under Amber's right hand and pry the hand up off the tape recorder on his knee were, in retrospect, evidently interpreted as an attempt at handholding or some other kind of physical affection, and apparently had a profound effect on Mrs. Moltke, for it was then that she brought her great head all the way around between Atwater's face and the steering wheel, and they were kissing — or rather Atwater was kissing at the left corner of Amber Moltke's lip, while her mouth covered nearly the entire right side of the journalist's face all the way to the earlobe. The fluttering motions of his hands as they beat ineffectually at her left shoulder were no doubt similarly misperceived as passion. The movements of Amber's rapid disrobing then began to cause the rented sedan to heave this way and that, and drove its starboard side even more deeply into the overlook's mud, and a very muffled set of what could have been either screams or cries of excitement began to issue from the tilted vehicle; and anyone trying to look in either side's window would have been unable to see any part of Skip Atwater at all.

4.

In New York it starts out as a puzzling marginal entry, 411 on Dish, 105 on Metro Cable. Viewers find it difficult to tell whether it's supposed to be commercial or Community Access or what. At first it's just montages of well known photos involving anguish or pain: a caved in Jackie next to LBJ as he's sworn in on the plane, that agonized Vietcong with the pistol to his head, the naked kids running from napalm. There's something about seeing them one right after another. A woman trying to bathe her thalidomide baby, faces through the wire at Belsen, Oswald crumpled around Ruby's fist, a noosed man as the mob begins to hoist, Brazilians on the ledge of a burning highrise. A loop

of 1,200 of these, four seconds per, running 5:00 PM–1:00 AM EST;
no sound; no evident ads.

A venture capital subsidiary of Televisio Brasilia underwrites The
Suffering Channel's startup, but you cannot tell that, watching, at first.
The only credits are photo ©s and a complicated glyph for O Verily
Productions. After a few weeks, stage one TSC also streams on the
Web at OVP.com\suff.~vide. The legalities of the video are more tor-
tuous, and it takes almost twice as long as projected for TSC stage two,
in which the still photo series is gradually replaced by video clips in a
complex loop that expands by four to five new segments per day, depending. Still in the planning phase, TSC stage three is tentatively
scheduled for experimental insertion during autumn '01 Sweeps, although, as is SOP with creative enterprises everywhere, there's always
flexibility and room to maneuver built in.

Like nearly all members of the paid press, Skip Atwater watched a
good deal of satellite TV, much of it marginal or late night, and knew
the O Verily glyph quite well. He still had contacts among R. Vaughn
Corliss's support staff because of the All Ads All The Time Channel
piece, which O Verily had ended up regarding as a fortuitous part of
its second wave marketing. The AAATC was still up and pulling in
a solid cable share, although response to the insertion of real paid ads
within the stream of artifact ads had not had the dynamic impact on
revenues that O Verily's prospectus had promised it very well might.
Like many viewers, Atwater had been able to tell almost immediately
which ads in the loops were paid spots and which were aesthetic objects, and regarded them accordingly, sometimes zapping out the paid
ads altogether. And while the differences between an ad as entertainment and an ad that really tried to sell something were fascinating to
academics, and had helped to galvanize the whole field of Media
Studies in the late 1990s, they did little for the All Ads Channel's
profitability. This was one reason why O Verily had had to outsource
capitalization for The Suffering Channel, which was in turn why TSC
had almost immediately begun positioning itself for acquisition by a
major corporation — the Brazilian VCs had required a 24 percent
return on a two year window, meaning that O Verily Productions

would retain only nominal creative control if its revenues did not reach a certain floor, which R. Vaughn Corliss had never, from the very start, had any intention of allowing to occur.

In Chicago, O Verily Productions operated out of north side facilities just a few blocks down Addison from WGN's great uplink tower, past which landmark Skip Atwater's rented Cavalier yawed and squeaked — pulling severely to the right from a bent transaxle that had worn one tire nearly bald on the trip up Interstate 65, and with the driver's side door bowed dramatically out from inside as if from some horrific series of impacts, about which neither Hertz Inc. nor *Style*'s Accounting staff would be pleased at all — on 2 July at 10:10 AM, nearly two hours late, because it had turned out that any highway speed over 45 mph produced a sound like a great deal of loose change rattling around inside the vehicle's engine.

As of June '01, The Suffering Channel was in the late stages of acquisition by AOL Time Warner, which was itself in Wall Street freefall and involved in talks with Eckleschafft-Böd over a putative merger that would in reality constitute E-Böd white knighting AOL TW against hostile takeover from a consortium of interests led by MCI Premium. The Suffering Channel's specs were thus already in the Eckleschafft-Böd pipeline, and it had required less than an hour of email finagling for Laurel Manderley to acquire certain variably relevant portions of them on behalf of her salaryman.

↓

Subj: **Re: Confidential**
Date: 6/24/01 10:31:37 AM Eastern Daylight Time
Content-Type: text/html; charset = us-ascii
From: k_böttger@ecklbdus.com
To: l_manderle@stylebsgmag.com
<!DOCTYPE html PRIV "-//W2C//DTD HTML 3.01 Transitional//EN">
Totalp CT: 6
Content-Transfer-Encoding: 7bit
Descramble-Content Reference: 122-XXX-idvM32XX
<head>
<title><title>

<head>

Condidential

Product: The Suffering Channel

Type: Reality/Gaper

Desc. of Product: Real life still and moving images of most intense available moments of human anguish

Production Lic.: O Verily Productions, Chicago and Waukegan, Ill

FCC Lic. Var. Status: [see Attachments, below]

Current Distribution: Regional/test through Dish (Chic., NYC), Dillard Cable (NE, SE grid), *Video Sodalvo* (Braz), Webstream at OVP.com\suff.~vd

Proposed Distribution: National via TWC Premium Options package (est. 2002), TWC and AOL key = SUFFERCH

Proposed Carryable Rate: Subsc. = $0.95 monthly stack on TWC Premium Options (= 1.2% increase) w/ prorate 22.5% per subscr. mo. 1-12. Variable projected prorate from Arbitron/Hale subsc Sweeps thereafter (standard) (Note: tracks MCI Premium's Adult Film Channel rate variance per prorate — see attached AFC spreadsheet from MCI source SS2-B4, below)

Bkg on O Verily Prod: CEO & Creative Executive, V. Corliss, 41, b. Gurnee, Ill, BA, Emerson College, MBA & JD, Pepperdine Univ. 3 yrs assoc producer, Dick Clark Prod./NBC, *TV's Bloopers & Practical Jokes*. 3 yrs line producer, Television Program Enterprises, *Lifestyles of the Rich and Famous, Runaway with the Rich and Famous*. 3 yrs exec prod., O.V.P., *Surprise Wedding! I-III, Shocking Moments in Couples Counseling! I-II*, 2.5 years exec producer, All Ads All The Time Channel [see Attachments, below]

Current O.V.P. Assets, Including Capital Equipment and Receivables: [See Attached LLC filing and spreadsheets, below] (Note: At counsel re photo and video permissions, releases [see USCC/F §212, vi-xlii in Attachments]: Reudenthal and Voss, P.C., Chicago and NY [see Attachments]

Precis of Sample Tape, 2-21-01 [Enclosure, acquisition specs Attached].

Contents:

(1) Low light security video, mothers of two children, aged 7 and 9, with late stage cancer, Blue Springs Memorial Hospital Palliative Care Unit, Independence, Mo.

(2) High light security video, 10 year old male owner (dog), elderly male owner (dog), adult female owner (cats) on Free Euthanasia Day, Maddox Co. Humane Society, Maddox, Ga.

(3) High light instructional video, 50 year old male coming abruptly awake on table during abdominal surgery, requires physical restraint. Audio quality very high. Brigham and Women's Hospital, Boston, Mass.

(4a) Handheld video, electroshock interrogation of adolescent male subject, *Chambre d'Interrogation,* Cloutier Prison, Cameroon (subtitles).

(4b) Appended low light video (quality poor), video clip (4a) is shown to subject's relatives (pres. parents?), one of whom is revealed as real subject of the interrogation (subtitles, facial closeups digitally enhanced).

(5) Covert (?) low light video, Catholic Outreach Services support group for families of victims of murder/violent crime, San Luis Obispo, Cal [rights pending, see Attachments].

(6) High light legal liability video, stage 4 root canal and crown procedure for 46 year old female allergic to all anesthetics, Off. Dahood Chaterjee DDS, East Stroudsburg, Penn.

(7) Unused BBC2 shoulder mount video clip of *Necklace Party,* Transvaal Civil Province C7, Pretoria, South Afr (audio excellent).

(8) Handheld video, middle aged Rwandan (?) couple murdered by group w/ agric. implements (no audio, facial closeups digitally enhanced).

(9) Handheld video, shark attack and attempts at resuscitation on 18(?) year old surfer, Stinson Beach, Cal [rights pending, see Attachments].

(10) High light videotaped suicide note and handgun suicide of 60 year old patent attorney, Rutherford, NJ.

(11) High light legal liability video, intake and assessment interview of 28 year old suicidal female, Newton Wellesley Hospital, Newton, Mass.

(12) Low light security video, parents identify remains of 13 year old raped/ dec. child, Emerson County Coroner's Office, Brentley, Tx.

(13) Webcam digital video, gang rape in dormitory room of 22 year old female designing real time *My Life* Web Site for college course, Lambuth University, Jackson, Tenn (video quality/FPS poor, high gain audio excellent, some faces digitally obscured [see Attachments]).

(14) High light security video, change of dressing for 3rd degree female (?) burn patient, Josephthal Memorial Hospital Burns Unit, Lawrence, Kan.

(15) Unused Deutsch 2DF shoulder mount video clip of Cholera Dispensary, Chang Hua Earthquake Zone, PRC.

2-01 Arbitron Rate for 1st Loop Serial Broadcast: 6.2 ± .6

2-01 Arbitron Rate for 2nd Loop Serial Broadcast: 21.0 ± .6

. . . and so forth.

↓

Ellen Bactrian had them out and arranged on Mrs. Anger's desk when the executive intern came in carrying her bicycle at 7:10. Three of the pieces were upright, one more base intensive and kind of spread out. Each sat on its own blank sheet of typing paper; it was the 20 pound rag bond used for executive letters and memos at *Style*. The pieces were in no particular order. The two editorial interns were in matching chairs in the room's two far corners. Ellen Bactrian had short dark blond hair and an arc of studs along the rim of one ear that every so often caught the light just right and flashed. On the wall near the office door, a large photorealist portrait depicted Mrs. Anger in a glove tight Saint Laurent suit and what almost looked like the kind of Capezio pumps professional dancers wore.

The executive intern, who had been student body president at both Choate and Vassar, always wore form fitting bike shorts for the commute and then changed in the executive lounge. It was another sign of her overall favor and influence that Mrs. Anger let her store the bicycle in her office, which locked. The executive intern's arrival that morning was ever so slightly late, because the SE2 issue had finally closed the previous day. Mrs. Anger herself rarely rolled in much before 9:30.

The executive intern stood there still holding her bike, which weighed only eight and a half pounds, and staring at the pieces while the smile she'd come in with emptied out. She was acknowledged as more or less defining the standard of excellence for interns at *Style*. At least 5'10" in flats, with long auburn tresses that shone in even the meanest fluorescence, she managed to seem at once worldly and ethereal, and moved through the corridors and semiattached cubicles of the magazine like a living refutation of everything Marx ever stood for.

'We decided you needed to see them,' Ellen Bactrian said, 'before anybody said anything to anybody one way or the other.'

'Great glittering God.' The executive intern's front teeth emerged and pressed lightly on her lower lip. She had unconsciously assumed the same position that Skip Atwater and Ellen Bactrian and many of the patrons of the soybean festivals and fair had — standing several feet away, her posture somewhat S shaped because of the twin impulses to approach and recoil. She had on a brain shaped helmet and a Vassar sweatshirt with the collar and cuffs removed and the white flocking of the interior allowed to show. Her athletic shoes had special attachments that evidently clipped to the racing bike's pedals. The shadow she cast back against the wall was complex and distended.

'Are they something?' Laurel Manderley said quietly. She and Ellen Bactrian had brought in some additional lamps from the conference room next door because something about the overhead lights hit the fixative wrong and produced glare. Each of the pieces was fully and evenly lit. The executive office area was much quieter and more dignified than the sixteenth floor, but also a bit cool and stiff, Laurel thought.

The executive intern still held the bicycle. 'You didn't actually . . . ?'

'They're sort of laminated. Don't worry.' Laurel Manderley had applied the additional fixative herself per instructions relayed through Skip Atwater, who was even then boarding a commuter flight to Muncie out of Midway. Laurel Manderley, who had also handled the whole rental car exchange unpleasantness, knew his timetable to the minute. She had declined the optional thing with the Saran, though. She felt like she might literally faint at any time.

'So was I jerking you off, or what?' Ellen Bactrian asked the executive intern.

Laurel Manderley made a little ta da gesture: 'It's the miraculous poo.'

One of her bicycle's wheels still idly turned, but the executive intern's eyes had not once moved. She said: 'Something isn't even the word.'

↓

Established fact: Almost no adult remembers the details or psychic fallout of her own toilet training. By the time one might have cause to want to know, it has been so long that you have to try asking your parents — which rarely works, because most parents will deny not only recollection but even original involvement in anything having to do

with your toilet training. Such denials are basic psychological protection, since parenting can sometimes be a nasty business. All these phe-
nomena have been exhaustively researched and documented.

R. Vaughn Corliss's most tightly held secret vision or dream, dating
from when he was just beginning to detach from Leach and TPE and
to conceive of reinventing himself as a force in high concept cable: a
channel devoted wholly to images of celebrities shitting. Reese With-
erspoon shitting. Juliette Lewis shitting. Michael Jordan shitting.
Longtime House Minority Whip Dick Gephardt shitting. Pamela
Anderson shitting. George F. Will, with his bow tie and pruny mouth,
shitting. Former PGA legend Hale Irwin shitting. Stones bassist Ron
Wood shitting. Pope John Paul shitting as special attendants hold his
robes' hems up off the floor. Leonard Maltin, Annette Bening,
Michael Flatley, either or both of the Olsen twins, shitting. And so on.
Helen Hunt. *The Price Is Right*'s Bob Barker. Tom Cruise. Jane Pauley.
Talia Shire. Yasser Arafat, Timothy McVeigh, Michael J. Fox. Former
HUD Secretary Henry Cisneros. The idea of real time footage of
Martha Stewart perched shitting amid the soaps and sachets and color
coordinated linens of her Connecticut estate's master bathroom was so
powerful that Corliss rarely allowed himself to imagine it. It was not a
soporific conceit. It was also, obviously, private. Tom Clancy, Margaret
Atwood, bell hooks. Dr. James Dobson. Beleaguered IL Governor
George Ryan. Peter Jennings. Oprah. He told no one of this dream.
Nor of his corollary vision of the images beamed into space, digitally
sequenced for maximum range and coherence, and of advanced alien
species studying this footage in order to learn almost everything necessary about planet earth circa 2001.

He wasn't a madman; it could never fly. Still, though. There was
Reality TV, which Corliss himself had helped lay the ground floor of,
and the nascent trend toward absorbing celebrities into the matrix of
violation and exposure that was Reality: celebrity bloopers, celebrities
showing you around their homes, celebrity boxing, celebrity political
colloquy, celebrity blind dating, celebrity couples counseling. Even serving time at Leach's TPE, Corliss could see that the logic of such programming was airtight and led inexorably to the ultimate exposures:

celebrity major surgical procedures, celebrity death, celebrity autopsy. It only seemed absurd from outside the logic. How far along the final arc would Slo Mo High Def Full Sound Celebrity Defecation be? How soon before the idea ceased being too loony to mention aloud, to float as a balloon before the laughing heads of Development and Legal? Not yet, but not never. They'd laughed at Murdoch in Perth, once, Corliss knew.

Laurel Manderley was the youngest of four children, and her toilet training, which commenced around 30 months, had been casual and ad hoc and basically no big deal. The Atwater brothers' own had been early, brutal, and immensely effective — it was actually during toilet training that the elder twin had first learned to pump his left fist in self exhortation.

Little Roland Corliss, whose nanny was an exponent of a small and unapologetically radical splinter of the Waldorf educational movement, had experienced no formal toilet training at all, but rather just the abrupt unexplained withdrawal of all diapers at age four. This was the same age at which he had entered Holy Calvary Lutheran Preschool, where unambiguous social consequences motivated him to learn almost immediately what toilets were for and how to use them, rather like the child who is rowed way out and then taught to swim the old fashioned way.

↓

BSG is magazine industry shorthand for the niche comprising *People, Us, In Style, In Touch, Style,* and *Entertainment Weekly.* (For demographic reasons, *Teen People* is not usually included among the BSGs.) The abbreviation stands for big soft glossy, with soft in turn meaning the very most demotic kind of human interest.

As of July 2001, three of the six major BSGs are owned by Eckleschafft-Böd Medien A.G., a German conglomerate that controls nearly 40 percent of all US trade publishing.

Like the rest of the mainstream magazine industry, each of the BSG weeklies subscribes to an online service that compiles and organizes all contracted stringers' submissions to both national wires and Gannett, of which submissions roughly 8 percent ever actually run in the major news dailies. A select company of editorial interns, known sometimes as shades because of the special anodized goggles required by OSHA for intensive screen time, is tasked to peruse this service.

Skip Atwater, who was one of the rare and old school BSG journalists who actually pitched pieces as well as receiving assignments, was also one of the few paid staffers at *Style* who bothered to review the online service for himself. As a practical matter, he did so only when he was not in the field, and then usually at night, after his dogs had again gone to sleep, sitting up in his Ball State Cardinals cap with a glass of ale and operating his home desktop according to instructions which Laurel Manderley's predecessor had configured as a special template that fit along the top of the unit's keyboard. An AP stringer out of Indianapolis, filing from the Franklin County Fair on what was alleged to be the second largest Monte Cristo sandwich ever assembled, had included a curio about displays of extremely intricate and high class figurines made out of what the stringer had spelled fasces. The objets d'art themselves were not described — they had been arrayed in glass cases that were difficult to get near because of the crowds around them, and people's hands and exhalations had apparently smeared the glass so badly that even when you did finally shoulder your way up close the interiors were half obscured. Later, Skip Atwater would learn that these slanted glass cabinets were acquired from the tax sale of a failed delicatessen in Greensburg IN, which for decades had had a small and anomalous Hasidic community.

It was a word padding aside in a throwaway item unflagged by any of *Style*'s shades, and from his own native experience Atwater was disposed to assume that the things were probably crude little Elvises or Earnhardts made of livestock waste . . . except the display banner's allegedly quoted *Hands Free Art Crafts* caught his eye. The phrase appeared to make no sense unless automation were involved, which, as applied to livestock waste, would be curious indeed. Curiosity, of course, being more or less Skip Atwater's oeuvre with regard to WHAT IN THE WORLD. Not curiosity as in tabloid or freakshow, or rather all right sometimes borderline freakshow but with an upbeat thrust. The content and tone of all BSGs were dictated by market research and codified down to the smallest detail: celebrity profiles, entertainment news, hot trends, and human interest, with human interest representing a gamut in which the occasional freakshow item had a niche — but the rhetoric was tricky. BSGs were at pains to distinguish themselves from the tabloids, whose target market was wholly different. *Style's* WITW items were people centered and always had to be both credible and uplifting, or latterly there at least had to be ancillary elements that were uplifting and got thumped hard.

Atwater could thump with the best. And he was old school and energetic: he ran down two or three possible WITW stories for every one that got written, and pitched things, and could rewrite other men's copy if asked to. The politics of rewrites could get sticky, and interns often had to mediate between the salarymen involved, but Atwater was known around *Style's* editorial offices as someone who could both rewrite and get rewritten without being an asshole about it. At root, his reputation with staffers and interns alike was based in this: his consistent failure to be an asshole. Which could, of course, be a double edged sword. He was seen as having roughly the self esteem of a prawn. Some at *Style* found him fussy or pretentious. Others questioned his spontaneity. Sometimes the phrase queer duck was used. There was the whole awkward issue of his monotone wardrobe. The fact that he actually carried pictures of his dogs in his wallet was either endearing or creepy, depending whom you asked. A few of the sharper interns intuited that he'd had to overcome a great deal in himself in order to get this far.

He knew just what he was: a professional soft news journalist. We all make our adjustments, hence the term well adjusted. A babyfaced bantam with ears about which he'd been savagely teased as a boy — Jughead, Spock, Little Pitcher. A polished, shallow, earnest, productive, consummate corporate pro. Over the past three years, Skip Atwater had turned in some 70 separate pieces to *Style,* of which almost 50 saw print and a handful of others ran under rewriters' names. A volunteer fire company in suburban Tulsa where you had to be a grandmother to join. When Baby Won't Wait — Moms who never made it to the hospital tell their amazing stories. Drinking and boating: The other DUI. Just who really *was* Slim Whitman. This Grass Ain't Blue — Kentucky's other cash crop. He Delivers — 81 year old obstetrician welcomes the grandchild of his own first patient. Former Condit intern speaks out. Today's forest ranger: He doesn't just sit in a tower. Holy Rollers — Inline skateathon saves church from default. Eczema: The silent epidemic. Rock 'n' Roll High School — Which future pop stars made the grade? Nevada bikers rev up the fight against myasthenia gravis. Head of the Parade — From Macy's to the Tournament of Roses, this float designer has done them all. The All Ads All The Time cable channel. Rock of Ages — These geologists celebrate the millennium in a whole new way. Sometimes he felt that if not for his schipperkes' love he would simply blow away and dissipate like milkweed. The women who didn't get picked for *Who Wants to Marry a Millionaire:* Where did they come from, to what do they return. Leapin' Lizards — The Gulf Coast's new alligator plague. One Lucky Bunch of Cats — A terminally ill Lotto winner's astounding bequest. Those new home cottage cheese makers: Marvel or ripoff? Be(-Happy-)Atitudes — This Orange County pastor claims Christ was no sourpuss. Dramamine and NASA: The untold story. Secret documents reveal Wallis Simpson cheated on Edward VIII. A Whole Lotta Dough — Delaware teen sells $40,000 worth of Girl Scout cookies . . . and isn't finished yet! For these former agoraphobics, home is not where the heart is. Contra: The thinking person's square dance.

At the same time, it was acknowledged that Atwater's best had sometimes been those pieces he ran down himself and pitched, items that often pushed the BSG envelope. For 7 March '99, Atwater had submitted the longest WITW piece ever done for *Style,* on the case of a U. Maryland professor murdered in his apartment where the only witness was the man's African gray parrot, and all the parrot would repeat was 'Oh God, no, please no' and then gruesome noises, and on the veterinary hypnotist that the authorities had had working with the parrot to see what more they could get out of it. The UBA here had been the hypnotist and her bio and beliefs about animal consciousness, the central tensions being was she just a New Age loon along the lines of

Beverly Hills pet therapists or was there really something to it, and if the parrot was hypnotizable as advertised and sang then what would be its evidentiary status in court.

Very early every morning of childhood, Mrs. Atwater's way of waking her two boys up was to stand between their beds and clap her hands loudly together, not stopping until their feet actually touched the bedroom floor, which now floated in the depths of Virgil Atwater's memory as a kind of sardonic ovation. Hopping Mad — This triple amputee isn't taking health care costs lying down. The meth lab next door! Mrs. Gladys Hine, the voice behind over 1,500 automated phone menus. The Dish — This Washington D.C. caterer has seen it all. Computer solitaire: The last addiction? No Sweet Talkin' — Blue M&Ms have these consumers up in arms. Dallas commuter's airbag nightmare. Menopause and herbs: Exciting new findings. Fat Chance — Lottery cheaters and the heavyweight squad that busts them. Seance secrets of online medium Duwayne Evans. Ice sculpture: How do they *do* that?

Atwater's best regarded piece ever so far, 3 July '00: A little girl in Upland CA had been born with an unpronounceable neurological condition whereby she could not form facial expressions, normal and healthy in every way with blond pigtails and a corgi named Skipper except her face was a flat staring granite mask, and the parents were starting a foundation for the incredibly over 5,000 other people worldwide who couldn't form normal facial expressions, and Atwater had run down, pitched, and landed 2,500 words for a piece only half of which was back matter, plus another two columns' worth of multiple photos of the girl reclined expressionless in her mother's lap, stony and staring under raised arms on a roller coaster, and so forth. Atwater had finally gotten the go ahead from the bimanual associate editor on the Suffering Channel piece because he'd done the '99 WITW fluffer on the All Ads All The Time Channel, which was also O Verily, and could truthfully posit a rapport with R. Vaughn Corliss, whose eccentric recluse persona formed a neat human hook — although the associate editor had said that where Atwater was ever going to find the UBA in the TSC story was anyone's guess and would stretch Atwater's skill set to the limit.

5.

The first of the dreams Laurel Manderley found so disturbing had occurred the same night that the digital photos of Brint Moltke's work had appeared on the floor below the fax and she had felt the queer twin impulses both to bend and get them and to run as fast as she could from the cubicle complex. An ominous vatic feeling had persisted throughout the rest of the evening, which was doubly unsettling to Laurel Manderley, because she normally believed about as much in intuition and the uncanny as US Vice President Dick Cheney did.

She lay late at night in the loft, her bunkmate encased in Kiehl's cream beneath her. The dream involved a small house that she somehow knew was the one with the fractional address that belonged to the lady and her husband in Skip Atwater's miraculous poo story. They were all in there, in the like living room or den, sitting there and either not doing anything or not doing anything Laurel Manderley could identify. The creepiness of the dream was akin to the fear she'd sometimes felt in her maternal grandparents' summer home in Lyford Cay, which had certain closet doors that opened by themselves whenever Laurel was in the room. It wasn't clear what Mr. and Mrs. Moltke looked like, or wore, or what they were saying, and at one point there was a dog standing in the middle of the room but its breed and even color were unclear. There was nothing overtly surreal or menacing in the scene. It seemed more like something generic or vague or tentative, like an abstract or outline. The only specifically strange thing was that the house had two front doors, even though one of them wasn't in the front but it was still a front door. But this fact could not begin to account for the overwhelming sense of dread Laurel Manderley felt, sitting there. There was a premonition of not just danger but evil. There was a creeping, ambient evil present, except even though present it was not in the room. Like the second front door, it was somehow both there and not. She couldn't wait to get out, she had to get out. But when she stood up with the excuse of asking to use the bathroom, even in the midst of asking she couldn't stand the feeling of evil and began running for the door in stocking feet in order to get out, but it was not the front door she ran for, it was the other door, even though she didn't know where it was, except she must know because there it was, with a decorative and terribly detailed metal scarab over the knob, and whatever the overwhelming evil was was right behind it, the door, but for some reason even as she's overcome with fear she's also reaching for the doorknob, she's going to open it, she can see herself starting to open it — and that's when she wakes. And then almost the totally exact same thing happens the next night, and she's afraid now that if she has it again then the next time she'll actually open the front door that isn't in front . . . and her fear of this possibility is the only thing she can put her finger on in trying to describe the dream to Siobhan and Tara on the train ride home Tuesday night, but there's no way to convey just why the two front door thing is so terrifying, since she herself can't even rationally explain it.

↓

The Moltkes were childless, but their home's bathroom lay off a narrow hallway whose east wall was hung with framed photos of Brint and Amber's friends' and relatives' children, as well as certain shots of the Moltkes themselves as youngsters. The presence in this hallway of Atwater, a freelance photographer who wore a Hawaiian shirt and smelled strongly of hair cream, and a Richmond IN internist whom Ellen Bactrian had personally found and engaged had already disarranged some of the photos, which now hung at haphazard angles and revealed partial cracks and an odd set of bulges in the wall's surface. There was one quite extraordinary shot of Amber at what had to have been her wedding's reception, radiant in white brocade and holding the cake's tiered platform in one hand while with the other she brought the cutter to bear. And what at first glance had looked like someone else was a Little League photo of Moltke himself, in uniform and holding an aluminum bat, the artist perhaps nine or ten and his batting helmet far too large. And so on.

Atwater's new rental car, a pointedly budget Kia that even he felt cramped in, sat in the Moltke's driveway with the MD's Lincoln Brougham just behind it. Moltke's company van was parked in the duplex's other driveway, which bespoke some kind of possible arrangement with the other side's occupant that Atwater, who felt more than a little battered and conflicted and ill at ease in Mrs. Moltke's presence, had not yet thought to inquire about. The artist's wife had objected strenuously to a procedure that she said both she and her husband found distasteful and degrading, and was now in her sewing room off the kitchen, whence the occasional impact of her foot on an old machine's treadle shook the hallway and caused the freelance photographer to have to readjust his light stands several different times.

The internist appeared to stand frozen in the gesture of a man looking at his watch. The photographer, for whom Atwater had had to wait over three hours in the Delaware County Airport, sat Indian style in a litter of equipment, picking at the carpet's nap like a doleful child. A large and very precise French curl of hair was plastered to the man's forehead with Brylcreem, whose scent was another of Skip Atwater's childhood associations, and he knew it was the heat of the arc lights that made the hair cream smell so strong. The journalist's left knee now ached no matter which way he distributed his weight. Every so often he pumped his fist at his side, but it was in a tentative and uninspired way.

In the wake of a slow moving front, the area's air was clear and dry and the sky a great cobalt expanse and Tuesday's overall weather both hot and almost autumnally crisp.

The Moltkes' home's bathroom door, a fiberboard model with interior hinges, was shut and locked. From its other side issued the sound of the sink and tub's faucets intermixed with snatches of conservative talk radio. Her husband was an intensely private and skittish bathroom individual, Mrs. Moltke had explained to the MD and photographer, due without doubt to certain abuses he'd suffered as a tiny child. Negotiations over the terms of authentication had taken place in the home's kitchen, and she had laid all this out with Mr. Moltke sitting right there beside her — Atwater had watched the man's hands instead of his face while Amber declaimed about her husband's bathroom habits and childhood trauma. Today she wore a great faded denim smock thing and seemed to loom in the periphery of Atwater's sight no matter where he looked, rather like the sky when one's outside.

At one point in the negotiations, Atwater had needed to use the bathroom and had gone in there and seen it. He really had had to go; it had not been a pretense. The Moltkes' toilet was in a small de facto alcove formed by the sink's counter and the wall that comprised the door jamb. The room smelled exquisitely of mildew. He could see that the wall behind the sink and toilet was part of the same east load bearer that ran along the hallway and sitting room and conjoined the duplex's other side. Atwater preferred a bathroom whose facilities were a bit farther from the door, for privacy's sake, but he could see that the only way to accomplish this here would have been to place the shower unit where the toilet now was, which given this shower's unusual size would be impossible. It was difficult to imagine Amber Moltke backing herself into this slender recess and settling carefully on the white oval seat to eliminate. Since the east wall also held the interior plumbing for all three of the room's fixtures, it stood to reason that the bathroom on the other side of the duplex abutted this one, and that its own plumbing also lay within the wall. For a moment, nothing but an ingrained sense of propriety kept Atwater from trying to press his ear to the wall next to the medicine cabinet to see whether he could hear anything. Nor would he ever have allowed himself to open the Moltkes' medicine cabinet, or to root in any serious way through the woodgrain shelves above the towel rack.

The toilet itself was a generic American Standard, its white slightly brighter than the room's walls and tile. The only noteworthy details were a large crack of some sort on the unpadded seat's left side and a rather sluggish flushing action. The toilet and area of floor around it appeared very clean. Atwater was also the sort of person who always made sure to put the seat back down when he was finished.

Evidently, Ellen Bactrian's brain trust had decided against present-

ing a short list of specific works or types of pieces they wanted the
artist to choose from. The initial pitch that Laurel Manderley had
been directed to instruct Atwater to make was that both the MD and
photographer would be set up in there with Brint Moltke while he
produced whatever piece he felt moved on this day to create. As predicted, Amber declared this totally unacceptable. The proffered compromise, then, was the presence of just the MD (which in fact was all
they'd wanted in the first place, *Style* having no possible use for in medias photos). Mrs. Moltke, however, had nixed this as well — Brint
had never produced an artwork with anyone else in the room. He was,
she iterated once more, an incorrigibly private bathroom person.

During the parts of her presentation he'd already heard, the journalist noted in Gregg shorthand that the home's kitchen was carpeted
and deployed a green and burgundy color scheme in its walls, counters,
and cabinets, that Mrs. Amber Moltke must almost certainly have had
some type of school or community theater experience, and that the
broad plastic cup from which the artist had occasionally sipped coffee
was from the top of a Thermos unit that was not itself in evidence. Of
these observations, only the second had any bearing on the piece that
would eventually run in *Style* magazine's final issue.

What had especially impressed Ellen Bactrian was Laurel Manderley's original suggestion that Skip pick up a portable fax machine at
some Circuit City or Wal Mart on the way down from Muncie with
the photographer — whose equipment had required the subcompact's
seats to be moved forward as far as they would go, and who not only
smoked in the nonsmoking rental but had this thing where he then
fieldstripped each cigarette butt and put the remains carefully in the
pocket of his Hawaiian shirt — and that the unit be hooked up to the
Moltkes' kitchen phone, which had a clip outlet and could be switched
back and forth from phone to fax with no problem. This allowed the
MD, whose negotiated station was finally fixed at just outside the
bathroom door, to receive the piece fresh ('hot off the griddle' had
been the photographer's phrase, which had caused the circle of
Moltke's digital mudra to quiver and distend for just a moment), to
perform his immediate field tests, and to fax the findings directly to

Laurel Manderley, signed and affixed with the same medical authorization number required by certain prescriptions.

'You understand that *Style* is going to have to have some corrobora-
tion,' Atwater had said. This was at the height of the ersatz negotiations in the Moltkes' kitchen. He chose not to remind Amber that this
entire issue had already been hashed out in the enmired Cavalier two
days prior. 'It's not a matter of whether the magazine trusts you or not.
It's that some readers are obviously going to be skeptical. *Style* cannot
afford to look overcredulous or like a dupe to even a fraction of its
readers.' He did not, in the kitchen, refer to the BSGs' concern with
distinguishing themselves from tabloids, though he did say: 'They
can't afford to let this look like a tabloid story.'

Both Amber Moltke and the photographer had been eating pieces
of a national brand coffee cake that could evidently be heated in the
microwave without becoming runny or damp. Her forkwork was deft
and delicate and her face as broad across as two of Skip's own placed
somehow side by side.

'Maybe we should just go on and let some tabloid do it, then,' she
had replied coolly.

Atwater said: 'Well, should you decide to do that, then yes, credibility ceases to be an issue. The story gets inserted between Delta Burke's
all fruit diet and reports of Elvis's profile in a photo of Neptune. But
no other outlet picks up the story or follows it up. Tabloid pieces don't
enter the mainstream.' He said: 'It's a delicate balance of privacy and
exposure for you and Brint, I'm aware. You'll obviously have to make
your own decision.'

Later, waiting in the narrow and redolent hallway, Atwater noted in
Gregg that at some point he and Amber had ceased even pretending
to include the artist in the kitchen's whole back and forth charade.
And that the way his damaged knee really felt was this: ignominious.

↓

'Or here's one,' Laurel Manderley said. She was standing next to the
trayless fax machine, and the editorial intern who had regaled the pre-

vious day's working lunch with the intracunnilingual flatus vignette was seated at the other WITW salaryman's console a few feet away. Today the editorial intern — whose first name also happened to be Laurel, and who was a particularly close friend and protégé of Ellen Bactrian — wore a Gaultier skirt and a sleeveless turtleneck of very soft looking ash gray cashmere.

'Your own saliva,' said Laurel Manderley. 'You're swallowing it all the time. Is it disgusting to you? No. But now imagine gradually filling up a juice glass or something with your own saliva, and then drinking it all down.'

'That really is disgusting,' the editorial intern admitted.

'But why? When it's in your mouth it's not gross, but the minute it's outside of your mouth and you consider putting it back in, it becomes gross.'

'Are you suggesting it's somehow the same thing with poo?'

'I don't know. I don't think so. I think with poo, it's more like as long as it's inside us we don't think about it. In a way, poo only becomes poo when it's excreted. Until then, it's more like a part of you, like your inner organs.'

'It's maybe the same way we don't think about our organs, our livers and intestines. They're inside all of us —'

'They *are* us. Who can live without intestines?'

'But we still don't want to see them. If we see them, they're automatically disgusting.'

Laurel Manderley kept touching at the side of her nose, which felt naked and somewhat creepily smooth. She also had the kind of sick headache where it hurt to move her eyes, and whenever she moved her eyes she could not help but seem to feel all the complex musculature connecting her eyeballs to her brain, which made her feel even woozier. She said: 'But partly we don't like seeing them because if they're visible, that means there's something wrong, there's a hole or some kind of damage.'

'But we also don't even want to think about them,' the other Laurel said. 'Who sits there and goes, Now the salad I ate an hour ago is entering my intestines, now my intestines are pulsing and squeezing and moving the material along?'

'Our hearts pulse and squeeze, and we don't mind thinking about our heart.'

'But we don't want to see it. We don't even want to see our blood. We faint dead away.'

'Not menstrual blood, though.'

'True. I was thinking more of like a blood test, seeing the blood in the tube. Or getting a cut and seeing the blood come out.'

'Menstrual blood is disgusting, but it doesn't make you lightheaded,' Laurel Manderley said almost to herself, her large forehead crinkled with thought. Her hands felt as though they were shaking even though she knew no one else could see it.

'Maybe menstrual blood is ultimately more like poo. It's a waste thing, and disgusting, but it's not wrong that it's all of a sudden outside of you and visible, because the whole point is that it's supposed to get out, it's something you want to get rid of.'

'Or here's one,' Laurel Manderley said. 'Your skin isn't disgusting to you, right?'

'Sometimes my skin's pretty disgusting.'

'That's not what I mean.'

The other editorial intern laughed. 'I know. I was just kidding.'

'Skin's outside of us,' Laurel Manderley continued. 'We see it all the time and there's no problem. It's even aesthetic sometimes, as in so and so's got beautiful skin. But now imagine, say, a foot square section of human skin, just sitting there on a table.'

'Eww.'

'Suddenly it becomes disgusting. What's *that* about?'

The editorial intern recrossed her legs. The ankles above her sling-back Jimmy Choos were maybe ever so slightly on the thick side, but she had on the sort of incredibly fine and lovely silk hose that you're lucky to be able to wear even once without totally ruining them. She said: 'Maybe again because it implies some kind of injury or violence.'

The fax's incoming light still had not lit. 'It seems more like the skin is decontextualized.' Laurel Manderley felt along the side of her nostril again. 'You decontextualize it and take it off the human body and suddenly it's disgusting.'

'I don't even like thinking about it, to be honest.'

↓

'I'm just telling you I don't like it.'

'Between you and I, I'd say I'm starting to agree. But it's out of our hands now, as they say.'

'You're saying you'd maybe prefer it if I hadn't gone to Miss Flick with them,' Laurel Manderley said on the telephone. It was late Tuesday afternoon. At certain times, she and Atwater used the name Miss Flick as a private code term for Ellen Bactrian.

'There was no other way to pitch it, I know. I know that,' Skip Atwater responded. 'Whatever's to blame is not that. You did what I think I would have asked you to do myself if I'd had my wits about me.' Laurel Manderley could hear the whispery whisk of his waist level fist. He said: 'Whatever culpability is mine,' which did not make that much sense to her. 'Somewhere some core part of it got past me on this one, I think.'

The *Style* journalist had been seated on the bed's edge on a spread out towel, checking the status of his injured knee. In the privacy of his motel room, Atwater was sans blazer and the knot of his necktie was loosened. The room's television was on, but it was tuned to the Spectravision base channel where the same fragment of song played over and over and the recorded voice of someone who was not Mrs. Gladys Hine welcomed you to the Mount Carmel Holiday Inn and invited you to press Menu in order to see options for movies, games, and a wide variety of in room entertainment, over and over; and Atwater had evidently misplaced the remote control (which in Holiday Inns tends to be very small) required for changing the channel or at the very least muting it. The left leg of his slacks was rolled neatly up to a point above the knee, every second fold reversed to prevent creasing. The television was a nineteen inch Symphonic on a swiveling base that was attached to the blondwood dresser unit facing the bed. It was the same second floor room he had checked into on Sunday — Laurel

Manderley had somehow gotten Accounting to book the room straight through even though Atwater had spent the previous night in a Courtyard by Marriott on Chicago's near north side, for which motel the freelance photographer was even now bound, at double his normal daily rate, in preparation for tomorrow's combined coverage spectacle.

On the wall above the room's television was a large framed print of someone's idea of a circus clown's face and head constructed wholly out of vegetables. The eyes were olives and the lips peppers and the cheeks' spots of color small tomatoes, for example. Repeatedly, on both Sunday and today, Atwater had imagined some occupant of the room suffering a stroke or incapacitating fall and having to lie on the floor looking up at the painting and listening to the base channel's nine second message over and over, unable to move or cry out or look away. In some respects, Atwater's various tics and habitual gestures were designed to physicalize his consciousness and to keep him from morbid abstractions like this — he wasn't going to have a stroke, he wouldn't have to look at the painting or listen to the idiot tune over and over until a maid came in the next morning and found him.

'Because that's the only reason. I thought you knew she'd sent them.'

'And if I'd called in on time as I should have, we'd both have known and there would have been no chance of misunderstanding.'

'That's nice, but it's not really my point,' Laurel Manderley said. She was seated at Atwater's console, absently snapping and unsnapping a calfskin barrette. As was SOP with Skip and his interns, this telephone conversation was neither rapid nor clipped. It was shortly before 3:30 and 4:30 respectively, since Indiana does not adhere to the DST convention. Laurel Manderley would later tell Skip that she had been so tired and unwell on Tuesday that she'd felt almost translucent, and plus was upset that she would have to come in on the Fourth, tomorrow, in order to mediate between Atwater and Ellen Bactrian re the so called artist's appearance on The Suffering Channel's inaugural tableau vivant thing, all of which had been literally thrown together in hours. It was not the way either of them normally worked.

Nor had *Style* ever before sought to conjoin two different pieces in process. It was this that signified to Skip Atwater that either Mrs.

Anger or one of her apparatchiks had taken a direct hand. That he felt no discernible trace of either vindication or resentment about this was perhaps to his credit. What he did feel, suddenly and emphatically in the midst of the call, was that he might well be working for Laurel Manderley someday, that it would be she to whom he pitched pieces and pleaded for additional column inches.

For Laurel Manderley's own part, what she later realized she had been trying to do in the Tuesday afternoon telephone confab was to communicate her unease about the miraculous poo story without referring to her dream of spatial distortion and creeping evil in the Moltke couple's home. In the professional world, one does not invoke dreams in order to express reservations about an ongoing project. It just doesn't happen.

Skip Atwater said: 'Well, she did have my card. I gave her my card, of course. But not our Fed Ex number. You know I'd never do that.'

'But think — they got here Monday morning. Yesterday was Monday.'

'She spared no expense.'

'Skip,' Laurel Manderley said. 'Fed Ex isn't open on Sunday.'

The whisking sound stopped. 'Shit,' Atwater said.

'And I didn't even call them for the initial interview until almost Saturday night.'

'And Fed Ex isn't apt to be open Saturday night, either.'

'So the whole thing is just very creepy. So maybe you need to ask Mrs. Moltke what's going on.'

'You're saying she must have sent the pieces before you'd even called.' Atwater was not processing verbal information at his usual rate. One thing he was sure of was that he now had absolutely zero intention of telling Laurel Manderley about the potentially unethical fraternization in the Cavalier, which was also why he could say nothing to her of the whole knee issue.

A person who tended to have very little conscious recall of his own dreams, Atwater today could remember only the previous two nights' sensation of being somehow immersed in another human being, of having that person surround him like water or air. It did not exactly take an advanced clinical degree to interpret this dream. At most, Skip Atwater's mother had been only three fifths to two thirds the size of Amber Moltke, although if you considered Mrs. Atwater's size as it would appear to a small child, much of the disparity then vanished.

After the telephone conversation, seated there on the bed's protective towel, one of the other things that kept popping unbidden into Atwater's mind was the peculiar little unconscious signifier that Brint Moltke made when he sat, the strange abdominal circle or hole that he formed with his hands. He'd made the sign again today, in the home's kitchen, and Atwater could tell it was something Mr. Brint Moltke did a lot — it was in the way he sat, the way all of us have certain little trademark styles of gesturing when we speak or arranging various parts of our bodies when seated. In what he felt was his current state, Atwater's mind seemed able only to return to the image of the gesture again and again; he could get no further with it. In a similar vein, every time he had made a shorthand note to himself to inquire about the other side of the Moltkes' duplex, he would then promptly forget it. His stenographer's notebook later turned out to include a half dozen such notations. The clown's teeth were multicolored kernels of what Atwater's folks had called Indian corn, its hair a spherical nimbus of corn chaff, which happened to be the single most allergenic substance known to man. And yet at the same time the hands' circle seemed also a kind of signal, something that the artist perhaps wished to communicate to Atwater but didn't know how or was not even fully aware he wished to. The strange blank fixed smile was a different matter — it too was unsettling, but the journalist never felt that it might be trying to signify anything beyond itself.

Atwater had never before received any kind of sexual injury. The discoloration was chiefly along the leg's outside, but the swelling involved the kneecap, and this was clearly what was causing the real pain. The area of bruising extended from just below the knee to the lower thigh; certain features of the car door's armrest and window's controls were directly imprinted in the bruise's center and already yellowing. The knee had felt constricted in his slacks' left leg all day. It gave off a radioactive ache and was sensitive to even the lightest contact. Atwater examined it, breathing through his teeth. He felt the distinctive blend of repulsion and fascination nearly all people feel when examining a diseased or injured part of themselves. He also had the feeling that the knee now somehow existed in a more solid and emphatic way than the rest of him around it. It was something like the way he used to feel at the mirror in the bathroom as a boy, examining his protuberant ears from all different angles. The room was on the Holiday Inn's second level and opened onto an exterior balcony that overlooked the pool; the cement stairs up had also hurt the knee. He couldn't straighten his leg out all the way. In the afternoon light, his calf and foot appeared pale and extremely hairy, perhaps abnormally hairy. There were also spatial issues. He had allowed it to occur to him that the bruising was actually trapped blood leaking from injured blood vessels under the skin, and that the changes in color were signs of the trapped blood decomposing under the skin and of the human body's attempts to deal with the decaying blood, and as a natural result he felt lightheaded and insubstantial and ill.

He was not so much injured as sore and more or less pummeled feeling elsewhere, as well.

Another childhood legacy: When anything painful or unpleasant happened to his body, Skip Atwater often got the queer sense that he was in fact not a body that occupied space but rather just a bodyshaped area of space itself, impenetrable but empty, with a certain vacuous roaring sensation we tend to associate with empty space. The whole thing was very private and difficult to describe, although Atwater had had a long and interesting off the record conversation about it with the Oregon multiple amputee who'd organized a series of high profile anti HMO events in 1999. It also now occurred to him for the first time that 'gone in the stomach,' which was a regional term for nausea he'd grown up with and then jettisoned after college, turned out to be a much more acute, concise descriptor than all the polysyllables he and the one legged activist had hurled at one another over the whole interior spatial displacement epiphenomenon.

There was something essentially soul killing about the print of the vegetable head clown that had made Atwater want to turn it to the wall, but it was bolted or glued and could not be moved. It was really on there, and Atwater now was trying to consider whether hanging a bath towel or something over it would or would not perhaps serve to draw emotional attention to the print and make it an even more oppressive part of the room for anyone who already knew what was under the towel. Whether the painting was worse actually seen or merely, so to speak, alluded to. Standing angled at the bathroom's exterior sink and mirror unit, it occurred to him that these were just the sorts of overabstract thoughts that occupied his mind in motels, instead of the arguably much more urgent and concrete problem of finding the television's remote control. For some reason, the controls on the TV itself were inactive, meaning that the remote was the only way to change channels or mute the volume or even turn the machine off, since the relevant plug and outlet were too far behind the dresser to reach and the dresser unit, like the excruciating print, was bolted to the wall and could not be budged. There was a low knocking at the door, which Atwater did not hear over the repetitive tune and message because he was at the sink with the water running. Nor could he remember for certain whether it was heat or cold that was effective for swelling after almost 48 hours, though it was common knowledge that ice was what was indicated directly after. What he eventually decided was to prepare both a hot and a cold compress, and to alternate them, his left fist moving in self exhortation as he tried to recall his childhood scouting manual's protocol for contusions.

The second level's ice machine roared without cease in a large utility closet next to Atwater's room. His tie reknotted but the left leg of his slacks still rolled way up, the journalist had the Holiday Inn's distinctive lightweight ice bucket in his hand when he opened the door and stepped out into the ambient noise and chlorine smell of the balcony. His shoe nearly came down in the message before he saw it and stopped, one foot suspended in air, aware at the same time that chlorine was not the only scent in the balcony's wind. The "*HELP ME*" was ornate and calligraphic, quotation marks sic. In overall design, it was not unlike the cursive *HAPPY BIRTHDAY VIRGIL AND ROB, YMSP2 '00*, and other phrases of decorative icing on certain parties' cakes of his experience. But it was not made of icing. That much was immediately, emphatically clear.

Holding the bucket, his ears crimson and partly denuded leg still raised, the journalist was paralyzed by the twin urges to examine the message's workmanship more closely and to get far away as quickly as possible, perhaps even to check out altogether. He knew that great force of will would be required to try to imagine the various postures and contractions involved in producing the phrase, its detached and plumb straight underscoring, the tiny and perfectly formed quotation marks. Part of him was aware that it had not yet occurred to him to consider what the phrase might actually mean or imply in this context. In a sense, the content of the message was obliterated by the over-whelming fact of its medium and implied mode of production. The phrase terminated neatly at the second E's serif; there was no tailing off or spotting.

A faint human sound made Atwater look hard right — an older couple in golfing visors stood some yards off outside their door, look-ing at him and the balcony's brown cri de coeur. The wife's expression pretty much said it all.

←

All salarymen, staff, and upper level interns at *Style* had free corporate memberships to the large fitness center located on the second under-ground level of the WTC's South Tower. The only expense was a monthly locker fee, which was well worth it if you didn't want to schlep a separate set of exercise clothing along with you to the offices every day. Two of the facility's walls were lined with mirrored plate. There were no windows, but the center's cardio fitness area was replete with raised banks of television monitors whose high gain audios could be accessed with ordinary Walkman headphones, and the channels could be changed via touchpad controls that were right there on the consoles of all the machines except the stationary bicycles, which themselves were somewhat crude and used mainly for spinning classes, which were also offered gratis.

At midday on Tuesday 3 July, Ellen Bactrian and Mrs. Anger's executive intern were on two of the elliptical training machines along the fitness center's north wall. Ellen Bactrian wore a dark gray Fila unitard with Reebok crosstrainers. There was a neoprene brace on her right knee, but it was mostly prophylactic, the legacy of a soccer injury at Wellesley three seasons past. Multicolored fairy lights on the machines' sides spelled out the brand name of the elliptical trainers. The executive intern, in the same ensemble she'd worn for biking in to the *Style* offices that morning, had programmed her machine to the same medium level of difficulty as Ellen Bactrian's, as a kind of courtesy.

It being the lunch hour, the center's cardio fitness area was almost fully occupied. Every elliptical trainer was in use, though only a few of the interns were using headsets. The nearby StairMasters were used almost exclusively by midlevel financial analysts, all of whom had bristly cybernetic haircuts. Not for over 40 years had the crewcut and variations upon it been so popular; a SURFACES item on the phenom was not long in the offing.

Certain parts of a four way internal email exchange Tuesday morning had concerned what specified type(s) of piece the magazine should require the Indianan to produce under tightly controlled circumstances in order to verify that his abilities were not a hoax or some tasteless case of idiot savantism. The fourth member of this exchange had been the photo intern whose mammoth engagement ring at Tutti Mangia had occasioned so much cattiness during yesterday's SE2 closing. Some of the specs proposed for the authenticity test were: A 0.5 reproduction of the Academy Awards' well known Oscar statuette, G. W. F. Hegel's image of Napoleon as the world spirit on horseback, a WWII Pershing tank with rotating turret, any coherently identifiable detail from Rodin's *The Gates of Hell*, a buck with a twelve point rack, either the upper or lower portion of the ancient Etruscan *Mars of Todi*, and the well known tableau of several US Marines planting the flag on an Iwo Jiman atoll. The idea of any sort of Crucifixion or *Pietà* type piece was flamed the moment it was proposed. Although Skip Atwater had not yet been given his specific marching orders, Mrs. Anger's executive intern and Ellen Bactrian were both currently leaning toward a representation of the famous photograph in which Marilyn Monroe's skirts are blown upward by some type of vent in the sidewalk and the expression on her face is, to say the least, intimately familiar to readers of *Style*.

Some of the internal email exchange's topics and arguments had carried over into various different lunchtime colloquies and brainstorming sessions, including the present one in the World Trade Center's corporate fitness facility, which proceeded more or less naturally because an axiom of elliptical cardio conditioning is that your target heartrate and respiration are to stay just at the upper limit of what allows for normal conversation.

'But is the physical, so to speak handmade character of a piece of art part of the artwork's overall quality?'

That is, in elliptical training you want your breathing to be deep and rapid but not labored — Ellen Bactrian's rhetorical question took only a tiny bit longer to get out than a normal, at rest rhetorical question.

The executive intern responded: 'Do we all really value a painting more than a photograph anymore?'

'Let's say we do.'

The executive intern laughed. 'That's almost a textbook petitio principii.' She actually pronounced principii correctly, which almost no one can do.

'A great painting certainly sells for more than a great photograph, doesn't it?'

The executive intern was silent for several broad quadular movements of the elliptical trainer. Then she said: 'Why not just say rather that *Style*'s readership would not have a problem with the assumption that a good painting or sculpture is intrinsically better, more human and meaningful, than a good photo.'

Often, editorial brainstorming sounds like an argument, but it isn't — it's two or more people thinking aloud in a directed way. Mrs. Anger herself sometimes referred to the brainstorming process as dilation, but this was a vestige of her Fleet Street background, and no one on her staff aped the phrase.

A woman about their mothers' age was exhibiting near perfect technique on a rowing machine in the mirror, mouthing the words to what Ellen Bactrian thought she recognized as a Venetian bacarole. The other rowing machine was vacant. Ellen Bactrian said: 'But now, if we agree the human element's key, then does the physical process or processes by which the painting is produced, or any artwork, have anything to do with the artwork's quality?'

'By quality you're still referring to how good it is.'

It is difficult to shrug on an elliptical trainer. 'Good quote unquote.'

'Then the answer again is that what we're interested in is human interest, not some abstract aesthetic value.'

'And yet isn't the point that they're not mutually exclusive? How about all Picasso's affairs, or the thing with van Gogh's ear?'

'Yes, but van Gogh didn't paint with his ear.'

By habit, Ellen Bactrian avoided looking directly at their side by side reflections in the mirrored wall. The executive intern was at least three inches taller than she. The sounds of all the young men's legs working the StairMasters were at certain points syncopated, then not, then gradually syncopated again. The two editorial interns' movements on the elliptical trainers, on the other hand, appeared synchronized down to the smallest detail. Each of them had a bottle of water with a sports cap in her elliptical trainer's special receptacle, although they were not the same brands of bottled water. The fitness center's sonic environment was basically one large, complex, and rhythmic pneumatic clank.

Between breaths, an ever so slightly peevish or impatient tone entered Ellen Bactrian's voice: 'Then, say, the *My Left Foot* guy who painted with his left foot.'

'Or the idiot savant who can reproduce Chopin after one hearing,' the executive intern said. This was an indirect bit of massaging on her part, since there had been a WITW profile of just such an idiot savant in an issue the previous summer — the piece's UBA was that the retarded man's mother had battled heroically to keep him out of an institution.

Under the diffused high lumen lights of the cardio fitness area, the executive intern's quads and delts seemed like something out of an advertisement. Ellen Bactrian was fit and attractive, with a perfectly respectable body fat percentage, but around the executive intern she often felt squat and dumpy. An unhealthy part of her sometimes suspected that the executive intern liked exercising with her because it made her, the executive intern, feel comparatively even more willowy and scintillant and buff. What neither Ellen Bactrian nor anyone else at *Style* knew was that the executive intern had had a dark period in preparatory school during which she'd made scores of tiny cuts in the tender skin of her upper arms' insides and then squeezed reconstituted lemon juice into the cuts as penance for a long list of personal shortcomings, a list she had tracked daily in her journal in a special numerical key code that was totally unbreakable unless you knew exactly which page of *The Bell Jar* the code's numbers were keyed to. Those days were now behind her, but they were still part of who the executive intern was.

'Yes,' Ellen Bactrian said, 'although, although I'm no art critic, Skip's guy's pieces are also artworks of surpassing quality and value in their own right.'

'Although of course all the readers will get to see is photos —'

'*Maybe.*' Both interns laughed briefly. The issue of publishable photos had been one they'd all agreed that morning to table — there were, as the WITW associate editor sometimes liked to quip, bigger fish on the front burner.

Ellen Bactrian said: 'Although remember that even photos, if Amine's to be believed, if absolutely properly lit and detailed so that —'

'Except hold on, answer this — does this person have to actually be *familiar* with something to represent it the way he does?'

Both women were at a node of their computerized workout and were breathing almost heavily now. Amine Tadić was *Style* magazine's associate photo editor; her head intern had served as her proxy in the morning's email confab.

Ellen Bactrian said: 'What do you mean?'

'According to Laurel, this is a person with maybe like a year or two of community college. How on earth would he know Boccioni's *Unique Forms of Continuity in Space,* or what Anubis's head looks like?'

'Or for that matter which side the Liberty Bell's crack's on.'

'I sure didn't know it.'

Ellen Bactrian laughed. 'Laurel did. Or she said she did — obviously she could have looked it up.' Ellen Bactrian was also, on her own time, trying to learn how to type completely different things with each hand, à la the WHAT IN THE WORLD section's associate editor, for whom she had certain feelings that she knew perfectly well were SOP transference for an intelligent, ambitious woman her age, since the associate editor was both seductive and a textbook authority figure. Ellen Bactrian liked the associate editor's wife quite a lot, actually, and so took great pains to keep the whole bimanual thing in perspective.

The executive intern was able to reach down and hydrate without breaking rhythm, which on an elliptical trainer takes a great deal of practice. 'I'm saying: Does the man have to see or know something in order to represent it? Produce it? Let's say that if he does and it's all totally conscious and intentional, then he's a real artist.'

'But if he doesn't —'

'Which is why the unlikeliness of a Roto Rooter guy from Nowhere Indiana knowing futurism or the *Unique Forms* is relevant,' the executive intern said, wiping her forehead with a terry wristband.

'If he doesn't, it's some kind of, what, a miracle? Idiot savantry? Divine intervention?'

'Or else some kind of extremely sick fraud.'

Fraud was a frightening word to them both, for obvious reasons. One consequence of getting Mrs. Anger's executive intern in on the miraculous poo story was that Eckleschafft-Böd US's Legal people were now involved and devoting resources to the piece in a way that Laurel Manderley and Ellen Bactrian could never have caused, even given the WITW associate editor's own background in Legal. BSG weeklies rarely broke stories or covered anything that other media hadn't already premasticated. The prospect was both exciting and frightful.

The executive intern said: 'Or else maybe it's subconscious. Maybe his colon somehow knows things his conscious mind doesn't.'

'Is it the colon that determines the whole shape and configuration and everything of the . . . you know?'

The executive intern made a face. 'I don't know. I don't really want to think about it.'

'What is the colon, anyhow? Is it part of the intestines or is it technically its own organ?'

Ellen Bactrian's and the executive intern's fathers were both MDs in Westchester County NY, though the two men practiced different medical specialties and had never met. The executive intern periodically reversed the direction of her elliptical trainer's pedals, working her quadriceps and calves instead of the hamstrings and lower gluteals. Her facial expression throughout these periods of reversal was both intent and abstracted.

'Either way,' Ellen Bactrian said, 'it's obviously human interest right out the wazoo.' She then related the anecdote that Laurel Manderley had shared with her in the elevators on the way back down from the 82nd floor early that morning, about the DKNY clad circulation intern at lunch telling everybody that she sometimes pretended her waste was a baby and then expecting them to relate or to think her candor was somehow hip or brave.

For a moment there was nothing but the sound of two syncopated elliptical trainers. Then the executive intern said: 'There's a way to do this.' She blotted momentarily at her upper lip with the inside of her wristband. 'Joan would say we've been thinking about this all wrong. We've been thinking about the subject *of* the piece instead of the angle *for* the piece.' Joan referred to Mrs. Anger, the Executive Editor of *Style*.

'The UBA's been a problem from the start,' Ellen Bactrian said. 'What I told —'

The executive intern interrupted: 'There doesn't have to be a strict UBA, though, because we can take the piece out of WHAT IN THE WORLD and do it in SOCIETY PAGES. Is the miraculous poo phenomenon art, or miracle, or just disgusting.' She seemed not to be aware that her limbs' forward speed had increased; she was now forcing her workout's program instead of following it. SOCIETY PAGES was the section of *Style* devoted to soft coverage of social issues such as postnatal depression and the rain forest. According to the magazine's editorial template, SP items ran up to 600 words as opposed to WITW's 400.

Ellen Bactrian said: 'Meaning we include some bites from credible sources who think it *is* disgusting. We have Skip create controversy in the piece itself.' It was true that her use of Atwater's name in the remark was somewhat strategic — there were complex turf issues involved in altering a piece's venue within the magazine, and Ellen Bactrian could well imagine the WITW associate editor's facial expression and some of the cynical jokes he might make in order to mask his hurt at being shut out of the story altogether.

'No,' the executive intern responded. 'Not quite. We don't create the controversy, we cover it.' She was checking her sports watch even though there were digital clocks right there on the machines' consoles. Both women had met or exceeded their target heartrate for over half an hour.

A short time later, they were in the little tiled area where people toweled off after a shower. At this time of day, the locker room was steamy and extremely crowded. The executive intern looked like something out of Norse mythology. The hundreds of tiny parallel scars on the insides of her upper arms were all but invisible. It is a fact of life that certain people are corrosive to others' self esteem simply as a function of who and what they are. The executive intern was saying: 'The real angle is about coverage. *Style* is not foisting a gross or potentially offensive story on its readers. Rather, *Style* is doing soft coverage on a controversial story that already exists.'

Ellen Bactrian had two towels, one of which she had wrapped around her head in an immense lavender turban. 'So Atwater will just rotate over and do it for SOCIETY PAGES, you're saying? Or will Genevieve want to send in her own salaryman?' Genevieve was the given name of the new associate editor in charge of SOCIETY PAGES, with whom Ellen Bactrian's overman had already locked horns several times in editorial meetings.

The executive intern had inclined her head over to the side and was

combing out a shower related tangle with her fingers. As was something of an unconscious habit, she bit gently at her lower lip in concentration. 'I'm like ninety percent sure this is the way to go,' she said.
'*Style* is covering the human element of a controversy that's already
raging.' At this point, they were at their rented lockers, which, in
contradistinction to those on the men's side, were full length in order
to facilitate hanging. Painstakingly modified with portable inset shelving and adhesive hooks, both the women's locker units were small
marvels of organization.

Ellen Bactrian said: 'Meaning it will need to be done somewhere
else first. SOCIETY PAGES covers the coverage and the controversy.'
She favored Gaultier pinstripe slacks and sleeveless cashmere tops
that could be worn either solo or under a jacket. So long as the slacks
and top were in the same color family, sleeveless could still be all
business — Mrs. Anger had taught them all that.

In what appeared to be another unconscious habit, the executive intern sometimes actually pressed the heel of her hand into her forehead
when she was thinking especially hard. In a way, it was her version of
Skip Atwater's capital flush. The opinion of nearly all the magazine's
other interns was that the executive intern was operating on a level
where she didn't have to be concerned about things like color families
or maintaining a cool professional demeanor.

'But it can't be too big,' she said.

'The piece, or the venue?' Ellen Bactrian always had to pat the ear
with all the studs in it dry with a disposable little antibiotic cloth.

'We don't want *Style* readers to already know the story. This is the
tricky part. We want them to feel as if *Style* is their first exposure to a
story whose existence still precedes their seeing it.'

'In a media sense, you mean.'

The executive intern's skirt was made of several dozen men's neckties all stitched together lengthwise in a complicated way. She and a
Mauritanian exchange student in THE THUMB who wore hallucinato-
rily colored tribal garb were the only two interns at *Style* who could get
away with this sort of thing. It was actually the executive intern, at a
working lunch two summers past, who had originally compared Skip

Atwater to a jockey who'd broken training, though she had said it in a light and almost affectionate way — coming from her, it had not sounded cruel. Over Memorial Day weekend, she had actually been a guest of Mrs. Anger at her summer home in Quogue, where she had reportedly played mahjongg with none other than Mrs. Hans G. Böd. Her future seemed literally without limit.

'Yes, though again, it's delicate,' the executive intern said. 'Think of it as not unlike the Bush daughters, or that thing last Christmas on Dodi's driver.' These were rough analogies, but they did convey to Ellen Bactrian the executive intern's basic thrust. In a broad sense, the cover the extant story angle was one of the standard ways BSGs distinguished themselves from both hard news glossies and the tabloids. On another level, Ellen Bactrian was also being informed that the overall piece was still her and the WHAT IN THE WORLD associate editor's baby; and the executive intern's repeated use of terms like tricky and delicate was designed both to flatter Ellen Bactrian and to apprise her that her editorial skill set would be amply tested by the challenges ahead.

Gaultier slacks held their crease a great deal better if your hanger had clips and they could hang from the cuffs. The voluptuous humidity of the locker room was actually good for the tiny wrinkles that always accumulated through the morning. Unbeknownst to Ellen Bactrian, lower level interns often referred to her and the executive intern in the same hushed and venerative tones. A constant sense that she was insufficient and ever at risk of exposing her incompetence was one of the ways Ellen Bactrian kept her edge. Were she to learn that she, too, was virtually assured of a salaried offer from *Style* at her internship's end, she would literally be unable to process the information — it might well send her over the edge, the executive intern knew. The way the girl now pressed at her forehead in unconscious imitation of the executive intern was a sign of just the kind of core insecurity the executive intern was trying to mitigate by bringing her along slowly and structuring their conversations as brainstorming rather than, for instance, her simply outright telling Ellen Bactrian how the miraculous poo story should be structured so that everyone made out. The executive intern was one of the greatest, most intuitive nurturers of talent Mrs. Anger had ever seen — and she herself had interned under Katharine Graham, back in the day.

'So it can't be too big,' Ellen Bactrian was saying, first one hand against the locker and then the other as she adjusted her Blahniks' straps. She now spoke in the half dreamy way of classic brainstorming. 'Meaning we don't totally sacrifice the scoop element. We need just enough of a prior venue so the story already exists. We're covering a controversy instead of profiling some freakoid whose b.m. comes out in the shape of Anubis's head.' Her hair had almost completely air dried already.

The executive intern's belt for the skirt was two feet of good double hemp nautical rope. Her sandals were Laurent, open toe heels that went with nearly anything. She tied the ankles' straps with half hitches and began to apply just the tiniest bit of clear gloss. Ellen Bactrian had now turned and was looking at her:

'Are you thinking what I'm thinking?'

Their eyes met in the compact's little mirror, and the executive intern smiled coolly. 'Your salaryman's already out there. You said he's shuttling between the two pieces already, no?'

Ellen Bactrian said: 'But is there actual suffering involved?' She was already constructing a mental flow chart of calls to be made and arrangements undertaken and then dividing the overall list between herself and Laurel Manderley, whom she now considered a bit of a pistol.

'Well, listen — can he take orders?'

'Skip? Skip's a consummate pro.'

The executive intern was adjusting the balloon sleeves of her blouse. 'And according to him, the miraculous poo man is skittish on the story?'

'The word Laurel says Skip used was excruciated.'

'Is that even a word?'

'It's apparently totally the wife's show, in terms of publicity. The artist guy is scared of his own shadow — according to Laurel, he's sitting there flashing Skip secret signs like No, please God, no.'

'So how hard could it be to represent this to Atwater's All Ads person as comprising bona fide suffering?'

Ellen Bactrian's mental flow charts often contained actual boxes, Roman numerals, and multiarrow graphics — that's how gifted an administrator she was. 'You're talking about something live, then.'

'With the proviso that of course it's all academic until this afternoon's tests check out.'

'But do we know for sure he'll even go for it?'

The executive intern never brushed her hair after a shower. She just gave her head two or three shakes and let it fall gloriously where it might and turned, slightly, to give Ellen Bactrian the full effect:

'Who?' She had ten weeks to live.

6.

In what everyone at the next day's working lunch would agree was a masterstroke, the special limousine that arrived at 5:00 AM Wednesday to convey the artist and his wife to Chicago was like something out of a *Style* reader's dream. Half a city block long, white the way cruise ships and bridal gowns are white, it had a television and wet bar, opposing seats of cordovan leather, noiseless AC, and a thick glass shield between passenger compartment and driver that could be raised and lowered at the touch of a button on the woodgrain panel, for privacy. To Skip Atwater, it looked like the hearse of the kind of star for whom the whole world stops dead in its tracks to mourn. Inside, the Moltkes faced each other, their knees almost touching, the artist's hands obscured from view by the panels of his new beige sportcoat.

The salaryman's Kia trailing at a respectful distance, the limousine proceeded at dawn through the stolid caucasian poverty of Mount Carmel. There were only faint suggestions of faces behind its windows' darkened glass, but whoever was awake to see the limousine glide by could tell that whoever was in there looking out saw everything afresh, like coming out of a long coma.

↓

O Verily was, understandably, a madhouse. The time from initial pitch to live broadcast was 31 hours. The Suffering Channel would enter stage three at 8:00 PM CDT on 4 July, ten weeks ahead of schedule, with three tableaux vivant. There were five different line producers, and all of them were very busy indeed.

It was not Sweeps Week; but as the saying goes in cable, every week is Sweeps Week.

A 52 year old grandmother from Round Lake Beach IL had a growth in her pancreas. The needle biopsy w/ CAT assist at Rush Presbyterian would be captured live by a remote crew; so would the activities of the radiology MD and pathologist whose job was to stain the sample and determine whether the growth was malignant. The segment entailed two separate freelance crews, all of whom were IA union and on holiday double time. The second part of the feed would be split screen. In something of a permissions coup, they'd have the woman's face for the whole ten minutes it took for the stain to set and the pathologist to scope it. She and her husband would be looking at a monitor on which the pathology crew's real time feed would be displayed — viewers would get to see the verdict and her reaction to it at the same time.

Finding just the right host for the segments' intros and voiceovers was an immense headache, given that nearly every plausible candidate's agent was off for the Fourth, and that whomever The Suffering Channel cast they were then all but bound to stick with for at least one stage three cycle. Finalists were still being auditioned as late as 3:00 PM — and *Style* magazine's Skip Atwater, in a move whose judgment was later questioned all up and down the editorial line, ended up devoting a good part of his time, attention, and shorthand notes to these auditions, as well as to a lengthy and somewhat meandering Q&A with an assistant to the Reudenthal and Voss associate tasked to the day's multiform permissions and releases.

In 1996, an unemployed arc welder was convicted of abducting and torturing to death a Penn State coed named Carole Ann Deutsch. Over four hours of high quality audiotape had been recovered from the suspect's apartment and entered into evidence at trial. Voiceprint analysis confirmed that the screams and pleadings on the tapes — which were played for the jury, though not in open court — belonged to the victim. This tableau's venue was a hastily converted OVP conference room. For the first time, Carole Ann Deutsch's widowed father, of Glassport PA, would listen to selections from those tapes. There with him for support are the associate pastor from Mr. Deutsch's church and an APA certified trauma counselor whose sunburn, only hours old, presents some ticklish problems for the segment's makeup coordinator.

Longtime *People's Court* moderator Doug Llewellyn hosts. After lengthy and sometimes heated negotiations — during which at one point Mrs. Anger herself had to be contacted at home and enjoined to speak directly by cell to R. Vaughn Corliss, which Ellen Bactrian later said made her just about want to curl up and die — representatives of both the ACLU and the League of Decency are on hand for brief interviews by Skip Atwater of *Style*.

It is a clear Lucite commode unit atop a ten foot platform of tempered glass beneath which a video crew will record the real time emergence of either an iconically billowing and ecstatic Monroe or a five to seven inch *Winged Victory of Samothrace*, depending on dramatic last minute instructions. Suspended from the studio's lighting grid to a position directly before the commode unit, a special monitor taking feed from below will give the artist visual access to his own production for the first time ever in his career. He believes what he sees will be public.

In point of fact, the piece's physical emergence will not really be broadcast. The combined arguments of *Style*'s Ellen Bactrian and the Development heads of O Verily Productions finally persuaded Mr. Corliss it would be beyond the pale. Instead, the artist's wife has been interviewed on tape respecting Brint Moltke's abusive childhood and the terrific shame, ambivalence, and sheer human suffering involved in his unchosen art. Edited portions of this interview will compose the voiceover as TSC viewers watch the artist's face in the act of creation, its every wince and grimace captured by the special camera hidden within the chassis of the commode's monitor.

A consciência é o pesadelo da natureza.

It is, of course, malignant. Subsequently, though, Carole Ann Deutsch's father discomfits everyone by seeming less interested in the tapes than in justifying his appearance on the broadcast itself. His purpose for being here is to inform the public of what victims' loved ones go through, to humanize the process and raise awareness. He repeats this several times, but at no point does he share how he feels or what he feels he's gone through just now, listening. In the context of what he and the viewers have just heard, Mr. Deutsch's reaction comes off as almost obscenely abstract and disengaged. On the other hand, Doug Llewellyn's own evident humanity and ad lib skill in getting everyone through the segment testify to the soundness of his casting.

A slow chain pulls the commode assembly up an angled plane until the unit locks into place atop its Lucite pipe. Mrs. Moltke's been allowed in the control room. Virgil 'Skip' Atwater and the Reudenthal and Voss paralegal are back against one wall, out of the arc lights' wash, the journalist's whole face flushed with ibuprofen and hands folded monkishly over his abdomen. At the base of the plane, *Style*'s freelance photographer is down on one knee, going handheld, still in the same Hawaiian shirt. The famously reclusive R. Vaughn Corliss is nowhere in view. Doug Llewellyn's wardrobe furnished by Hugo Boss. The Malina blanket for the artist's lap and thighs, however, is the last minute fix of a production oversight, retrieved from the car of an apprentice gaffer whose child is still nursing, and is not what anyone would call an appropriate color or design, and appears unbilled. There's also some eleventh hour complication involving the ground level camera and the problem of keeping the commode's special monitor out of its upward shot, since video capture of a camera's own monitor causes what is known in the industry as feedback glare — the artist in such a case would see, not his own emergent *Victory*, but a searing and amorphous light.

"Breathtakingly smart. . . . David Foster Wallace writes so beautifully, is so show-offishly smart, and understands the intricacies of human emotion so keenly that a reasonable person can only hope he is terribly unhappy. . . . Even stripped-down Wallace is epic modernism: big plots, absurd Beckettian humor, and science-fiction-height ideas portrayed vis-à-vis slow, realistic stream of consciousness."
— Joel Stein, *Time*

"*Oblivion* argues convincingly that the short story is Wallace's true fictional métier. . . . *Oblivion* puts stylistic idiosyncrasy to better use than any of its predecessors."
— Jan Wildt, *San Diego Union Tribune*

"A peerless combination of intelligence, compassion, and lyricism that needs no apology or qualification."
— Carlene Bauer, *Elle*

"The real joy of reading these stories is not in having Wallace ferry us from point A to point B, but in watching his reptilian intelligence slither and snake across the page, flicker out its forked tongue, and nab yet another linguistic fly off the wall."
— John Freeman, *Denver Post*

"*Oblivion* is yet another tug on the envelope of fiction and a fresh excursion into weird and wired consciousness. . . . A psychological and verbal tour-de-force."
— Mark Shechner, *Buffalo News*

"David Foster Wallace's brilliance lies in his ability to expose a character with a mass of bubbling afflictions and life-sustaining neuroses yet make the reader care deeply for him and his absurd existence."
— *Chicago Tribune*

"Many of *Oblivion's* rewards come by way of Wallace's sheer mastery of craft. His sentences crackle and swoon, patiently peeling back layers of artifice that cloak the Big Questions."
— Andy Battaglia, *The Onion*

"The stories of the infinitely talented David Foster Wallace transport the lucky reader into an absurd and magnificent Oblivion."
— Elissa Schappell, *Vanity Fair*